To Rosie, for introducing me to my adult self.
And to Natalie, for making it all make sense.

I won't be the lonely one.

Glasvegas, 'Daddy's Gone'

Prologue

The four-year-old boy stirs in the backseat of the station wagon, his body little more than a bump beneath the blanket draped over him, his hip sore where the seat belt's buckle presses into it.

He sits up, rubbing his eyes in the morning light, and looks around, confused.

The car is pulled to the curb, idling beside a chain-link fence. His father grips the steering wheel, his arms shaking. Sweat tracks down the band of flushed skin at the back of his neck.

The boy swallows to wet his parched throat. 'Where . . . where's Momma?'

His father takes a wheezy breath and half turns, a day's worth of stubble darkening his cheek. 'She's not . . . She can't . . . She's not here.'

Then he bends his head and begins to cry. It is all jerks and gasps, the way someone cries who isn't used to it.

Beyond the fence, kids run on cracked asphalt and line up for their turn on a rusted set of swings. A sign wired to the chain-link proclaims, IT'S MORNING AGAIN IN AMERICA: RONALD REAGAN FOR PRESIDENT.

The boy is hot. He looks down at himself. He is wearing jeans and a long-sleeve T-shirt, not the pajamas he'd gone to bed in. He tries to make sense of his father's words, the unfamiliar street, the blanket bunched in his lap, but can focus on nothing except the hollowness in his gut and the rushing in his ears.

'This is not your fault, champ.' His father's voice is high-pitched, uneven. 'Do you understand me? If you remember . . . one thing . . . you have to remember that nothing that happened is your fault.'

He shifts his grip on the steering wheel, squeezing so hard his hands turn white. His shirt cuff has a black splotch on it.

The sound of laughter carries to them; kids are hanging off monkey bars and crawling around the beat-up jungle gym.

'What did I do?' the boy asks.

'Your mother and I, we love you very much. More than anything.'

His father's hands keep moving on the steering wheel. Shift, squeeze. Shift, squeeze. The shirt cuff moves into direct light, and the boy sees that the splotch isn't black at all.

It is bloodred.

His father hunches forward and his shoulders heave, but he makes no sound. Then, with apparent effort, he straightens back up. 'Go play.'

The boy looks out the window at the strange yard with the strange kids running and shrieking. 'Where am I?'

'I'll be back in a few hours.'

'Promise?'

His father still doesn't turn around, but he lifts his eyes to the rearview, meets the boy's stare for the first time. In the reflection his mouth is firm, a straight line, and his pale blue eyes are steady and clear. 'I promise,' he says.

The boy just sits there.

His father's breathing gets funny. 'Go,' he says, 'play.'

The boy slides over and climbs out. He walks through the gate, and when he pauses to look back, the station wagon is gone.

Kids bob on seesaws and whistle down the fireman's pole. They look like they know their way around.

One of the kids runs up and smacks the boy's arm. 'You're it!' he brays.

The boy plays chase with the others. He climbs on the jungle gym and crawls in the yellow plastic tunnel, jostled by the bigger kids and doing his best to jostle back. A bell rings from the facing building, and the kids fly off the equipment and disappear inside.

The boy climbs out of the tunnel and stands on the playground, alone. The wind picks up, the dead leaves like fingernails dragging across the asphalt. He doesn't know what to do, so he sits on a bench and waits for his father. A cloud drifts across the sun. He has no jacket. He kicks the leaves piled by the base of the bench. More clouds cluster overhead. He sits until his rear end hurts.

Finally a woman with graying brown hair emerges through the double doors. She approaches him, puts her hands on her knees. 'Hi there.'

He looks down at his lap.

'Right,' she says. 'Okay.'

She glances across the abandoned playground, then through the chain-link, eyeing the empty parking spots along the curb.

She says, 'Can you tell me who you belong to?'

NOW

Chapter 1

Mike lay in the darkness, his gaze fixed on the baby monitor on the nightstand. He had to be up in three hours, but sleep wasn't coming any easier than it usually did. A blowfly had been circling the bedroom at irregular intervals as if to ensure his continued alertness. His mother used to say that a blowfly in the house meant that evil was stalking the family – one of the only things he remembered about her.

He took a moment to catalog some less morbid memories from his early years. The few imprints he'd retained were little more than sensory flashes. The scent of sage incense in a yellow-tiled kitchen. His mother bathing him. How her skin always seemed tan. Her smell, like cinnamon.

The red light bars fanned up on the monitor. A crackle of static. Or was that Kat coughing?

He nudged the volume down so as not to wake Annabel, but she shifted around beneath the sheets, then said hoarsely, 'Honey, there's a reason they call it a *baby* monitor.'

'I know. I'm sorry. I thought I heard something.'

'She's eight years old. And more mature than either of us. If she needs something, she'll march in here and announce it.'

It was an old argument, and Annabel was right, so he muted the volume and lay morosely staring at the damn thing, unable to click it off altogether. A little plastic unit that held a parent's worst fears. Choking. Illness. Intruders.

Usually the sounds were just interference or crossover noise from other frequencies – a charge in the air or the neighbor's toddler snuffling from a cold. Sometimes Mike even heard voices in the rush of white noise. He swore there were ghosts in the thing. Murmurs from the past. It was a portal to your half-conscious mind, and you could read into its phantom whisper whatever you wanted.

But what if he turned it off and this proved to be the night Kat *did* need them? What if she awakened terrified and disoriented from a nightmare, sudden paralysis, the blowfly's evil spell, and lay stricken for hours, trapped alone with her fear? How do you choose the first night to take that risk?

In the early hours, logic and reason seemed to fall asleep before he did. Everything seemed possible in the worst kind of way.

He finally started to drift off, but then the blowfly took another loop around the night-light, and a moment later the red bars flared again on the muted unit. Kat crying out?

He sat up and rubbed his face.

'She's fine,' Annabel groaned.

'I know, I know.' But he got up and padded down the hall.

Kat was out cold, one slender arm flung across a stuffed polar bear, her mouth ajar. Chestnut hair framed her serious face. She had her mother's wide-set eyes, pert nose, and generous lower lip; given her looks and whip-smart demeanor, it was sometimes hard to tell whether Kat was an eight-year-old version of Annabel or Annabel a thirty-six-year-old version of Kat. The one trait that Kat had received from Mike was at least an obvious one – one brown eye, one amber. Heterochromia, they called it. As for her curls, who knew where she got those?

Mike leaned over her, listened for the whistle of breath. Then he sat in the glider chair in the corner and watched his daughter. He felt a stab of pride about the childhood he and Annabel had given her, the sense of security that let her sleep so soundly.

'Babe.' Annabel stood in the doorway, shoving her lank hair off her forehead. She wore a Gap tank top and his boxers and looked as good in them as she had a decade before on their honeymoon. 'Come to bed. Tomorrow's a huge day for you.'

'Be there in a moment.'

She crossed, and they kissed quietly, and then she trudged off to bed again.

The movement of the glider was hypnotic, but his thoughts kept circling back to the unresolved business of the coming day. After a time he realized he wasn't going to be able to sleep, so he went into the kitchen and made a pot of coffee. Back in the chair, sipping contentedly from his mug, he soaked in the pale yellow walls, the raft of dolls on the floating shelf, his daughter in angelic repose. The only interruption was the occasional buzz from the blowfly, which had stalked him down the hall.

Chapter 2

Kat skidded through the kitchen, her ponytail loose and off center. Annabel paused above the omelet pan and regarded the fount of curls. 'Your father did that, didn't he?'

Kat shoved her stuffed polar bear into her backpack and climbed onto a counter stool next to Mike. Annabel slung the omelet onto Kat's plate, then leaned over and readjusted her daughter's hair tie with a few expert flips and tugs. She dropped the pan into soapy water, mopped the leak beneath the farmhouse sink with a foot-held paper towel, and moved back to finishing Kat's lunch, cutting the crust off her peanut-butter – no jelly – sandwich.

Slurping at his third cup of coffee and watching his wife, Mike felt like he was moving in slow motion. 'I'll fix the sink tonight,' he said, and Annabel gave him a thumbs-up. He noted the furry white arm protruding from his daughter's backpack. 'May I ask why you packed a polar bear for school?'

'I have a report today.'

'Another report? Aren't you in third grade?'

'It's for that enriched-learning thing after class. I'm talking about global warming—'

Annabel, sarcastic: 'No kidding.'

'—and this isn't just *any* polar bear.'

Mike lifted an eyebrow. 'No?'

Kat pulled the white bear from her backpack and presented it theatrically. 'This is no longer Snowball, my favourite stuffed animal. *This* . . . this is Snowball, the Last Dying Polar Bear.' She removed her eyeglasses from their case and put them on. The round red rims added gravity to her expression. Not that she needed the help. 'Did you know,' she asked, 'that polar bears will probably be extinct by the time I'm a grown-up?'

'Yes,' Mike said. 'From that Al Gore movie. With the melting icecaps and drowning polar bears. You cried for two days.'

Annabel said, 'Eat your omelet.'

Kat picked at the edge. Mike gave the nape of her neck a squeeze. 'Want me to walk you to class today?'

'Dad, I'm *eight.*'

'So you keep reminding me.' Mike tugged his sturdy cell from his pocket and hit 'redial.' A few rings, and then the bank manager picked up. 'Hi, Mike Wingate again. Did the wire hit?'

'Just a minute, Mr Wingate.' The sound of keyboard typing.

As Kat and Annabel negotiated how many more bites Kat had to eat, Mike waited, drumming his fingers nervously on the counter.

It had taken him thirteen years to work his way from hired hand to carpenter to foreman to contractor. And now he was on the brink of closing out his first deal as a developer. He'd taken some ulcer-inducing risks to get here, leveraging their house and maxing out a handful of loans to buy a section of undeveloped canyon at the edge of town. Lost Hills, a Valley community thirty miles northwest of downtown Los Angeles, had a number of advantages, the main one being that real estate was merely expensive, not obscene. Mike had carved the land into forty generous parcels and built a community of ecological houses that he had named, uninventively, Green Valley. Not that he was a die-hard ecofreak, but Kat had shown an interest in environmental stuff from an early age and he had to admit that those futuristic computer-generated photos of Manhattan flooded due to sea-level rise scared the hell out of him.

The state's offer of green subsidies had helped the houses sell quickly, the cash from the final cluster of sales due to be wired from the title company this morning. This wire would get him out from under the bank – finally, entirely – after three and a half years and meant they'd no longer have to eyeball their checking-account balance before deciding to go out to a meal.

The bank manager's breath whistled over the line. The typing stopped. 'Still nothing, Mr Wingate.'

Mike thanked him, clicked his cell closed, and ran the sweat off his forehead with the heel of a hand. The little nagging voice returned: What if, after all this work, something *did* go wrong?

He caught Annabel looking at him, and he said, 'I shouldn't have bought that stupid truck yet.'

She said, 'And what? Duct-taped the transmission together on your beater pickup? We're fine. The money's there. You've worked hard. *So* hard. It's okay to let yourself enjoy it a little.'

'And I certainly didn't need to drop eight hundred bucks on a suit.'

'You've got a photo shoot with the governor, honey. We can't have you show up in ripped jeans. Besides, you can wear it again at the award ceremony. Which reminds me'. She snapped her fingers. 'I need to pick it up from the tailor this morning after class. Kat's got that back-to-school checkup this morning. Can you take her on your way in? Meet back here at lunch?'

In the past year, their schedules had gotten more complicated to coordinate. Once it had become clear that Kat and third grade were getting along, Annabel decided it was time to go back to Northridge University for her teaching degree. State-school tuition was manageable, as long as they bent the budget here and there.

Mike flipped his phone open and checked the screen in case he'd missed the bank calling back with good news. He rubbed a knot out of his neck. The stress, still holding on. 'I don't know what was wrong with my old sport coat.'

Kat said, 'I don't think anyone wears plaid jackets anymore, Dad.'

'It's not *plaid*. It's windowpane.'

Annabel nodded at Kat and mouthed, *Plaid*.

Mike had to smile. He took a deep breath. Tried for a full exhale. The money was already at the title company. What could go wrong?

Annabel finished at the sink, tugged off her rings, and rubbed lotion into her hands. The engagement ring, a fleck of pale yellow diamond that he'd scraped together two paychecks to afford, gave off a dull sparkle. He loved that ring, like he loved their nice little house. The American dream distilled into two bedrooms and fifteen hundred square feet. Having money come in would be great, sure, but they'd always known to be grateful, to appreciate how fortunate they were.

Annabel reached for his hands. 'Come here, I got too much lotion.' The light from the window was pouring over her shoulders, bronzing her dark hair at the edges, and her eyes, picking up the frost blue of her shirt, looked translucent.

He raised the cell phone, framed her in the built-in camera, and snapped a picture. 'What?' she said.

'Your hair. Your eyes.'

Annabel rolled her hands in his.

'Gawd,' Kat said. 'Just kiss and get it over with already.'

The Ford F-450 gleamed in the garage like a spit-polished tank. The four-ton truck guzzled enough diesel to offset whatever help Green Valley was lending the environment, but Mike couldn't exactly haul gear to a construction site in a Prius. The truck was extravagant – irresponsible, even – but he had to confess that when he'd driven it off the lot yesterday, he'd felt more delight than seemed prudent.

Kat hopped into the back and stuck her nose in a book, the usual morning procedure.

Pulling out of the driveway, Mike gestured at the roof-mounted TV/DVD player. 'Stop reading. Check out the TV. It's got wireless headphones. Noise-canceling.'

He sounded like the brochure, but couldn't help himself; the new-car smell was making him heady.

She put on the headphones, clicked around the channels. 'Yes!' she said, too loud since the volume was cranked up. '*Hannah Montana.*'

He coasted up the quiet suburban streets, tilting down the sun visor, thinking about how nervous and yet excited he was about today's photo shoot with the governor. They passed a jewelry shop, and he looked at all the glimmering ice in the storefront window and thought that once that wire hit, just maybe he'd stop by and get something to surprise Annabel.

As they neared Dr Obuchi's, Kat's face darkened, and she tugged off the headphones. 'No shots,' she said.

'No shots. It's just a checkup. Don't freak out.'

'As long as there are no needles, there will be no freaking out.' She extended her hand with a ceremony beyond her years. 'Deal?'

Mike half turned, and they shook solemnly. 'Deal.'

'I don't believe you,' she said.

'Have I ever broken a promise to you?'

'No,' she said. 'But you could start.'

'Glad to see I've built up trust.'

Her mouth stayed firm for the rest of the drive and all the way into the examination room, where she shifted back and forth on the table, the paper crinkling beneath her as Dr Obuchi checked her reflexes.

The doctor finished the physical and eyed Kat's chart. 'Oh. She never got her second MMR, since Annabel wanted me to spread out the vaccines.' She tugged at a lock of shiny black hair. 'We're late on it.' She fussed in a drawer for the vial and syringe.

Kat's eyes got big. She stiffened on the table and directed an imploring stare at her father. 'Dad, you *swore.*'

'She prefers to get ready for shots,' Mike said. 'Mentally. A little more notice. Can we come back later in the week?'

'It's September. Back to school. You can guess what my schedule looks like.' Dr Obuchi took note of Kat's glare. Unwavering. 'I *might* have a slot Friday morning.'

Mike clicked his teeth together, frustrated. Kat was watching him closely. He put his hands on his daughter's knobby knees. 'Honey, I'm wall-to-wall with meetings Friday, and Mom has class. It's my worst day. Let's just do this now and get it over with.'

Kat's face colored.

Dr Obuchi said, 'It's just a prick. Over before you know it.'

Kat tore her gaze from Mike and looked at the wall, her breath quickening, her arm almost as pale as the latex glove gripping it. Dr Obuchi dabbed some alcohol on Kat's biceps and readied the needle.

Mike watched, his discomfort growing. Kat kept her face turned away.

As the stainless-steel point lowered, Mike reached out and gently stopped the doctor's hand. 'I'll make Friday work,' he said.

Mike drove, chomped Juicy Fruit, and tried to keep from checking in with the bank manager for the fourth time that morning. As they approached Kat's school, he rolled down the window and spit his gum into the wind.

'*Dad.*'

'What?'

'That's not good for the environment.'

'Like if a bald eagle chokes on it?'

Kat scowled.

'Okay, fine,' he said. 'I won't spit any more gum out the window.'

'Snowball the Last Dying Polar Bear thanks you.'

He pulled up to the front of the school, but she just sat there in the backseat, fingering the wireless headphones in her lap. 'You're getting some award thing for the green houses, aren't you?' she asked. 'From the governor?'

'I'm being recognized, yeah.'

15

'I know you care about nature and stuff, but you're not, like, *really* into it, right? So why'd you build all these green houses?'

'You really don't know?' He angled the rearview so he could see her face.

She shook her head.

He said, 'For you.'

Her mouth came open a little, and then she looked away and smiled privately. She scooted across and climbed out, and even once she was halfway across the playground, he could see that her face was still flushed with joy.

Letting the breeze blow through the rolled-down window, he took in the scene. A few teachers were out supervising the yard. Parents clustered among the parked cars, arranging play dates, coordinating car pools, planning field trips. Kids whooped and ran and tackled one another on the grass.

It was a life he'd always dreamed about but barely dared to believe he could have for himself. And yet here it was.

He dialed, raised the cell phone to his face. The bank manager sounded a touch impatient. 'Yes, Mr Wingate. I was about to call. I'm pleased to tell you that the wire came through just this instant.'

For a moment Mike was rendered speechless. The phone sweaty in his grip, he asked for the amount. And then asked the bank manager to repeat it, just to make sure it was real.

'So the loan is paid off now, yeah?' Mike said, though he knew he had just received enough to close out the remaining debt five times over. 'Fully paid off?'

A note of amusement in the man's voice. 'You are free and clear, Mr Wingate.'

Mike's throat was tightening, so he thanked the manager and hung up. He tipped his face into his hand and just breathed awhile, worried he might lose it here in the middle of the Lost Hills Elementary parking lot. It was the money, sure, but it was so much more than that, too. It was relief and pride, the knowledge that he'd taken a gamble and put nearly four years of nonstop effort behind it, and now his wife and daughter would never have to worry about having a roof over their heads and food in the refrigerator and overdue tuition bills tucked into the desk blotter.

Across the playground, her image split by the cross-hatching of the chain-link fence, Kat climbed to the top of a fireman's pole and dinged the top bar with a fist. The sight of her made his heart ache. Her safe little world, composed of small challenges, open horizons, and boundless affection.

Late for work, he sat and watched her play.

Chapter 3

The workers clustered around Mike's truck as soon as he pulled onto the job site.

'Whew-wee!'

'Boss got a new *vee*-hicle.'

'What'd this baby run ya?'

Mike climbed out, waving off the questions to hide his discomfort. He'd never fully adjusted to being a boss and missed the easy camaraderie that came from working beside the guys day after day. 'Not as much as you think.'

Jimmy leaned on the hood with both hands, one fist gripping a screwdriver.

Mike said, 'Watch the paint,' and immediately regretted opening his mouth.

Jimmy put his hands in the air, stickup style, and the others laughed.

'All right, all right,' Mike said. 'I deserve that. Where's Andrés?'

His irritable foreman trudged over, stirring a gourd with a stainless-steel straw. The gourd held yerba maté, and the straw – a *bombilla* – filtered out the loose leaves so Andrés could suck the bitter tea all day without spitting twigs. He shooed the workers off. 'Well, what you wait for? You supposed to loaf when the boss *leave*, not when he show up.'

The workers dispersed, and Andrés set down his maté gourd on the truck's bumper. 'Aargh,' he said without inflection.

'Aargh?'

'It is National Talk Like a Pirate Day. What a country. All these holiday. Take Your Kid to Work Day. Martin Yuther King Day.'

An import from Uruguay, Andrés was finally applying for naturalization and had become a walking repository of obscure U.S. trivia.

Mike said, 'I've heard they called him Martin *Luther* King.'

'That what I say, matey.'

They headed up the slope into the heart of the planned community. The forty houses, framing a parklike sprawl of grass in the canyon's dip, stretched up the slope on either side, rising in altitude and sticker price. At first glance they looked like ordinary houses, but closer inspection revealed bioswales for storm-drain runoff, roofs scaled with photovoltaic cells and breathing with vegetation, vitrified-clay pipes instead of nondegradable, toxin-leaking PVC. Even with all that, the houses had barely squeaked by to get the coveted Leadership in Energy and Environmental Design green certification. But they had, and now, aside from some final electrical and trim work and a few cosmetic flourishes, the job was done.

They crested the rise and walked down into the park. It was Mike's favorite part of Green Valley, positioned in the center where parents could look out their kitchen windows and see their kids playing. The development was zoned for two more lots there, but he couldn't bring himself to build over that land.

They headed for the hole at the far edge of the park, already prepped for the pouring of the fire pit's foundation. 'What are we waiting for?' Mike asked.

'That tree-hugger concrete take longer to mix,' Andrés said. 'But my control-freak developer boss don't let me use the normal kind.'

This was their routine – an old couple, bitter and exasperated, but in it together to the end.

'The LEED certification is too tight. We don't have the wiggle room.' Mike grimaced, ran a hand over his face. 'Jesus, who knew what a pain this would be?'

Andrés took another pull through his *bombilla*. 'What we gonna build next?'

'A coal factory.'

Andrés snickered, poked the stainless-steel straw into the gourd. 'I tole you, we no do this green, we could've pull another twenty-percent profit off the top. Then we *all* drive new trucks.'

As they approached, Jimmy waved and started backing up a concrete mixer to the fire-pit hole. Andrés lifted an arm in response, the *bombilla* flying from his gourd into the pit. He frowned down as if this were only the latest in a string of the day's disappointments. 'Forget it. I buy another.'

Staring at the reed-thin steel straw stuck in the mud, Mike heard Kat's voice in his head, chattering about trash and decomposing metals. His conscience reared up annoyingly.

Jimmy was just about to tip the drum of concrete when Mike shouted to him and pointed. Jimmy rolled his eyes and stepped off for a smoke while Mike hopped down. The hole was about five feet with sheer walls; they'd gone deep for the gas lines. As Mike crouched to pluck up the straw, he spotted an elbow of drainpipe protruding from the dirt wall. The water main.

He froze.

His stomach knotted. The metal straw fell from his hand. The mossy reek of moist earth and roots pressed in on him, crowding his lungs.

At first he thought he was mistaken. Then he fingered around the crumbling dirt, and dread finally broke through the shock.

The pipe wasn't the environmentally friendly vitrified clay he'd paid a small fortune for.

It was PVC.

'How much was used?' Mike stood at the edge of the hole now with Andrés, trying to keep the panic from his voice. He'd sent the other workers away.

Andrés said, 'I don't know.'

'Get the van here,' Mike said. 'I want to run plumbing cameras through the sewage and drain lines.'

'The day rate for that van—'

'I don't care.'

Mike grabbed a shovel from a nearby mound of decorative rock, jumped down into the hole, and started chiseling at the wall. He'd retained his laborer's build – muscular forearms, strong hands, broad enough through his chest to stretch a T-shirt – and he made impressive progress, but still the packed earth didn't give way under his shovel as it might have a few years ago. Andrés called for the van, then stood with his arms crossed, chewing his cheek, watching. Mike's grunts carried up out of the hole.

After a few moments, Andrés picked up a second shovel and slid down there with him.

The plumbing van idled in the middle of the street, a pipe video camera snaking through the laid-open rear doors and dropping down a manhole. Despite the hour the workers, except for Jimmy, had been sent home. Aside from the occasional passing bird, a pervasive stillness lingered over the development. The community of shiny new houses, beneath the late-morning sun, seemed like a fake town awaiting an atomic test blast.

Inside the van, crammed beside the hose reel, their clothes muddy, their faces streaked with dirt, Mike and Andrés watched a live feed on a small black-and-white screen – a grainy, endoscopic view of black piping. The hose reel next to their heads turned with a low hum as the camera continued its subterranean crawl, transmitting footage so consistent it seemed looped. Meter after meter of PVC pipe, stretching out beneath the hillside, beneath the streets, beneath the concrete slabs of the houses.

Light from the screen flickered across the men's faces. Their lifeless expressions did not change.

Jimmy crawled up from the manhole, his dark skin glistening with sweat, and peered through the open van doors. 'We done?'

Mike nodded, his eyes distant. Barely able to register the words. 'Thanks, Jimmy. You can go now.'

Jimmy shrugged and walked off. A moment later an engine turned over with a familiar growl, and then the men listened to Jimmy putter off in Mike's old truck.

When Mike finally spoke, his voice was cracked. 'PVC is the worst of all of it. The chemicals leak into the soil. The shit migrates. They find it in whale blubber. They find it in Inuit breast milk, for Christ's sake.'

Andrés leaned back, resting his head against the wall of the van.

'How much would it cost?' Mike asked.

'You kidding, no?'

'To make it right. To replace it with vitrified clay.'

'It's not just under the street. It's under the slabs. Under the houses.'

'I know where pipes go.'

Andrés sucked his teeth and looked away.

Mike registered a dull ache at the hinge of his jaw and realized he was clenching. Tearing up the houses would be a nightmare. A lot of the families had already sold their old places. They were middle-income folks who wouldn't have the money for a rent-back or a prolonged hotel stay. Hell, that had been a big part of this – to help families get into nice houses. Many of the properties he'd placed not with the highest bidders but with people who needed them – single mothers, working-class couples, families who needed a break.

Mike said, 'How did you not notice this?'

'*Me*? You choose the grading contractor. Vic Manhan. The guy roll in with thirty workers and do the whole thing over Christmas break. Remember – you were thrilled.'

Mike stared across at his Ford with resentment and enmity. A fifty-five-thousand-dollar pickup – what the hell was he thinking? Would the dealership take it back? His anger mounted, the fuse burning down. 'You got Manhan's number there?' he asked.

Andrés scrolled through his cell phone, hit 'send,' and handed it off to Mike.

As it rang, Mike ran a dirty hand through his sweaty hair, tried to slow his breathing. 'This prick better carry a hefty insurance policy. Because I don't care what it costs. I'm gonna hit him with as many lawsuits as I can—'

'*This number is no longer in service. If you believe you have reached this recording in error—*'

Mike's heart did something in his chest.

He hung up. Clicked around in Andrés's phone. Tried Manhan's cell.

'*The Nextel subscriber you are trying to reach is no longer—*'

Mike hurled the phone against the side of the van. Andrés looked at him, then leaned over slowly, retrieved his phone, eyed the screen to make sure it still worked.

Mike was breathing hard. 'I checked his goddamned license myself.'

'You better check again,' Andrés said.

His shirt sticking to his body, Mike made a chain of calls, jotting down each new number on the back of an envelope. The picture swiftly resolved. Vic Manhan's license had expired five months ago, shortly after he'd finished the job for Mike. Manhan had let his general-liability insurance lapse before that, so it had not been in effect when he'd laid in the PVC pipes. The policy documents he'd produced for Mike had been fraudulent. Which meant – in all likelihood – no money to cover damages.

For the first time in a long time, Mike's mind went to violence, the crush of knuckles meeting nose cartilage, and he thought, *How quickly we regress.* He lowered his head, made fists in his hair, squeezed until it stung. His breath floated up hot against his cheeks.

'You can't be *that* surprised,' Andrés said. 'About finding the PVC.'

'What the hell kind of thing is that to say? Of *course* I'm surprised.'

'Come on. Vitrified clay is heavier than cast iron. More expensive to make, to truck, to install. So how you think Manhan's quote come in thirty percent below everyone else's?' The brown skin at Andrés's temples crinkled. 'Maybe you didn't *want* to know.'

Mike looked down at his rough hands.

Andrés said, 'You got forty families moving in. This week. Even if you want to spend all the money to replace, what are you gonna do? Jackhammer through all their houses? Their streets?'

'*Yes.*'

Andrés lifted an eyebrow. 'To switch one set of pipes with another?'

'I signed,' Mike said. 'My name. Guaranteeing I used vitrified-clay pipes in place of PVC. My *name.*'

'You didn't do anything wrong. This guy screw us.'

Mike's voice was hoarse: 'Those houses are built on a lie.'

Andrés shrugged wearily. He climbed out of the van with a groan, and a moment later, Mike followed, his muscles feeling tight and arthritic.

They faced each other in the middle of the street, blinking against the sudden brightness like newborns, the canyon laid out before them, beautiful and steep and crusted with sagebrush. The air, crisp and sharp, tasted of eucalyptus. The green of the roofs matched the green of the hillside sumac, and when Mike squinted, it all blended together and became one.

'No one will know,' Andrés said. He nodded once, as if confirming something, then started for his car.

Mike said, 'I will.'

Chapter 4

Mike sat on the hearth of their small bedroom fireplace, his back to the wall, staring at the cordless phone in his lap. Debating with himself. Finally he dialed the familiar number.

A strong voice, husky with age. 'Hank Danville, Private Investigations.'

'It's Mike,' he said. 'Wingate.'

'Mike, I don't know what else to tell you. I said I'd call if I found anything, but I've got nowhere else to look.'

'No, not that. Something new. I have a guy I need you to track down.'

'I hope it's something I can actually make headway with this time.'

'He's a contractor who screwed me.' Mike gave him a brief rundown. He could hear the faint whistle of Hank's breathing as he took notes. 'I need to know where he is. To say it's urgent is an understatement.'

'How much you in for?' Hank asked.

Mike told him.

Hank whistled. 'I'll see what I can do,' he said, and hung up.

Mike was used to searching for information he probably didn't want to know, but that didn't make the waiting any easier. He got into the shower and leaned against the tile, blasting himself with steaming water, trying to pressure-wash away the stress. As he was drying off, the phone rang. Towel wrapped around his waist, he picked it up, sat on the bed, and braced for bad news.

'Vic Manhan's last-known puts him in St. Croix,' Hank said. 'A bounced check at a bar two months ago. God knows where he is now. His wife left him, he was staring at an expensive divorce, all that. Probably figured pulling a last job and splitting with his cash would be a better way to go. I'm not sure how he dummied the insurance papers and the databases, but there were no real policies backing him when he did your job.'

Mike closed his eyes. Breathed. 'You can't find where he is now?'

'The guy's on the run from the cops and his wife's lawyers. He probably hightailed it to Haiti by now. He's not findable.'

Bitterness rode the back of Mike's tongue. 'Come on. The guy's hardly Jason Bourne.'

'You're welcome to have someone else try. I thought I did pretty good for fifteen minutes.'

'It's just another dead end, Hank. We seem to keep hitting them.'

Hank's voice sharpened with indignation. 'Oh, we're back to that now? I told you when you first came in that what you were asking for would be next to impossible. I *never* promised you results.'

'No, you sure didn't.'

'You can be displeased with the facts, but I'm too old to have my character questioned. Come by the office and pick up your file. We're done.'

Mike held the phone to his face until the dial tone bleated, regret washing through him. He'd acted like an asshole, looking for someone to blame, and he owed Hank an apology. Before he could hit 'redial,' he heard the door to the garage open and then Annabel breezing through the kitchen. He tossed the phone onto the bed just before she swept in, his suit slung over her shoulder.

'Sorry I'm late. He pressed the pants wrong, made them look like Dockers. Come here. Grab a shirt. Put this on.' She jangled her watch around her wrist until the face came visible. 'We can still get you there on time.'

The photo shoot. Right.

He obliged, moving on stunned autopilot. He couldn't figure out how to stop getting dressed and start telling her.

Annabel moved around him, tugging at the lapels, straightening the sleeves. 'No, not that tie. Something darker.'

'It used to be I could pick out my own tie,' Mike murmured. 'When did I become so useless?'

'You were always useless, babe. You just didn't have me around to point it out.' She went on tiptoes, kissed him lightly on the cheek. 'You look *amazing*. The governor will be impressed. Might hit on you, even. Could be a scandal.' She stepped back, appraised him. 'Certainly beats that plaid jacket.'

'Windowpane,' Mike said weakly. 'Listen . . .'

'*Lord*.' She'd spotted his work clothes, kicked off on the bathroom floor. 'What'd you do, crawl through a sewer?'

She went over and scooped up the grimy clothes. A small brown box fell from the pocket of the jeans, bounced on the linoleum, and spit out a ring – the two-carat diamond he'd chosen at the jewelry store after dropping Kat off at school. He'd forgotten about it.

Annabel's hand went to her mouth. She crouched reverently over the ring, plucked it up. Her eyes glimmered with tears. 'The deal closed!' She laughed and ran over, embracing him. 'I *told* you it would all work out. And this ring. I mean, Mike, are you kidding?' She slid it onto her right hand, splayed her fingers to admire the stone. The joy on her face was so absolute that the notion of breaking the spell tightened his throat, made it hard to breathe.

He set his hands gently on her shoulders. Her bones, delicate and fragile beneath the skin.

She looked up at him. Her gaze sharpened. 'What's wrong?'

There he was, in their tiny walk-in closet, wearing a jacket and shirt with no pants. 'The pipes. Remember the pipes?'

'Vitrified clay. Arm and a leg. Of course.'

'The subcontractor screwed us and took off. I just found out.

Everything stubbed up through the slabs is vitrified clay. That's how we passed environmental inspection.' He moistened his lips. 'But everything buried beneath the surface is PVC.'

A flicker of understanding crossed Annabel's face. 'How much? To fix it?'

'More than we'll make.'

She took a step back and sat on the bed. Her hands were clasped and her eyes on that big diamond sticking out, gleaming even in the faint light of the bedroom. She and Mike breathed awhile in the silence.

'I love my old ring anyway,' she finally said. 'You married me with it.'

Something in his chest unraveled a bit, and he felt suddenly much older than his thirty-five years.

'It's you and me,' she said. 'And Kat. We don't need more money. I can put school on hold, get a job for a while. Just until, you know. We'll find room in the budget. We can pull Kat from that after-school enrichment program. We'll live in a condo. I don't care.'

He pulled on his pants, slowly, his legs heavy and numb, like they didn't belong to him. He couldn't meet Annabel's eyes because he was scared of what that would make him feel.

'You are always true,' she said. She took off the two-carat ring, set it on the duvet beside her, and managed a smile. 'Make this right however you have to.'

The suite in the Beverly Hills Hotel was the largest Mike had ever seen. Bill Garner sat behind an antique letter desk, cocked back thoughtfully in a leather chair that seemed designed for musing. He studied the photo, a computer printout that showed PVC pipe protruding into the ditch.

Through the open door to the sitting room wafted laughter, tidbits of conversation, and the occasional camera flash. The recipients of the community-leadership award were to mingle now and take some PR photos to lay the media foundation for the formal ceremony Sunday evening. Aside from the governor, who – judging by the chorus of salutations – had just swept in, Mike had been the last to arrive.

Garner rose, strode across, and poked his head through the doorway. 'Are the setups ready? Okay, give us a minute here.' He closed the door and resumed his spot behind the desk. His face, teenage smooth, registered nothing but pleasant optimism, as it had the entire time Mike had explained the problem.

Garner templed his fingers. 'You're going to pay for the fix?'

Mike said, 'I am prepared to do that.'

'Those PVC pipes. Where do you think they'll go once you dig them up?'

'I hadn't given that much thought,' Mike said.

'Into a landfill, I'd guess. So you want to move pipes from the ground back into the ground in another location? And use a lot of gas-guzzling machinery to do it?' He smiled affably. 'Sounds a bit silly, doesn't it?'

Mike became suddenly aware of his new suit. 'Yes. But honest, at least.'

'These houses you've built, they're ninety-nine-percent green. There's a lot to be proud of.'

Mike studied him a moment, trying to read his face. 'I don't see it that way.' He shifted on the plush armchair, uncomfortable in the dress clothes. 'I'm not sure I'm following the direction this conversation is taking.'

'The governor's hung his hat on this project, Mike. You know how strong he is on the environment. And your housing community, with our pilot subsidy program, shows that a green model can work not just for rich assholes – that it can make sense for working folks. Green Valley is the governor's baby. He's been talking it up in the press for *months*.'

'I understand that this is an embarrassment,' Mike said. 'I'm sorry.'

'The subsidies are a pilot program, tenuous at best. The governor is under fire from both sides of the aisle. If we don't parade out a community model to show the energy benefits – soon – those subsidies will be off the table. You're aware of the election in a month's time? The governor's got a host of ballot initiatives he's put his neck on the line for. That's why we timed the press, the photo shoot, the award ceremony this Sunday.' He pursed his lips. 'How long will it take you to switch out these pipes?'

Discomfort glowed to life in Mike's stomach, crept up his throat. 'Months.'

'And your award for outstanding community—'

'Obviously, you'll have to withdraw that.'

'See,' Garner said, 'that's the thing. No award ceremony means no press. No press means no public support. No public support means no state subsidies for those home buyers.'

Mike's mouth went dry.

'How much are the subsidies?' Garner asked. 'Three hundred thousand per family?'

'Two seventy-five,' Mike said faintly.

'And these are middle-class families you have moving in there. I mean, that was the point, really. And now you're gonna tell these folks that not only can they not move into their new houses for *months* but that the subsidies upon which they've based their financial planning will no longer be there for them?' He grinned ruefully. 'That they will have to come up with nearly *three hundred grand* more apiece? Or were you planning on covering that as well?'

Mike swallowed to wet his throat. 'I don't have anywhere near that kind of money.'

'Then are you sure you want to pass on this problem to those families?'

For the first time, Mike had no ready answer.

Garner placed a manicured fingertip on the Polaroid and slid it slowly back across the antique desk.

Mike stared down at it.

An impatient knock on the door. A young aide leaned into the room and said, 'We need him *now*. The photographer's restless, and I have to get the governor on a plane back to Sacramento.' From behind him Mike could make out the governor telling a joke, the firehose-pressure vowels of the Austrian intonation. Garner held up a finger. The aide sighed, said, 'You got thirty seconds,' and withdrew.

Mike and Garner regarded each other, the silence cut only by the ticking of a carriage clock and muffled conversation from the sitting room.

'So what do you say?' Garner leaned forward on the desk, a flash of skin peeping through the slit in his shirtsleeve. 'For the benefit of forty families, think you can smile for a few cameras?'

He gestured toward the sitting room, his gold cuff link glittering.

On his knees, Mike peered into the flickering fire. It threw an orange glow across his face, the carpet, the white duvet of their bed. In his hand he clutched the Polaroid showing that telltale elbow of PVC. Ridiculously, it struck him that his posture was that of a shamed samurai.

Annabel stood behind him, still absorbing the scene. Kat, thankfully, was in her room with the door closed, engrossed in homework.

Annabel hadn't spoken. Not since he'd trudged in, tugged off his suit jacket, and taken his spot on the floor. She didn't have to. She already knew and was just waiting for him to tell her.

'They don't want a delay,' he said. 'They need the PR from the award ceremony. They threatened that the families will lose the subsidies.'

'Then we should absorb the cost for them,' Annabel said. 'How much is it? On top of the pipe replacement costs?'

'Eleven million dollars.'

31

He heard the breath leave her.

'So what . . . what are we going to do?' she asked.

He held out his hand, dropped the Polaroid into the flames. The picture curled and blackened.

'Okay.' Her voice was faint, crestfallen. 'I guess I'll buy a new dress.'

The bathroom door clicked shut behind her. He stared into the fire, wondering what the hell else a lie like this could open up.

Chapter 5

A baby's sputtering cry split the night air, rising from the basket placed on the front porch. Folds of fluffy blue blanket poked up from the woven straw. All was still, save the flecks of circling gnats in the yellow smudge of the porch light. Night-blooming jasmine, trellised up the porch, perfumed the air. SUV bumpers gleamed up and down the street. Every third house was being remodeled, the lowboy Dumpsters as much a mark of the neighborhood's affluence as the Boxsters slumbering beneath car covers.

The intermittent cries strengthened into a wail. Finally footsteps came audible within the house, then the beep of an alarm being turned off. The front door cracked so far as the security chain allowed, and a woman's sleep-heavy face peered down. A gasp, then the door closed, the chain unclasped, and she stepped out onto the porch. A well-kept woman in her fifties, she clasped a blue bathrobe shut at her throat. Stunned. Her knees cracked as she crouched to grab the basket with trembling hands.

The blanket was twisted over itself, and she tugged at the folds frantically but gently, the cries growing louder, until finally she pulled back the last edge of fabric and stared down, dumbfounded.

A microcassette recorder.

The red 'play' light beamed up at her, the baby's squawks issuing from the tiny speakers.

The crunch of a dead leaf floated over from the darkness of

the front lawn, and then a man's massive form melted into the cone of porch light. A gloved fist the size of a dumbbell flew at her, shattering her eye socket and knocking her back into the front door, rocketing it inward so hard the handle stuck in the drywall.

A moment of tranquillity. Even the crickets were awed into silence.

The large man stood at the edge of the porch, breath misting, shoulders slumped, his very presence an affront to the quiet suburban street. His plain, handsome face was oddly smooth, almost generic, as if his features were pressed through latex. He held a black duffel bag.

Another set of footsteps padded across the moist lawn, a second man finally entering the light. He was lean and of normal height, but he looked tiny next to his counterpart. He shuffled as he walked, one foot curled slightly inward, matching the awkward angle of his right wrist. As he finished tugging on his black gloves, his arms jerked ever so slightly, a symptom of the illness.

Ellen Rogers grunted on the foyer floor where she'd landed, one eye screwed off center, the skin dipping in the indentation where her cheekbone used to be. Her nose was split along the bridge, a glittering black seam. One leg was raised off the tile, paddling as if she were swimming. Her breaths were low, animal.

The men stepped inside, closed the door behind them, stared down at her. The lean one, William, said gently, 'I know, honey, I know. Dodge can put some muscle behind a punch. I'm sorry for your face. Don't think we wanted this any more than you.'

She whimpered and drooled blood onto the tile.

When Dodge dropped the duffel, it gave a metallic clank. He placed two cigarettes in his mouth, cocked his head, got them going with a cheap plastic lighter plucked from his shirt pocket, and passed one to his colleague. William sucked an inhale past yellowed teeth, closed his eyes, let a ghostly sheet of smoke rise from his parted lips.

34

'Mr Rogers,' he called down the hall. 'Can we please have a word?'

The muted light thrown from the Tiffany lamp seemed the only thing holding darkness at bay. The office's mallard-green walls dissolved into black; they might as well have not been there at all. Beyond the lip of the desk, a stock-ticker screen saver glowed out of nowhere. An artful black-and-white framed on the sofa's console table showed the family a few years earlier posed cute-casual on the rear deck: proud parents leaning over beaming teenage son and daughter, matching smiles and pastel polos. A nautical motif suffused the room – burnished brass compass, gold-plated telescope, antique loupe pinning down the parchment pages of a leather-bound atlas. It was the office of a man who fancied himself the captain of his own destiny. But William and Dodge hadn't chosen the room for the design.

They'd chosen it because it was soundproof.

Ted Rogers propped up his wife on the distressed-leather couch, which Dodge had covered entirely with a plastic tarp. Ted had a softness befitting a man his age and circumstances. A fine, well-fed belly, spectacles accenting a round face, a close-trimmed white-gray beard – all jiggling now with grief and terror. When William had asked him into the study, he'd taken one look at Dodge and complied with all instructions.

Ellen shuddered in her husband's arms, murmuring incomprehensibly. Her neck kept going slack, Ted's plump hands fussing to keep her head upright.

'Boss Man is displeased.' William scratched calmly at the patchy scruff on his neck. 'That little move of yours, it's gonna prove costly to him.'

Old cigar smoke had settled into the furnishings, sweet and comforting.

'I . . . Listen, please, tell him I'm sorry,' Ted said. 'I understand, now, the gravity—'

William held up a finger. 'What did Boss Man tell you?'

'I can get it all back first thing tomorrow. I swear to you.'

'What. Did. Boss. Man. Tell. You?'

Ted's chest jerked beneath his bathrobe. 'If I did anything to betray his trust, he'd kill me.'

William moved his hand in a circle, prompting, cigarette smoke swirling like a ribbon. '*How* would he kill you?'

Ted leaned forward, gagged a bit, wiped his mouth. His voice came out unnaturally high. 'Painfully.' His hand rose, chubby fingers splayed, a man used to resolving conflict, to meeting halfway, to finding sensible solutions. 'Look' – his rolling eyes found William again – 'you can take *anything*. Whatever this has cost him, I can set right. I mean, he can't possibly *prefer* to . . . to . . .' He sputtered to a stop, an engine winding down.

William and Dodge just stared down at him.

Ted's tongue poked at the inside of his lip, making that well-trimmed beard undulate. 'I was in some trouble and made a stupid decision. But I can undo it. I will pay for whatever the costs of the fallout will be. I can take a third mortgage on the house. I have equity in . . . in—'

Beside him his wife keeled over, her bruised face pushed into the cushion. Ted began to weep. 'Look at her. Let me get her to a hospital. Let me call 911. We won't say what happened. There's still time. We can still get everything straightened out.'

William turned the cigarette inward, studying the cherry. Then he ground it out against his front tooth. He placed the butt carefully into a Ziploc bag, which he returned to his pocket, then continued as if there had been no interruption. 'My uncle used to tell me: All we have is our word. All we have is what we promise we will do. Our employer is a man of his word. And I'm a man of mine. Ethics, see? So we're in a predicament here. We don't like hurtin' folks, but we have to do what we say. Following orders, like in the armed services, or the whole damn thing falls apart. It's a sad business all around, but that's how it's gotta be.'

His close-set eyes never faltered. Strands of facial hair, strawberry blond and wiry, fringed the sallow skin of his jawline. The smell coming off him was medicinal and sour. 'In our business you gotta make sure a man's promise to you is upheld. If it's *not*, you gotta set precedent. You, Ted, are that precedent.'

Ted thumbed back Ellen's eyelid. The pupil, dark and dilated. 'Can you, please, *please*' – his hand tightened into a fist – 'take her to the hospital? She had nothing to do with this. She knew nothing about—'

The gunshot, even muffled, brought him upright on the couch. Ellen's head bobbed, and then, through the fresh tear in the drop cloth, a single feather floated up from the cushion, flecked crimson. Shock at the sight overtook Ted instantly – glazed eyes, spread mouth, ice-water tremble of his muscles, like a horse flank shuddering off flies. A small, shapeless noise escaped him, a vowel sound drawn out and out.

Dodge leaned over, reached into the unzipped duffel, and rummaged inside. Objects clanked.

'We need to take pictures,' William explained. 'At various stages. So we can show them to the next guy, see, who thinks he can get one over on Boss Man.'

When Dodge's gloved hand emerged from the duffel, it was gripping a ball-peen hammer.

Ted moaned softly.

William said, 'I need you to sit over here. So we have room. The angle, you see. No, here. There you go. Thank you.' Stunned, Ted complied. William stepped back, admired his positioning. 'Dodge here, he gets impatient. So we're gonna get going. Dodge, where you want to start?'

Dodge hefted the ball peen, let it slap the leather of his palm. 'Joints,' he said.

The white van rattled up the dirt road, veering side to side on wide, trash-littered switchbacks. The ground finally leveled off, the headlights sweeping past an endless chain-link guarding a disused auto-wrecking yard. Vehicles smashed into neat rectangular bales were stacked treetop high, the unlit aisles running as long and true as cornrows. Caught wrappers and plastic bags wagged in the barbed wire. Rust ground into the hilltop dirt had turned the soil an Indian red.

Past the wrecking yard, beyond a massive setback of dead weeds, rose a two-story clapboard house. It had settled westward, resigning itself to the wind. A blue oak twisted up out of the brown earth like something from a painting.

The van halted in front of the house, dust clouding around the tires. The breeze picked up to a faint moan. Dodge climbed out, slammed his door, stretched his spine. It was early-morning dark, the hilltop as desolate as an abandoned mine.

A light clicked on upstairs in the house.

William was a bit slower getting out. Wincing, he fumbled a pill from his pocket and downed it dry, then rubbed at the backs of his legs. He palmed a handful of sunflower seeds into his mouth, his jaw shifting with machine precision, then spit a few hulls in the dirt. He'd started at eleven years old with tobacco dip, but a few years ago someone had shown him a video of people with holes in their lips and cheeks, and so sunflower seeds it was. He had enough problems already without a sieve for a jaw.

He walked around the van, running a hand along the chipped white paint, and opened the back door. Ted lunged out, bellowing, his voice strained through the pillowcase tied over his head. William sidestepped, his wilted leg nearly buckling, and Ted tumbled off the rear bumper into the dirt. He screamed, arms flopping boneless at his sides, shattered at the shoulders and elbows.

He used his chin to shove himself up, shuffling and grunting like a blind bear, then bolted. The pillowcase was spotted red around the mouth where William had punched a knife through to give him some air; it was hard to be precise when they struggled.

About twenty yards away, Ted tripped and fell. Found his feet. Kept on.

William's brother, Hanley, emerged from the front door and paused on the rickety porch, staring out across the Sacramento Valley. Morning edged over the horizon, a thin plane of gold. Hanley gave a half nod to the new day, stepped down, and peered into the back of the van. A body neatly wrapped in plastic drop cloth, one leather couch cushion seared from a bullet, rags soaked with bleach strong enough to make the eyes sting. When Hanley nudged the couch cushion to explore the bullet hole, the microcassette beside it clicked to life, a few baby squalls escaping until he stopped the recording again.

The footing of the sprawling front yard was uneven, ground squirrels doing their work beneath cover of the weeds. Ted ran, tripped, knee-crawled, ran. He blazed a frantic, meandering path, making poor progress. The three men paid him no mind.

Hanley drew a hand across his mouth, his stubble giving off a rasp. The family resemblance was apparent, though Hanley was clearly a healthier version of his older brother. Well-defined muscles, smooth pale skin, no kink in the posture or tweak in the limbs. 'Nice work, brother,' he said. 'Dodge do his thing?' Eagerness showed in his voice. This was new for him, and more than a little exciting.

'He did indeed,' William said.

Dodge was rooting in the duffel bag. He'd donned a rubber butcher's apron and slaughterhouse goggles. The apron, pulled tight across his massive chest, held the marks of jobs past. He paused from cataloging his implements and drew himself upright, towering a full head above the van's roof. That mannequin face, blank as a turned-off TV.

Behind them Ted collided with the trunk of the oak and went down hard with a grunt, vanishing into the waving foxtails. He struggled back up and stumbled onward at a new trajectory.

William nodded, bunched his lips. 'We'll prep the cellar,' he said.

The brothers started toward the house, Hanley helping William up the stairs.

Somehow Ted had navigated his way across the giant stretch of yard. His ragged breaths carried back on the wind. He was sobbing something unintelligible, trying to form words.

Dodge shouldered the duffel and started calmly after him.

Leaning heavily on his brother, William dragged his lame leg up, one step at a time. They reached the porch, and he glanced down at a plastic-wrapped edition of the *Sacramento Bee*. He jerked to a halt.

Hanley said, 'What, brother? You all right?'

William's cheek twitched to one side, a dagger of teeth showing in the wire of his beard. He pointed down at the newspaper's front-page photograph. 'The face,' he said.

Hanley looked down. Dumbstruck. 'It's not possible. It can't be.'

William's eyes hardened. He spit seeds across the black-and-white print. 'Sure as hell *looks* like it. We'll find out. We'll make sure.'

'And then?'

Down below they heard Dodge catch up to Ted. A crunch of bone and tendon, followed by a thin, wavering scream. A grunt as Ted was hoisted onto a shoulder and then the scrabble of arms flailing weakly against Dodge's back.

'Coming,' Dodge said.

THEN

Chapter 6

'What's your name? Can he hear? Is he listening? Hello? Hey there. Your name?'

'Michael.'

'Okay, great, kid. Last name? Can you tell me your last name?'

'He's in shock, Detective.'

'You don't know your last name? How about your dad's name? Do you know your dad's name?'

'John.'

'Good, that's good. And your mom? You remember your mom's name? Hello? What's your mom's name?'

'Momma.'

'Okay. Okay. That's fine. John and Momma. It's a start, right?'

'I don't see how sarcasm's going to help either of you, Detective. Michael, honey, how old are you?'

'Four. And a quarter.'

'Good, kid, that's good. We need to figure out how to get you home. Do you understand?'

'I think we should give him some more time, Detective.'

'Time is of the essence, ma'am. Son, do you live nearby? Do you know – Hey, kiddo, over here. Look at me.'

'I really think I should complete my assessment before—'

'What town are you from? Michael? Michael? Do you know the name of the town you live in?'

'The United States of America.'

'Jesus.'

Chapter 7

The first year passes in bits and pieces, fragments with sharp edges. It is defined by voices. Conversations. Like this one:

'How about a street? C'mon, help us out here. You must remember a street sign, *some*thing.'

And him pointing to the letter *X* on an alphabet puzzle. 'Like that.'

'Hey, Joe, you know any street names start with the letter *X*?'

'How 'bout Fuckin' Xanadu?'

'I think that starts with a *F*.'

And this one:

'My dad's coming back.'

'Sure, shithead. My momz, too. *All* our parents is coming back. We gonna have a big fat Thanksgiving turkey dinner and fall asleep 'round the fireplace.'

There are flashes, too – light and movement, photographs that can be strung together to form herky-jerky story lines. There is the Trip to the Hospital, him trembling in the sterile white hall, terrified that he'd been brought here to be put down like the neighbor's Doberman who'd bitten a Sears repairman. (Which neighbor? Why remember a Sears repairman but not his own mother's name?) The doctor comes for him, towering and imperious and breathing Listerine, and leads him to a tiny room. He goes passively to his death. They count his teeth, assess his fine motors skills, X-ray his left hand and wrist to check bone development. Then they give him a birthday.

A week later he gets a last name.

Doe.

A random assignment by a faceless clerk in an unseen office. The fact that a brand like that, a goddamn *name* could be yoked to him forever seems the punctuation mark on a lifelong sentence he will have to serve for a crime he didn't commit. Michael Doe. Reborn and renamed and left to build from scratch.

Over the months he has added to the memories here, amended them there, losing pieces to the shock that preceded and followed. He had rubbed the narrative curve to a high polish, like river rock, wearing in contours, revealing new seams in the excavated quarry, until what remained, what he beheld, may not even have been the same shape anymore, until he'd freed a different sculpture from the same marble block. But this – this bastardized fusion of past and later – is all he has. This is his imperfect history. This is how it lives in his bones.

Then there is nothing but a snowstorm.

When it clears, he is six.

A run-down house at the end of a tree-shaded lane. He is kneeling at a bay window, nose to the glass, elbows on the sill, fists chubbing up his cheeks. Waiting. The yellow plaid cushion beneath his knees reeks of cat piss. Waiting. A car pulls up, and his spirits fly to the stars, but the car keeps on driving, driving away. Waiting.

A girl's voice from behind him, 'Shithead still thinks Daddy's comin' back.'

He has told no one about his mother. That he suspects her dead. His mind flits like a butterfly over poisonous flowers. *Did his father kill her? Did he use a knife? What is his bloody inheritance?*

He doesn't turn from the window, but his thoughts have moved to the kids gathering behind him, sneakers shuffling on worn carpet. One voice rises above the others, boy-cruel and high with prepubescence: 'Get over it, Doe Boy. Daddy didn't want you.'

Mike tries to slow time. He makes a conscious decision to form a fist, the steps of curling, tightening, where to put the thumb. He will use this, his hand, to smash. But then anger bleeds in, overtakes him. A frozen expression of surprise on Charlie Dubronski's face as Mike charges. A fist, fatter than his, blotting out the bright morning. A whirl of rust-colored carpet and a dull ache in his jaw. And then Dubronski leaning over him, hands on dimpled knees, leering red face. 'How's the weather down there, Doe Boy?'

Mike thinks, *Calmer next time.*

And then, weeks later, he is in the bathroom at three in the morning, the one time it is unoccupied. He needs a stool so he can lean forward over the sink, to see his face in the dim nightlight glow. Looking in the mirror, he sees a missing person. He examines his features. He does not have his mother's high cheekbones. He does not have her beautiful black-brown hair. His skin does not smell like cinnamon, and his clothes do not carry the faintest whiff of patchouli as did hers. With the exception of the final imprint, his memories of his father are all good ones, gentle ones. But memories are weighted by quality, not quantity. He pictures his father's hands gripping the steering wheel. That splotch of red on his shirt cuff.

He cannot help fearing just how much like his father he might be.

He does not know his last name. He does not know in which state he was born. He does not know what his room looked like or what toys he had or if his momma ever kissed him on the forehead like the mothers in children's books. But he does know, now, that he is sixish years old and being raised in an overcrowded foster home in the smog-draped Valley of 1982.

Daylight. The Couch Mother lays in her hermit-crab shell of corduroy sofa, bleating instructions, giving off great wafts of baby powder and something worse, something like decay. An ashtray surfs of its own accord between formless breast and thigh, adrift on a sea of gingham. Ginger hair done in a sixties flip, easy smile, that Virginia Slims voice rattling after them down the hall: *Charlie dear, pick up the bath mat. Tony dear, wash the dishes. Michael dear, empty my ashtray.*

The communal dresser. He hates the communal dresser. Hates when he's the last one to get dressed for school and winds up with the salmon-colored shirt that is cruelly mistaken – the day long – for pink. He hoards shirts at night, sleeps with them. But this night, when he gets back from brushing his teeth, his pillow is turned aside; the blue-striped shirt is gone. Dubronski, cross-legged on his bed, is smiling. And of course Tony Moreno, skinny sidekick, is laughing with implausible vigor.

Mike says, 'Give it back.'

Dubronski holds out his fat bully hands as if catching rain. 'Give what back?'

This, to Tony M, is high comedy.

'You can't even fit it,' Mike says.

'Then why don't you take it?' Dubronski says. 'Oh – that's right. Because I'll give you a beat-down.'

Something hard and gemlike flares in Mike's chest. It is blue-hot, but this time as controlled as a pilot light. He leans forward, says, 'Yeah, but you have to sleep sometime. And my bed is right next to yours.'

Dubronski's face changes. Tony M stops laughing. Dubronski recovers, quickly, with tough words. He cannot give up the shirt, not now, not with six sets of eyes watching from the surrounding cots. But the stench of his fear lingers in the room after dark. The spell has been broken.

The next day Dubronski limps to school. Mike is the Wearer of the Blue-Striped Shirt.

He is in the bay window as usual. Waiting. *Michael dear, go outside and play – you practically* live *in that window.* There is a new kid, skin and bones, with huge feet like a puppy's paws. When he arrived, his hair was curly and long, but now it is close-cropped like everyone else's. Head lice make their rounds with such frequency that the Couch Mother has ruled for crew cuts; she wields a pair of clippers with the impersonal proficiency of a bureaucrat denying a request. Function over form, always.

The new kid has a dog name to go with the puppy paws – Shep. Right now Dubronski and Tony M are pummeling him. From his perch on the cushion, Mike watches him get back up, lips bleeding. Another punch. Dubronski's mouth moving: *Stay down, ya little faggot.* The neighbor's kids are at their windows; they are used to the Roman theater that is 1788 Shady Lane. Shep struggles, finds his feet. Dubronski draws back his fist for the fifth or fifteenth time. The Couch Mother's voice sails from the living room – '*Diii*–ner' – terminating the day's festivities.

The new kid's voice is funny, too loud – *Hey, Retard Voice, why you sound like such a* ree-*tard* – so he doesn't talk much. He eats at the long kitchen table, head down, shoveling, his rail-thin body burning off the calories before he finishes chewing. The Couch Mother arises to refill her jug of Crystal Light, and Dubronski leans across the table and swats Shep's fork as it goes into his mouth. Shep emits a faint bark. The Couch Mother whirls. 'What's wrong, Shepherd dear?' He winces, shakes his head. When Couch Mother disappears again behind the refrigerator door, he dips his mouth into a napkin, drools blood.

A dream. Beneath flickering eyelids Mike's mind dances with fantasies of domesticity, of waffle irons and cream-white linens. He wakes up cramped on the too-small cot, staring at a ceiling blotched seaweed brown from water damage.

Back on the yellow plaid cushion. Waiting. Shep out front. Couch Mother engrossed in a talk show and a cantaloupe in the TV room. Outside, Dubronski hammers Shep into the dirt. Shep gets up, jeans torn, knees bloodied. Even Tony M can horn in on the action, can knock the small kid down. Mike can hear Dubronski shouting, exasperated, 'Stay down, douchebag! Stay down.' Shep rises again. Mike turns his eyes to the end of the road. There is no station wagon there.

Now it is sloppy-joe night. Zucchini was on sale yesterday, so it substitutes for onions. Zucchini bits are not meant to appear in sloppy joes, with good reason. But the foster children are hungry; they eat with relish. The Police da-da-da from the crackly radio by the toaster. Dubronski has just taken his insulin – *Remember, Charlie darling: Cold and clammy, you need some candy. Dry and hot, you need a shot* – so he must wait fifteen minutes to eat. When the time is up, he scrambles to the kitchen. On his way back, he pauses behind Shep, extends his overladen tray above Shep's head, lets it clap to the table in front of him. The sound is like a gunshot in a bank vault, but Shep doesn't so much as blink. A spray of runny meat spatters his face. Unfazed, he scoops a fingerful off his cheek and pops it into his mouth. The Couch Mother looks at him sidewise, her chins ajiggle, and the next day Shep arrives late to school wearing hearing aids from the Shriners Hospital. On the playground at recess, Dubronski heat-seeks his target. 'Hey, look at the old man! Shep needs hearing aids like a *old man!*' A crowd has gathered. Shep pulls the flesh-colored units from both ears, drops them to the asphalt, crushes them under a sneaker. His stare is level, Zen-like, and for once his voice is even. 'I don't need anything.'

A rumor makes its rounds, something involving Shep's drunk of a dad and a gun with blanks. Like a stubborn shellfish, Shep will not let himself be pried open, will not let his treasure spill. Whereas Mike has strength, Shep has will, and Mike is sharp enough to know which is the rarer commodity.

Time scribbles forward a few months and there Mike is, still on the piss-smelling yellow cushion, nose pigged against the bay window. An unearthly light pervades 1788 Shady Lane, turning it slate gray; it is a black-and-white movie. The street is empty. A station wagon makes the turn, and Mike feels his heart soar. It nears and – *yes* – pulls to the curb and – *yes* – that is a man, a solitary man who climbs out – *yes* – and makes his way up the walk, and a fall of light breaks through the trees and the slate gray pall, lighting his face in full color and – *yes* – it is his father. Mike runs to the door and is swept up in strong arms, he and his father spinning like a shampoo-commercial couple in a field of foxtail yellow, and he hugs him, feels the cheek warm against his own, the grit of stubble beneath the clean shave, the crinkle of the starched collar. His father sets him down and says, *I am so sorry. I came back for you at the playground, and you were gone. I've been looking for you all these months, every waking hour, forgoing food and sleep, and look –* he holds out his shirt cuff with the bloodred blotch – *this is just a splash of cranberry juice, and look –* he points to the car, and there, waving from the passenger seat, his mother, her smile sending out a light all its own and –

Mike is shaken awake. He tugs away, buries his face in the pillow, rooting out remnants of the dream. But the wide hand is persistent. He rolls onto his back, stares up at the perfumed face, lax with gravity. 'Michael dear, come with me.' Instantly he is drenched in panic sweat – *another move, another abandonment –* but he is walking, in underwear, on ice-numb bare feet, following Couch Mother to doom or desertion. She moves on hushed footsteps; the house creaks under the weight of her. Into the kitchen, into a slant of yellow thrown by the outdoor security lamp, and Mike squints and sees on the table: a cake. His name frilled in frosting. He looks at Couch Mother, but she is watching the cake, her eyes alight. This is their little secret. His mind sputters. 'It's not my birthday.' 'No,' Couch Mother says, 'it's *our* birthday. A year to the day I got you.' His breath leaves him in a huff. He lunges to her, hugs, burying his face in the soft folds of her nightgown. He says, 'I love you,' and she says, 'Let's not get carried away.'

The next day he finds himself again on the cushion. Waiting. The bay window, smudged with a thousand marks from his nose and forehead. A thousand and one. Waiting. He thinks back on the time he has passed on this cat-piss cushion and wonders if this is all life is, one year after the last, nothing memorable, a sun-baked torment. Outside, Shep is receiving his daily beating. He lies on his back in the fall-gorgeous leaves, Dubronski brandishing a fist over his face. 'Stay the fuck down, runt. Stay *down*.' Shep finds his feet. Mike's eyes move through the arcade of yellow-orange leaves and their geometric patterns to the end of the street, to the station wagon that has still not appeared. Waiting. He tries to stop time, to freeze the image like a photograph, this unextraordinary moment, just to have it, just to have something he can hold on to, something he can keep. He waits for his father.

And then, at once, he hates him.

Shep is standing again – no, not anymore. Tony M, inexplicably wearing an Angels batting helmet, is cackling that idiotic laugh, thumping Dubronski's shoulders, leaping with joy. Shep manages to get to all fours, but he has halted there. For the first time, he has lost momentum. Dubronski jeering, 'I told you, you fuckin' deaf runt. I told you I'd make you stay down.' Shep looks up at him, the looming fist, unable to rise to it. Mike knows now that if Shep doesn't rise, something beautiful will die out there on the browning front lawn of 1788 Shady Lane.

Mike walks outside. Dubronski stands over Shep, victorious. Tony M and three others have formed a half circle around Dubronski, crowing victoriously. They turn when the screen door bangs. Mike crosses to them, Dubronski's unease registering on his broad features. Mike walks in front of the half circle, stands facing Dubronski, two feet away, the distance of an uppercut. Shep is behind Mike, still on all fours; Mike can feel the heat of him against the backs of his calves.

Mike says, loudly, 'Get up.'

He hears Shep breathing hard. He hears Shep grunt with exertion. And then Mike reads the shadow.

Shep is standing.

Dubronski's face flushes. 'You queers deserve each other,' he says, but he is backpedaling, knocking through the others,

51

dispersing them. They go inside. All is quiet at 1788 Shady Lane. Dusk is coming, and there will be dinner soon.

Shep brushes himself off, as composed as a businessman lint-rolling a suit. Mike heads up the walk.

Shep follows.

'Where did you get these?' The Couch Mother stands over them, legs trembling from the exertion, the mini liquor bottles dwarfed in her flushed, pillowy palm.

Mike and Shep are ten. They are now the same height, but Mike is wider still, more solid, whereas Shep's body, pulled thin like taffy, can't seem to catch up to him.

Shep says, 'What?'

He has learned to speak softly to control his voice, to over-compensate for his bad hearing, for the guttural bursts and blurred consonants. People lean toward him to distinguish his words. They take a step or two in his direction. He draws the world to him, if it is interested. Generally it isn't. So he has learned something else. He has learned to use his semideafness to his advantage.

That is never clearer than at this moment.

The Couch Mother's gaze shifts from Shep, zeroing in on Mike. He stares at her ash-speckled crocheted sweater, grimaces, and says, 'Valley Liquor.'

The Couch Mother frowns, her face folding in and in around her lips. 'We are going back there to return these, and you are both going to apologize and take whatever punishment you are due. Do you understand me?'

Mike watches the fifty-milliliter nips of Jack Daniel's disappear into her elephantine purse. 'Yes, ma'am,' he says.

Shep says, 'What?'

The Couch Mother is not fooling, because she marches them outside and lowers herself into her long-suffering Pontiac. Mike has seen her drive only a few times before, and only to the hospital when someone needs stitches or a fever won't break. The passenger seat is stripped to the coils, and her seat is shoved back so far that Shep has to sit on Mike's lap in the back. With dread they watch the scenery roll by while the Couch Mother navigates streets, grunting against the non-power steering, her stomach adding friction to the wheel.

In no time they are behind the counter at the liquor store, standing at attention before Mr Sandoval, who never lets them handle the comic books, who grimaces when he counts their change for Dr Pepper bottles, who hates them. Mike mumbles out an apology, and Mr Sandoval, who has set aside his cursing, hateful self before the Couch Mother, makes a big show of patronizing magnanimity.

It is time for Shep to apologize, but Mike knows that he will not. Shep is not like him or anyone else; he is made of steel and concrete; he cannot be broken.

'Shepherd dear, your turn.'

'What?'

'You're not going to play this game with me. Now, apologize to Mr Sandoval this instant.'

'What?'

It escalates until Mike is uncomfortable, until he backs away so his shoulder brushes the real-size liquor bottles on the shelves behind them. He notices a picture Mr Sandoval keeps taped to the cash register – his daughter. It is school-picture day, and she beams proudly, but her little skirt is stained and tattered at the edges. It reminds Mike of the communal shirts in the dresser, and he is flooded with guilt, his assumptions cracking apart one after another, like dropped eggs. But his remorse is temporary, because the Couch Mother's voice has risen so as to drown out all thought.

Just when it seems Shep will triumph, that he has worn them down into defeat, he mutters, 'Sorry.'

Mike is shocked. He has never seen Shep cave in, and he fears the act will diminish him irrevocably. On the ride home, Mike pouts. Shep turns on Mike's lap, studies his face, his own expression unreadable. And then his lips twist in his version of a smile. Tugging up his shirt furtively, Shep flashes the pint bottle of Jack Daniel's he has shoved down his pants.

A blurred half decade, and they are fourteen. Shep has taken to wearing a pendant of St. Jerome Emiliani – patron saint of orphans – that he stole from a pawnshop. While Mike awaits his growth spurt, Shep has, at last, grown into his feet. He towers, husky with premature muscle. Despite some acne, he now buys Jack Daniel's without getting carded. At the home, Charlie Dubronski lives and breathes in constant fear, but Shep has never laid a hand on him. He just looks at him now and then, and that is enough.

Mike and Shep have ridden the bus over to Van Nuys Park, where the ice-cream man forgets to lock the back of his truck, so Bomb Pops can be stolen while he's distracted with paying customers. They have made their way over to the far baseball diamond, where a father, son, and grandfather play ball. The boys lean against the chain-link by the backstop and watch cynically. The grandfather pitches, the son bats, and the father plays somewhere between shortstop and left field, retrieving the ball and tossing it back. They have a pretty good system down. The boy, who is about their age, dribbles a grounder to his father.

Mike says, 'He can only hit the pull,' and Shep remarks, ''Cuz he's not good enough to go the other way.'

The father's car, a straight-off-the-lot forest green Saab, is pulled up onto a patch of dirt behind the fence, and the boy's bike, an expensive-looking ten-speed, leans against the bumper.

Mike says, 'Nice set o' wheels,' and Shep says, 'The 900's a piece of shit.' Mike agrees out loud but secretly loves the Saab, its sleek lines, its odd angles, how it's not afraid to be ugly and beautiful at the same time. The car reeks of affluence and power, of accomplishment and control. In its unblemished paint, he sees his own wavery reflection, his idealized self, a future he cannot

yet discern. The dealer's plate stares out at him – WINGATE DEAL-
ERSHIP: WE HAVE WHAT YOU WANT! – and he thinks the name, like
the car, boasts of success. Wingate. Win-*gate*. It has a ring.

A voice from the baseball field shatters Mike's reverie, the
father calling out, 'Ready for a Fudgsicle?' For an instant, in his
disorientation, Mike mistakes the man as speaking to him. But
then the son smiles and tosses aside his bat and three generations
set out across the park for the ice-cream truck Mike and Shep
just looted.

Mike watches them walking away. The boy's longish blond
hair curls out from beneath his cap and makes Mike ashamed of
his and Shep's buzz cuts. He hates that his whole stupid appearance is a concession to head lice.

Shep walks around the fence and picks up the bat. He comes
back. Kicks over the kid's bike. 'Wanna piss on it?'

This is something they have done before.

Mike shakes his head.

Shep says, 'Car first?' He never uses extra words.

Mike stares at the beautiful Saab, and it seems a shame, but
there is something burning deep in his chest that wants a way
out. He's not sure what it is, but it has to do with the white gleam
of the father's teeth when he called to his son about getting a
Fudgsicle. Mike says, 'I don't know.'

Shep says, 'Why?'

He is embarrassed, but it is Shep, and he can tell Shep anything. 'I mean, if my mom *is* alive, I owe it to her not to wind up
in—'

Shep says, 'There is no past.'

Mike coughs out a laugh. 'No past?'

Shep's lips part, showing off the slight overlap of his front
teeth. 'There are only two things in life: loyalty and stamina.
Everything else is just a distraction.'

'What about responsibility?' He is channeling the Couch
Mother and hates himself for it.

55

Shep speaks quietly, as always. 'You're not a son. You're not a brother. No one wants you. So. Make it your own. You can be whatever you want to be. And right now? You're a man with a task.'

Mike takes the bat. One headlight goes with a satisfying pop. The moon-crescent ding distorts the shine of the hood, the next even more so. He is lost in a haze, in something sticky sweet and unslakable.

Mike's forearms ache. He stops, pants. Across the park, on someone's boom box, Bon Jovi is going down in a blaze of glory.

Shep takes the bat. He beats down on the bicycle, wheels denting, spokes flying, metal clanging.

A voice from behind them. 'Hey, loser. *Hey*. That's my bike.'

The boy has run ahead of his father and grandfather.

Shep says, 'What?' The boy steps forward, repeats himself. Shep says, 'What?' The boy leans in for a third try. Shep headbutts him, and the boy goes down screaming and the father is running at them, and Mike is frozen; he has fought plenty, but an old-fashioned respect for adults has locked him up. The father grabs Mike around the neck, hard, with both hands, and Shep blurs over, closing the space in no time, and then the father is bent backward, choking, Shep's hand clamped over his throat.

Shep says, in his trademark hush, 'I'm gonna let go of you. But don't touch him again. Understand?'

The father nods. Shep releases him. Offers the boy his hand, helps him up. Says, 'Don't call me a loser.'

There are sirens. Shep's mouth is Bomb Pop red, and Mike is quite certain his is, too.

At the station the desk cop says, 'The Shady Lane boys, what a surprise.'

Mike and Shep are sent to different interrogation rooms. Alone, Mike stares at the wall, memories of similar rooms flooding back. *You remember your mom's name? Hello? What's your mom's name?* A detective comes in, sits down, reads the report, sighs, and throws it on the wooden table. 'You're not worth the chair you're sitting in, you foster-home piece of shit.'

Mike thinks, *Make it your own.*

'You did about fifteen thousand dollars of damage.'

His stomach clutches at the figure. It might as well be a million. Mike knows at that moment: his life is over.

He looks down at his wrists, cinched in flexible plastic handcuffs – kid handcuffs – because the steel ones kept slipping off at the park.

'Before we ship your ass to sentencing,' the detective continues, 'your victims want to confront you.'

Panic overtakes dread. 'I don't want to see them.'

'Well, guess what? When you're a lawbreaking degenerate, you don't get to choose your options.'

Mike closes his eyes. When he opens them, the kid is there, freckled cheeks tight with disdain, the detective and the father at his elbows. The grandfather stands in the back, arms crossed. 'You gonna apologize?' the kid asks.

Mike knows it is in his self-interest to do so, but he looks at the kid's ironed shirt, the smudge of chocolate in the corner of his mouth, and can think only, *Never.*

The kids points at Mike. 'You're a *nothing*. You wreck my stuff because you don't have anything and you'll never be anything. Well, guess what? It's not my fault your life sucks.'

Mike closes his eyes again, for a very long time. He hears footsteps, the door creak open and click shut. When he opens his eyes, the grandfather is sitting across from him. Alone. The man says, 'That was my car.'

Mike says, 'I thought it was your son's.'

The grandfather laughs. He has a white mustache, impeccably maintained. 'That would have made it okay?'

Mike stares down at the wooden table. Someone has etched into it, POINT OF NO RETURN, MOTHAFUCKA.

'I grew up in the Depression. You know what that means?' The man waits for a response but, getting none, continues, 'If we spotted roadkill on the side of the road, my pop used to pull over so we could cook it for dinner. For a time we slept in the car. We went two long years without a roof over our heads.'

Mike says, 'You can't have everything.'

The grandfather spreads his hands. 'Why not?'

'I don't know. People like us, we don't get to.'

'People like us?'

'Like me and Shep.'

'How about me?'

'You have a Saab.'

'I see.' The grandfather folds his hands across his old-man's paunch and nods. 'How do you think I got that car?'

'How would *I* know? That's the first time I've been within ten feet of a car that nice.'

'You're the predator here, not a victim. Let's be clear about that.' His eyes are hard now, and Mike is awed by the force of his conviction.

Mike looks down at his hands. His thumb has a sticky blue streak from the Bomb Pop. He pictures that beautiful, spotless Saab (WINGATE DEALERSHIP: WE HAVE WHAT YOU WANT!), and for a moment the car and the man before him become of a piece; they become two elegant, polished parts of the same whole. Shep's words come back to him: *You can be whatever you want to be.* Mike rethinks the question posed to him a moment ago – *How do you think I got that car?* – and he is speaking, softly, before his brain can catch up: 'When I get out of juvie, I will work to pay you back for wrecking your car.'

The grandfather closes his eyes, his face beatific and soft, and Mike doesn't understand his reaction at all. Then the man says, 'No. You won't. I'm not pressing charges. And you won't be held responsible for the damages.'

Mike is certain he is being mocked.

'I will pay to fix my car,' the man says. 'But I'm buying something for that money. Would you like to know what it is?'

Transfixed, Mike nods.

'I am buying your not getting to feel sorry for yourself about this.'

Incredulous, Mike asks, 'What's that accomplish?'

The man says, 'Wait and see.'

Mike and Shep walk out free men, and from that day forward Mike sees things a little differently. He and Shep remain thick as thieves, closer than brothers because they are all parts of a family to one another, though this remains unspoken. Because Shep did not bend and repent in that interrogation room, he has to work off the price of the boy's bicycle by bagging groceries; he does this in double time by peddling cigarette packs he boosts from behind the counter.

As they grow older, they run liquor stores with fake IDs, get bulletproof drunk, and raise hell, but Mike is spending more time with his nose in textbooks – *Michael dear, you'll be my first to go to college* – then studying for the SATs, taking practice tests, scoring somewhere between retarded and stupid. But slowly, over his junior year of high school, he has brought his scores up to average, and when the acceptance letter arrives from Cal State L.A., he doesn't even tell Shep right away; he goes out to the backyard when everyone is sleeping and sits with it beneath the golden glow of the security light, reading and rereading it, cherishing it like hidden treasure.

For a few blissful months, the path ahead seems illuminated. The Couch Mother is proud; his plans for college reflect well on them both. Dubronski and Tony M, never deep on originality, start in with the nickname – *Hey, College, you gonna grow a mustache like Alex Trebek?* – and Mike recognizes their mocking as a form of flattery.

Every year more kids have come, young and damaged, but for the first time Mike realizes that he has become, oddly, a role model. And Shep has, too – a role model of another kind. As an almost-adult, Mike gains a different understanding of the workings of the foster home. How the Couch Mother gets money from the state for every kid under her roof. How on occasion she gets a birth certificate fudged with a little help from well-placed women of like minds and body type to ensure that her children are protected from abusive mothers or molester uncles. It strikes him how fortunate he is to be a cog in the wheels of this particular system.

For a high-school senior, he is young at seventeen. Shep has taken advantage of his first four months as an eighteen-year-old to rack up two strikes under the California penal code. A third felony will land him in jail for twenty-five to life, which seems a bit much for a stolen VCR and beating up some snot-nosed private-school kid who welshed on an arm-wrestling bet. But Shep, as ever, is not worried – *Two strikes is nothing. You've seen me play ball.*

One day Shep walks into the shared bedroom carrying what appears to be a wall safe, his substantial biceps bulging under the weight of it. Mike is rereading his worn SAT practice book, because he is convinced that he will arrive at college next fall and not know how to communicate with kids actually smart enough to be there. He hopes against logic that knowing words like 'bedight' and 'acetate' might help close that gap.

Incredulous, he looks up from the vocab section at Shep. 'Where'd you get that?'

Shep says, 'A wall.'

Mike conveys another bite of SpaghettiOs from can to mouth, using the flat edge of a butter knife since all the forks and spoons are dirty. 'Shep,' he mumbles around the mush, 'you can't do that shit.'

'You get half of whatever's in it.'

'I don't want half.' Mike rolls up the workbook and smacks it against his forehead. 'I want to know what "flagitious" means.'

'Of or like a flag.' Shep sits Indian style on the floor, knocks on the safe at various points, then removes from his back pocket folded graph paper and an actual stethoscope. Mike watches with fascination. Shep ducks into the earbuds and twists the dial, listening with medical interest. Given his hearing, he seems to be having trouble perceiving the clicks. The EKG line of his graph doesn't progress beyond a few peaks and valleys. He sets the stethoscope aside, goes out, and returns a moment later with a hammer and chisel.

Mike's mouth comes slightly ajar. '*Really*?'

Round Two. Shep starts beating the hell out of the safe. The ringing of course does not bother him. The others are all ostensibly at a Dodgers game, so Shep and Mike enjoy relative privacy.

Until the Couch Mother, who has been groaning through a bout of colitis in the mephitic fog of her bedroom, calls down the hall, 'Michael dear, what's that *noise*?' She has learned not to shout to Shep.

Shep says quietly, 'I'm fixing a carburetor.'

Mike shouts, 'He's fixing a carburetor!'

Shep does not have a car.

'Don't make a mess!' Couch Mother bellows.

'He won't!' Mike has set aside his workbook. 'What are you gonna do with your share?' he mocks.

'Vegas,' Shep says. 'Hookers. You?'

'A house. Thirty-year mortgage, fixed. A yard. I want a garage workshop with tools.'

'How old are you again?' Shep sits back on his heels, arms sweat off his brow. 'Look,' he mutters, not really talking to Mike. 'Look at that. Hammering off the hinges doesn't do shit. I need to find where the lock-in lugs slide into the sides of the frame.' He leans over, tongue poking from the side of his mouth, and jots something onto the back of the failed graph.

A few hours later, the safe looks exhausted, and Shep has sketched what amounts to an engineering diagram. He has been hammering at the seams, meticulously marking the lug locations and projecting new ones. Mike has watched this venture evolve from whimsy to science.

Sometime later Shep has created a hole in the back wall of the safe and peeled up the sheet metal. Beneath is a layer of concrete, which crumbles under the hammer, then sheet metal again. This is Round Eleven, and maybe Round Twelve as well.

From down the hall, the Couch Mother's voice sounds exasperated and dehydrated. 'Aren't you done fixing that carburetor yet?'

Shep says softly, 'Just about.'

After another flurry of force and leverage, the back wall finally gives way. Shep tosses the loot, a bunch of old coins, aside. He is not interested in them; he is interested in the safe. He mumbles to himself, checks the lugs he hadn't guessed at, writes down the brand and make of the safe. 'The concrete's for weight,' he mutters.

Mike asks, 'Don't you want your priceless coins?'

Shep chews his lip, marveling at the reinforced door. He says, 'What?'

The next day they are walking past a pawnshop and Shep pulls one of the coins from his pocket and hands it to Mike.

Mike says, 'Why don't you?' and Shep says, 'They got my picture behind the register.'

Mike hesitates a moment. He thinks of that grandfather's admonishment years ago and recalls his own wavery reflection in the unblemished forest green paint of the Wingate Dealership Saab, but it's one old coin and it's Shep, so he takes it and goes inside. The security camera behind the bulletproof glass makes him antsy, but he writes a fake name and address on the invoice ticket and tells himself again, *It's one old coin and it's Shep*. Mike comes out with twenty bucks, which he stuffs into Shep's large hand. 'That was worth it,' he smirks.

Shep hands him ten back.

That night the cops roll up on 1788 Shady Lane. The senior officer brings a still shot from the pawnshop security camera, and this time the set of handcuffs he wields are adult-size.

NOW

Chapter 8

There was no front-office woman, just a front office. No sign, no venetian blinds, no noir stenciled lettering announcing HANK DANVILLE, P.I. Mike stepped past the bare wooden desk, tapped on the inner office door, and opened it.

Hank was behind his desk, pants dropped, withdrawing a needle from the pale white skin of his thigh. He looked over his shoulder, grimaced, and barked, 'Goddamn it!'

Mumbling an apology, Mike skipped back and closed the door. A moment later Hank yanked it open again. Tucking in his shirt, he returned to his desk, Mike shadowing him across the room on a cautious delay, both men avoiding eye contact. Hank slumped into his chair and gestured at the worn love seat opposite, where Mike had sat many times over the past five years.

Hank had an old-fashioned build, the kind they don't make anymore – tall and lanky, scarecrow shoulders broad enough to hang a linebacker's frame on. He was balding pleasantly and evenly, his hair receded midway on his head, which extended, turtlelike, on a ropy neck. It was an intellectual head – academic, even – built for peering at dusty tomes and longhand letters. It matched neither his powerful forearms nor the taciturn cop's demeanor he'd perfected during the thirty-some years he'd spent behind a badge before going private to limited success.

Hank's dry lips wobbled as he tried to come up with an explanation. No easy task, given what Mike had walked in on. Hank cursed under his breath, shoved back from his desk, and stood, cuffing his sleeves. Mike noticed that he was wearing his years a bit more heavily than when they'd last face-to-faced. Hank never gave his age. He was old enough to wobble here and there but young enough to get pissed off if you tried to steady his elbow.

He crossed to the window, shoved it open, and leaned on the sill, his suspenders drawing tight across his back. He'd quit smoking but still forgot sometimes, leaning out windows as if to exhale. His cat, an obese tabby, looked up from the radiator at him with indifference.

Mike cleared his throat awkwardly. 'I wanted to apologize for yesterday when—'

'I'm dying,' Hank said. He remained leaning over the sill, staring off at the Hollywood sign in the distance, the fabric of his shirt bunching between his shoulder blades. 'Lung cancer. I gave 'em up, hell, fifteen years ago. Thought I was in the clear. Amazing how something like that can boomerang back on you.'

He strode over and tapped the little needle kit on the desktop. 'That's what this poison is for. Neupo-something. Supposed to stimulate my last two white blood cells.'

Hank eased down into his chair, his gaze shifting, unsure where to land. At closer glance he looked not just slender but downright gaunt. Mike had never seen him uneasy, let alone floundering. Empathy left Mike tongue-tied. It was always hard to find the right words when someone parted the curtains like that, when you were given a glimpse into the inner workings of a life. So Mike said the first thing that came to mind: 'What can I do?'

Hank sneered a little. 'You gonna start coming by the house Wednesdays with baked casserole?'

'If I baked a casserole,' Mike said, 'it would kill you for sure.'

Hank tilted his head back and laughed, and Mike recognized him again. That quiet dignity, the wise-man smirk in the face of it all.

'Aw, hell,' Hank said. 'Your expression when I had my pants around my ankles just about makes dying worth it.'

'Maybe—'

'We stopped chemo. Last week. It's in the bone now.' A wry grin lost its momentum, flared out on Hank's face. He swiveled slightly in his chair, bringing into view a wallet-size school photo of a young boy, maybe six years old, thumbtacked to the otherwise blank wall behind him. Mike had politely inquired during an early meeting, and Hank had made clear: Any discussion about the photo was off-limits. That Hank was unmarried and had never mentioned children only added to the photo's curiousness. The picture was worn, wrinkled with white lines. The boy's striped, snap-button shirt had late sixties written all over it. Something in the shrinelike placement of the picture – so low as to be a private reminder – suggested that the boy was dead. An estranged son? A victim from an unsolved case that Hank couldn't let go of?

Mike averted his focus before Hank could key into it. Hank read Mike's face, then broke the mood by floating a hand Fonzie style over the remaining strands straggled back on his shiny scalp. 'Least the new-generation chemo let me keep my hair.'

Mike leaned back, shot a breath at the ceiling. 'Shit, Hank,' he said.

'Yeah, well, everyone's ticket gets punched sometime. I know better than to take it personally.' Hank tugged a fat file from a bottom drawer and thunked it on the desk, causing the cat to leap from the radiator and stalk along the baseboards. 'You came by to pick this up?'

Mike regarded the file like an artifact, giving it its due before reaching over and pulling it into his lap. It held the record of the private investigator's search for Mike's parents. Its girth was impressive, given that Mike remembered so little to set Hank on his investigative course. John and Momma. Approximate ages. No last name to work with, no city, no state. Abandoned-child investigations back then weren't what they are now. Nor were computer records. Half of what Hank had dug up was on crumbling microfiche, and none of the missing-person reports on record fit what little Mike remembered. For decades he had lived with the gnawing conviction that it was his mother's blood that had darkened his father's sleeve that morning. Maybe he'd have to live with it forever.

He leafed through the file, memories and possibilities rising from the print. The geographic spread of the search was large, since he didn't know how far his family home had been from the preschool playground he'd been left at; his father could have driven a few blocks or all through the night. There were investigation reports and phone transcripts, crime blotters and clipped obits from small-town papers. Mug shots of scowling men named John, all of an age, all of whom were not his father. By now he knew most of these strangers' faces by heart. The sight made him cringe, made him wonder what children these men had left behind, what women they had destroyed. But what really put a hook into his gut were the morgue photos, a Technicolor parade of women who'd been murdered in 1980 and unclaimed bodies that had turned up for years after that. He'd become acquainted with a virtual dictionary of shrug-off terms for corpses – floaters, crispy critters, headless horsemen.

He closed the file and tapped it with a fist. A scrapbook of a failed investigation. Years of dead ends. Years of high hopes and corrosive disappointments, a deep-seated yearning running through each day like a habit you can't quite quit.

It occurred to him that this file, with its cop-house chicken scratch, bluing flesh, and flashbulb misery, had become all he had of his parents.

Hank drew a hand across his face, tugging his features down into a basset droop. 'I'm sorry I couldn't do better by you, Mike.'

Over the years there had been quite a few other investigators, but none as committed.

'I didn't come by today for this,' Mike said, tapping the file again. 'I came to apologize. I was up against it when we talked.

I know how to handle stress better than that. Things have been good long enough that I forgot what it's like to be graceful when they're not.'

Hank studied him. Gave a nod. The tabby jumped up into his lap, and he dug his fingers into its scruff, the cat going limp and squint-eyed. 'You gonna be all right with this pipe business?'

'It's my own goddamned fault. I liked the price and didn't perform due diligence, and now I'm a liar and a cheat.'

'What's that mean?'

Hank was still regarding him curiously, but Mike just shook his head. No use getting worked up. He'd made a decision, and now he had to put it in the rearview mirror. He stood with the file and offered his hand across the desk. 'You always did fine work for me, Hank.'

They shook, and Mike left him there, staring out the window, the cat purring in his lap.

Jimmy was waiting in Mike's truck, passenger window rolled down, elbow stuck out, radio blaring. Mike had brought him along because they needed to select rock for the fire pit, and Hank's office was en route to the stone yard, a good drive from the site.

Mike climbed into the truck and tossed the enormous file onto the vast plane of the dashboard. Jimmy eyed the file but said nothing. Mike had told him he needed to run an errand, and it was clear enough he hadn't wanted to say more than that.

The music was all ska rhythm and subbaritone bleating. Mike turned down the volume, but kept the channel in a show of largesse. 'Thanks for waiting.'

Jimmy shrugged, bopping to the tunes. 'You the boss, Wingate.' Pulling out, Mike watched him poke at the buttons on the console, turning on the seat warmer – a seat warmer in fucking California. 'Hey,' Jimmy said, 'can I have this truck, too, when you done with it?'

'Not if you play this music in it.'

Jimmy made a dismissive sound, tongue clicking against his teeth. 'Shaggy's shit so smooth, you get VD just *listenin'* to his ass.'

'That's by way of recommendation?'

'Better than your James Taylor shit.'

'*My* James Taylor shit?' Mike rolled the knob in protest. A few channels over, Toby Keith was crooning that he should've been a cowboy, a sentiment not shared by Jimmy, judging by the sour twist of his mouth.

Mike loved music, but particularly country with its twang and swagger, its paternal America, its celebration of hardworking men who punch a clock their whole lives and don't ask for nuthin'. Parents were heroes, and if a man put his sweat into the land, he could have a shot at an honest life and good woman's love. *An honest life.* Those PVC pipes bobbed up through Mike's thoughts like a corpse that wouldn't sink, and for the rest of the drive and the baking walk through the stone yard he was distracted and useless.

On the drive back, they passed a cemetery Mike hadn't seen before, so he pulled off the frontage road and turned in.

Jimmy looked across at him, displeased. 'We don't got enough to finish today that you gotta do this again?'

Mike said, 'Two minutes.'

The guard in the shack kicked back on a stool, reading the *L.A. Times.* Mike rolled down the window and was surprised to confront himself in a grainy black-and-white photo beneath a headline reading, GOVERNOR SHOWS FOR THE GREEN. Yes, that was Mike, grinning in all his lying, hypocritical glory, his arm stretched around the governor's considerable shoulders. The paper rustled and tipped, the guard's ruddy face appearing. The guy waved Mike through without asking any questions. There was a time when Mike got stopped at every checkpoint and reception booth, but now he was legitimate, with a knockoff Polo shirt and an overpriced fucking truck.

He parked under an overgrown willow, and they climbed out, Jimmy tapping down his pack of smokes. 'The hell you look for in all these graveyards anyway?' Jimmy asked.

'John.'

'Just John?'

'That's right.'

And a woman born in the late 1940s.

'There a lotta Johns out there, Wingate,' Jimmy said.

'Five hundred seventy-two thousand six hundred ninety-one.'

The cigarette dangled from Jimmy's lower lip. His eyebrows were lifted nearly to his dense hairline. He took a moment, presumably to ponder Mike's sanity. 'In the country?'

'State.'

'You know he dead, though? Just John?'

Mike shook his head, thought, *Wishful thinking.* He grabbed the file off the dash, because he didn't need Jimmy nosing through it, and headed off.

The sod yielded pleasantly underfoot, and the dense air tasted of moss. A snarl of rosebush plucked at his sleeve. He found his first one three rows in – John Jameson. The dates were a stretch, but you never knew. Two more rows, the file growing heavy in his arm. Tamara Perkins. *Maybe you.* A gravestone at the rear fence, lost beneath dead leaves. He swept them with his foot, unearthed another cold, carved name. *Maybe you.* He scrutinized dates and wondered. He closed his eyes, breathed in the familiar scents, and dreamed a little.

He knew, of course, that neither of his parents was in this cemetery or any of the countless others at which he'd stopped over the past twenty years. He couldn't even be certain that they were dead. Given that splash of blood on his father's cuff, he assumed that his mother was. And his father could well have been brought down by any variety of perils. But even if one or both of Mike's parents was in the ground, and even if through some marvel of chance and guesswork he arrived at the correct cemetery, he could stroll straight over the right grave and still not know. So what the hell was he looking for here on these lush swells? The rites that were denied him? After all, he never got the deathbed visit, the box and shovel, the ash-filled urn.

He passed the aftermath of a service, people breaking off in solemn twosomes and quartets. A rubbed-raw exhaustion hung over the gathering, all those universal fears and vulnerabilities laid bare. And Mike at the periphery, traipsing between gravestones like a zombie, trying to convince himself that he came from somewhere, anywhere. Trying to convince himself that as a four-year-old boy he might have been something worth keeping.

Your mother and I, we love you very much. More than anything. Feeling intrusive, he gave the widow a wide berth and a gentle nod. *It's Morning Again in America.* Walking up a jagged path of broken stone, he pictured the way Hank's dress shirt had bagged between his shoulders in the back, slack from his lost bulk. *Nothing that happened was your fault.* He sensed the phantom bite of the station-wagon seat belt's buckle beneath his hip, saw the sweat tracking down the flushed back of his father's neck, felt that void in his four-year-old gut. *Where's Momma?* He thought of the high curve of his mother's cheekbones, his eyes misting, and then he became aware of his arm, sweating under the weight of the file.

It was an absurdity, the file. A collection of random men and women who shared a birth year or a first name or a vague set of descriptors. He'd always kept it at Hank's. What was he gonna do now? Take it home? Leaf through it with Kat?

A pastor's voice, cracked and portentous, carried down the hill from a second service: the age-old incantation, ashes to ashes, dust to dust.

Something in Hank's illness had jarred loose a new awareness, a harsh reality Mike couldn't help but meet head-on. Maybe it was the symbolism of his sole remaining accomplice in the search being stricken with a death sentence, but it hit him with sudden, vicious certainty that failure was inevitable and that it had always been inevitable. He'd been searching for a needle in a stack of needles.

He would never know.

A trash can appeared around the turn, a sign from the accommodating universe, and Mike looked down at the bulging file, trembling in his too-firm grip. He held it over the mouth of the can, closed his eyes. Ashes to ashes. Dust to dust. He let it fall. The twangy rattle echoed off the surrounding stone.

Case closed.

Chapter 9

The baby monitor, with its soothing blue trim and newborn-soft edges, was designed to project calm. Its red lights – five of them, like an equalizer bar on an old-fashioned stereo – were designed for the opposite effect. An emergency flare, harsh red, coded by man and nature for fire, danger, blood.

The first bar flickered on, then came steady, laying a crimson glow across Mike's face. Bar one meant static, usually. The color, a perfect match for the alarm-clock digits, currently showing 3:15. Annabel slept soundly, her breath a faint whistle.

Now the second bar joined its counterpart, climbing the ladder, adding weight and force to the alert. With a thumb, Mike nudged up the volume until he could faintly discern the rush of white noise. The air-conditioning vent kicking on in Kat's room? When he'd last checked on her, she'd been as still as a scone beneath the sheets, tucked in with the polar bear, both heads sharing the pillow.

A muted hush of air leaked from the monitor, a dragon exhaling.

Then a voice, faint as a whisper, sandblasted with static: *She looks so peaceful when she sleeps.*

Mike went board-stiff, frozen, his thoughts spinning, looking for traction. Was he dreaming?

But then, again, fuzzed at the edges: *Like an angel.*

He bolted upright, hurling back the covers, Annabel yelping beside him. He was running down the hall, feet pounding the floorboards, his wife calling after him. Skidding through Kat's door, tensed for combat, fighting for night vision, he took in the room in a single scan.

Nothing.

He slapped the light switch.

Kat sleeping as contentedly as he'd left her. Annabel was behind him now, breathing hard. 'What? What is it?' She was whispering hoarsely, though you couldn't wake Kat with a jack-hammer when she was out like this.

'I thought I heard a voice.'

'That said what?' She clicked off the rocker switch with the heel of her hand, and the room fell dark. 'What did it say?'

He pinched his eyes, the afterglow of the ceiling lamp hanging on in the darkness. He could hear the crickets sawing in the creek bed that ran behind the property line. Annabel stroked his back.

'I thought it said . . .' He was shaking now, rage burned out, leaving behind adrenaline and a vague kind of terror. He felt his muscles, each one individually, taut and bull-strong.

'What, babe?'

'"She looks so peaceful when she sleeps."' Repeating it put a charge into him, made it real again.

'You've had a lot going on lately.' Annabel rested a hand on his cheek. Her face held empathy and – he feared – pity. Despite his embarrassment, he was compelled to draw back the curtain and check the window. Locked.

Annabel said, 'What are you . . .?'

He made a snorkel mask with his hands, peering through the glass at the dark backyard. 'The window autolocks, so someone could've slipped back out and lowered it.' From the side he could feel the weight of Annabel's stare. 'I'm just saying it's *possible*. They could have been in here, whispering at me through the monitor.'

'Mike,' she said, 'who'd want to do something like that?'

Chapter 10

When Mike picked Kat up from school the next day, she carried a jar containing a twig and a baby lizard. She climbed into the back, slid the headphones on, and clicked around the TV channels. He watched her in the rearview, figuring you know you're doing a good job as a parent when they take you for granted.

'Take those things off and say *hello*.'

'Wireless,' she said. 'Noise-canceling. I'm just trying to get our money's worth.' She held the jar aloft, showing off the lizard. 'Look! I caught him. And Ms Cooper helped me make a home for him.'

'I'm not sure he can breathe in there, baby.'

She pulled off her red-frame glasses and folded them carefully in their case. 'I poked holes in the lid. He's fine.'

'He needs more oxygen than that. He'll die if you keep him.'

She shrugged. 'I like him, though.'

The trapped lizard bothered Mike more than seemed rational. His irritation grew. Kat was so mature generally that it was easy to forget the ways in which she was age-appropriate. One of the hardest parts of parenting, he'd found, was keeping his mouth shut the times when he wanted to control her, to step into her brain and throw the levers.

'Where we going?' Kat asked.

'I have to pick up some cabinet handles from the Restoration Hardware on the Promenade. Figured we'd walk around a little, grab a bite.'

In the backseat her face lifted with excitement and the sun caught her eyes – one amber, one brown, both vibrant with hidden hues. His anger dissipated instantly.

They drove for a while, and then she tugged off the headset and said, 'Sorry I didn't say hi when I got in the car.'

He noted the smart-ass set of her mouth – she was prompting him to play the Bad-Parenting Game – so he said, 'It's not your behavior that's bad. It's *you*.'

'It is,' she said, enjoying herself, 'an innugral part of who I am.'

'As your father I must *grind* the self-esteem out of you. Scour it from the corners—'

'Of my black little heart.' Her giggle caught fire.

By the time they reached Santa Monica, they'd been joking long enough that he'd forgotten about PVC pipes and baby monitors and Sunday's dreaded award ceremony with the governor. They walked holding hands along the Promenade, except when he had to carry her past the headless mannequins in the Banana Republic display window. She hadn't been scared of mannequins, he suspected, since she was four, but a ritual is a ritual.

He picked up the cabinet handles, and they bought some French bread and horseradish cheddar from a farmers' market outpost and sat on a metal bench by the stegosaurus fountain and listened to a busker playing 'Heart of Gold' with genuine, street-burnished soul. A homeless man reclined opposite, lost in a heap of dirt-black clothes. Mike thought the guy was long gone but then noticed he was mouthing the lyrics, smiling to himself as if remembering an old lover. The man put his hand inside his ragged jacket and made his heart flutter, and Kat laughed, her mouth full of food.

The busker was wailing, blowing that harmonica on its hands-free brace, and the homeless guy shouted observations and facts at them, as if in argument. 'This guy does Neil Young better'n Neil Young!' 'I had a little T-shirt shop in NYC.' 'My daughter's a dental hygienist in Tempe, married that guy, said I can visit *whenever I want.*'

A woman in clown makeup twisted balloon animals – only two bucks a pop. Mike peeled a few dollars off his money clip and handed them to Kat. 'You want to get one?'

Kat scooted off the bench, walked past the balloon lady, and handed the bills to the homeless guy, who stuffed them into his beggar's cup with a wink.

She returned and slid up next to Mike, and he marveled a moment at her intuition. The busker had moved on to 'Peaceful Easy Feeling,' and the setting sun stayed warm across their faces. Mike's thoughts for once were on nothing but the moment at hand.

He carried Kat on his shoulders back to his truck, both of them humming along to different songs. They'd stopped for french fries and milk shakes, and Kat, still munching, buckled into the backseat with a glazed expression of contentedness that made Mike smile. She said, 'What?' and he said, 'Someday you'll know.'

As he turned onto San Vicente, she piped up. 'I lost Snowball the Last Dying Polar Bear.'

A glance at the rearview showed that she was upset. Mike asked, 'Where'd you have him last?'

'I don't know. I realized at school. Ms Cooper had the whole class help me look for him. But we couldn't find him anywhere. Then I remembered bringing him back home. I looked every-where in my room, but ...' She gazed out the window, distressed, then shrugged. 'I'm getting too old for stuffed animals anyways.'

'Not Snowball,' he protested.

She said, 'Maybe it's time,' and a part of his heart cracked off and blew away.

He was formulating a response when he spotted, three cars back, a black sedan. He'd noticed it before, pulling out after him when he'd exited the parking lot. He turned left. The sedan turned left. That pilot light of paranoia flared to life in his chest.

His eyes glued to the rearview, he signaled right but drove past the turn. The sedan neither signaled nor turned. Headphones on, Kat was lost in the TV screen, swaying with the truck's movement. The air was grainy with dusk, pricked with headlights, so he couldn't get a clear glimpse of make or plate. The muscles of his neck had contracted back to remembered form; how quickly it felt as though they'd never relaxed at all.

When Mike glanced down from the mirror, the stopped cars at the streetlight were zooming back at them fast – too fast. He hit the brakes hard, Kat's milk shake flying from her grip onto the seat next to her. '*Motherf*—crap.' They stopped inches from the bumper in front of them.

'Motherfffcrap?' she repeated, giggling.

He tore off his T-shirt, tossed it back to her. 'Here, use this to mop it up.'

'Sorry, Dad.'

'Not your fault, honey.' He angled the mirror. The sedan was still there, idling behind a minivan, one headlight peeking into view. The edge of the hood looked dinged up, dust clouding the black paint.

'—or the moon?' Kat was asking.

'Sorry, what?'

'Which do you like better, Mars or the moon? I like Mars, because it's all red and—'

The light changed, and Mike waited a moment before trickling off the line. The minivan changed lanes, and he caught a glimpse of the sedan's tinted windshield and front grille – looked like a Grand Marquis – before a Jeep slotted in between them.

He turned off onto a residential street and gunned it.

'Dad. Dad. *Dad.*' Kat had a long french fry she needed to show him.

'Cool, honey. That's a big one, huh?' In the band of reflection, just beyond her uplifted fry, he saw the Mercury turn off after them.

Kat adjusted the headset and sank back into her TV show.

Mike wheeled around the corner, accelerated, turned again, and reversed up an alley. He turned off the car, killed the lights.

'What are we waiting for, Dad?'

'Nothing, honey. Just need to think for a minute. Watch your show.'

She shrugged and complied.

Night had come on abruptly, dogs barking, security lights glaring, living-room windows lit with TV-blue flickers. Being shirtless made him feel oddly vulnerable, the vents blowing cool air across his torso. He looked down at his hands, white on the steering wheel, which brought him back to –

Headlights turned up the street. Prowling. Approaching.

Mike found a wrench in the center console. He cupped his fingers around the door handle, bracing himself. The headlights swept into direct view, blaring into his face, and just as he was about to leap out, the garage door next to them started shuddering open. The beams shifted, and he saw the car behind them – not a dark sedan but a white Mercedes. It pulled in to the driveway, the man at the wheel offering a suspicious glare.

Mike breathed. In the backseat Kat's face glowed from the screen, her blinks growing longer. After another minute he eased out onto the empty street. Cautiously, he took the next turn. Nothing.

As his breathing returned to normal, he thought about the route he'd taken from Santa Monica – a major thoroughfare back to the freeway, save the final detour. What was that, really? Three turns? Had the Grand Marquis actually done anything out of the ordinary? Or was he jumping at imagined threats?

He gave a chuckle, palming sweat off the back of his neck. *Officer, a Grand Marquis drove behind me for a few blocks. Made a couple turns, even. No, I didn't catch a license plate, but maybe you could track it down using satellite imagery.*

His guilt about the fraudulent green houses was working over-time, creating stalkers that weren't there, making him cast a suspicious eye at everything from a baby monitor to traffic patterns. Besides, the only people who knew about the PVC pipes were complicit in one way or another, so who would come after him for that? And why? No one. No reason. No worries.

He watched the rearview the rest of the way home.

'She's scratching her head. All the time. Didn't you notice?'

Mike watched Annabel picking through Kat's hair. 'No,' he admitted.

'It's been going around school, and she seems to be the first in line every time.' Annabel firmed Kat's head beneath her grip, angled her into the strong bathroom light. It was late, and they were all tired. 'Stay still, monkey.'

'Don't be mad at me,' Kat said. 'It's not like I said, "What can I do to bug Mom today? Oh – I know. I'll get *head lice*."'

Mike set down his keys on the kitchen counter – he'd just dashed out to the drugstore – and pulled the treatment bottle from the bag.

Kat eyed the ominous red label. 'What's *in* that stuff anyways?'

Mike held up the bottle, squinted at the ingredients: 'Gasoline, skunk juice, battery acid—'

'*Mom.*'

'He's kidding.'

'But there's bad stuff in it. It'll give me skin burns. And mutation.'

'It won't make you mutate,' Annabel said wearily.

But as usual their daughter outnegotiated them, so they wound up using a home remedy Annabel found online – mayonnaise combed through Kat's hair, turban-sealed with Saran Wrap. The getup accentuated Kat's smooth features, the smiling elf face. Mike went into the master bathroom to dig mayo out from under his nails and listened on the monitor to Annabel singing Kat to sleep, the lullaby sweet and soft and, as always, way off key. '*Lay thee* down *now and* rest, *may thy* slum-*ber be blessed.*' He smiled to himself before remembering the dirty black Grand Marquis he'd managed to convince himself was a tail, and he pictured how the milk shake had flown from Kat's hand when he'd hit the brakes at the streetlight and – *Shit*.

The lizard.

He rushed out to the truck, finding the peanut-butter jar wedged beneath the passenger seat. The baby lizard, dead inside, thin and curled like a feather.

He carried in the jar as Annabel emerged from Kat's bedroom. She said, 'I laid a hand towel over her pillow so—' She caught sight of the jar.

'She wanted to keep him,' Mike said.

Annabel shrugged. 'How else will she figure it out?' She crossed her arms, leaned against the wall. 'Do we tell her?'

They'd been through it with hamsters and goldfish and a frog, but as Kat had grown older and more aware, each time seemed to be worse.

'Yes,' Mike said. 'Have to.'

'I know. You'll do it?'

'Sure.'

Mike set the jar down in the hall, entered, and sat on the edge of Kat's bed. She peered up at him, puckish and vaguely alien in her mayo wrap. He pressed his fingertips into the comforter. 'I will never lie to you, right?'

She nodded, and immediately the image of those buried PVC pipes came at him, the lie of the cover-up, the lie of the houses, the lie of the coming award. But this was not the time for that. This was the time for an eight-year-old and a dead lizard.

'Your lizard died.'

'Dead?' She blinked. 'Like, lizard heaven?' Despite the wise-crack, her bottom lip trembled ever so slightly. A flash of remorse moved across her face, but then she bit her lip, forced it still. 'Well, you can say "told you so" now.'

He hated to see how well she could rein in her emotions. He looked down at his hands, trying to figure out a way in. The Bad-Parenting Game?

'We don't talk about feelings,' he said. 'We swallow them and cram 'em down inside of us so they turn into hidden resentments and fears.'

Kat half smiled, her eyes glassy, and then her face broke and tears fell at once, spotting her cheeks. 'I want my baby lizard not to be dead.'

He hugged her, rubbed little circles on her back, and she sputtered a bit against his shoulder. Finally she pulled back. 'Can I see him?'

He retrieved the jar, and she held it in her tiny hands, tilted it so the lizard slid stiffly around the twig. 'What happens to his body?'

'Well, we can bury him in the backyard and—'

'No,' she said. 'Zach Henson.'

It took a moment for Mike to pluck the name from memory – fifth-grader, leukemia, last year. Mike and Annabel had gone to the funeral just to shake hands with the parents and helplessly say the only thing one could – 'If you need *any*thing.' After, they'd sat in the truck in the church parking lot, awed into a muted sort of terror, Annabel weeping quietly, him gripping the wheel, watching the relatives trickle by, faces chapped, posture eroded. As usual, Annabel put words to his thoughts and said, 'Anything else I think I could live through, but if something happened to her, I think I would die.'

Now, Mike cleared his throat, set his hand on Kat's tiny knee, and said, 'Zach's body has probably gone back into the earth by now.'

Kat scratched at her head through the sheath of mayonnaise and cling wrap, her face somber and thoughtful, and asked, 'What if you and Mom die?'

'We'll be fine. You have plenty of time to worry about stuff like that when you're older. Your job right now is to be a kid and have fun. We will always protect you. Until you can protect yourself.'

Kat rolled over, poked the pillow in the spot where her polar bear used to sleep. 'But what if you just disappear one day, like *your* parents did? What would happen to me?'

The question cut the breath off halfway down his throat, and it was a moment or two before he could reassure her and kiss her good night. Walking down the hall to bed, he could have sworn he heard the buzz of that blowfly, portending ill, but when he turned, there was nothing at the seams of the ceiling except darkness.

Chapter 11

Mike's oversize, pixelated face greeted him and his family one step into the Braemar Country Club. Tuesday's *Los Angeles Times* article, blown up to the size of a door and mounted on foam, leaned against the entrance to the main dining room. Lined beside it like enormous dominoes were similar clippings from the state's other major papers, giving the effect of tabloid wainscoting. Itching in his eight-hundred-dollar suit, Mike paused, uncomfortable.

Despite the newspaper photo's clearly showing Mike's heterochromia, the journalist had referred to his 'blazing brown eyes,' ignoring the fact that one of them was technically 'blazing amber.' But the oversight was nothing next to the fraud at the core of the politicized hype – Mike's receiving an environmental award for houses that shouldn't have passed the green code. Scanning the puff piece, which praised his work to the ozone-depleted heavens, Mike felt a rush of guilt and – feeling his daughter's tiny hand in his – shame.

Annabel finally tugged at his arm, breaking him from his thoughts. Reluctantly, he entered, nodding at various well-dressed folks, many of whom beamed at him with recognition. Kat kept pace, clutching her backpack full of books, which she'd brought in case she got bored. Waiters circled with glasses of champagne and hors d'oeuvres he couldn't recognize. He popped a pastrylike item into his mouth just to have something to do and scanned the crowd for a familiar face.

Kat had already engaged Andrés's kids in a game of tag. Annabel looked stunning in a red dress with a cutout back. He watched her drift effortlessly into a circle of heavily made-up women, moving with the grace bestowed by a proper upbringing and natural confidence. The woman was a marvel; each situation brought out a new facet of her. But even as he watched with pride, her ease seemed only to underscore how out of place he felt. It seemed the one place he fit in effortlessly was with his family.

He started toward his wife, but an older woman with a clipboard appeared between them, facing Annabel. 'Michael Wingate's wife, right?' she asked. 'I need to borrow you for a picture.' She clasped Annabel's hand in hers, leading her away. Annabel shrugged in mock helplessness and went with a smile.

Mike made his way across the room and caught the bartender's attention. 'Can I get a Budweiser?'

The bartender, a handsome aspiring-actor type, gestured at the bottles in the ice bucket behind him. 'Only Heineken. You're at the wrong party.'

Mike took the cold bottle. The bitter beer felt great going down. The last two days had dragged out, made slower by how much he'd been dreading tonight.

Gazing across the swirls of people, Mike spotted Andrés at one of the elegantly set tables by the dais. Carrying his wife's purse and looking bored senseless, Andrés rolled his eyes, and Mike had to look away to hide his smile.

The sight of the governor's chief of staff holding court one table over made the half grin go brittle on Mike's face. Catching Mike's eye, Bill Garner offered him a head tilt that he couldn't help but interpret as conspiratorial. Were other people looking at him that way, too? He couldn't get a handle on his uneasiness. For a week now, he'd been jumping at shadows.

At the far end of the room, floor-to-ceiling windows looked out across a sloping golf course, now dark. Mike angled his way through the crush, offering greetings to passing faces. Getting to the fringe of the gathering and having a view of the horizon calmed him a bit.

Just as he'd started to unknot his concerns, someone collided into him from the side. Stumbling to regain his footing, he spilled beer down the leg of his trousers.

A voice floated over his shoulder. 'Oh, sorry.' A wiry man with a patchy beard leaned in at him, gripping his arm. 'I have CP.'

The man had breath like a birdcage, his lips spotted with black flecks. Sunflower seeds? He reached into a ratty brown sport coat and withdrew a handkerchief. Mike took it and swiped at the wet mark on his thigh, but the liquid had already seeped through the fabric.

'Cerebral palsy,' the man said. 'Bad balance, you know? Again, I'm real sorry for that.'

'That's okay. I hate this suit anyway.'

The man's sport coat looked like Salvation Army – corduroy, worn elbow patches, frayed sleeves. Mike offered back the handkerchief, and the man hooked it in a hand curled like a monkey's paw. His eyes, set in a jaundiced face, twitched from side to side.

A hulking man stood idly several feet away, not uncomfortable but not at ease – not anything at all, in fact. He was so detached that it took Mike a moment to register that the two were together.

'I've had my Achilles tendon lengthened eight times, my hamstring five,' the man in the sport coat continued. 'Eleven tendon releases in my right foot alone. Forty-four surgeries in all. That don't even count Botox injections into spastic muscles. Then there's the seizure meds, then the meds for med side effects, and . . . well, hell, you get the picture.'

Mike loosened his tie, wondering what the guy wanted. The big man remained immobile, looking at the draped walls, at nothing. Was he even listening?

'And still the muscles tighten. I walk a little worse each year. Need a few more snips and cuts. Expensive as hell. Keeps me working, that's for sure.' He brought a wineglass up to his chin and spit sunflower seeds into it. A soggy wad had collected in the bottom of the glass, steeping in a quarter inch of leftover red wine. 'All this 'cuz I didn't get enough oxygen when I was riding down that birth canal. No fault o' my own. But I gotta pay anyways, day after day.' He snickered. 'Karma's a bitch, ain't it, Mike? Catches up to us all.'

Mike studied the guy's face. 'How do you know my name?'

The man nodded at the newspaper blowups. 'Man o' the hour.'

'And you are . . .?'

'William.'

'William . . .?'

William smiled, showing off yellowed teeth. 'My kid cousin had scars like that.' He nodded at Mike's knuckles. 'Old-fashioned fighting.'

Mike slid his hands into his pockets. 'Had?'

'People with knuckles like that don't generally make it to happy middle age.'

Kat ran by, chasing Andrés's son, shrieking laugher.

William gestured at them with his chin. 'Look at the little ones. I could watch 'em play all day.'

The way William was looking at the kids made Mike squirm.

'Cute girl,' William said. 'Must be yours – strong resemblance, those cat eyes. You can tell *she* ain't adopted.'

A creepy remark, creepier still since Mike didn't think he and Kat looked all that much alike. Why would the guy give a damn if Kat *was* adopted? Had Mike heard wrong, or had William actually placed extra emphasis on the 'she'? A veiled reference to Mike's foster-home past? Meaning what? And how could William know? Mike felt a pulse beating in the side of his neck.

'So who do you know here?' Mike asked.

'Well, Mike, now I know you, don't I?'

'Sure,' Mike said evenly. 'But who invited you?'

Someone made an announcement, and they all began settling

into their chairs. The woman with the clipboard waved Mike toward his seat by the podium, her gesture emphatic: *We need you here* now.

'Better get going,' William said. 'Looks like they want you onstage.'

There was no denying it; this second evasion was intentional. Something had shifted in the air, gone sour.

And Mike's patience had worn thin. He swallowed, tried to rein in his irritation. 'You didn't answer my question. How are you hooked into this?'

'I'm just a guy who likes a party.' William kept his eyes on Mike and spit out another sunflower shell, this time over the lip of the cup onto the carpet. 'Plus, there's a whole mess of fine-lookin' women around.' He gestured, again with his scraggly chin. 'Look at that slice o' pie there.' Annabel was sitting at the edge of the banquet table up on the dais. Her chair was pulled sideways as she spoke with one of the waiters. Though her legs were closed, her dress was hitched on a knee, and from their lower vantage they could see a little triangle of white silk between her legs.

Mike felt his face go hot. He stiffened, and the big man, never shifting his blank gaze from the far wall, sidled a half step toward them.

Mike felt a surge of old instinct rising in him, gathering heat. His face was close enough to William's that he could smell the stink leaking through his teeth.

The woman with the clipboard called Mike's name. He untensed his muscles and stepped calmly away. Walking up onto the dais, he whispered in Annabel's ear, and she straightened her dress, smoothing it over her knees. The lights dimmed, save those beating down on the banquet table, illuminating Mike and the other award recipients. Squinting out at the room, he could discern little more than shadowy figures around the far tables.

The governor made a grand entrance, his frame dwarfing the

podium. He threw out a few opening cracks, a broad grin showing off the trademark gap in his front teeth. Mike registered the crowd's titters but little else; his eyes were picking over the crowd. Annabel, misreading his tension, squeezed his hand supportively. Kat waved from Andrés's table down in the front.

The other honorees got up and made brief speeches, but Mike couldn't concentrate on what they were saying. He thought he spied William's form moving across the back, but then there was an awful silence and he realized everyone was staring at him. The familiar woman, sans clipboard, said Mike's name again into the microphone. Annabel urged him to his feet, and, walking on wooden legs, he took the podium.

'I, um—' A feedback squawk; his mouth was too close to the mike. The wet fabric from the spill felt cold against his thigh. He did his best to put the bizarre confrontation out of mind. 'I don't really deserve to be here,' he said.

At the VIP table, Bill Garner looked up at him, head cocked, lips wearing a tense little smile.

'I mean, to give me an award when I already feel so lucky for what I have and what I get to do. I wake up every day thinking I've won the lottery.' Finally relaxing a bit, Mike glanced at his wife. She was looking back at him with adoration. 'Because I have. I mean, my wife, my daughter, steady work that I love.'

Mike glanced down at the podium. 'And it's not like building Green Valley was all selfless. It was a paying job.' Eager to break the tension, a few people laughed, thinking he was joking. 'I'm no great environmentalist,' he said. 'I just don't want my daughter and grandkids to look back at me decades from now and be angry that I didn't do the right thing.'

Annabel's new diamond ring glinted, the big rock seeming to sum up how full of shit he was. As if reading his thoughts, she slid her hands into her lap and looked away, trying to keep her composure. Seeing her upset completely threw him, and for a moment he lost track of where he was. The silence stretched out uncomfortably as he grasped for words. He almost just came clean, admitted the lie, and walked off to start shoveling his way out of the hole he'd dug for himself and forty families, but instead he heard himself say, 'Thank you for this recognition. I'm honored.' Annabel closed her eyes, and he saw her heartbeat fluttering the thin skin of her temple. To applause, he stepped out of the spotlight, touched her gently on her shoulder, and murmured, 'Let's go.'

The lights were up now in the dining room, the ceremony over. Mike scanned the space, but there was no sign of William or the big guy anywhere. He felt ill, his mind racing, his stomach churning from the altercation earlier, from the phony award, from the way Annabel had averted her gaze when he was up there, as if she couldn't meet his eye. He wanted to get home, burn off the night with a scalding shower, and put all this behind them.

A photographer approached: 'We need you for one more set of pictures—'

'Sorry,' Mike said. 'We really have to be going.'

Nodding curtly at well-wishers, he grabbed Kat's hand and led her and Annabel to the door, Andrés calling after him, 'What the big hurry?'

Kat was beaming. 'Dad said he built Green Valley for *me*.'

Annabel forced a smile. Mike rushed on, trying to leave Kat's remark behind. A few guests had trickled outside, but for the most part the parking lot was empty of people. Gleaming foreign cars and a good number of hybrids. Mike hurried Kat and Annabel up and down the aisles, searching for that black Mercury Grand Marquis that he'd thought had followed him earlier in the week.

'Mike' – Annabel shifted the award plaque in her arms, nearly dropping it – 'what's going on?'

'Just give me a minute.'

At the far edge of the lot, slant-parked across two spaces, a

91

dingy white van stood out distinctly among the sleek vehicles. Wedged between windshield and dash was a torn-open bag of David's sunflower seeds. Mike halted twenty or so feet from the van. The driver's and passenger's seats were empty, but beyond them the cabin was dark.

No front license plate.

Mike turned to his wife. 'Take her, get into the truck, and lock the doors.'

Annabel's forehead crinkled with concern, but she took Kat and hurried back toward the truck. Though a few more people were making their way to their cars, here in the farthest row it was dark and still.

Tentatively, Mike circled the van. An old Ford, late-seventies model. Checked drapes covered a high-set rear window, slid open to a dusty screen. With relief he saw there was a back plate, an old-fashioned California model with a blue background, the yellow numbers and letters so faded he had to crouch to read their raised outlines – 771 FJK.

The voice came at him, unnervingly close. 'You let your *wife* go out dressed like that?'

Mike whipped upright. William's face, leering out the van's rear window, wore the checked drapes like falls of hair. The back door came ajar with a creak, Mike peddaling back, heart jerking in his chest. William unfolded painfully from the dark interior, the big man sliding out to loom behind him.

Mike's breath fired hot in his lungs. 'I don't *let* her do any-thing.'

A car alarm chirped nearby, and Mike noted with relief more people heading to their cars, spreading out through the lot. Had the men been hiding in the van, waiting to follow him home?

With a little smirk, William lurched toward Mike in an odd, toe-in gait. 'Why you harassing us?' He swirled the wineglass, packed with half-chewed sunflower shells, for emphasis. 'Following us out here, spying on our van.' William spit a sunflower shell on the asphalt near Mike's feet. He jerked his chin, a gesture he seemed to overuse. 'Better get back to your family.'

Mike's gaze moved uneasily from William to the big man, who stood silently, log arms crossed, his unreadable features half lost to shadow. 'The hell does that mean?'

'It means a family man like you's got better things to do than stand out here jawing with a buncha lowlifes.' He peered around Mike, and Mike turned.

From the passenger seat, Annabel peered anxiously through the windshield. The truck was two rows away, but Kat was visible in the rear, standing up, fussing with her backpack. Both of them right there in plain view, exposed. The night air, crisp in Mike's lungs, tasted of mowed grass from the distant golf course. The faintest trace of cigar smoke laced the breeze. Annabel's eyes implored him.

Mike wheeled back. 'Is this about Green Valley?'

'Green Valley?' William looked genuinely confused.

'You've been following me,' Mike said.

William's eyes jittered from side to side rapidly, an almost mechanical tic. 'Sounds like you got people after you, Mr Wingate. Don't take it out on me and Dodge here.'

Neither broke off his stare. Mike took a few backward steps, then turned and headed swiftly to the truck, Annabel watching him tensely. A few passersby offered their congratulations, and he nodded, his face still burning with anger. As he neared, Annabel threw open her door. Kat was facing away from the scene, pointing out the side window and laughing. 'That lady has a *cra*-zy hat!'

Mike heard a pop behind him.

He turned. Pitifully, William clutched his trembling wrist, apologizing to the small cluster of folks who had gathered around, concerned. 'I'm sorry. It just slipped.' A man in a suit used a rolled magazine to sweep the broken glass away from his tires. Dodge crouched to help, his lips still sealed. Was he mute?

Annabel was out of the truck now. 'Mike, what the hell is going on?'

He grasped her biceps, reversing her protectively into the passenger seat. 'We're going. I'll explain in a second.'

'That's hurting my arm,' she told him quietly.

He let go. His grip had turned her skin red. She climbed in, and he started around the hood to the driver's seat.

But William and Dodge were on top of him already. He turned and caught Annabel's eye. She read his expression, her face draining of color. She moved her arm, and he heard the click of the automatic locks. In the rear Kat reorganized her books in her backpack, distracted.

William stepped up on Mike, moving swiftly. His hips dipped a bit when he walked, but it was nothing like the pronounced gait he'd put on display earlier. Mike wondered how much he used the illness to his advantage, the way Shep had his bad hearing.

Mike squared off as William sidled into reach and said, 'I see your CP cleared up some.'

William bared his yellow teeth. 'Thank the Lord Jesus.'

Dodge stood with one massive arm curled behind his back. Hiding a knife? A gun?

Adrenaline pounded through Mike, the rush leaving him light-headed. He could drop William in a heartbeat, but Dodge was a wild card. From the looks of him, he could snap Mike's neck with a twist of his hand. But Mike's only concern right now was Annabel and Kat. His daughter remained focused on her book bag, but she'd look up at any minute and take in whatever was going to happen here. He tried to will Annabel to scoot across the console and drive away, but he knew she'd never leave him here.

William spit a scattering of shells across Mike's shoes.

Mike said, 'Don't spit on me.'

William's tongue dug around his mouth and then poked into view, a black crescent riding the tip. He blew it into Mike's chest.

Mike said, 'One more time and we're gonna have a problem.'

William bunched his lips, the scruff of his chin bristling, his stare narrowing appraisingly. 'Aah. There it is.'

Oblivious, a woman in a fur coat, begging Mike's pardon, slid past him and climbed into a Jaguar. Her presence returned him to his senses. He exhaled, dissipating his rage. Then he took a step away, ceding ground, his eyes on the bulge of Dodge's shoulder, that arm curling out of view.

Mike glanced quickly over his shoulder. Kat's face pointed back at him, her sober expression a match of Annabel's. He grabbed for a line of reasoning. 'Look at all these people. This is an upscale gig. We don't want to fight here.'

'Fight? *Fight?*' William grinned, and even Dodge's face seemed to rearrange itself into an expression of amusement, a couple of spaced teeth peeking into view. 'There are generally a few more steps of escalation in there. Shouting, chest bumping, shoving. We don't want to skip all the foreplay, now, do we?'

'Yeah,' Mike said. 'We do. Whatever game you're playing, it ends here.'

'No,' Dodge said, the low voice, almost a vibration, surprising Mike.

Dodge moved his massive hand from behind his back and let fall a white stuffed polar bear.

Chapter 12

Mike's first reaction wasn't anger or fear but total disbelief. Everything slowed to a syrupy crawl – Dodge's hand, still open from the release; William's mouth bunching around the sunflower seeds with convalescent imprecision; Kat's polar bear rocking ever so slightly on the parking-lot asphalt, one furry arm gone sleek and dark from an oil puddle. It was surreal – disorienting, even – to see that animal in this context.

Mike's mind spun, cogs clattering, searching for purchase. The implications about how the polar bear had gotten here seemed too large for him to process.

'Where'd you get that?' he asked.

William, closest to him, said, 'Found it.' He popped a sly grin. 'It *is* Katherine's?'

Hearing his daughter's full name emerge from William's lips jogged something loose. The gears meshed. The scene – and Mike's thoughts – lurched back into motion at full speed. The voice through the monitor. Kat's autolocking window. These men, in his daughter's room?

His blood thrummed like a well-plucked string. His vision went impossibly sharp, then blurred as he lunged, driving his forehead into William's face. Bone clashed. William's breath left in a huff, intermingling with Mike's, their eyes inches away for a frozen instant, Mike catching a close-up of one brown pupil rolling obscenely in shock and pain.

William reeled back, howling, Mike feeling the man's sweat

across his own forehead. There was something so primitive about a headbutt, using your own face as a weapon. The street move, Shep's favored ambush, left Mike breathless and transported, suspended somewhere closer to Shady Lane than to the Braemar Country Club.

Dodge regarded him with level interest, a cat tracking a canary.

William was rolling on the ground, clutching at his cheek, crying out, 'Did you see? He *hit* me! This man *hit me!*'

Guests from the ceremony paused to gawk. Heads pivoted above car roofs. A few people stayed frozen at a ten-yard standoff, looking on, contemplating what the hell to do. William's bad leg scraped the asphalt stiffly.

Dodge's lips parted to show the thinnest sliver of teeth, but on him it seemed a massive display of kinetics.

Mike squared to meet him head on.

Somewhere he registered Kat screaming from the backseat of the truck. The sound broke through the muted rush of white noise pervading his head, knocking him back to the present. He halted, searching for restraint, breathing so hard his shoulders rose and fell with the effort.

Annabel was shouting for him to get into the truck, and he thought of her and Kat behind him, watching through the movie screen of the windshield. Everything he stood to lose seemed summed up in the countless glares pointed in his direction, all those well-dressed folks who'd watched him knock down a cripple.

Mike backpedaled to the truck, a few brave souls rushing in to aid William.

Dodge's gaze never faltered from his. 'Soon,' he said, the word sending a line of fire up Mike's spine.

Mike got into the truck, turned over the engine. A scrum of people now surrounded the two men, illuminated in the headlight glare. William, holding his face, was helped to his feet, but then his leg faltered and he collapsed again. Several women shot mortified glances at Mike.

Annabel asked, quietly, 'What just happened?'

Mike said, 'I don't know.'

Throwing an arm over the seat back, he reversed out of the space. Kat lay curled up in the backseat, her cheeks glittering. The cluster of people dissipated as Mike pulled away, keeping his stare fastened on the rearview mirror.

In the red light of the brakes, William stayed down, twisted over his limp legs. At his side, Dodge stood inhumanly tall, head tilted, his insensate eyes watching them drive off.

Chapter 13

'So we've got a William. And a . . . *Dodge*, was it?' The detective edged his coffee mug meticulously into one of many ring stains blemishing the surface of his too-small desk. The big man had a lantern jaw, a wide and crooked seam of mouth, and a Slavic family name – Markovic – printed across a peeling nameplate.

His partner, a study in contrast, had precise, focused features and smooth, dark skin. Simone Elzey wore a cheap button-up with her sleeves cuffed. Callused hands and a bull neck betrayed a propensity for the weight room. An angel tattoo walling the left side of her throat gave her an intimidating air, which Mike assumed was precisely the point. After they'd run through the essentials, she'd gone to the back office to key in an incident report, which sounded like deputy shorthand for doing fuck-all.

The Lost Hills Sheriff's Station, a few miles from the Wingates' house, was tumbleweed-dead. Eleven o'clock on a Sunday, and everyone had better things to be doing, Markovic and Elzey included. Mike and Annabel sat on stiff wooden chairs, Kat slumped with exhaustion in her mother's lap. They'd recounted the story a number of times, the detectives asking the same questions in different keys, a symphony of skepticism.

Since the confrontation had occurred in Tarzana, they'd been informed, LAPD would be called in if a formal investigation was opened. Because Mike and Annabel had agonized over what to do for most of the drive home, they'd wound up at their local station. It occurred to Mike that it was the only location he

99

actually knew. What a contrast with the Shady Lane years, when he and Shep knew intimately the interiors of every cop shop within a joyride of the Couch Mother's domain.

'Yeah. Like I said.' Mike rubbed his neck.

Markovic studied him with dull gray eyes. 'You get a last name?'

The question, in its third incarnation, knocked Mike further off-kilter. He felt unease, and an odd creeping guilt that defied explanation. Sensing his discomfort, Annabel reached over and rested a hand on his shoulder.

'A last name?' Markovic prompted again.

Finally Mike sourced the echo, his mind racing back to that first hazy memory after his father abandoned him. A similar station, questions lobbed at him like fastballs, one after another, driving him further into his amnesiac haze: *You don't know your last name? How about your dad's name? Do you know your dad's name?* Trying to regain his bearings, Mike soaked in the room around him – missing-children flyers, dark-complected men scowling from mug shots, the bitter scent of stagnant coffee. Parallel in so many ways. But – he reminded himself – completely different. He was an adult now. A taxpayer. A member of the community.

The Steve Miller Band, piped in through decades-old speakers, was flying like an eagle above the crackle of police scanners.

'No,' Mike said, perhaps a bit too firmly. 'Like I said. I figured that license-plate number would be good.'

'Like *I* said, the number you gave us is from a brown 1978 Eldorado last registered in 1991 to Jirou Arihyoshi, a gardener in Yuba City. So unless you made a mistake . . .'

'I didn't make a mistake.'

'Mmm.'

TV always made this look so easy. A book of mug shots, a fingerprint, and next thing you knew, Jack Bauer was kicking down a front door. But all Mike had was no last name, a white van, and

100

a plate number that had been out of circulation for two decades. He thought of how he'd felt in Hank's office when he'd confronted the File of Dead Ends. A needle in a stack of needles.

Annabel still didn't buy that William or Dodge had broken into the house at night to steal the polar bear and whisper into the monitor; she was more concerned about their general menace. The fact that they'd picked up the bear somewhere meant they were either following the family or snooping around behind Kat. Clearly, they wanted *something*.

Markovic flipped through his notes. 'You have this . . . stuffed polar bear?'

'No, I . . . no, we—'

Annabel said, 'We drove away and left it on the ground. It didn't seem wise to go back and get it.'

'Mmm.' The gaze settled on Mike. 'And you said *another* car followed you?'

Mike had mentioned the Mercury in passing, drawing a curious glance from Annabel. Now he regretted raising it at all. 'I think. But I can't be sure. On Wednesday. A Grand Marquis.'

'But these guys tonight, William and' – glance to the notepad – '*Dodge*, they had a van.'

'They could own two vehicles.'

'Sure. Of course.'

Mike pressed his fingertips to the sore spot on his forehead, testing the bruise. Markovic had zoned out, contemplating his notes. In the adjoining office, her tapered back turned to the interior window, Elzey was still tapping away on a keyboard. She was on an old-fashioned phone now, the coiled cord stretching up into view. She hung up, dialed someone else. Her neck was flexed, and Mike didn't like the intensity of her body language. She stepped to the doorway and curled a finger. 'Marko.'

Markovic pushed back, his chair offering a feeble squeak of protest, and joined her. Something about the way they were talking flicked at Mike's nerves. Faces close, teeth shut, lips barely moving. Elzey noticed him observing through the office window and closed the blinds with a single wrench of the turning rod.

Troubled, Mike refocused his attention on his family. Kat's eyes drooped, then finally closed. Annabel whispered, 'We gotta get this one home.'

'As soon as he comes back.'

'Do you think—' Annabel stopped. Mike nodded her on. 'Do you think this has anything to do with that sleazy contractor? Or the governor's agenda?'

'What are you guys talking about?' Kat had stirred to life again. 'What sleazy contractor?'

'Nothing, Kat,' Mike said. Then, to Annabel, 'I doubt it. It's hard to picture them doing this over that.'

'Over *what*?'

'Not now, Kat,' Mike said. 'Go back to sleep.'

She furrowed her brow at him before tilting her head against her mother's chest. Annabel stroked Kat's hair absentmindedly, her eyes fixed on Mike.

He *hoped* that this – whatever this was – had everything to do with PVC pipes and Bill Garner's latest PR campaign for his boss. That felt containable, known, a world of clear-cut motives and back-scratching. So Mike didn't say what he feared most: that this had nothing at all to do with Green Valley. That this was a whole different order of ugliness that had yet to reveal its face.

Markovic and Elzey returned, a fresh energy stiffening their strides. Elzey spun a chair around, mounted it like a Harley. 'We're encountering some difficulties nailing down biographical details,' she said. 'For you.'

Mike felt his pulse tick up a few beats. 'Why are you running *me*?'

'"Running" you.' Markovic gave an impressed frown. 'Look who's been watching *Law & Order*.'

'Listen,' Elzey said, 'a guy asks us to look into something, we look into it. You have a squeaky-clean record with a number of blank spaces. If you're really as concerned as you claim, you can probably fill in some of those blanks so we can know where to look.'

Mike pictured them shoulder to shoulder in that back office and wondered what they'd been discussing that had prompted them to take such an aggressive tack. He said, 'I have *no idea* where to point you.'

'Come on. There must be *some*thing. A bad deal, a weird overlap, a near miss . . . You've never bumped up against anything like that?'

'No.' Mike was out of shape when it came to this and was sure his face showed the lie. But he couldn't exactly spill here about PVC pipes and an implicit deal struck with the governor's office. Besides, he felt certain that the confrontation had nothing to do with that anyway. The near-surface violence, the circling-shark approach, the unspoken threat to his family – the whole thing was raising more red alerts than some PR bullshit involving subsidies and green houses.

Elzey held out her hands. 'We can't help you if you're not more forthcoming with us.'

'Wait a minute. Why are you making this about *him*?' Annabel came vertical in her chair, nearly pushing Kat out of her lap.

Kat grumbled a complaint, and Markovic leaned over and said to her, 'Why don't you go play on those chairs over there?'

'She's tired,' Annabel said.

'Then she can lie down.'

Kat dragged her backpack over to the row of chairs and slouched into one, her dangling sneakers a few inches off the flecked tile.

'Two men came after me in a parking lot,' Mike said. 'What's my background have to do with that?'

'You want to tell us?' Elzey's tone was polite, conciliatory. When she bent her head to listen, her angel tatt – black ink on dark skin – looked like an elaborate birthmark. 'Plus, it doesn't sound like they came after you any more than you went after them. So they were acting strange—'

'This wasn't just *strange*. It wasn't some game or random harassment.' Disheveled in his overpriced suit, Mike yanked his tie free and stuffed it into a pocket. 'These are dangerous men. I can tell the difference.'

'How?' Markovic matched Mike's stare. 'I mean, an upstanding businessman like you – where would you have learned to read men like that?'

'Anyone could've read these guys.' He was burned out, his fuse short, his words terse. 'Plus, they stole something from my daughter.'

'Sounds like they were trying to return missing property.'

'How do you think it *got* missing?' Annabel said.

'Your daughter had a backpack with her,' Elzey said. 'It couldn't have fallen out at the ceremony?'

Kat said, loudly, from across the room, 'I think I'd notice if there was a *stuffed polar bear* in my backpack.'

'Maybe she lost it at the ceremony and was embarrassed,' Markovic offered quietly. 'Or she was worried she'd get in trouble. Kids. Maybe she lied.'

'We don't lie in our family,' Mike said, before he could catch himself.

'It was stolen *days* before,' Annabel added.

'Maybe Katherine misplaced it. Like in your truck, by the door. You get to the party, open the door, it falls out . . .' Markovic's face said he was just painting a scenario, but his eyes said something else.

Mike's confidence faltered. He couldn't be certain that the detective was wrong. After all, Kat wasn't positive where she'd last seen her stuffed animal. He felt himself growing more defensive, shoring up his own case, which he knew was exactly what you're not supposed to do. He spoke low so Kat wouldn't hear but felt his teeth clenching around the whisper. 'No. They broke into our house and *stole* it.'

'Oh, good.' Markovic's face softened. 'So you filed a burglary report?'

Annabel cast a sharp look at Mike; she'd recommended, wisely, that he leave out the possible break-in. He looked away glumly. 'No.'

'Why not?' Markovic asked.

What was he going to say? *Because I thought I was hearing ghosts in the baby monitor? Because there wasn't a single sign of forced entry? Because maybe it was all in my head?*

Even though she didn't believe it herself, Annabel shouldered in in his defense, 'We may have heard something—'

Elzey's cop stare made her pause, the phrase – 'may have' – reverberating in the abrupt silence.

Annabel pressed on, trying to explain without making them seem crazy, but Mike stayed quiet, drawing into himself. He knew this drill, the feeling of being on the wrong side of an inter-rogation. Though it had been years since he'd been on the receiving end, he could still read the shifts that made clear that you were subject to the law, not being aided by it.

He stood, touched his wife on the back. 'Let's go.' He nodded at the detectives. 'Thank you for your time.'

'Sit down,' Elzey said.

Mike stayed on his feet. Waited a moment. When he spoke, his voice was perfectly even. 'I'll stand, thanks.'

Elzey stood, matching him eye to eye. Annabel rose, too, jostling Elzey a bit since the detective was standing too close to her. Markovic watched the whole thing with an air of been-there detachment that seemed weary and faintly amused all at once.

'The way this shit went down,' Elzey said, 'you better hope your boy William doesn't press charges against *you*.'

Her temper was up, her intonation shifting, dropping into a street cadence. She and Mike were different pages from the same book. She'd made good, gone legit, but the street kid was still in there, wanting to scrap, needing to prove something. She blinked once and looked away, uncomfortable under his gaze.

Mike said, 'You seem awfully dug into this all of sudden.'

Elzey made a pronounced shrug, all shoulders and spread hands. 'You came through *our* door.'

Annabel let out a single, mirthless laugh. 'My husband gets assaulted at a ceremony honoring his community service and you start investigating *him*?'

'"Assaulted"?' Markovic finally stood as well, the four of them now around shoved-back chairs like a huddle that wasn't huddling. 'From what you said yourself, they never so much as threatened you.'

Mike said, 'The whole *thing* was a threat.'

'Then help us figure out *why* you're being threatened,' Elzey said. 'Your records look like Swiss cheese. You just appeared outta thin air when you were nineteen, yeah?'

'I grew up locally.'

'What's "locally" mean? Strip mall across the street?'

'I haven't broken any laws. I'm fully in the system. Taxes, Social Security number. I don't need to report every fact from my childhood.'

'How 'bout *any* fact?' Elzey said.

'You've got my date of birth.' The one he'd been assigned along with the last name Doe. Even when he'd personalized his surname, he'd kept the birthday, since it was the only one he had.

'What about the rest? Parents? Childhood address? Grade school?'

'Why are you so interested in my past?'

Elzey's lips met in something like a smile. 'Me and Marko, we're just askin' questions here.'

Annabel took Mike's arm and said, 'Thanks for all your help.'

Kat was on her feet, watching anxiously, chewing on a backpack strap. She scurried across to meet them. The whole way to the door, Mike could feel the detectives' stares boring a hole through his shoulder blades.

THEN

Chapter 14

Three minutes past midnight, Mike sees the red lights against the window of the shared bedroom of 1788 Shady Lane and he knows. The neighboring cot is empty; Shep's been working as a bouncer at a crappy bar and won't be home for hours, if at all. Mike hears the Couch Mother's steps thundering toward the front door, a quickening drumroll of his own mounting anxiety. He burrows, wanting to bury his head beneath the sheets. On the plastic stool that serves as his nightstand rests a dog-eared copy of *The Grapes of Wrath* that some genius – no doubt Dubronski or Tony M – has scratched up so the cover reads *The rape of rat*. Around him the others stir. Mike thinks, *It's all over.*

A half hour later, he is in the all-too-familiar interrogation room, and this time, there will be no kindly Saab-owning grandfather to rescue his ass.

Yes, that is him in the security-still frame. Yes, he pawned the rare, stolen coin. Yes, he found it on the street.

As always, the detectives are faceless, nameless. They are adults in *Peanuts* cartoons. They are sounds and pointed information.

'You're a decent kid,' they say. 'We can tell. It's not too late for you.' They say, 'We been looking at your record. Some run-ins, sure, but a safecracking job? It doesn't add up. Now, we know you're buddies with Shepherd White, and that sounds like something more up *his* alley. That kid is bad news. He's going down sooner or later. You gonna let him drag you down with him?'

Mike thinks, *Loyalty*. He thinks, *Stamina.*

They say, 'You're on your way to college, trying to be a good citizen. Bright future. Shepherd White is a punk and a reprobate. You do the math.'

But Mike is working out a different equation. He is still seventeen years old. Shep is eighteen, and Shep has two felonies on his adult record. If Mike rolls on Shep, this will be Shep's third strike, and he will go away for twenty-five to life.

Mike knows the options, and both scare him so badly that he has sweated through his communal T-shirt.

The detectives are unimpressed with Mike's willingness to be exculpated. They say, 'If you don't want to play ball, here's how it goes. You've got a shit-stained rap sheet, and we've got an angry victim, one Mr Sandoval from Valley Liquors, willing to say what needs to be said. Juries love safecracking cases; in this day and age, they're quaint and easy to grasp. One way or another, we will nail your sorry foster-home ass. Even if we have to take a loss on the burglary, we can make receiving stolen stick as a felony. Which means you do time. So you better think long and hard about whether your pal is worth it.'

If Shep was present, he would speak up. He would serve a life sentence before letting Mike take the fall, because he is pure, unlike Mike, who is fighting with himself to do the right thing and wishing Shep were here to step in and take the choice away from him.

Mike's throat is dry and tight. He says, 'He is.'

The detectives are ready for this. They produce an application from Cal State L.A. and say, 'Read.'

Mike reads question 11b, which is highlighted in yellow: '*Have you ever been arrested for, convicted of, or forfeited collateral for any felony or Class A misdemeanor violation?*'

They say, 'That's right. This won't be done when you get out either. This is throwing away college. This is throwing away your future. Think it over.'

He is arraigned the next day and makes bail.

At home, as he heads up the walk, Mike sees Shep waiting in the bay window. They go out back, plunk down on the rotting swings.

Shep says, 'No way. I'm going in and telling them.'

Mike says, 'You go in, you're not coming back out, Mr Two-Strikes-You've-Seen-Me-Play-Ball.'

Shep's voice, for the first time in a long time, is loud. 'I don't care. This is your life. This is *college*. I'm going in.'

'If you go in, I'll never come visit you,' Mike says. 'I'll never talk to you again for the rest of my life.'

Shep's face changes, and for one awful instant Mike thinks he is going to cry.

As promised, receiving stolen property sticks. The judge is tired of kids like Mike, and he is assigned to six months in the Hall. The night before he is due to report, he asks for a moment alone in the bedroom. The others grant his last request. Shep's face shows nothing, but Mike knows he is devastated to be left out with the others. Mike cleans up around his space, makes his little cot a last time, then pauses to take stock of the room. Resting on the long-broken air conditioner is one of Shep's shoes, so big it looks like you could sleep in it. The drawers of the communal dresser tilt at all angles, the tracks long gone. There on the plastic stool is *The rape of rat*. He picks it up, runs his thumb across the tattered cover. Like the Saab, it seems to encompass everything he cannot have, everything he is not, everything he can never be. He reaches over and drops it into the trash can.

Dubronski is in the doorway; Mike thinks the asshole has WD-40ed the hinges for occasions such as this. Dubronski has been watching, but for once that fat bully face is not lit with schadenfreude. He pops a Jelly Belly for a sugar hit, plays with his pudgy hands. 'Hey, Doe Boy, I just wanted to say, this sucks ass. I always thought if you could make it, hell, maybe we *all* were worth something.'

And that makes Mike's insides crumble in a whole new way.

The Hall is tough, but not as violent as billed. Mike knows how to fight, so he doesn't have to much. But it is hell – the hell of utter neglect. The others, his peers, represent every dirty part of himself that he never managed to scrub clean. He watches his back all the time and suffers from vigilance burnout, waking every five minutes, spinning circles down the corridors, keeping his back against the chain-link during yard time.

The third week he gets summoned to the head office, where the superintendent waits. She is not a warden. Just like he is not serving a 'sentence' but a 'disposition', and the hulking guards are called 'counselors'. All those soft names don't seem to make the time any less hard.

She asks, 'How would you explain your state of mind, son?'

Mike says, 'Scared straight.'

'I understand you caught a bad rap. If you keep up the good behavior, I will make sure your time here is pleasant.'

'Yes, ma'am.'

'I will do my best to get you an early release. In the meantime don't make me look stupid.'

'Yes, ma'am.'

'And when you're out, don't make me look stupid then either.'

'Yes, ma'am.'

A few days later, a pie-faced guard wakes him at two in the morning and mumbles the news: The Couch Mother is dead.

Details are scarce. The rest of the night, Mike sits on his turned-back sheets with his bare feet on the icy tile, a wall of static blotting out thought and feeling.

In a hushed morning phone call with Shep, Mike learns that she had a stroke on a rare trip to the bathroom and cracked her head open on the lip of the tub. She had a good heart, a strong heart to push blood through all that acreage. But still, all hearts have their limits.

Hearing Shep's voice jars something loose in Mike's chest, and he hangs up and walks down the hall to the bathroom and locks himself in a stall. He sits on the closed toilet, doubles over, and sobs three times in perfect silence, his eyes clenched, both hands clamped over his mouth.

She may not have seemed like much, but she was what he had.

He is allowed to attend the funeral. Two sheepish uniformed cops, Mike's escorts, stand in the back of the airless chapel. As the service begins, the hearse from the previous funeral is still idling in the alley, visible through a side door, and the folks for the next one are waiting in the reception area. Mike walks the aisle, regards the refrigerator of a casket, and thinks, *I failed you.*

None of the foster kids will give a speech. The notion of ceremony, of formality, evades them all. Finally Shep gets up. Somber in an ill-fitting dress shirt, he takes the podium. His mouth is a stubborn line. Silence reigns.

'She was there,' he says, and steps down.

Though the by-the-hour pastor frowns, Mike knows that Shep means this as the highest compliment.

Nine weeks later Mike walks from the Hall with a bag of clothes and forty dollars from the state. Shep is waiting for him outside on the shoulder of the road, leaning against a dinged-up Camaro, arms crossed. Mike has no idea how Shep knew about the early release date; he just found out himself the morning before.

As Mike approaches, Shep tosses him the keys. 'You shouldn't have done that,' Shep says.

'Loyalty,' Mike says. 'And stamina.'

Over the next few months, he applies for a few real jobs, but that felony charge gets in his way, sitting there like a boulder in the middle of a canyon road. So he gets a job as a day laborer, working with prison-release guys twice his age, hauling soot out of firehouses. With his first paycheck, he hires a lawyer out of the yellow pages and has his juvenile record sealed. But he soon discovers that while prospective employers can't see his file, they will always know that it *is* sealed. And what they imagine his transgressions to be, he gleans, is worse than the reality.

At a dingy downtown government office, he stands in line with a bunch of domestic-abuse victims to get his last name and Social Security number changed. He is assigned a fresh number and a fresh surname, this time of his own choosing. He is Michael Wingate, and he has no past, no history. He has a clean start.

He gets a proper job as a carpenter, and nights he presses shirts in a purgatory of a dry cleaner. He and Shep drift, riding separate undercurrents. It is natural, gradual. It goes unspoken.

One day he walks past the window at Blockbuster and sees her standing there between Drama and Comedy. He stops to gawk. The sight of this woman makes him hurt in the worst way; it makes him *yearn*. But he is too intimidated to go in and talk to her, so instead he goes home and lies awake all night, cursing his unexpected timidity.

For the next few weeks, he goes back to Blockbuster before work, on break, between jobs. She has to return the movie sometime – two days, right, then late fees? He grows convinced that she has sworn off rentals, that she leaves the house only at inopportune times, that she saw him in the window leering like a stalker and was frightened into moving.

But one Sunday she reappears. Without figuring out what he is going to say, he rushes up to her in the parking lot, and only then does he stop and ask himself, *What are you* doing? She appraises him, panting and speechless, and before he can utter so much as a syllable, she bursts into laughter and says, 'Okay, lunch. But somewhere public in case you're an ax murderer.'

Lunch lasts through dinner. Engrossed in conversation, they forget to eat, the food no longer steaming on untouched plates. She works at a day-care center. Her smile makes him dizzy. She touches his arm, once, when laughing at something. He tells her his story, unedited, in a single breathless burst, how he was six kinds of stupid when he went into the Hall but has since gotten it down to three or four. He tells her about the Couch Mother and the Saab Grandfather and the Superintendent Warden, how they all gave him consideration before he really deserved it, how that probably saved his life, and how he hopes eventually to do the same thing for other people. He tells her he wants to build houses someday. She says, 'Dreams are a dime a dozen. But sounds like you actually have the backbone to get there,' and he burns with pride and says, 'Stamina.'

She lets him see her to her car, and they pause, nervous in the biting October night. Her door is open, the interior light shining, but she stands there, waiting. He hesitates, desperate not to blemish the perfect evening.

'If you had any guts,' she says, 'you'd kiss me.'

There is a second dinner, and a fifth. When she invites him over for a meal, he changes outfits three times, and still, to his eye, his clothes look worn out and blue-collar. As she sautés mushrooms, he patrols her apartment, picking up a sugar bowl, eyeing the rows of matching candles, fingering vanity curtains that are there only to provide a dab of lavender. He pictures his bare mattress, his cabinet lined with cans of SpaghettiOs, the poster of Michael Jordan thumbtacked above his garage-sale desk and realizes that no one ever taught him how to live properly.

That night they make love. She weeps after, and he is convinced he did something wrong until she explains.

She is very different from the girls he met during his tenure at 1788 Shady Lane.

At the movies one night, she giggles at his whispered joke, and the muscle-bound guy in the row in front of them turns and says, 'Shut *up*, bitch.' With a quick jab, Mike shatters his nose. They rush out, leaving the guy mewling in the aisle, his friends looking on helplessly, clones in matching college football jackets. Outside, Annabel says, 'I'd be lying to say I didn't find that charming and exciting in a fucked-up sort of way, but promise me you won't ever do something like that again unless you really have to.'

That's her – reverent and irreverent at the same time.

Confused, he acquiesces.

Later that week, exhausted, he dozes off at the shirt press and burns a tux vest. The customer, a coked-out dickhead in a blue Audi, shows up on his way to his black-tie event. 'Do you have any fucking idea how much that tux cost?' Mike apologizes and offers to file a damage claim. 'And what the hell am I supposed to wear to*night*?' The customer grows irate, leaning over the counter, jabbing a finger into Mike's chest. 'You stupid fucking clown, you couldn't pay for that with what you make in a *year*.' The guy shoves Mike, and Mike sees the angle open up, the downward cross to break the jaw, but instead he takes a step back. The guy's rage blows itself out, and he departs, peeling out and flipping Mike the bird. Mike still has a job, his knuckles aren't bruised, and there are no cops to contend with. For days he basks in this small triumph.

He is becoming socialized.

But still he fears Dinner with the Family. Her father is a bankruptcy lawyer. Her older sister is a domestic machine who produces baked goods and offspring at an alarming rate. Her brother has a Subaru and a weave belt. He gives to charity and complains about taxes, the kind of guy who probably played multigenerational baseball at the park around the time Mike and Shep were boosting Bomb Pops and urinating on Schwinns.

Mike minds his silverware, his elbows, his napkin in his lap. He thinks of those few domestic memories he has held on to – sage incense in a yellow-tiled kitchen, his mother's tan skin, the dust-and-oil smell of the station wagon's cloth seats. He feels uncomfortable, unworthy of sitting here at a nicely set table in a nice home. The parents, none too enamored, seem to agree. When her father passes the butter, he asks, 'Where did you go to college?' and Mike smiles nervously and says, 'I didn't.' The rest of dinner is consumed by stories of successful friends and neighbors who never went to college and were successful *anyway*, the two other siblings swapping anecdotes while the parents chew and sip and shoot each other shrewd glances. Annabel has to contain her laughter at the absurdity of it all, and when they leave, she says, 'I will never make you do that again.'

The next week, at dinner, she fiddles with her watercress. Her face is tight and flushed and quite unhappy. He braces himself for the speech he has been fearing. And sure enough she comes at him hard. 'What are we *doing* here?' She tosses down her fork with a clatter. 'I mean, I don't want to do this whole casual-dating thing—'

'I don't either.'

She bulldozes ahead, undeterred. '—where we agree we're allowed to see other people—'

'I don't want to see anyone else.'

'—and I pretend I'm okay with it.'

'I'm not okay with it.'

'I'm too old for that shit. I need security, Mike.'

'Then marry me.'

This time, finally, she hears.

They don't drink a drop of liquor at the ceremony but feel drunk with joy. The service is brief, some pictures after on the courthouse steps, Mom and Dad doing their best to muster smiles.

As he helps her mother gingerly into the car at the night's end, she pauses in a rare unfiltered moment, dress hem in hand, and says, 'The thing that doesn't add up with you – you're so gentle.' He replies, 'I spent enough years being not.'

He works hard, is promoted to foreman. In what is the single best day of his life, their daughter is born. She was to be Natalie, but when they meet her, she is Katherine, so forms must be reprocessed to ensure she has her proper name.

They settle into an apartment in Studio City. Prints of water lilies, matching linens, little seashell soaps for the bathroom. Through their back window, they can see the Wash, where the L.A. River drifts through concrete walls.

Out of the blue, Shep calls from a pay phone. It has been months – no, over a year. Both times he and Annabel met were excruciating, Shep's hearing putting a damper on what little conversation could be summoned. Annabel is protective of Mike, all too aware of the costs of the sentence he served, and Shep doesn't understand her; she is simply beyond his frame of reference. Mike remembers only long silences and sullen sips of beer, him in the middle, sweating worse than he did at that first dinner with her family.

Given Shep's hearing, this phone conversation, like all others, is awkward, filled with starts and stops. Shep has heard that Mike has a daughter, and he wants to come by. Kat is five months old, and Mike is nervous, still adjusting, but cannot bring himself to say no.

Shep arrives two hours late, well after Kat is down. 'Can I spend the night?' he asks at the door, before saying hello. 'I have a thing going on with my place.'

Mike and Annabel manage nods.

From his pocket Shep withdraws a gift – a wadded, unwrapped onesie sized for a three-year-old. Mike hates himself for wondering if it is stolen. He rubs his fingers over the butterfly pattern. It is the softest thing he has ever seen Shep hold.

Shep puts his feet on the coffee table and lights up, and Annabel says, apologetically, 'Would you mind not smoking in here? The baby.'

'Right,' Shep says. 'Sorry.' He walks to the window and leans out, blowing into the wind.

Annabel says to Mike, 'I think I'm gonna grab some sleep while I can.'

Mike goes over to Shep, wanting him to say good night, to be polite, to be gracious. He rests a hand on Shep's back, still ridged with muscle. When Shep flicks his cigarette and turns, Annabel is starting to pull out the couch bed, and he says quietly, 'Don't bother. I'll just sleep on it like it is.'

'It's really no trouble.'

He pauses a moment, processing. 'Couches are more comfortable,' he says. 'I sleep on a couch at home.'

'Oh,' she says. 'Okay.'

They stare at each other, Shep pinching his St. Jerome pendant between his lips.

'Well,' she says. 'Good night.'

Shep nods.

The bedroom door closes. Shep says, 'Go get a drink?' and Mike says, 'I'm pretty beat. The baby has us up a couple times a night, and I got work at five.'

Shep asks, 'Can I have a key?'

At three in the morning, the front door opens and closes loudly; Shep never hears doors well. Annabel wakes with a start, and Kat fusses through the monitor.

Mike stumbles out into the living room. Shep says, 'Alcohol? Bandages?'

Drawing closer, Mike sees that his cheek has been badly raked by fingernails. He tilts Shep's head, sees the white flesh glittering through the blood. He gets one of the matching hand towels from the bathroom and soaks it in warm water. When Shep pats on rubbing alcohol, he doesn't so much as flinch. They have done this many a night – staying up, whispering, cleaning wounds. For a moment Mike is lost in the sweet familiarity of the ritual. But the footsteps and movement wake Kat fully. Annabel emerges from the bedroom, pauses on her way to the nursery. 'What happened?'

Shep says, 'Crowded bar. I was having trouble, you know . . .' He gestures to an ear. Mike has never known him to speak directly about his hearing problem, and he isn't about to start now. 'Guy was playing with me. Sneaking up. He had a lot of friends. He sucker-punched me. The rest didn't go down how they wanted. His girlfriend jumped on my back somewhere in there. Cops showed up, so I split. It wasn't my fault.'

Someone bellows outside, 'You fuckin' asshole, get out here! We're gonna kill you!'

Kat is crying now in the nursery.

Mike says, 'Did you hear that?'

Shep says, 'What?' Mike points to the window. Shep crosses and sticks his head out. An instant later a bottle shatters against the wall near the window. The yelling, now a chorus, intensifies.

The phone rings, and Annabel snatches it up. 'Yeah, sorry, Mrs. McDaniels.' She points at the ceiling, in case Mike has forgotten where the McDanielses live. 'Everything's okay,' she says into the phone. 'Just some drunk out there. We'll handle it.' She hangs up, says to Mike, 'I don't want this going on here,' and disappears into the nursery.

Shep withdraws his head from the window, wiping beer spray from his face. 'Couple of his buddies must've followed me home,' he says. 'I'll handle it.'

Calmly, he goes outside. Sitting on the couch, Mike lowers his face into his hands. There is a crash. And then another. Then silence.

A moment later Shep reappears. 'My bad,' he says.

'Look,' Mike says, 'maybe you should split before more guys show up.'

'What?'

'I think maybe this isn't the best time . . .' He is grasping for words, stuck between a blood-sworn loyalty and what he owes that grandfather from the park who bought his soul for fifteen grand. He considers the Couch Mother, the superintendent, Annabel, Kat, himself. Obligation makes for tough sledding.

Shep says, 'The guy came at me. I was defending myself.'

Shep is a lot of things, but he is not a liar.

Mike thinks about his mother's faint cinnamon smell, his meandering graveyard walks, and Kat asleep in the next room. He will not – cannot – let anything put that child or her future at risk. And yet Shep is Shep, their friendship battle-tested like no other relationship Mike has ever known. Life is unfair; Mike knows this firsthand. But in this moment he hates that he is now on the high end of the seesaw, enjoying the better view.

He is sweating, unsure of himself, filled with self-loathing. He says, 'I know that, but it's not . . . safe. I mean, I got a baby now. The neighbors. I'm still trying to figure this whole thing out, you know?'

Shep snaps off a nod and stands, his face betraying nothing. Feeling like a heel, Mike walks him down. His broad frame cut from the slanting yellow of the streetlights, Shep heads toward the Wash, Mike a half step behind. A narrow footbridge extends across the river. Black water rustles against concrete banks below. Mike is hustling to keep up, calling after him – 'Shep. Shep. *Shep.*' – sure that Shep is, for the first time ever, mad at him.

But halfway across, when Shep finally hears and turns, his face shows no anger.

Bugs ping off the lights overhead. The eastern horizon has moved from black to charcoal. They are centered above a river moving invisibly beneath them.

Mike clears his throat. 'You told me once . . . you said, "You can be whatever you want to be."' He wants to cry – he almost is – and he doesn't understand himself. It is as though his face is having its own reaction to this while his heart stays resolute and hunkered down. 'Well' – he casts his arms wide – 'this is who I want to be.'

Shep's mouth moves a bit, forming something like a sad smile. Blood shines darkly in those claw marks beneath his eye. He says, 'Then it's who I want you to be, too.'

They both seem to sense the finality in those words, in this moment. The wind comes up, cutting through Mike's jacket.

Shep offers his hand, and they clasp, gripping around the thumbs.

'You're my only family,' Shep says.

He walks off before Mike can reply.

Mike watches Shep's shoulders fading into the early-morning dark. He bites his lip, turns back into the wet wind, and starts for home.

NOW

Chapter 15

Mike stood before the closet, finally stripping off that button-up shirt. One-thirty A.M., and he'd only just finished installing a second heavy-duty lock on Kat's window. Despite his prompting, Kat didn't want to sleep in their bedroom, and he could tell by the set of Annabel's mouth that she found his request a bit over the top as well. He wasn't so sure about an evidence-free home break-in anymore himself. But still, additional lock aside, he got a prickling beneath his skin when he contemplated the view of the dark backyard through Kat's window. He could have pressed the point and made Kat move, but he didn't want to give in to his fear that way. Or force them to give in to it.

He folded his dress pants, worked at the beer stain with a thumbnail, then gave up. Neatly folded clothes stared back from the crammed shelves. All those shirts. Such a long way from the communal dresser of his childhood. He regarded the closet with something like survivor's guilt.

Annabel sat on the bed behind him, kicked off her high heels with a groan, and rubbed her feet. 'I'm just saying,' she remarked, picking up the thread of the discussion they'd interrupted a half hour ago, 'They had an agenda, those detectives. When she was on the phone back there – Elzey – I didn't like her expression. How animated she was. And the way they came back out swinging at you.'

Down to his boxers, he turned. 'Something was off with those cops. No question. They're not gonna help us. We need to figure out how to protect ourselves.' He paused, wet his lips. 'Maybe I should call him.'

'Him? *Him* him?' She leaned back on her elbows, shook her head vehemently. 'No,' she said. 'Uh-uh. He scares me.'

'He would know what to do.'

'Or how to escalate things. Besides, you haven't talked to Shepherd in years.'

Except for the Couch Mother, Annabel was the only one who ever referred to Shep by his full name. Mike used to think it stemmed from her discomfort with Mike's past, not wanting to use the abbreviated name from the stories. But he'd figured out it was more of a maternal nod to the given name, to the boy – a mother's sympathy for that thin-necked kid who didn't jump when someone dropped a lunch tray six inches from his nose.

'And the way you left things,' she continued. 'What makes you think he'd be there?'

'Shep would be there,' Mike said firmly.

'We have *other* friends. Terrance next door. Barry and Kay—'

'What's Barry gonna do, portfolio-manage them into submission? This isn't the kind of problem you call people like our friends for.'

'Then why don't you talk to that private investigator, Hank? I mean, isn't that what a PI's supposed to do? Find out information on people? Look – just think about it. I don't think we want to release the bull into the china shop. Yet.'

'Hank's sick. I told you.'

'Hank never struck me as big on pity. You don't think it might help him to have something to do?' She pulled free a hairpin, shook out her mane. 'I'll go in to school tomorrow with Kat and update the contact and pickup lists, make sure they keep a close eye on her, all that.'

'And talk to her—'

'Of course. We've had the stranger-danger talk a million times, but I'll go over it again. Now, come here. Unzip me.'

She held up her hair, exposing the light down of her nape. He drew the zipper south, admiring the slash of flesh, and she shrugged out of the dress and draped it over the upholstered chair in the corner. They took the duvet off together as they had every night for years – fold, step, fold, step – a marital square dance. And then she went into the bathroom and emerged with her toothbrush poking out of her mouth and his sporting a bead of paste. Leaning over to tug off his socks, he paused, and she popped his toothbrush into his mouth before returning to the bathroom, wearing a clown mouth of foam. The everyday physics of intimacy.

Brushing his teeth, he walked down the hall to Kat's room. She was out cold, the curtain drawn, the locks secure.

He finished up in the bathroom, slid into bed next to Annabel, turned up the monitor, and exhaled. She had leaned his award plaque against the wall by the closet, no doubt unsure what to do with the thing. His name, etched in the bluish mirror beneath the seal of California. When he turned back, Annabel was studying him.

He said, 'What an asshole I was standing up there accepting that award.'

'And what an asshole *I* was sitting there playing the dutiful wife, clapping along.' She rolled over, her face soft, and rested a hand on his cheek. 'It's less lonely being assholes together.'

He caught her wrist, lifted her arm gently so he could see the broken capillaries from when he'd grabbed her in the parking lot. 'Did I do that?'

'Brute.' She twisted lazily in his grasp so the back of her wrist grazed his lips. 'All protective like that, leaving your handprints on me. It was *such* a turnoff.' Beneath the covers her foot found his calf.

Her touch brought a jolt of gratitude – even after stumbling through the past few days, he still got to spend the night in this bed with this woman.

He kissed the inner curve of her arm, delicately, where it was red. Her mouth found his, and they pushed up a little, propped on elbows, their lips joined. He shifted on top of her, stomach to stomach, both of them moving slowly, their exhaustion lending every touch and movement a dreamlike aspect. He moved into her, but she clenched with her arms and legs, held him still. Crossing her wrists behind his neck, her head hoisted a few inches off the mattress, she fixed her gaze on him and tilted her hips slowly, slowly, and he slid deeper until he stopped. She held him still again, perfectly still. He was up on his knees and hands, bearing his weight and most of hers, his arms trembling slightly.

'I want you to look at me,' she said. 'All the way through.'

And he did.

After, she lay as she always did, on her back, one arm thrown across her sweaty bangs, her stomach pale in the alarm clock's glow. He loved the faint ridge of scar tissue from her C-section, how it traced the pan of her hips, dividing erotic from merely sexy, a warrior's mark of a body well used.

She held up her hand, the dull diamond of her engagement ring managing a sparkle. The new one had disappeared into the jewelry box as soon as they'd gotten home. 'We've been married a decade, Wingate.' Her teeth pinched a bite of swollen lip. 'It doesn't feel like ten years in any of the bad ways. But it feels like it in all the good ways.'

She curled into him, slinging a leg across his stomach, and he stroked her back, her skin still fever-hot. He pressed his lips to her damp forehead and held her until she was asleep.

Lying on his back, cooling beneath the overhead fan, he couldn't linger in the aftermath. His mind kept returning to the confrontation at the Braemar Country Club, his shame at losing control that way, how his temper had ignited, how it had been right there like an old friend, like something atavistic. And the cold-sweat horror of Dodge's mouth shaping a single word: *Soon.*

He got up, padded down the hall, and carried Kat, limp and dead-heavy in his arms, back to their bed. He tucked her in in his place and paused, surveying mother and daughter in idyllic calm. Something glinted over by the closet. His award.

He crossed and turned the plaque around so it faced the wall.

Then he killed the baby monitor, walked down to Kat's room, and took up his post on the glider in the corner.

Soon, Dodge had promised.

Soon.

Chapter 16

Mike's office, a modular-classroom-style prefab dropped in the middle of a dirt lot, had all the basics. Phone, fax, high-speed Internet. Aggressively competent gum-smacking 'front-office girl,' rounded out with high hair and bosom. Fire-sale desks shoved up against corkboard-covered walls, onto which were pinned various blueprints, permits, geological surveys, and Sears photos of family members. It was a humming little operation, twenty-five by thirty-eight feet of efficiency, the nuts and bolts behind the facades they constructed elsewhere.

Mike sat at his desk, massaging away an incipient migraine and pretending to review a bid for an insurance job. He'd been preoccupied all morning, adrift on sour thoughts. He couldn't stop imagining William's black-flecked lips, the reek of his gut breath, the way his face had appeared in the back window of the van, a disembodied head floating between the curtains. Then there was the image of that oil-stained polar bear, rocking in slow motion on the parking lot's asphalt between Dodge's massive feet.

He rose abruptly and headed for fresh air. Pacing the weeds of the yard, he tried Hank for the third time, and at last the PI picked up.

'Want a distraction?' Mike asked.

'From dying?' Hank said. 'Whaddaya got?'

Mike told him about his run-in with Dodge and William and how oddly the sheriff's deputies had acted back at the station.

'Not much to go on,' Hank said, 'but I'll nose around, see what I come up with.'

Unsatisfied, Mike headed back inside. Andrés was at the copy machine, frustrated and pushing buttons indiscriminately. He came over, sat sideways at the edge of Mike's desk, and gazed across the office at Sheila's cleavage as she argued an insurance adjuster into telephonic submission. Andrés clicked down on Mike's desktop stapler with the heel of his hand a few times, just for fun. 'A guy come by the site, asking about you.'

'What do you mean, asking about me?'

'When you around. When you at the office versus the jobs. That kind of stuff. Like he making conversation. Maybe he looking to hire you.'

Mike's face grew hot. 'What'd the guy look like?'

'Dunno. Just a guy. Scruffy beard. Walk funny.'

Mike's heartbeat vibrated in his ears. That headache, picking up steam. He tugged open the top desk drawer to grab some Tylenol. 'What time was he—' The question caught in his throat as he stared down into the drawer. His calendar was to the left. Because the drawer seam there had cracked, pushing up splinters, he always kept the calendar snug against the right side, the habit ossifying over the past few months.

'Sheila?' He waited until she covered the phone and looked over. 'Did you need to go in my desk for anything this morning?'

She shook her head. He lifted the Tylenol bottle up, regarded it, then tossed it in the trash can. He rose abruptly, Andrés observing him with puzzlement.

Mike crossed to the front door, swung it open, and crouched to study the dead bolt. He'd selected the Medeco himself for its six tumblers and the fact that it took a multidimensional key that was hard as hell to duplicate with a pick set. He'd learned this, of course, from Shep. But he'd also seen Shep get one open with a can of spray lubricant and a pull-handle trigger pick gun that, in Shep's expert hands, could get the pin stacks to hop into alignment.

He hesitated a moment, almost fearful to know, then smeared a thumb across the keyhole. Sure enough, his print came away glistening with spray lubricant.

Someone had prepped this lock for a pick gun. Dodge or William.

Mike's mouth had gone dry. Getting through a Medeco was professional-level stuff, a job worthy of Shep. Which meant their coming through Kat's bedroom window wasn't as far-fetched as Mike had been trying to convince himself.

Why would they break into his *office*?

'Sheila,' Mike said, his voice gruff even to his own ears. Everyone in the office, he realized, was staring at him, crouched there in the front doorway. 'Can you tell *when* certain computer files were looked at?'

'Sure, Mr Wingate.' No matter how many times he told her to call him Mike, she insisted on addressing him formally. 'There's a "last accessed" time-stamp feature on most documents, though people usually never pay it any mind.'

He beckoned her to his desk, pulling out his chair for her. As he leaned over her shoulder, she clicked around, Andrés looking on from the far side of the desk.

'Was anything opened over the weekend?' Mike asked.

'I'm looking. But I have to go doc to doc. Anything in particular you want me to check?'

'Green Valley,' he said.

As she typed, Andrés tilted his head and said to Mike, 'Our files are all clean on that.'

'Why wouldn't they be?' Sheila asked, still focused on the monitor. Mike and Andrés exchanged a look. Before either could answer, she said, 'No, those files haven't been opened since twelve twenty-one P.M. last Thursday.'

That had been Mike, perusing the vitrified-clay invoice to torture himself over lunch break.

'But wait,' Sheila said. '*This* was opened Saturday night, one thirty-two A.M.'

'What is it?' Mike asked.

'The personnel files.'

A chill ran across the back of his neck. 'They looked through our personnel files?'

She clicked around some more. 'No,' she said. 'Just yours.'

He took a step back. Andrés and Sheila turned to him, their mouths moving but their words not registering. Dodge and William were digging for information not on some job but on *him*. Just as the sheriff's deputies had been.

Dodge and William, it seemed, wanted to know who he was just as much as he did.

He became aware, slowly, of his cell phone vibrating in his pocket. He wiggled it out and glanced at the screen, which showed a text message from Annabel: HI HON WHERES THE KEY TO THE SAFE DEPOSIT BOX AGAIN I FORGOT NEED TO GRAB SOMETHING OUT.

He stared at the message, that timpani thrum in his skull urging his headache to loftier heights. He and Annabel never texted; they were old-fashioned and preferred to use phones for talking.

He called his wife right away. It rang through to voice mail. *'Hi, it's Annabel. I'm probably digging around for my phone in that tiny space between the car seat and the door, so—'*

He signaled Andrés and Sheila to give him a minute and began pacing cramped circles around his desk as the home phone rang. Voice mail.

It took him a moment to realize that Sheila was talking to him. 'Mr Wingate. *Mr Wingate.* You're due to walk that undeveloped land in Chatsworth at two. Which means you have to leave now.'

'Can't do it, Sheila.' He barreled toward the door. 'I've got to get home.'

She pressed an irritated smile onto her face as he swept past, his jog turning to a sprint.

Chapter 17

Mike raced home, running red lights and stop signs, dialing and redialing the home line. Finally Annabel picked up. 'Hi, babe,' she said. 'I just walked in, and that kitchen sink's getting worse. I know, shoemaker's kids and all that, but—'

He cut her off. 'Did you text me?'

'When have I *ever* texted you? I'm not fourteen.'

'Where's your cell phone?'

'I've been looking for it all morning. I think I left it at school.'

He took a moment to level out his breathing, then said, 'They stole it. I got a text from your cell asking me where the safe-deposit key was.'

'In the tissue box in your nightstand. I wouldn't ask that.'

He told her quickly about the message, William's coming by the job site, and the break-in at the office. A dreary silence as she tried to catch up to the information. 'Okay . . . so they want into the safe-deposit box because that's where people keep private stuff they don't want to hide in the house.' Her voice trembled a bit. 'Which means they've searched the house.'

'They searched my office.' He turned onto their street. 'I'm here.'

Now, anger. 'How would they even *know* we have a safe-deposit box? It's not like everyone has one. Plus, bank records are confid—' She stopped. He could hear her breathing harder with the realization.

'The deputies,' he said. 'Law enforcement could get clearance to see those records, to know there's a safe-deposit box at our bank in my name.'

She was at the front door, walking the key out to him as he pulled in the driveway. He could see her mouth moving an instant ahead of the words in his ear. 'You think they're working together? These guys and the deputies?'

'*Someone's* prying around at a higher level, either officially or unofficially.' He was still talking into the phone, though she was now a few steps away.

He rolled down his window, and she leaned in, dropped the safe-deposit key in his lap, and kissed him firmly on the mouth.

When she pulled back, her gaze was tense, scared. 'Whatever this is, how do we get free of it?'

'Depends what they want,' he said.

'Seems like they want to know where you came from.'

He closed a fist around the key and put the truck in reverse. 'Don't we all.'

Walking past the gaze of his favorite prim-mouthed bank manager, Mike signed in and stepped into the privacy booth with his safe-deposit box. A deep breath before lifting the thin metal lid. A mess of pictures and documents greeted him. An abandoned child report. The county-issued form, three decades old, assigning him a new last name. Elementary-school transcripts. His old Social Security card. The Couch Mother's obituary. A few tattered photos of him and the Shady Lane boys. That college acceptance letter he'd prized so. A probation report, documenting his sentence served.

A chronicle of the imperfect history of Mike Doe.

A flood of nostalgia almost choked him. Here, before him, was everything that remained of his former self.

He dug through the contents, his fingers striking something hard and buried. He lifted it carefully to the light. A Smith & Wesson .357. Straightforward and easy to handle, it was the only make of gun he'd ever been comfortable with. Shep had given it to him for home protection when Mike had first gotten his own place. Mike had kept it in his nightstand drawer for years, finally moving it here at Annabel's behest when Kat was born. He'd never fired it away from a shooting range and hoped he never would. The heft of it in his hand felt familiar and dangerous.

He set it gently on the counter.

He pulled the empty plastic liner from the trash can beneath the counter and dumped the box's contents into it. Bag slung over his shoulder, he stared down at the revolver for a beat.

He pocketed it on the way out.

Mike crouched in a deserted alley, the shadows stretching dusk-long, the whine of traffic thrumming off the brick walls. The door to his Ford stood open, casting a triangle of light onto the ground. He leaned forward, broken glass crunching beneath his shoes, and touched the end of a lit match to a corner of the trash bag. His eyes glassy, he watched the flames catch and flare, peeling away the plastic and eating through all those photographs and documents.

There is no past.

And yet, clearly, there was.

It ended with a sad little pile of ash, which he kicked to the dead air, scattering it. He stamped out the embers, climbed into his truck, and drove away.

Dinner preparation on pause, Annabel sat on the kitchen counter and stared down at the .357 clutched nervously in her lap.

'It's a revolver,' Mike said. 'Easy to handle.'

She spoke in a hushed voice so Kat, busy with homework in her room, wouldn't hear. 'I'm worried about having it around her.'

'Let me show you how to use it.' As the pasta water boiled, he positioned his wife's slender hands around the grip, but she pulled back, leaving him with the revolver.

'It makes me uncomfortable.'

'We're past comfort now.'

Kat trudged in, eyeing her workbook. 'How annoying is long division? I mean, if they're teaching us to be smart, wouldn't smart people just use a calculat—' She looked up, her eyes pronounced behind the red frames of her glasses. 'Why do you have a gun? That's a gun, right? I mean, a gun in our kitchen? Is something wrong? Have you ever shot it? Can I hold it?'

'Go back to your room,' Annabel managed. 'Give us a moment here.'

Kat backed away, eyes on the Smith & Wesson.

Annabel turned to Mike. 'And there you have it.' She slid off the counter, turned down the stovetop heat, and eyed the lesson plan splayed in the cookbook stand, her feminine scrawl brightening the page margins. She was the only person he knew who could study and prep puttanesca simultaneously.

The phone rang. Mike snatched up the cordless.

Hank sounded burned out. 'I can't get anything on a Dodge or a William being at the award ceremony, but that's to be expected.' He cleared his throat, which turned into a coughing fit. 'Now, listen, there's something I gotta lay out for you here.'

Mike found the pause as unnerving as the tension in Hank's voice. 'What?'

Annabel turned, and he drew her toward him, turning the phone so they could both hear.

'Well, I don't know what,' Hank said. 'Yet. I called my hook at the sheriff's, and it seems there's some kind of alert out on you.'

'Alert? What does that mean?'

'Don't know. But your name's been flagged.'

'Flagged for *what*?' Mike's voice was rising.

'I already told you. I don't have those answers.' A deep rasp of a breath. 'Look, this could be local, limited to L.A. County

Sheriff's. Or it could be some other agency that's monitoring anything around your name, that wants to be informed if you have any run-ins.'

Mike thought of Elzey and Markovic's hushed conversation in the back office after she'd gotten off the phone, and how they'd come back out gunning for him.

'Like who? The FBI? CIA?' Mike choked out a laugh. 'How widespread is it? I mean, every station?'

'I can't get more just yet,' Hank said. 'Everyone's being a bit coy. Obviously, it's classified. I gotta massage this thing, nibble at the edges, come in at the right angle. Gimme a day or two.'

'Is there any agency that *doesn't* have me flagged?' Mike asked.

'I'm sure there are plenty. Agencies – and individual stations within agencies – are understaffed and overworked. So unless you went to sleepaway camp in the rugged northwest of Pakistan, it's not like you're at the top of morning roll call. We don't know the extent of this thing, but there's no reason to assume you've become public enemy *numero uno*.'

'What if we need help?'

'Well, that's the problem, isn't it? Until we determine how widespread the alert is and who put it out, how can you know who to trust?'

Mike swallowed dryly. 'And if Dodge and William make another move in the meantime?'

'From what I can read at this point, I wouldn't count on the authorities lending you a friendly ear.'

He signed off, and Mike and Annabel stared at each other.

Annabel reached down, took the revolver from Mike's hand. She raised it clumsily, waiting, her gaze steady. He exhaled a heavy breath, moved forward, and shaped her hands properly around the grip.

Chapter 18

The laundry room's back door had the weakest exterior lock, a dated Schlage that required only a half-diamond pick, a medium-torsion wrench, and a ninety-second attention span. With gloved hands, Dodge jiggled at it quietly. It yielded, and he stepped from night into the dull glow of the house. The old-fashioned wall clock above the dryer showed 9:27. Pocketing the tools, he moved forward into the kitchen, his size-fourteen feet surprisingly silent across the linoleum.

Mike Wingate's head and upper torso were tucked under the sink, tools spread out on a grease-stained bath mat beside his sprawling legs. He was banging away at the U-pipe with a hammer. Dodge glided past him, drifting within a yard or so of his bare feet. Without breaking stride, he plucked a flat, magnetized digital recorder from the top of the refrigerator, where he'd hidden it days earlier. Continuing into the hall, he passed the girl in her room, her back to the open door. She was hunched over her desk, chewing a pencil, and said, 'Mom, long division *sucks*,' to him without glancing up from her work.

He ducked into the bathroom farther up the hall and locked the door. From the back pocket of his cargo pants, he withdrew a Fujitsu tablet computer, a Japan-only model the size of a checkbook; Boss Man spared no expense when it came to matters such as these. Ducking to accommodate the sloped ceiling, Dodge set up the miniature laptop at the edge of the square pedestal sink and plugged the digital recorder into a port. Within seconds the download was complete.

The doorknob behind him twisted, the jangle pronounced in the small space. Then the wife said, 'Oh, you're in there. Sorry, honey. Brush your teeth and get ready for bed.'

Dodge didn't tense. His broad, flat features betrayed nothing. He kept on with his preparations.

As the footsteps padded away, Dodge tugged on a pair of clamp headphones and clicked 'play.' A sound graph came up on screen, charting every noise with a green flare, stretched out like a spiky caterpillar. He nudged the tracking button along a little ways to test sound.

Katherine's voice: *'Don't be mad at me. It's not like I said, "What can I do to bug Mom today? Oh – I know. I'll get* head lice."'

Dodge popped open a search window, typed in, *KEY.*

High-pitched noise scribbled in his ears. And then the wife spoke, the search feature elevating the volume on the last syllable of her sentence: '*Stay still, monKEY.*'

Dodge clicked *Find Again.* More chipmunk babble and then, '*I got a text from your cell asking me where the safe-deposit KEY was.*' Dodge waited, and then a feminine voice replied, '*In the tissue box in your nightstand. I wouldn't ask that.*' The time stamp was from earlier today, shortly after they'd sent Mike the sham text message.

Dodge folded up the equipment, distributed it to various pockets, and pressed his ear to the door. From the kitchen he heard tool meet metal again, and he stepped out into the hall and headed down to the master bedroom.

The bathroom door was cracked, the shower running. As he passed the open slice of doorway, he saw the flesh-colored outline of Annabel, blurry behind the steam-clouded glass. He opened the nightstand drawer. Inside, a Kleenex box encased in a plastic decorative cover. He reached through the slit, fingers digging around the tissue. Nothing. He lifted the plastic cover, and there, taped to the underside, was the safe-deposit key. He wiggled it free, pulled a similar-looking key from his pocket, and wormed the replacement into the spot beneath the bubbled strip of Scotch tape.

As he eased the cover back down, a glint in the rear of the drawer caught his eye. He pulled the drawer all the way out. A Smith & Wesson .357. Using only one hand, he removed it, thumbed the lever to release the wheel, and flicked it, setting it spinning. Cocking his head, he stared down the sights. His lips twitched in a sneer.

The water stopped. The shower door creaked open. He tilted his wrist, the wheel clicking home, and set the revolver back beside the new cellophane-wrapped package of bullets. When he closed the drawer, it made a soft thump.

'Babe, you about done with that sink?'

Dodge made an agreeable noise in his throat.

'Man, this steam.' Her hand tapped against the bathroom door, and it swung open another foot or two.

Standing a few feet to the hinge side, out of view, he withdrew a ball-peen hammer from the deep thigh pocket of his cargo shorts. He waited, but she did not appear.

Moisture wafted across his face as he took a step out in front of the open door. Annabel was doubled over, twisting her wet hair into a towel, her eyes on the floor. He swiveled back, his face affectless, and walked out of the room. Moving down the hall, he slid the hammer into his pocket again.

Katherine was in the small bathroom, toothbrush in tiny fist, leaning over the sink to spit. He floated past her, his mirror reflection passing above her bent head, and walked back into the kitchen.

Mike remained angled up into the cabinet beneath the sink as if it were devouring him headfirst. His legs were bent, hips raised, braced for traction. A muffled clang issued through the wood, and Mike said, 'Damn it.' His hand poked out, groping around on the bathmat, tapping across various tools.

Dodge's boot scuffed the threshold bar between kitchen and laundry room, and Mike said, 'Hey, babe?'

Dodge halted.

'Get me the pipe wrench, would you?'

Dodge hesitated, facing the rear door. Then he reversed, trod back across the kitchen, and plucked the hefty tool from the bath mat. He bent over and slapped it into Mike's waiting hand.

Then he walked calmly out through the laundry-room door, slipping back into the night. Hands in his pockets, he started up the sidewalk. The white van sputtered to life a half block away and crept up on him, the rolling door sliding open to swallow him whole.

Chapter 19

Dodge and William waited by the Dumpster in the midnight-dark back parking lot of Union L.A. bank. The rear door had been shut and relocked, but a light shone through a high interior window. Despite the cold, Dodge wore his short-sleeved button-up open, revealing a clean white wife-beater. Eyes on the building, William shifted impatiently from leg to leg.

He cracked a sunflower seed between his front teeth and blew out the shell. 'Cigarette,' he said.

Dodge's cheap plastic lighter flared, and then two cherries burned at his mouth. He removed one cigarette and handed it over. William sucked an inhale and closed his eyes, savoring it before letting white smoke trickle from the corner of his mouth.

Dropping the lighter into his shirt pocket, Dodge drew hard on the cig, the burn crackling down a third of its length.

The inside light clicked off, and a moment later William's brother appeared at the back door with a nervous security guard, who glanced around before stepping outside.

Hanley scurried over to them, the guard on his heels. 'It's fucking *empty.*' He tapped the safe-deposit key on his knuckles so hard it made a wooden knocking sound.

William drew back his lips, bit down on the cigarette. 'Empty?'

'He must've figured out the text was fake and cleared out whatever was in there.' Hanley was bouncing from tiptoes to heels until Dodge blanketed his shoulder with a hand, firming him to the ground.

'Listen . . .' The guard fussed with his hands at the periphery of the triangle Dodge and the brothers had formed. 'I did my job, right? I glitched the security recording, nothing written on the safe-deposit log – covered all the bases. So my sister's cool? Accounts balanced and all that?'

'Yeah.'

'She can't go down again, man. She got three kids under the age of ten. I mean, she's staring at ten to fifteen. Are you sure? You *positive* your guy can—'

'Boss Man says he'll square it,' William said, 'then he'll square it.'

'You guys are angels, man. Guardian fuckin' angels.'

'We didn't get what we wanted here,' William said. 'So what do you say you take the party elsewhere?' He flicked the cigarette over the guard's shoulder, sparks cascading down the front of the uniform shirt.

The man's face changed. He looked at Dodge, who had moved to stand apart, staring at the black edge of the parking lot with no apparent interest. 'Okay.' The guard held out his hands. 'I never saw you. You never saw me.' Shoring up his posture, he headed back inside, loop-de-looping his mass of keys on its retractable cord. The Plexiglas door closed after him. His pale face stared out at them as he turned the locks, and then he was gone.

'God*damn* it,' Hanley said. 'All that and the fucking thing's empty?' He hurled the safe-deposit key into the darkness. It clicked off the side of the van, then skittered across the asphalt.

Dodge's head turned. 'Get it.'

'Look, I—'

'Now.'

Hanley went over and searched for a time on his hands and knees. Dodge lit two more cigarettes and he and William smoked them down.

Finally Hanley brought the key over to Dodge. Dodge dropped it on the ground, kicked it into a sewer grate.

'Sorry,' Hanley said.

'Relax.' William slung a hand over to cup the back of his brother's neck. 'We were a step late.'

'I know this is a big job, and—'

'No.' Dodge's gaze was cold and steady.

'Well, now.' William showed his teeth. 'Is it *a* job or The Job? That's what we have to find out.'

'How?' Hanley asked.

'How do we always get answers?' William said. 'Slow, steady pressure, watch 'em crumble. We gotta poke at him and poke at him. Till he shows us the way. He's on edge, right? Wingate? Well, guys on edge make mistakes. He'll reveal who he is.'

Without Dodge's hand weighing him down, Hanley was back to bouncing. 'I say we just fuck it and handle'm now.'

'We can't take down a guy 'cuz he *looks like* a guy. We got standards. Every time you do a job, there's a mess. We gotta make sure this is a mess worth making.'

Hanley turned and spit, hard, into the wind. Rolled his lips over his teeth and bit down. 'Fucker beat us. He beat us to that safe-deposit box.' He did a double take. 'What? What are you smiling about?'

William started back for the van. 'The night is young.'

Chapter 20

'*We know who you are.*'

Mike stirred in bed, the hoarse, whispered voice in his ear. Next to him, the heat of Kat burrowed into his kidney.

His eyes cracked open. The baby monitor, eye level on the nightstand, stared him in the face.

The red bars flared again, rising and falling like a painted mouth. '*The question is, do you?*'

And then an earsplitting screech ripped Mike fully awake. It was the sound made when the receiver in Kat's room came unplugged, but in the darkness, unexpected, it sounded like nothing so much as a shriek.

He sprang out of bed, digging in his drawer for the revolver and bullets. Beside him Kat rolled over with a scream, banging into Annabel, and then both were flailing upright, frantic in the sheets, the monitor still wailing until Annabel grabbed it and tugged free the cord. Sprinting down the hall, crashing into walls, Mike fought bullets into place, dropping some, kicking others and sending them pinballing across the floorboards.

Leading with the .357, he swung into Kat's room. A dreary stillness – made bed, orderly books, vacuum-striped carpet. The only movement was the curtain fluffing up with the breeze. On numb legs he moved forward, sweeping the curtain aside.

Both locks unfastened. The window, cracked open several inches. Black square of night looking back at him through the glass.

He shoved the window the rest of the way open and popped out the loosened screen, which flew to nestle in the moist bushes below. Leaning out, he aimed left and then swung right, but there was only stillness and the faint hiss of sprinklers along the perimeter.

Annabel called from the hall, her voice trembling. 'Mike?'

'I'm going outside. Take Kat, lock yourselves in the bathroom, bring the cordless phone, and call 911 if you hear shots.'

He hopped through the window and dashed to the side of the house. A few steps down the concrete run, he could make out the wooden gate, unlatched and swaying in the breeze. The cold blew across him, and he noticed that he was barefoot, wearing boxers and a T-shirt.

He ran to the gate, steeled himself, then shouldered into it hard, springing into the driveway with the .357 braced in both hands. No one there.

He jogged across the front lawn, revolver at his side, and stopped, wet grass chilling his feet. The bug zapper on the Martins' porch across the street hummed and threw off a smudge of burnt orange. Towering like witches' hats, the cypresses at the property line nodded in the wind. He listened, but the breeze was up, branches and leaves rustling all around.

'Where are you?' It felt strange speaking to an empty street. 'You want to hide?' Fueled by anger, his voice steadied. 'I'm not afraid. Here I am. *Right here!*' More rustling, but nothing else. 'You think you know who I am?' He spun, shouting to the night. 'Who am I, then? *Who am I?*'

The bedroom light clicked on next door at the Epsteins'. He could hear Kat crying inside. Crickets twitched on blades of grass at his ankles. After a time their chirping resumed.

Hearing a crackling of car tires, he turned sharply, greeted by a single burp of police siren. A sheriff's-deputy car coasted up in front of his mailbox, and he eased his arm behind his back to hide the revolver. The window glided down to reveal Elzey's dark face. She hopped out, slammed the door.

'What are you holding?'

Turning away, Mike shoved the .357 into the waistband of his boxers, praying that the weight wouldn't cause it to fall through one of the leg holes. He held his bare hands to either side.

'I know what you put back there, Wingate.' Elzey moved forward across the curb, the heel of her hand riding the butt of her hip-holstered pistol. 'You don't have any registered guns in your name, so you're in serious shit if you're holding.'

'I didn't give you permission to come onto my property.'

She halted. The yard was dark, and shadow caught in her face, made her look hard and rawboned. Markovic was out of the squad car now, too, staring at him across the white roof. The taste of autumn – decaying leaves, mulch, dew – was strong at the back of Mike's throat. A faint sliver of moon cast meager light.

'Step back,' Mike said. 'Or show me a warrant.'

'You sure you want to play like this?' Elzey asked.

Mike said, 'Why are you here?'

'After you left the station,' Markovic said, 'we were concerned.'

'So concerned that you're right outside, keeping an eye,' Mike said.

'That's right,' Markovic said. 'We were cruising by, checking on the house.'

'You didn't happen to check my backyard, too, just now? My daughter's window? The inside of her bedroom?'

The deputies' faces pointed at him out of the darkness. Markovic jabbed a finger at the lens pegged to the rearview mirror in the cruiser. 'We've got time-stamped in-car footage and GPS, both of which show our entire patrol tonight, so you'd better watch what kind of accusations you throw around.'

'Someone just broke into my daughter's room.'

'You sure you're not hearing things?' Elzey asked. 'I mean, running around half naked with a gun in your underwear at one in the morning doesn't exactly unconfirm our suspicions.'

'Half naked, sure. But no gun.'

'Okay,' Elzey said. 'So if there *was* a break-in, we'll need to come onto your property if you want us to take an incident report.'

'Another incident report?' Mike said. 'No thanks. Let's wait and see what kind of headway you make on that first one.'

Elzey shrugged. 'Suit yourself.'

Mike walked backward to the gate to keep an eye on her and the revolver hidden. She watched with amusement. When he moved through the gate, she climbed into the passenger seat, the door slamming at the same time gate hit post.

The engine turned over, and the squad car drifted away.

The front yard was still.

Crouched in the dappled shadow of heavy-headed fronds at the far edge of the house, William leaned back against the dew-beaded sill of the kitchen window. His grin sprang into being, floating in the dark like the curve of a sickle.

Chapter 21

Kneeling on the frilly bed, Mike finished nailing Kat's window closed and used his shirt to blot the sweat from his forehead. The dirt at the base of the window was hard packed and, as before, yielded no footprints. He pulled the curtains closed and sat on the mattress. In the master bedroom, Annabel was trying to settle Kat down, lying beside her, petting her to sleep.

Across on the bookshelf, Kat's treasure chest caught his eye. A shoe box she'd wrapped in cloth and bedecked with stickers in preschool, it held her most cherished items. He retrieved it, placed it on his knees, and lifted the fabric-padded lid. Annabel's plastic bracelet from the maternity ward. A sterling-silver baby cup with a lamb imprinted on the side. That missized butterfly onesie that Shep had brought over the last time Mike had seen him. He picked it up and unfolded it, remembering how Shep had pulled it from his pocket and offered it unwrapped at the door. It was so big then, sized for a three-year-old, not a new-born, and yet now it looked so tiny. Those first months they'd used it as a burp cloth, and then Kat had attached to it the way she did and dragged it around as a blankie. She'd never worn it, even when she'd grown enough that she could have.

He poked through the relics of pale yellow and baby-girl pink. There was a sanctity here in this sloppily decorated shoe box, in this room, in this house.

He set the treasure chest back and walked down the hall. Kat was sprawled on the tousled sheets, asleep, Annabel curled beside her, gazing down, a drape of dark hair framing both their pro-files.

Annabel got up, pushed herself back against the headboard. 'They want us to be scared, right? Well, I'm scared. And if we can't go to the cops right now, we need to be creative and figure something out. I can call my folks, have them come here.'

'With your mom's new hip, she's gonna jump on an Airbus?'

'There are a ton of flights every day from Tampa. My dad knows the law. He can—'

'Your father is a retired bankruptcy attorney. And I can only imagine their take on this. They have *never* trusted me—'

'We don't need to get off onto that. I'm just saying there are still some legitimate channels to—'

'There is no legitimate anymore. Guys like this, they don't listen to reason. They listen to force.'

They listen when you wake them up with your fists after they steal your shirt from under your pillow. They listen when you stand within the reach of an uppercut and tell them to quit knocking a kid to the dirt.

'Or they respond with *more* force,' she said.

'What do you propose, then? Our hands are tied. We can't go to the cops until we know which agencies are gunning for me and why.'

'I'm just saying, this thing could spin out of control.'

'Annabel. Are you watching what's going on here?'

'Yes. And I'm doing my best to figure out what it is.'

'What does *that* mean?'

She pulled the blanket up over Kat, gestured that they should keep their voices down. '"We know who you are." That's what he said, right? Through the monitor?'

'And?'

'I know you pulled some stuff back in the day. With Shepherd. Is there anything you did that might be coming back to haunt us now? Anyone you stole money from, hurt, whatever?'

The question struck him deep, in a place he'd kept insulated for so long he'd forgotten that it was vulnerable. He squeezed his eyes shut and pictured that moment he'd frozen in time decades ago, the view out the bay window through the arcade of yellow-orange leaves to the end of the street, to the station wagon that never appeared. The snapshot was his and his alone, and he retreated now into the safety of it. It had shown him that he would be okay if that station wagon never appeared, because he could have something that no one could take from him, and as long as he had that, he wouldn't need anyone ever again.

But he was no longer seven. He had a wife and a daughter, and he needed them as much as they did him. He opened his eyes, fighting to keep his anger on low simmer.

'No,' he answered. 'We were petty hoods, not pulling off bank heists.'

'Are you sure there was *nothing*?'

'You don't believe me. All these years I'm still some street kid underneath everything.'

'Of course not.'

'How could you ask me that? I've never lied to you about anything.' He turned, his gaze sticking on that award plaque leaning against the wall.

She blew out a breath and refocused. 'Because these men are coming after our family, Mike. Given that, nothing is off-limits, not between us. And if there's anything—'

'You don't think I've been racking my brain? There's nothing. *Nothing*. It was shoplifting, spray-painting shit on walls. Nothing that men like this would grudge-hold this long.'

Kat mumbled a sleepy complaint, and Annabel came off the bed, gripped his arm, and pulled him a few steps into the bathroom. Having Kat out of sight, even this close, made him nervous, and he knuckled the door open a few more inches so he could see her.

Annabel's voice was low but intense, pushed through clenched teeth. 'When you wrong someone, you don't get to say which grudges people may or may not hold.'

She was coming at him, her head canted forward on her neck. He realized that his posture was the same. 'Some threat arises, and all of a sudden you married Scarface? I never did *anything* that damaged people. I made some dumb choices, sure, but that's it. We didn't all grow up in the fucking Cleaver household.'

Her arm swung out and smashed a perfume bottle off the counter. It skipped once and shattered against the base of the tub, and a moment later the bathroom filled with the sickly-sweet aroma. Her stare, her face – inches from his – never moved.

The sound of the exploding bottle continued to reverberate around the bathroom.

Annabel took a deep breath. Held it. When she exhaled, her voice was perfectly calm. 'Okay, let's try this again. The office break-in today, the file they looked at, pretty much shows that this doesn't involve Green Valley. Whatever it is, it's centered on you and your past. If it's got nothing to do with your so-called petty-hood years, then there's only one option left.'

His throat was scratchy. 'You don't think I know that?'

'What happened when you were four—'

'For once,' Mike said, 'let's just call it what it was. My father killed my mother.' He had never said it so bluntly, and it caused a shift in the muscles beneath his face. The skin hung on like a mask, but the words had set the real him beneath on fire.

Had he known all along? That the trail of red flags would lead back, eventually, to that spot of crimson on his father's shirt cuff? He pictured his father's ghost hands tensing and shifting on the station wagon's steering wheel. *Nothing that happened is your fault.* Nothing that happened. What the hell had his father done?

Annabel swallowed, wet her lips. She had one hand up, fingers slightly spread. 'We don't know the whole story.'

'I know enough of it. I know that whatever he did is coming back on us.'

'Maybe it was something else. Maybe something happened that made him—'

'*Made* him? Nothing could have *made* him do something like that. There is *no excuse*—' He caught himself. It was all up, piling on top of him, a barrage of words and images: *Morning Again in America. Shithead still thinks Daddy's comin' back. You wreck my stuff because you don't have anything and you'll never be anything. Look at that slice o' pie there. Your records look like Swiss cheese. We know who you are.*

On the bed Kat mumbled something and rolled over.

Mike fought his voice level: 'What kind of a man leaves his kid? Just *leaves* him somewhere? There is no forgiving a parent who could do that to a child.'

Annabel kissed him. Long and tender, mouth closed, on the lips. 'Stop,' she said. 'Breathe.'

He did.

She said, 'You get whatever resources here that you need to face this thing.'

He kissed her on the forehead, and she wrapped his waist tightly in a hug.

In the kitchen he paced beneath the harsh fluorescent glow with the cordless phone pressed to his mouth. Finally he dialed. The last number he had in his book was no longer in service, but the recording gave a forwarding number with a Reno area code.

It rang and rang. Though it had been seven years, the voice was just as he remembered, quiet and a touch hoarse. 'Yeah?'

'I need you here.'

'What?'

'I need you here,' Mike repeated, a bit more loudly.

A rustling sound. A second or two of silence. Shep said, ''Kay.' There was a click, then the dull blare of the dial tone.

154

Chapter 22

Five hours and fifty-seven minutes later, the doorbell rang.

The family lay nestled on the master bed, slats of morning light linking their bodies. Mike and Annabel hadn't fallen asleep until some time around 5:00 A.M., when the adrenaline had finally ebbed, leaving behind mounting dread and stripped-bare exhaustion. He'd drowsed off fully clothed, revolver in one hand, fistful of bullets in the other.

Mike's eyes fluttered, and he lifted his head, which seemed to have taken on weight during the night. The alarm clock read 7:47 A.M. – late for school and work, not that any of that mattered today. Revolver at his side, he trudged down the hall. Since there was no peephole, he opened the front door the length of the looped security chain and drew back his head, surprised.

Reno was more than five hundred miles away – what should have been an eight-hour drive. After Mike called, Shep must've put the phone down, walked straight out to his car, and pushed the needle to ninety the whole way.

For the first time in recent memory, Mike felt relief. He set the .357 beside the empty vase on the accent table, unfastened the security catch, and pulled the door wide. Shep blocked out the rising sun. Behind him a '67 Shelby Mustang sat steaming in the driveway like a horse in lather, the air above the hood wavering from the heat. Midnight blue, two white racing stripes laid lengthwise across the top and right down the hood.

Shep shifted, and the sun came across his right shoulder, striking the side of his face. He had a new scar, a twist of hard tissue beneath his ear – shattered bottle, maybe, though Mike knew that it was something they'd never talk about. Shep still kept his hair short, a little longer than a buzz, the right length to avoid foster-home head lice. He wore a V-necked undershirt, the St. Jerome pendant, rubbed faceless like an old coin, swaying on its thin silver chain. The muscles ridging the top of Shep's chest were as distinct as those that used to frame the bottom of Mike's a decade ago. Though Mike was still in good shape for his age, the contrast made it clear: He had softened.

That slight overlap of Shep's front teeth – the familiarity – was comforting. It felt like home. But there were differences, too, beyond the purpled seam of scar tissue. The muscle of Shep's neck had hardened, grown sinewy with age, and his features looked more pronounced; they had a lean, hungry intensity that was almost wolfish. Regarding him across the threshold, Mike was all too aware of the missed years.

Shep said, 'Well?'

Mike said, 'You got any stuff?'

'Nope.'

Kat's footsteps pattered on the tile behind Mike. Shep brushed past him and crouched, bringing his head level with hers. 'The eyes,' he said.

'You're big,' Kat said. And then, to Mike, 'He's big.'

'Kat, this is Shep.'

Her hand looked tiny shaking his. Annabel came around the corner, smoothing her shirt. Her posture firmed when she saw Shep.

'Thanks for coming,' she said. 'The way Mike and I have been going, I need someone new to fight with.'

Shep looked at her blankly.

'That was a joke,' she said. 'Except for the thanks part.'

They moved into the kitchen. With a yawn Annabel tugged the omelet pan from the rack. She looked at it wearily, set it aside on the counter, then poured coffee for the adults and cereal for Kat. 'Eat fast, monkey. We gotta get you to school.'

'I don't know that I want her going today,' Mike said.

'You think those guys are coming after *me*?' Kat's cheeks looked hollowed out, dark fingerprints beneath her eyes. They'd filled her in on what had happened, keeping the details as vague as they could get away with. She needed to know that dangerous men were focused on them; she didn't need to know that they'd crawled into her bedroom while she was sleeping.

'No, honey,' Mike said. 'They want to mess with me. But you can't be too safe.'

Annabel said, 'The teachers are on alert, the playgrounds are fenced, they have three supervisors out there at all times, and frankly, it seems they're finding it easier to break into our h—' She caught herself and shot Kat a quick look, but Kat was busy staring at Shep. It occurred to Mike, with some regret, that Kat had never met anyone like him. 'Plus,' Annabel continued, 'even sitters and relatives *on* the pickup list have to sign out the kids with ID. She's probably safer at school than she is here.'

'So it's *not* safe here?' Kat asked.

Shep sipped his coffee and stared straight ahead, playing up his deafness. He could retreat like that when strategic or convenient. Mike would bring him up to speed when the time was right, and until then all this was none of his concern.

'You are safe,' Mike said. 'We will keep you safe. Your mom's right. School's safe, too.'

Annabel took Kat by the shoulders, steering her toward the hall. On her way out, Annabel caught sight of her textbook – *Experience & Education* – on the phone table and groaned. 'I was supposed to write up a mock lesson plan for today. Dr Skolnick's gonna be annoyed with me.'

'We'll get things back on track,' Mike said.

Annabel eyed Shep, still gazing blankly forward, taking his coffee one deliberate sip at a time. 'Promise?' she said.

The telephone rang, and Mike crossed, rubbing sleep from his eyes, and picked up.

A woman's voice said, 'Michael Wingate?'

'Yes.'

'My name is Dana Riverton,' she said. 'I knew your parents.'

Riverton hadn't given any more information or revealed why she wanted to meet. She'd said only that she'd rather handle their business in person. Mike had picked a café nearby, and they'd agreed to meet at noon. Shep would watch from the shadows and follow the woman home to get an address.

Mike had asked Sheila to clear his schedule for the day, a directive that was met with passive-aggressive cheer. He'd called Hank, eager to find out who the hell had put the alert out on him and which law-enforcement agencies *didn't* have him flagged. Hank was still grinding away, hitting walls everywhere he looked, the whole thing feeling more ominous by the hour. Waiting on several return calls, he swore up and down he'd phone back the minute something broke. Before hanging up, Mike had told him to also see what he could find out about a Dana Riverton.

The few hours since then, Mike had spent filling in Shep, who'd listened intently, interrupting here and there to ask highly specific questions that Mike couldn't always answer – 'These guys have any jailhouse ink?' 'Did Dodge square up on you like a boxer or a streetfighter?' 'Who's the senior detective, Markovic or Elzey?' Then he and Shep had walked the property, spending extra time at Kat's window – 'You need a sturdy check rail with the sash lock or you can slide in a flexible form hook and pop the latch. See the scratch marks here? They ain't from a chicken.'

Now they sat in the family room, Shep ready at last to weigh in on the big picture. 'Your locks suck,' he said. 'That Schlage in the laundry room, you could get through with a wet noodle. We'll change the ones that need changing after we handle this Riverton broad. The side gates need padlocks. I have a friend who trains attack rottweilers in Fort Lauderdale, I can have one out in two days.'

'An attack rottweiler? What about Kat?'

'I'm thinking of Kat. That's why we need an attack rottweiler. You can keep him out back.'

'How will we—'

'I'll handle him.' Shep pulled two sleek black cell phones from his pocket and set one on the coffee table in front of Mike. 'These are only for us. Don't use it for anything else. Let me repeat that: Don't use it for *anything else*. Each is programmed with the other's number.'

'Can I give Annabel your number? In case . . .?'

'Her and no one else. Keep this phone with you at all times. Text me if possible. I don't like talking.'

Mike knew that the issue for Shep wasn't talking but hearing. On the facing sofa, Mike leaned back, picked at his shoe. It was ten forty-five, his apprehension growing the closer he got to that meeting with Dana Riverton. First Dodge and William, then all of a sudden she shows up? Pretty big coincidence. Her claim that she'd known his parents *had* to be a manipulation; he despised himself for wondering – hoping – that maybe it was something else.

Refocusing, he plucked the Batphone from the coffee table and slid it into a pocket. Shep leaned forward, the pendant dangling, and laced his rough hands together.

The first lull since he'd arrived.

Another awkward minute crept by, and Mike asked, 'What have you been doing?'

Shep shrugged. 'Cracking jobs mostly, still. A lot of cash floating around Reno, 'cuz, you know, the gambling. I did a bank once, but no guns. Went through a back wall at night, covered the sound with a fake street crew jackhammering the curb out front.' He shook his head. 'But that was a onetime thing.'

'I bet you're something to watch now,' Mike said. 'Going at a safe.'

'You wouldn't believe your eyes.' Shep leaned back, stretched his arms across the top of the couch.

Mike thought of the others. Charlie Dubronski, serving a life sentence for armed robbery. Tony Moreno, overdosed on black tar in a truck-stop bathroom. All those wrong turns, all those dead ends. And here was Mike Wingate of the Ford F-450 and the land-development deal, with his pure-of-heart wife and bright daughter. He'd been lucky as hell. Until now.

Mike said, 'What next?'

'Go get me your cell phone. Your real one, I mean.'

When Mike retrieved his phone, Shep clicked around, then held up the screen. The highlighted entry read A'S CELL. 'This the one they have?'

'Yeah, that's hers.'

Shep hit *speaker* and dialed. Straight to voice mail. '*Hi, it's Annabel. I'm probably digging around for my phone in that tiny—*'

Shep hung up. Heat crept into Mike's face. The notion that they had even her recorded voice in their possession made him angry. He pictured her cell phone in William's sweaty hand, in Dodge's oversize pocket, riding on the dash of that dingy white van.

'Tell her not to report her phone missing,' Shep said. 'We want to keep it active.'

'Why?' Mike asked.

He was punching buttons, so Mike crossed and looked over his shoulder. He'd typed a text message: WHAT DO U WANT?

He looked at Mike. Mike nodded. Shep clicked 'send', pulled out a pad, and jotted down the time. He set the cell on the glass surface of the table.

'They're only turning on her phone at intervals,' he said. 'Harder to track.'

'Impossible?' Mike asked.

'Harder.'

They sat. Shep, never one for small talk on a job, stared

straight ahead. Mike did his best not to fiddle with his hands. Ten minutes passed, then twenty. Pretty soon they'd have to start thinking about heading out to that café. Mike checked his watch, cleared his throat, about to suggest they get moving.

The clatter of the cell phone against the glass made his breath catch in his chest. It was loud enough for him to feel in his teeth, but Shep barely blinked.

Mike leaned over and picked it up, his hands shaking slightly as he read the new text.

U REALLY GOT NO IDEA, DO U?

A chill did a slow crawl up Mike's back. He started to say something, but Shep ticked his finger once to silence him. Shep checked his watch, jotted down the time, then pointed at the phone.

Mike keyed in, NO.

He set the phone back on the table and leaned back. Both men stared at it for what seemed a very long time, Mike bracing for the ring this time. The anticipation only made him start worse when it finally did sound.

He pried open the cell. His hands were trembling even more, but he no longer cared what Shep might think. The message stilled them instantly – it seemed his whole body, his heart, was frozen in a moment of suspended alarm.

JUST WAIT.

Chapter 23

Driving through his neighborhood, Mike was struck by its suburban genericness. This was not Hollywood of the palm trees
and starred sidewalks, Venice Beach of the hippie conspiracists
and incense burners, Beverly Hills of the Sunday Bentley and
nine-dollar cupcake. Lost Hills was built, block after block, of
ranch-style family homes, a community of gleaming mailboxes
and bright yellow play structures. It was for folks who craved
Southern California's endless summer, who could not afford
Malibu real estate but wanted to live a short drive from the
Pacific, who didn't need the paparazzi glare of Los Angeles but
enjoyed the bright-light glow from a distance. Neighborhood
Watch signs, hammered into every third street corner and front
lawn, served as amulets against shadowy men with sinister hats
and white slits for eyes. Bad things weren't supposed to happen
here.

He could not see Shep anywhere on the road, impressive given
the Mustang's conspicuousness. He got to the café five minutes
early and took an outside table, as planned. Sipping an orange
juice, he waited, his nerves frayed. Two women in their fifties
dressed like they were in their twenties sashayed in, rat dogs
peeping from their handbags. A well-dressed man carried on a
domestic dispute through a Bluetooth earpiece. Glancing around
the parking lot and surrounding buildings, Mike looked for
some sign of Shep, but still nothing.

He turned at the clop of her heels. A middle-aged woman

approached, clutching a tatty leather briefcase and wearing a short-sleeved silk blouse and a bark-colored skirt. Librarian's spectacles with a beaded chain offset a soft, jowly face. Frizzy brown hair spilled to her shoulders. Her big arms had once held muscle. Whatever Mike was expecting, it was not her.

'Michael?'

'Mike's fine.'

She sat. 'I'll cut right to it, as I imagine you're fairly eager after all these years to know what this is about.'

Her curt, businesslike manner was something you'd encounter at a customer-service desk.

'I think you may have me confused with someone else,' Mike said.

'Your father passed a few years ago. John. John Trenley.'

Hearing the first name, he felt a flare of excitement. But *Trenley*? It meant nothing to him.

'Your mother's been gone about a decade now.'

That didn't square with the blood on his father's sleeve. But then again, with everything going on, he didn't know what he knew anymore.

Riverton unsnapped her briefcase and laid it open. 'Danielle.'

Mike could see only the raised lid and the hinges of the briefcase. His mind raced, but he kept his mouth pressed closed. *Danielle. My mother was named* Danielle.

'I was appointed the executor of their estate.' She smiled self-effacingly. 'I'm a paralegal. I lived next door to you, was close to your parents. I remember when your mother brought you home from the hospital. I was eleven. I fed you a bottle once.'

Mike's throat was dry. 'Your maiden name?' he asked.

'Gage.'

The name sailed through three decades to strike a cord, setting his insides on vibration. The Gages next door. Mint green trim on a white house. Where the Doberman had bitten the Sears repairman.

He kept his face impassive, though she was still rustling through her paperwork and not looking at him. He reminded himself that this had to be another play in the scheme they were running on him. Even so, the temptation to respond, inquire, react burned in him like a calm rage.

'There's some money, a good amount of money, that's due you. And, obviously, an explanation of epic proportion. But I need to ascertain that you are who I think you are.'

And there it was.

Her arms wobbling, Riverton withdrew a file from her brief-case, '*Michael Trenley*' written across the red tab. A few photographs fell free – crisp real-estate shots of a house. 'Oh, sorry. We had to put the house up, of course. It sold last year, but I can still take you by once we handle the logistics.'

He tried to still his hand but it reached of its own accord and plucked up the top photo. The steps were wider than he recalled and the roof lower, but it tripped a memory.

His childhood house.

The first concrete evidence of his past life. He felt the blood leave his face, but fortunately she was still digging through papers, focused on them. He struggled to show minimal inter-est, to choke back the horde of questions crowding his throat.

He dropped the photo casually on the café table as Riverton perused the folder. The waiter came by – 'Hi, take your order?' – and Mike said, 'Give us a minute, please.' He waited until the man had retreated, then said, 'I'm confused. Why do you think I'm related to these people?'

'Well, you'll see it was *prit*-ty obvious.' Riverton laid the file open. A newspaper photograph of Mike from the PR shoot with the governor. The same one that the *Los Angeles Times* had run, but the headline showed that this one had been clipped from the *Oregonian*. 'And . . .' She slid out from under it a grainy Kodak from the seventies.

Mike's father as a young man.

Their faces were remarkably similar, right down to the pronounced Cupid's bow of the upper lip. The family resemblance was strong, if not undeniable.

The reality hit him, twisting his gut: The newspaper picture of him had shone like a flare on the horizon. It was how they – whoever *they* were – had picked up his trail after all these years. It wasn't the green houses that weren't green that had led those men to his door; it was his decision to swallow the truth, to play party to the fraud, to put his arm around the governor's shoulders and smile for the cameras.

Guilt seethed. Had he listened to Annabel and his own best instincts, this whole threat would have been avoided.

The woman studied him for a moment, then continued. 'When your father was in the hospital at the end, he confessed to abandoning you when you were four. He explained why he had to. That *is* your story, right? Abandoned at age four? Because if it's not . . .' She closed up the file and put it away.

Mike just looked at her, his jaw tensed, debating whether it was worth it to spill. That red-tabbed file was sitting there just out of reach, tucked into her well-worn briefcase, temptation incarnate. *Could* she really be the estate executor? Was she trustworthy?

'Look.' She grasped his forearm across the table. 'I understand the pain you've suffered over this. I mean, the loss, waiting for a parent, searching for them your whole life, just wanting to know. I can only imagine. I have the answers for you. Your parents' estate is waiting for you. I only need to confirm the story of where you came from.'

His breath quickened, her words working on him. Shep was out there watching, but right now it felt as though it were only the two of them, Mike Doe and Dana Riverton alone in the world. He wrestled himself back to calmness. He would not ask questions. He would not appear curious. He would let Shep follow her home and get an address, and they would proceed slowly and with caution.

He looked down, and she withdrew her hand swiftly and put it in her lap. But not before he saw, beneath the makeup foundation she'd pancaked on, the tiny jail tattoo on her thumb webbing. A tombstone with a number 7 on it – the number of years she'd spent inside.

On the edge of his finger was a small flesh-colored streak where her foundation had rubbed off. His heart racing, he cupped his hands so she wouldn't see.

'I'm afraid you have the wrong person.' He rose, dropped a ten on the table, and walked away.

Chapter 24

'Don't you need, like, camo sheets?'

'No.'

'Dad, doesn't he look funny in there, I mean, with my pink sheets?'

'Shep's fine, honey.'

'You knew Dad when he was a kid?'

'Yup.'

'I thought no one knew him as a kid. I thought maybe he never *was* a kid. What was he like?'

'Opinionated.'

'Did he drink? Like, beer and stuff?'

'Sometimes.'

'Did he smoke?'

'He tried.'

'Dad smoked!'

'Not really, honey. I didn't always act—'

'Did he have girlfriends?'

'Dozens.'

'Really?'

'No.'

Mike smirked and headed down the hall to get ready for bed, leaving Kat and Shep. Kat cocked her head, eyeing Shep as if readying to paint his portrait. He looked ridiculous crammed into her bed.

'So why are you here?'

'I owe your dad.'

'You do? For what?'

'He saved my life.'

'Like, pulled you out of a burning car?'

'There are different ways you can save someone's life.'

'Like how?'

Shep blinked a few times wearily.

'Ms C says there are no stupid questions.'

'Ms C is wrong,' Shep said.

'Let him sleep!' Annabel, passing in the hall, called out.

Kat waited for her mom's footsteps to fade. 'Like how?' she repeated.

'He expected more out of me than I expected out of myself.'

'So you owe him forever?'

Shep laid back and stared at the ceiling.

'I can do long division, you know.'

'Is that so.'

'And name the constellations. And the planets, in order. Except Pluto, which isn't a planet anymore. How sad is that? One day you're a planet, the next oh, well, sorry.'

'Pretty sad.' Shep lifted his shirt, pulled a Colt .45 from the waist of his jeans, and rested it on his chest.

'Wow. Just . . . *wow*. Can I touch it?'

'Sure.'

She crossed tentatively, reached out a finger, and poked the steel barrel.

'Kat, we need you in bed with us *now*. I've got practicum tomorrow, which I'm *already* flunking, and if—' Annabel wheeled around the corner, Kat looking up at her, finger extended, red-faced. Annabel's own face tightened. 'Please don't let her handle that.'

Shep said, 'Okay.'

Annabel pointed. Kat marched. Annabel followed. The master door closed, firmly. Raised voices hummed through the walls. A

168

few minutes later, Mike was in the doorway, forearm across the jamb.

'Nice dust ruffle. Matches your personality.' Mike came in, sat.

Shep moved up against the headboard, laid the Colt across his lap. He nodded at the window. 'Don't worry. You can sleep tonight.'

'I know.' Mike took a deep breath, gestured through the wall at their bedroom, then at the pistol. 'Sorry 'bout that. It's been a rough couple days. We've never dealt with something like this.'

'*She* hasn't, you mean.'

Mike moistened his lips. 'You don't like her,' he said. 'Annabel.'

'I didn't say that.'

'Technically.'

'She loves you,' Shep said. 'That's all I need to know.'

Mike looked at his feet. Shep stared at the seam where wall met ceiling.

'Look,' Mike finally said. 'How things were left. I never—'

Shep waved a hand. 'The past don't interest me. You need me now. So here I am.'

'I didn't know how to handle things,' Mike said. 'How to reconcile . . .' He sensed Shep's disinterest and trailed off.

'You've come a long way,' Shep said.

'And not so far, too.' The stymied conversation left Mike feeling like he wanted to say something more, but he didn't know what. 'We did some good work today.'

And they had. Shep had followed Dana Riverton back to an apartment in Northridge. From across the street, he'd watched her enter a second-floor place. He'd found an elderly neighbor out walking her schnauzer, who'd told him that no Dana Riverton lived in the complex. Mike had left the address, as well as the other bits of information or misinformation on Hank's old-fashioned answering machine at the office. In the afternoon Shep had applied his focus and Mike's tools to the house, getting the locks secure as only a safecracker could ensure.

Shep looked relieved at the turn in conversation. Back to logistics. Safer ground. 'Tomorrow,' he said, 'I'm gonna go see about tracking that cell-phone signal.'

'How?'

'I called a guy who knew a guy.'

'Long shot?'

'Yup.' Shep tugged back on the pistol's slide, and the round reared up its brass head. He released it again, put it back on his chest. They were, it seemed, out of things to talk about. For once Shep broke the silence. 'She's a live wire, Kat.'

'Yeah. Yeah, she is.'

'What's it like? Being a parent.'

The question, a bit vague for Shep, caught Mike off guard.

'Besides the obvious stuff,' Shep added.

'They're yours,' Mike said. 'All yours. And then you're letting them go for the rest of your life. You move them out of your bed. They walk on their own, don't want to be held the same. You stop cutting their food for them. They go off to school. Pretty soon some jackass in a car'll be out front, wanting to take her to a concert.'

Shep said, 'We were once that jackass.'

'Let's hope she does better than *that*.'

'No shit, huh?' Shep scratched his cheek with the pistol barrel. 'I guess if you do your job well,' he said, 'you get to let go of her again.'

All the smart stuff Shep ever said came packaged like that, wisdom smuggled in simplicity. Gratitude welled in Mike, and he realized just how much he'd missed him. Again he found himself searching for words. 'All this' – his gesture encompassed the room, the house, his family – 'I got because of what you taught me.' He looked around, his words echoing in his head – *all this* – and he realized with chagrin that it may have seemed as though he were bragging, a big shot. On one level – logistics, security, shorthand – he and Shep had fallen right back into sync, but at the same time a part of Mike couldn't seem to get comfortable.

Shep said, 'I didn't teach you shit.'

'Stamina.' Mike couldn't bring himself, just now, to list 'loyalty'.

Shep's eyes pulled to a photo on the bookshelf, Kat at three, hair in her eyes, blowing bubbles. 'Nah, you were always smart enough to know there's more than that.'

'But we needed it. Stamina.'

Shep said, 'That's because we didn't have anything else.'

He closed his eyes, though Mike knew he was just resting, not asleep.

After a time Mike rose quietly and headed back to his family.

Two sleepless hours later, Annabel stood at the refrigerator getting water from the door dispenser, one thumb hooked inside the cup to sense in the darkness when it was full. Turning, she froze at a man's shape in the living-room doorway. Her hand went white around the glass.

'Shep?' The word came out strangled.

'Yuh.'

She shuddered. 'You scared me.'

'Didn't mean to.'

They stood there, two faceless silhouettes.

'You don't want me here,' he said.

She wet her lips. 'Yeah, but I'm generally wrong half the time, so don't pay me any mind.' She cocked her head slightly and seemed to consider him, up and alert at her footsteps, keeping watch. 'You know what? I don't know *what* I want right now. This has been so horrifying. And you're here, aren't you? In it with us.'

'Sorry.' He shifted on his feet, a rare show of discomfort.

Her face softened; his politeness, his out-of-placeness, seemed to tug at her. 'You and I have had our differences, but I want you to know that I'm grateful to you for coming.'

Shep said, 'Okay.'

'And it means the world to Mike. I'm worried about him. He's been really . . . angry. I've never seen him like this.'

'You don't worry about Mike when he's mad,' Shep said. 'You worry about him when he's *quiet*.'

Chapter 25

'There's someone new at the house.'

'Good. Movement.' Boss Man, on the phone, was even more abbreviated than in person.

'He showed up in a Shelby Mustang, the '67, a beaut,' William said. 'It's got that wide grille, makes her look like she's scowlin' at you.'

He sank to the bed, freeing a cloud of dust from the threadbare blanket. Hanley sat opposite, a mirror image, their knees nearly touching. The motel room's lights were off, but the blinking FIVE ADULT CHANNELS!! sign outside threw a neon glow through the curtains, lighting up patches of their faces, their bodies, the dreary furnishings. Dodge was on the floor by the bathroom, his back to the wall, flipping through one of his comics, some violent tale featuring a guy with jester tattoos on either shoulder. The bathroom door was slivered open behind him, a fall of light laid across the open pages. The stink of mildew hung in the air.

'When did he get there?' Boss Man asked.

'We picked up on him this afternoon, but he may have come in earlier.'

'He's formidable,' Boss Man said.

'Yes.'

'We'll see about that. How'd it go with our estate executor?'

'Wingate didn't bite.'

'I figured. We need confirmation on this soon, before it gets out of hand.'

William could hear the whistle of his breathing through his nose.

'What's he doing?' Boss Man continued. 'This new fella.'

'Switching locks. Checking the fences. Looks like they're waiting.'

'For what?'

'Us.'

Boss Man said, 'Name.' A request, not a question.

'Don't have one yet,' William said. 'We ran the plates this afternoon, came back fake.'

'How 'bout that.'

'But Hanley went back and pulled the VIN off the dashboard, so we can check on that tomorrow.' William nodded reassuringly at his brother. 'He's been doing good work on this, Hanley. Helping us achieve the mission directive.'

'What's the VIN?'

William told him the number.

'I'm not waiting until tomorrow. I'll have someone handle it now.'

Click.

William said, to the dead line, 'Okay, I'll be sure to do that, sir.' He clicked the cell shut and said to Hanley, 'He says you're doing good.'

'He did? What'd he say?'

'That you're doing good.'

Dodge made a noise. William figured him for amused, though whether by the comic book or the conversation he didn't know. He and Dodge got on so well because they never tried to figure each other out. William's talents were a complement to Dodge's – mouth and muscle, two interlocking pieces that formed a perfect whole. When Dodge was serving a nickel in Pelican Bay on a battery-assault beef, he'd celled with William's uncle. 'When Dodge bumps you,' Uncle Len had said, 'it's like you're eight years old and he's a Buick.' Uncle Len had been impressed, and that was saying something. He was the one who had started it all, who had introduced William to his distinct philosophy of brutality. Even on his deathbed in the prison infirmary, Uncle Len had held to his code. And passed on his obligations. 'Burrells see to their commitments,' he'd told William on visiting day. 'But I'm leaving a piece of unfinished business. Only thing I didn't get done.' He'd hacked a few times and spit green into a bedpan. 'One job. The Job.' William's only birthright, aside from cerebral palsy and Uncle Len's shattered pocketwatch, had been to complete the task.

Dodge had gotten out a year later, around the time William's osteoporosis had kicked in, his increasing fragility threatening to sideline him. With mounting medical bills, William couldn't afford to be sidelined. A team-up was in order. When he'd brought Dodge onto Boss Man's payroll, Dodge was happy for the work. He'd appeared at the clapboard house William and Hanley had moved into after their grandmother passed, and taken up on a mattress in the cellar, where he read his graphic novels and meditated in thunderous silence. He had a sick mom in a home somewhere – or maybe an aunt who'd raised him – and all his cash went to that. Dodge wasn't about the money, though. He was about the work. William suspected he wouldn't know how to spend a hundred bucks at one time unless he was buying implements. Him and that ball peen. He liked the hammer because he could work for a long time and keep someone conscious. It seemed a good fit for his patience, his deliberateness. William always figured you could read a man by his choice of weapon. Rash, sharp, and to the point, Hanley preferred a knife. As for William, the only weapons he used these days were his words.

The Morse-code flicker of the motel neon was starting to get to him. William leaned over and used a knuckle to work the stiff muscle of his left thigh. If his legs stiffened too much, they'd scissor when he lay down. The pain was so exquisite they even had a name for it: high-tone, like the record company.

He'd learned to live with pain from a young age. Maybe that's why he was such an expert in its application. He'd walked on his knees at first, until a staph infection over one cap forced him upright. By four he'd figured out a gait that didn't require braces. His first memory was shuffling down the shag-carpeted hall, Hanley doing an infant crawl at his side so he could lean into him when he got wobbly. Despite his test scores, William's kindergarten teacher thought he was retarded, because of his loose articulation. During his second hospital stay for pneumonia, his nurse had gotten him speech therapy to help pass the endless bedridden hours. Even as a seven-year-old, he'd known he would be grateful to her for the rest of his life. He spent his time reading dime novels about soldiers and war heroes, fetishizing a military that would never have him. He loved the muscular heroics and derring-do, G.I. Joes charging into the fray, strong of back and square of jaw, their ramrod postures unbending in the face of fair-haired krauts, underhanded Japs, or jungle gooks. When William was discharged, he learned that his parents had moved into a fourth-floor apartment in a complex with no elevator. It didn't take him long to wind up in a boys' home, Hanley following shortly after in solidarity.

William clutched the sheet as a wave of spasticity rippled over him like a prolonged sneeze. The toughest part about cerebral palsy was its unpredictability. Some nights he'd go to bed tight and wake up feeling athlete-strong. Other times he'd be sailing through weeks without symptoms and drop off the cliff, a period of exacerbation coming on fast and hard without warning.

Like right now.

'Dodge' – his voice box felt locked down – 'can you give me a minute alone?'

Dodge stood and walked out. His footsteps clopped down the outdoor hall, and then a door opened and closed.

William flopped back on the mattress, stared at the ceiling, and emitted a low-throated groan.

Hanley said, 'What do you need?'

'The baclofen. It's in my bag.' William tilted his head forward when his brother approached, and popped the muscle relaxant dry. It tasted bitter as sin, but it gave him no bad side effects like the Dilantin he took to prevent seizures, which made his eyes jerk like a fun-house effect. He held on as another spasm worked its way through his lower back and legs, and then he dug a thumb into the knot in his left calf, working it. 'Okay,' he told himself. 'Okay.'

Hanley's forehead furrowed, deep lines between the brows just like William's. He grabbed William's ankle-foot orthosis from the bag and tossed it onto the bed. The flesh-colored plastic brace, with its footlike base and high shin strap, looked anachronistic, something out of the polio-scare fifties. During bouts William wore it at night to stretch his left Achilles tendon.

William stared at it with enmity.

Hanley said, 'Need help with your pants?'

'No,' William said bitterly.

Hanley nodded and headed for the door. When he got there, William said, quietly, 'Yes.'

Hanley came back, helped William out of his clothes, and got the orthosis strapped on.

William said, 'Put the phone near. Boss Man's callin' back.'

Hanley set the phone on the mattress beside William, then pulled the sheets over him and turned out the light.

William listened to his brother walk into the room next door. He heard the shower start, the pipes humming in the wall. He felt a cramp start in the arch of his left foot, but his back was too tight for him to lean forward and fight the orthosis off. The tightness spread until he was corkscrewed in the sheets, his back arched so only his shoulder blades and right hip were touching the mattress. Sweat dotted his face. He waited, prayed, waited. Finally the shower turned off.

Using all the strength he could muster, he dragged a fist

through the sheets and banged on the wall above his headboard. His eyes squeezed shut, he heard Hanley knocking around his room, tugging on clothes, then the sound of running, and – finally – Hanley barged through the door.

His little brother rushed over, tugged off the sheets, and pulled William's limbs this way and that, stretching out the cramps, massaging away gnarls. William grimaced and grunted, releasing the pain with short bursts of breath.

Hanley drew a bath, poured in epsom salts, and carried William over, naked as a baby. He settled into the steaming water with a cry of relief. And then he was floating, weightless, the muscles letting go. In water he was just like everyone else. Hanley sat on the toilet, flicking dirt from under his nails with their father's folding lock-back hunting knife, the one thing he'd left to either of them.

William said, 'I wonder sometimes if this isn't heaven. And then I remember, it's just how everyone else feels all the time.'

The bedsheets muffled the cell phone's ring in the other room.

'Fetch it for me,' William said.

Hanley retrieved the phone, and William flipped it open, warm water sloshing around his neck and shoulders. 'Yes, sir?'

'The Mustang's registered to a Shepherd White. He was in a foster home in the San Fernando Valley from late 1981 to 1993. Another boy lived there during that time, named Mike Doe. Doe popped up in the system as a four-year-old with little memory and no records, abandoned by his father. Guess when?'

William said, 'October 1980.'

'He's our missing person.'

In the excited silence, William could sense, after all these years, what this meant to Boss Man. The Job.

But it didn't take him long to get down to business. 'Hanley goes point on this. The family knows your face and Dodge's. You two can play janitor afterward.' He hung up.

William shut the phone, set it on the edge of the tub, and settled back into the warmth, inhaling the saline vapor from the epsom bath. His muscles felt relaxed, limber, ready.

Hanley was leaning forward, eyes bulging with excitement. 'Well?'

William said, 'We're green-lit.'

Chapter 26

'Dana Riverton's a fake name all right,' Hank said, his old-man voice sounding scratchier over the phone. 'The lease agreement on the apartment was signed by a Kiki Dupleshney.'

'That's her *real* name?' The sharpness in Mike's voice caused Sheila to glance up from her desk across the office.

'Implausibly, yes. She's got your typical con-artist rap sheet – pigeon drops, mail-order nudie stuff, a phony city-inspector routine targeting nest-eggers for home repairs. She doesn't run a regular team, looks to be a gun for hire.'

'Let's go talk to her about her recent employer.'

'She cleared out last night. Manager said she was on a week-to-week. Waiting to time a meeting with you, I'm thinking.'

Ten minutes prior Shep had texted Mike from downtown saying that his contact couldn't get anywhere tracking Annabel's stolen cell phone. William and Dodge either had dumped it or were keeping it mostly turned off, so there was nothing anyone could do. Mike's frustration had hit a high-water mark, but now it looked like it had plenty more room to rise.

'So she's gone?' Mike asked.

'Into the ether. We'll have to wait for her to rear her head. Good news is, we know she uses her real name now and again.'

Mike glanced down at the fat telephone directory spread on his desk. For the hell of it, he'd flipped through the white pages and circled a few names. Thirty-seven Gages, four Trenleys, none with first initial *J* or *D*.

'How about Gage?' he asked. 'A Gage family lived next door when I was a kid. I *know* she didn't make that up.'

'Yeah, but we need a first name, and I'm guessing she invented the Dana. I checked anyway, and I'm getting no Dana Gages who fit our demographics. And when we start looking at Gages, no first name, without specifying region . . . well, you can imagine what those numbers look like.'

As bad as John and Momma.

Mike asked, 'You get anything on John and Danielle Trenley?'

'Nothing helpful,' Hank said. 'There are a handful of John Trenleys, but race and age rule them out. The only Danielle Trenley the database turned up is a teenager in South Carolina.'

Mike thumped a fist down on the phone book, the sound echoing through the office, causing heads to swivel. Mike did everything he could to keep his voice low. 'How about the law-enforcement alert?'

'I'm making some headway – emphasis on "some". I got to a desk officer at Sheriff's Headquarters Bureau. I guess because they oversee Lost Hills, your hometown, the stations were put on alert. Thus the warm reception you got from Elzey and Markovic. There's a standing request for any deputy who comes into contact with you to obtain biographical details from your childhood.'

Mike realized he'd stopped breathing. So William and Dodge had baited him into going to the sheriff's station, where Elzey and Markovic had been instructed to hammer him on his past. But were the four of them working in concert? It seemed a stretch that a law-enforcement agency would use muscle like William and Dodge to intimidate a family.

'And report back where?' Mike asked. 'Who put the alert out on me? Which agency?'

'I still don't have an answer. It seems there's a weird routing request—'

'What does that mean, "routing request"?'

'What it sounds like, son. Take a breath. We're working around some clearance issues here, and a misstep could draw the wrong attention and shut us down. Catch more bees with honey and all that. Plus, I'm trying to see if LAPD or anyone else is looped in on it, too. These things take time.'

Mike signed off, pressed the heels of his hands into his eyes, and ground at them.

His nerves were frayed – another restless night, another 5:00 A.M. wake-up augmented the whole day long with coffee. He'd been running on caffeine and adrenaline for too long now, and he felt his mood getting wobbly.

Sensing his workers' eyes on him, he rose and headed out to the weed-scraggly front lot. He climbed into his truck, turned on the radio, scrolled through a few commercials and shitty songs, and smacked it off angrily. He gripped the wheel hard and took a few deep breaths.

His cell phone vibrated in his pocket. He hoped it was Shep with an update on *something*.

The words blinking on the screen of his cell sent a wash of coldness over him.

A'S CELL.

He clicked *ACCEPT*.

The screen pulsed, then went live with a video feed. Through his shock it took a moment for Mike to recognize the cracked asphalt, the laughing children, the wooden benches.

The playground at Lost Hills Elementary.

His heart felt like a pulsing fist in the base of his throat.

The image tilted jerkily up. There Kat was, jumping rope.

Mike's mouth was moving, sounds coming out.

A hulking figure stepped out from the cover of a jungle gym behind her, his features lost in the glare of the midday sun. The man moved closer.

Dodge.

Mike's foot dropped like a weight onto the accelerator, his tires spinning in the dirt before finding purchase.

Dodge headed for Kat briskly. She continued to play, oblivious.

Mike was shouting at the phone, crushing it in his hand, juggling it against the wheel so he could steer and watch at the same time.

Dodge was five feet away and closing fast from behind. Kat was giggling, counting as she skipped, the rope tracing a rainbow arc overhead.

Mike screeched out of the lot, swiping the gate, throwing up rooster tails of dirt and rock.

Dodge came up on top of her, barely brushing her with a hip, knocking her to the ground.

Mike bellowed.

The screen went black.

Chapter 27

He remembered calling 911 and shouting for the cops to get to Lost Hills Elementary, though his office was seven blocks away and he knew he'd get there first. He remembered reaching the school's answering machine two, three times and bellowing at the electronic voice reciting endless options. He remembered calling Annabel's cell phone, instinctively. When the voice mail kicked on – '*Hi, it's Annabel. I'm probably digging around for*' – he recalled that they had just contacted him from the very phone he was calling and, cursing his stupidity and horn-blaring through a red light, he dialed home. Voice mail there, too. Annabel wasn't back from practicum? At the beep he heard himself saying, '—they got her at her school I called 911 I'm three blocks away now two goddamn it I *knew* we should've kept her out of school—' He was furious with himself for letting Kat out of his sight, for listening to Annabel, all that blind fear and rage seeking an outlet to blast out of him.

He skidded into the school parking lot, narrowly missing a mom unloading a birthday cake from her trunk and Kat's first-grade teacher, who stared after him as he left the truck with two tires up on the curb. Door open, dinging behind him, he sprinted through the attendance office – 'Where's Katherine Wingate my daughter where is my' – and through the side door onto the playground, leaving behind a panorama of startled faces. No kids – recess was over.

The multicolored jump rope lay on the asphalt, limp and snakelike.

His shirt plastered to his body, he dashed over, spinning circles, shouting his daughter's name. He crashed to his knees over the jump rope, hard ground tearing his jeans, and lowered his head.

Through the cacophony in his brain, he thought he heard her voice, high and pure. *Daddy?*

And then again, 'Daddy!?'

He turned. She was on a picnic bench at the edge of the quad, the nurse crouched before her, tending to a bloody knee.

It couldn't be true.

He was running to her, but he wouldn't believe it until he touched her.

The nurse stood, startled, as he approached.

'Hey, Dad – your knee's cut up. Just like mine.'

He gripped Kat's arms, clutched her to him.

'Ow. Dad. Dad. My knee. That hurts.'

'How did this happen?' he said.

'Kids skin their knees on playgrounds,' the nurse replied dryly.

'No, there was a grown man who knocked her over.'

'How did you see?' Kat asked. 'He was huge. He just kept walking. Didn't say sorry or *anything.*'

'We're having some work done on the gymnasium,' the nurse said. 'I'm sure one of the workers accidentally—'

Mike hurried Kat off the playground, through the stunned-silent front office, and around his crash-parked truck to the passenger door.

Tires screeched as a vehicle barreled into them. Mike swept Kat behind him out of the way and met the lurching hood with a spread hand, Superman holding back a bullet train. The acrid scent of burning tire. The metal grille of a van, hot against his palm. Two feet more and he'd have been under the carriage.

The color of the van – white – dawned slowly. With a slow-burning terror, Mike lifted his gaze to the windshield. William at the wheel, his pupils jittering, a slash of a grin breaking the sallow oval of his face. In the passenger seat, his eyes fixed on Mike, Dodge raised two forked fingers to his throat and jabbed them into the pale skin above his trachea.

The engine revved, and Mike strong-armed Kat all the way up onto the curb. As the grille shoved forward, he rolled off the side, catching a glimpse of Dodge's face, staring out at him, expressionless.

'Holy crap, Dad, that guy almost killed us.'

Hidden behind his back, Kat hadn't registered who was driving.

'Buckle in,' he said. 'We gotta go.'

'It's just a knee, Dad. I don't have to go home.'

'We're gonna take the day off, honey.'

'Is this more of what—'

'I need you to trust me right now. I'll explain everything to you later.'

He sped out of the parking lot, dialing home. Voice mail.

In the mirror he watched Kat's expression as she worked through her worries and moved on to other matters. 'So today in class, Kyle Safranski wouldn't be quiet during reading group, and he kept talking, and finally Bahar was like, "Shut up, Sa*fartski*!"'

Redial. Voice mail. Hearing Annabel's calm voice on the recording, he was hit with a flood of remorse for venting about her decision on the previous message – *Goddamn it I* knew *we should've kept her out of school.*

'I got her,' he said into the phone. 'She's okay. We're coming home.'

'Like *Safranski*, but with *fart*.'

He scanned the road ahead, checked the mirrors, but the white van was long gone. 'Yeah, I got that honey.'

The image kept flashing in his mind: Dodge pressing two fingers into his neck, indenting the flesh, those shark eyes black and inscrutable. It was a prison sign, its meaning obvious: *You are marked.*

He adjusted the rearview, checked the oncoming traffic. He couldn't wait to get home, behind locked doors, calling in Shep, shoring up their defenses.

'—spilled her grape juice all over Sage's leg. Shouldn't she?'

He dug in the center console, reached back with the head-phones. 'Honey, do you want to watch a show?'

'Out of school early *and* I get to watch *Hannah Montana*?' She pulled the headphones on and settled back contentedly.

His hands drummed the steering wheel at the stoplight. Finally he was turning onto their street, pulling in to their drive-way. Annabel's car was there in the garage. She must've just gotten home, was probably listening to his messages now.

He waited for the garage door to close safely behind them, then turned to face Kat in the backseat. 'You want to stay and watch till your show is over?' He didn't want her to get scared when he explained to Annabel.

'What?'

He leaned over, lifted a headphone away from her ear, and asked again. She nodded and slipped back into a TV-induced haze.

He stepped out into the garage, wiping his palms on the thighs of his jeans, working out how to tell Annabel. The door from garage to kitchen swung open on well-greased hinges.

He gulped in the scene at once, undigested.

His wife's purse and satchel bag, dumped on the kitchen counter beside the omelet pan. Way across on the family-room hearth, a man crouched, unaware, his bowed back facing Mike. A blood-streaked knife jittering in a fist at his side. A horrible wheezing from beyond. A pale feminine leg poking into view around the man's left haunch, a familiar tan sandal strapped to the foot.

Annabel, bleeding out on the family-room floor.

Chapter 28

Noises filtered through the shock.

Annabel, wheezing. A ragged sound that seemed to come not from her mouth but directly from her body.

The agitated murmur of the man's voice. 'Shit oh shit. Look what you made me do.'

The faintest creak of the doorknob, clenched in Mike's frozen fist.

And then smells.

Dish soap.

Men's deodorant.

Cordite.

Mike's .357 lay in view, nestled in the carpet by the fireplace rocks. The man, facing away, was rocking slightly, agitated, cursing. Still, Mike couldn't see Annabel's head and upper torso. His angle was offset so he could make out only the faintest edge of the man's profile. The guy's cheek was raked open, fingernail gouges so deep they looked like claw marks. He was William and *not* William. The features seemed too even, the musculature too formidable. His arm looked to have been nicked by a bullet, a pencil-thick groove of skin bored from the curve of his biceps where presumably Annabel's shot had skimmed him.

Bunched on the floor to the side of them was, surreally, a plastic drop cloth. Mike's spinning brain couldn't yet attach meaning to it, couldn't fasten onto the ramifications. He remained motionless a half step into the house, one hand still behind him on the doorknob, his hip a few inches off the kitchen counter, the handle of the omelet pan poking his forearm.

The man fell to his knees, the jolt shuddering his shoulders, and Mike caught a glimpse of Annabel's blanched face above his shoulder. Then the man shifted, and only her arm and hip were in view, her sleeveless shirt hiked up from her fall, bra strap misaligned. Ink gurgled from a slit in her left side, just below the ribs.

'You couldn't just listen and sit on the couch and wait for him to get here.' At first it seemed the guy was whispering like a lover, but then Mike caught the tension – no, *fear* – in his voice. The man reached forward, working the bra strap like a rosary, his skin wet and shiny, stress popping out of his pores. 'This is too messy, too messy. We were supposed to wait. I wasn't supposed to . . . What am I gonna . . .? What am I gonna tell . . .?' Eyes squeezed shut, he twisted his head back and forth, a child's vehement *no*.

In total, maybe three seconds had passed.

Surreally, the silence was split by a Muzak version of 'The Blue Danube.' The man dug a shitty plastic phone from his pocket, the ringtone ceasing when he clicked to answer. 'Hello?'

His voice jarred Mike from his stunned suspension. Grabbing the protruding handle of the omelet pan, he closed the distance in four or five massive strides and tomahawked the disk of stainless steel at the man's head. The guy registered Mike's footsteps late, his head craning around to look over his shoulder, his eyes flying open a second before impact. He emitted a terrified noise like a whinny.

Mike caught him at the corner of his jaw with all his force, the momentum twisting his head back around his neck the wrong way, the brutal sound like the snap of a stick wrapped in wet cotton amplified ten times over. The guy toppled over, body hitting carpet as a single rigid piece and giving off a deadweight vibration.

Sobs flashed across Annabel's face – downturned lips, then normal, a strobelight of pain. Her mouth came open, but there was no sound. Air moved through the hole in her side. Mike clamped both hands over the wound. She pawed at his shoulder, missing, missing, and then hooked his neck. He leaned over, pressed his forehead to hers.

Mike took her hand and firmed it over the wound. 'Hold this. Hold this tight.'

To her side lay her attacker, his eyes turned to glass, one boot obscenely touching her calf. His shitty cell phone, an untraceable throwaway model, lay on the carpet where he'd dropped it. Mike pulled back, Annabel's fingers trying weakly to hold him there, and snatched the phone off the floor, remembering only now that there had been a live call going. The connection had been severed, and he wondered who had—

—but then he was dialing 911, not giving a shit about alerts, which agency suspected him of what or how this would play, not giving a damn about anything except—

'—an intruder stabbed her bleeding everywhere get someone here our address is—'

—her fingers were loose over the hole, though the stream had stopped, and then he had his hands, wet with blood to the wrists, back on her and—

Annabel rested a hand against his cheek. He was, he realized, choking back sobs, his breath seizing in his throat. With a groan she tilted her head to take in the blood slick that had robbed the carpet of its texture. 'Oh, Jesus. This isn't gonna . . . work.' The words leaked out of her, breathy, hoarse. Her legs cycled against the floor, one sandal loose at the heel, the other kicked off.

'Where's Kat? Is she—'

'She's fine she's okay I have her in the truck.'

'I got your message. Sorry I . . . didn't listen and keep her . . . home.'

'It's not your fault didn't mean what I said not your fault.'

Jesus, she'd listened to his message blaming her, the last words she'd heard before—

'. . . said he was a cop,' she murmured. 'I thought he had news about Kat. Opened to check his badge—'

'None of that matters you didn't do anything wrong.'

If he hadn't left the message, she wouldn't have been worried enough to open the door to someone who said he was—

'Where's my baby?'

'The garage she's in the garage.'

'I don't want her to see . . . to remember me like . . .'

'It's okay you'll be okay don't talk like—'

'Get her away from . . . all of . . . Leave . . . with her . . . now. Promise me.'

'Don't worry, we'll get you to the hospital and—'

She grabbed his face in both hands, a burst of strength. '*Promise me.*'

'I promise.'

Her hands fell away from his face.

She said, 'I'm scared.'

He was breathing hard, pressing uselessly. 'It's okay it's okay it's okay.'

'But I *am* scared.'

He stilled. Looked at her. Held that gaze, those eyes. 'I know,' he said.

She lay back, shuddered, and was motionless.

Her lips were bluing already, or was it just a trick of the eye? His vision dotted; he reminded himself to breathe.

Wrist. No pulse.

Neck. No pulse.

Chest. No pulse.

His own heart seemed to halt in stunned sympathy. He heard a low, frustrated bellow – from his own mouth? – and then leaned over and vomited on the rug.

No pulse.

He squeezed her cheeks, her lips opening with a faint pop. Was it *breathe breathe* then *push*? Where the *hell* were the –

The cheery three-note chime of the doorbell.

He shoved himself up, sneakers losing their purchase on the bloody carpet, and sprinted around the corner to the entryway. Shards of glass gleamed on the floor tile; it took him a moment to piece them together as the empty vase that used to sit on the accent table. Ripped from the front door, the slide catch dangled from the end of the security chain. Both dead bolts remained unfastened. Annabel must have opened to the length of the chain – no peephole – and the man had kicked in the door, knocking down the table. She'd fled into the house, turned, and gotten off a shot. And then he'd stabbed her. Flying over the glass, Mike reconstructed the event with one part of his brain while the rest hummed with senseless panic.

No pulse.

He flung open the front door. A man with thick black hair and stubble so dense it looked as if his skin changed shade around his mouth and cheeks. Average height, compact build crammed into a rumpled suit. Deep wrinkles split his forehead like cracks. In the midst of the nightmarish chaos, those wrinkles were something Mike could fasten onto; they said this was all real.

The man wiggled a badge in front of Mike's nose. 'Rick Graham.'

'You're not the ambulance where's the ambulance?'

'Dispatch sent a request. I was the closest responder—'

Mike grabbed him, pulled him inside. 'Help her in here do you know CPR?'

Graham jogged back, keys jingling in his pants pocket. He came around the corner and drew up, grimacing at the dead man's head, twisted around on his neck at that impossible angle. 'Jesus, Mary, and—'

Mike steered him down to a knee. 'Here she needs . . . she needs—'

As Graham checked her vitals, Mike glanced at the door to the garage. Kat out there, plugged into her TV show. He could see the light of the screen flashing on the windshield. He had to get this on some kind of footing before she—

'I'm sorry.' Graham stood, rubbing his hands together in what seemed a misplaced show of humility. A new network of lines knit that empathetic forehead. He was older than he'd appeared at first glance, maybe early fifties, with some gray threaded through his black hair and puckers at the edges of his lips. 'She's dead.'

'She's not,' Mike said. 'She's just got no pulse.' Tears were gliding down his cheeks, but his breathing stayed smooth, not fitful – a statue draining through the eyes. If he didn't move, if he didn't breathe, it wouldn't be true.

'I'm sorry. You're in shock. The paramedics'll be here any minute to take care of you. But right now I need to know . . .'

The voice faded off in Mike's head, as if someone had lowered the volume. He looked down at Annabel, his stomach clutching. Her skin had gone dusky, her fingertips mottled gray tinged with mauve, like the edge of a bruise. The blood flow from the stab wound below her ribs had ceased, leaving a distinct black cigar-burn hole.

Graham placed a hand on his elbow, shook him a little, and Mike heard his voice like a tinny echo. 'Is anyone else here, sir? I need to know if anyone else is—'

'My daughter. She's . . .'

Graham said, 'I'd better safe the house.'

It hadn't occurred to Mike that there might be other intruders. Nothing had occurred to him.

Graham drew a Glock from his hip holster and moved cautiously down the hall, out of view. Mike turned an agitated circle. His wife at his feet. His daughter in the garage, still mercifully unaware. He looked down at the blood smears marking his shirt, his hands, even the bulge of the dead man's cell phone he'd shoved into his pocket. Kat couldn't see this. She couldn't find out by seeing him painted with her mother's blood. He tore himself away from his wife's side. Pulling off his shirt, he staggered to the kitchen sink, blasted his hands with hot water, running it up his forearms, scrubbing at his jeans, dripping everywhere. The swirling water, against the porcelain, was tinged salmon pink. A gym shirt was balled up on the phone table by the oven. He pulled it on, thrust open the curtains over the sink, but still there was no ambulance.

Something seemed wrong with the view, but his overtaxed brain couldn't lock on to what. It was the same view it had always been – stretch of curb, row of cypresses, Martins' throwback porch. He glanced at the oven clock, realized that though an eternity had passed since he'd entered the house, less than six minutes had actually gone by.

Rick Graham had arrived with impossible speed.

It struck him, abruptly, what was wrong with that stretch of road in front of their house.

No vehicle at the curb.

Why would Rick Graham have parked out of view?

Down the hall Mike heard a closet door thump open. He could have sworn that Graham was a cop; twelve years at Shady Lane had taught him to read that vibe. But the badge Graham had flashed – Mike couldn't recall which agency it belonged to. He was about to shout back to ask when a chill froze the question in his mouth.

He reached down to his pocket, withdrew the disposable cell phone he'd taken off the body. Phone book empty. Outgoing calls wiped. There was one incoming call, seven minutes ago, the one the guy had answered.

Mike pressed "call back" with his thumb, a rim of crimson showing beneath the tip of his nail. The ringing came through the cell phone's receiver. Once. Twice.

And finally it was matched by a flat-toned version of 'The Blue Danube' from deep in the house.

Rick Graham's voice came in concert through the walls and in Mike's ear. 'Hello?'

Graham had gone back there not to safe the house but to wipe out any witnesses.

Mike looked longingly at the revolver lying beside Annabel's waxy arm, but already Graham's footsteps were headed back down the hall toward him. Mike moved swiftly to the rear door, throwing it open hard enough that it banged against the side of the house. The distant sound of sirens rode the breeze. He retreated and hid behind the kitchen island, peeking out as Graham bolted into the family room, lowering from his ear a cell phone – a match for the throwaway Mike had just dialed from.

The whiteness of Graham's fingers was momentarily shocking, until Mike realized that he'd donned latex gloves. In his right hand, Graham gripped not the service pistol he'd been holding when he'd stepped out of view but what looked like a cheap .22. His right pant cuff was snagged in the top of his black dress sock, revealing the ankle holster from which he'd removed the untraceable throw-down gun.

Graham stepped over the bodies and paused at the threshold to the kitchen, spotting the open back door. He cursed under his breath.

The concern in his tone did not match the purposefulness with which he sighted on the open back door. 'Mike? You okay?'

Mike had not given his name.

The sirens were getting louder. In the garage the door to Mike's truck opened and closed, the noise faint beneath the rising wail of the sirens. Mike bit his lip, drawing blood, but it seemed Graham did not hear. In his crouch Mike was closer to the garage, and he knew the vibrations of the house. He sensed Kat's approaching footsteps and he readied himself to leap out, but then Graham swore again and dashed out into the backyard.

Pressing "redial", Mike left the phone open on the kitchen counter. He swung toward the door to the garage, catching it as it opened and pushing Kat gently off the step. 'Come on, honey. Back in the truck. We gotta go.' He turned her, commanding her back into the dim light of the garage.

'What's—'

'Listen to me, Kat. Get back in. We gotta go.'

She climbed in. 'Daddy' – she only called him that when she was scared – 'you changed your shirt.'

'Yeah, the other one got stained.'

'With *what*?'

As he smacked the wall opener, sending the garage door shuddering up, he noticed a trail of blood curling from his pinkie to his elbow. Light was streaming in, a veil lifting. He grabbed a rag from a shelf and turned away, scrubbing at his arm.

Was he really leaving his wife's body alone? The image of her, still and cool as alabaster, nearly sent him sprinting back inside. He had to see her again.

An echo of Annabel, her dying request. *Leave . . . with her . . . now. Promise me.*

Kat peered out from the massive truck, her voice tremulous and thin. 'Daddy? Daddy?'

'Hang on a sec, honey.' Staggering backward to the driver's door, still swiping at his arm, he didn't recognize the timbre of his own voice. 'Be right there.'

Dropping the rag, he fell into the driver's seat. The key waited in the ignition, left there to keep the TV on, and he twisted it violently and reversed out, nearly skimming the roof against the still-opening door. He braked with a screech and peeled forward.

The sirens were screaming now. Couldn't be more than a few blocks away.

Hidden behind the row of cypresses at the property line was Graham's car.

A dinged-up, black Mercury Grand Marquis. Just like the car that had followed him leaving the Promenade.

Mike skidded up beside it, grabbed his Leatherman from the

glove box, and hopped out, unfolding the longest blade from the compact tool. Crouching so Kat wouldn't see, he jammed the blade through the front tire, ripping forward. Hot air hissed across his knuckles.

Faintly, from the backyard, piped the melody of 'The Blue Danube.' Growing louder.

Stuffing the tool into his pocket, Mike rushed to check out the back license plate. Sure enough, preceding the numbers, an *E* with an octagon around it jumped out at him – the "exempt" mark carried by cop cars and G-rides. Beyond the cypresses, the side gate banged open, and Mike bolted before he could memorize the number.

He jumped back into the truck and floored the accelerator before he got his door closed, that *E* sizzling on his brain like a brand. Rick Graham was a cop or an agent. He was involved in Annabel's murder. He wanted to kill Mike and was willing to off an eight-year-old girl as well just to keep it clean. How many other officers were in on it with him? How deep did this thing go? And where could Mike take his daughter that would be safe?

Kat's face bobbed up in the rearview mirror. 'What'd you just do?'

Through the back window, he saw Graham jog out into the street and crouch by that front tire. He tugged off his gloves, took a few steps away from the curb, set his hands on his hips, and stared after Mike's truck. He was too far away for Mike to read his expression, but his posture showed equal parts amusement and exasperation.

No pulse.

'I had to . . . do something to that car.'

He turned the corner, and they passed an ambulance and a line of cop cars, lights flashing, the noise splitting the air, loud enough to make him cringe. His head jerked to keep the vehicles in sight – windows, side mirror – as they rocketed past.

Kat sat rigid in the backseat, a departure from her usual loose-limbed flopping. Dread had turned her voice hoarse. 'Where's Mom?'

Again came the nightmare repetition, except this time it was not from his father's mouth but his own. 'She's not . . . here.'

He was trying to watch the road, trying to grip the wheel steadily, trying to keep himself from flying apart. It took everything he had, and still he was coming up short.

'Daddy,' she said. 'What's wrong with your voice?'

'Daddy,' she said. 'The light's green.'

'Daddy,' she said. 'Why are you breathing funny?'

Chapter 29

Kat had retreated into a ball of fear and resentment in the backseat. He needed to get them somewhere private before he explained to her about her mother. At least that's what he told himself. Maybe he was just at a comprehensive loss for how to break the news. While driving he'd done his best to make his voice work and comfort Kat, but she was smart enough to take his generic reassurance as worse news, so finally he'd shut up, locking down his body to keep his grief from exploding out of him.

He pulled into a gas station, a dark voice needling him: *The last time I filled up my tank, I had a wife.* Taking a few steps from the truck, he flipped open his phone to call Shep. There Annabel was in the screensaver picture: the photo he'd snapped of her in the kitchen the morning he'd found out about Green Valley. He remembered the warmth of the sun across his shoulders, how she'd rolled her lotioned hands in his.

What?

Your hair. Your eyes.

The last quiet moment they'd shared before the PVC pipes, his decision to indulge the governor's lie by lying himself, the hell that choice had brought down on them.

For the benefit of forty families, think you can smile for a few cameras?

That smile had cost him Annabel.

His thumb twitched, wanting to call her. Catching the

instinct – and the blast of reality that came with it – was a fresh hell. It couldn't be real. He couldn't do it without her – navigate through this threat, parent, live.

He hauled his attention back to the eight-year-old waiting, needing him to take care of her. Shep. Game plan. He realized he had to use the sleek black Batphone, so he swapped them before dialing.

Shep picked up on the first ring.

'My wife is dead.' Saying it caused Mike's face to break. He turned away from the truck, did his best not to double over.

Shep said, 'What?'

Mike glanced over his shoulder, but Kat was still buckled in, staring blankly into space. He forced the words out. 'She's dead. William and Dodge made a threat against Kat, and I took the bait. I went running to her and left Annabel open. I left her alone.'

'Who?'

'A guy, William's brother or cousin. I killed him.'

The memory set Mike's teeth on edge. The vibration sent from the man's skull through the omelet pan had left his arm throbbing, the kind of bone-deep ache you felt getting jammed by a fastball. The sound was inhuman. It was a construction-site noise, the complaint of material yielding. He had taken a man's life. He had no remorse and would do it again unflinchingly, but the hard fact of it extinguished something in his chest.

Shep had spoken – 'How do you know he's related to William?' – and it took Mike a long moment to retrieve the question.

He thought of that grainy Kodak of his father at the age Mike was now. How Dana Riverton had laid it beside the newspaper photo that had announced Mike to whoever had been waiting for him to appear. 'Resemblance.'

'He *planned* to kill Annabel?'

'She fought.' The man's words played again in Mike's head. *You*

couldn't just listen and sit on the couch and wait for him to get here.
'He wanted to kill *me*, not her.'

'So why misdirect you to Kat?'

'So he could . . . I don't know . . . have time to set up in the house. So it would be quiet and no one would know. Maybe he wanted them there for leverage. To get me to talk.'

'About what?'

'I have no idea.'

'What happened after you killed him?'

'A cop showed up – Rick Graham. They were in on it together. Graham called to warn him I was coming.' Mike explained about the incoming call and how he'd phoned back. 'Graham came in to kill me, I think. To clean up. I grabbed Kat and took off. So I'm probably wanted by the *proper* authorities now, too, because of how I left. I don't know who I can trust.'

Shep said, 'Money.'

'I can't think about that right now. I haven't even told Kat yet. Later we can—'

'There won't be a later,' Shep said.

'Okay. Okay.'

'You have your gun?'

'No. That's the one Annabel—'

Shep cut him off. 'You need to turn off your cell phone – not this one but your original one. It's under your name, and they can track it if you leave it on too long.'

Mike powered it down, glancing around. Vehicles flew by on the busy intersection. Two underage kids smoked by the drive-through car wash. A woman left her VW Beetle at the gas pump behind him and waddled to the convenience store.

Shep was talking. '—and your truck.'

'My truck?'

'You've got satnav, right? That means they can track you down through your own GPS system. Get rid of it.'

Discarding the truck seemed like losing a last, essential part of himself. The passenger seat still retained Annabel's settings – slid forward toward the dash, slight recline, headrest low on its prongs. Crumbs from a PowerBar she'd eaten en route to the award ceremony were still caught in the leather seam.

'Right now?' The gas pump clicked off, and Mike tugged it from the tank.

'They've gotta deal with a private company for the trace. It'll take them some time to pull a warrant. Money first. Go.'

Shep hung up.

Mike crouched in a private office at the bank, moving stacks of hundreds into a black vinyl bag the prim-mouthed bank manager had provided. Kat was waiting in the driver's seat in a front parking space, locked in, one hand at the ready on the horn.

'Can we provide some other service, Mr Wingate, to make you reconsider?'

'This isn't about your service.'

'It seems a shame, given your recent influx, to—'

'Why can't I withdraw more?'

'I think under the circumstances, our producing three hundred thousand dollars cash on zero notice is rather impressive. With computerized banking we don't stash as much cash in the vault as we used to. As I said, I'd be happy to arrange for a transfer of the balance to any—'

A cautious knock on the door, and then an attractive woman in a crisp pantsuit opened the door a crack. 'Excuse me, sir. You have a phone call.'

'You know very well, Jolene, that when the door to the back office is closed—'

'I was told it's *very* important.'

A red light blinked on the telephone sitting on the corner desk.

The manager stiffened. He nodded at Mike and turned for the desk.

Mike threw the remaining bundles into the bag and walked briskly out.

'Daddy, why are we here? These people are scary.'

'We're going to catch a ride out of here in a second, Kat.'

'Are you gonna tell me what's going on?'

'Yes. Yes, I am. Soon.'

South of Devonshire in Chatsworth. The shortest distance to the shittiest neighborhood. Weeds rose through cracked sidewalks, vining their way through fallen chain-link. Kicked-in front doors were spray-painted with blood reds and metallic greens: *INS* with a *Ghostbusters* bend sinister through it; gang symbols; the see-no-evil monkey with his two cronies. Clustered in doorways, meth heads vibrated, skeletal arms poking from puffy jackets, blackened fingers working toothless gums. Falling dusk gave the whole stretch of sordid real estate a haunted-house vibe.

Mike was horrified that he'd brought Kat here. But he was more horrified of what might happen to her if he allowed whoever was chasing them to catch up.

The gleaming Ford crawled along, drawing stares, a few people shouting at them, their words blurred to senselessness by the purr of the engine. A knock on the back window startled Kat into a shriek. A bony face loomed, caved cheeks and suppurating smile, the outside door handle click-clicking against the lock.

Mike accelerated, the bony face falling away, and turned the corner. An elderly man backed an ancient Volvo out of a driveway and Mike pulled tight behind him, blocking him in. The man climbed out indignantly to meet him, scraggles of gray hair fringing the drooping line of his jaw.

'Boy, don't you think you can intimidate me. I been living here since before your daddy's—'

Mike held up three hundred-dollar bills. 'This is for you to wait for us. Two minutes. We'll come back. I'll pay you double this to give us a ride.'

'I was born at night, boy, but not *last* night. You want more'n a ride for that money.'

Mike stuffed the money into the man's wrinkled hand. 'Just a ride.'

He drove back to the worst run of meth houses, stopped in the middle of the street and climbed out, leaving the driver's door open and the engine running. Slinging the bank bag over a shoulder, he scooped up Kat from the backseat as he used to when she was an infant. Terrified, she buried her face in his neck. He jogged with her, her breath steaming against his throat.

Reaching the quiet intersection, he looked back. Stick figures circled the pickup, flickering past the bright beams, heads cocked. It would only be a matter of time. And Dodge or William or Graham could spend the night running down a junkie joyride while Mike got Kat somewhere safe.

He turned and jogged to where the elderly man stood waiting.

He and Kat cut across Jimmy's ragged front lawn, dodging car parts and a rusting lawn mower that had deteriorated into the brown grass. Mike had asked the old man to drop them off several blocks away, and they'd run to cover the distance.

Kat hid behind Mike's back as he rang Jimmy's bell.

Jimmy tugged the door open, facing away toward the interior. '—get the damned armchair off the front lawn.'

A disembodied feminine voice. 'Why should you care?'

'Because I ain't havin' no duct-taped La-Z-Boy on my lawn, that's why.'

Shelly appeared in the hall, pale slender fingers forked around an ash-heavy cigarette. 'You're a credit to your race.' Her gaze shifted, taking note of Mike before Jimmy did, and then she pinched her bathrobe closed and trudged back out of sight.

Jimmy's head swiveled. 'Wingate? What the hell you doing here?'

'I need help.'

204

'Fight with the wife? Shit, I don't blame you. Ever since Shelly and I got back together . . .' Jimmy growled a low note of frustration. 'You know when she wants to have sex? *Tomorrow*. That's when.'

Kat moved into view behind Mike, and Jimmy said, 'Shi*hoot*. Hi, sweetheart. Didn't see you.'

Mike said, 'I need something to drive.'

'You want your truck back?'

'I'm in trouble, Jimmy.'

Jimmy looked from Mike to Kat, seeming to register the severity of the situation.

A minute later they were in the quiet of Jimmy's garage. Mike settled Kat into the passenger seat of the Toyota, the familiar smell of his old pickup a badly needed piece of comfort. He pointed at the toolbox mounted over the wheel well. 'We need to empty that?'

'Nah,' Jimmy said. 'It's all your shit anyways.'

'Can I switch the plates?' Mike asked. 'With the Mazda?'

'It's Shel's car, but hell, I pay the note on it.'

He helped Mike replace the plates, and then Mike shook his hand. 'Thank you, Jimmy. I'll make this up to you.'

'Nothing you haven't done for me already.'

Jimmy stood and watched as Mike backed out. 'Going to find Just John?' he called out.

Mike drove off thinking, *I guess I am.*

The Days Inn required a credit card, so they'd wound up closer to the city in one of the run-down motels across from Universal Studios. From what Mike gleaned, the place catered to thrifty tourists and people looking to rent a bed in hour intervals. A single-story strip of rooms lining a narrow parking lot, it was the Bates Motel sans taxidermy victims. Car exhaust and the screech-and-honk of Ventura Boulevard two blocks away assailed the senses. The front-desk clerk, a collection of tattoos shaped like a man, was only too happy to take a cash deposit.

The overnight parking form asked for a vehicle license number, making Mike glad he'd switched the plates in Jimmy's garage. In the room he dropped the bag of cash in the corner and emptied his pockets onto the bedspread. Two cell phones, money clip, change, a half-used ChapStick he carried for Kat. He closed the blinds. An internal door connected to a room next door, which he'd also rented so Kat would have somewhere to sleep undisturbed while he conducted whatever grim business the night would hold.

Kat lay curled in the fetal position on the bed, and he sat to pet her head. She made a little noise and shifted so she could hug him around the waist. He bent and gathered her clumsily into his arms, smelling her hair, taking her in. Her warmth. The tiny fingers. The fragile stalk of neck. That smooth skin – not a crease, not a wrinkle. He looked up to keep his tears from falling, did his best to freeze his chest so she wouldn't sense the shift in his breathing.

He owed her an explanation – *now*.

He went into the bathroom to shore himself up. Leaning over the chipped sink beneath the flecked mirror, he took his reflection's measure. He was nearly unrecognizable. Pink-rimmed eyes, pasty flesh, sweat-dark hair swirled this way and that. No wonder Kat was so terrified.

With horror he saw that blood had dried beneath the fingernails of his left hand. He dug at the black crescents with his other nails, shoving his fingers under the stream of boiling water, but the flakes were stubborn and would not budge. He stopped suddenly, steam rising from the sink, moistening his cheeks. The dried blood beneath his nails was the only part of Annabel he had left.

A memory swept through him, so vivid it seemed he could fall into it: the last time they made love, Annabel's arms crossed at the wrists behind his neck.

I want you to look at me. All the way through.

He cried as silently as he could, banging a fist gently on the lip of the sink. Then he sucked in a breath and forced his face still. Staring down his reflection, he murmured, 'Get it together. Talk to her.'

He splashed bracingly cold water over his face. He still didn't like what he saw in the mirror, but it was as good as it was gonna get.

When he stepped out, Kat was sitting against the headboard with her knees pulled up to her chin. She was staring down at Mike's phone, her face drawn and terrified.

Mike rushed over. 'We can't turn that phone on.'

'I was calling Mom, and . . . and . . .' She started crying.

He snatched the phone from her. The block letters of text message crossed the LED screen.

YOU'RE NEXT.

His stomach went to ice. He threw the cell phone on the floor, crushed it under heel.

She shoved herself farther away, as if to escape the phone's toxicity. 'What does that mean? I want to talk to Mommy.'

He crouched at the edge of the bed, took her hands. 'You can't talk to Mom right now, honey.'

'Why not? *Why not?*'

'She can't . . . she can't talk.'

'That's *not* an answer. Dad – that's *not* an answer!'

'Honey, listen. Mommy . . .' He took a deep breath, let it out as evenly as he could. The last photo he had of his wife was in the phone he'd just smashed into the thin carpet. 'Mommy is—'

The other cell, the sleek Batphone, rang. Mike snapped it up. 'Shep?'

'Yeah,' Shep said. 'It's me.' A rare hesitation.

'What?' Mike said. 'What is it?'

Shep said, 'She's alive.'

Chapter 30

'Don't you dare,' Mike said. 'Don't you fuck with me.'

'I'm at the hospital,' Shep said. 'They have her at Los Robles Med Center.'

'I saw her. I *saw* the body.' He was fighting, now, through a different sort of denial. Hope felt too dangerous, a wobbly tightrope.

'The body?' Kat's voice, flat with dread. 'What happened to Mommy?'

Mike covered the phone. 'She was . . . hurt.'

'How bad?'

'I don't know.' Back to the phone. 'I need to see her.'

'You can't come here,' Shep said. 'Cops crawling all over the place.'

'She needs me—'

'She doesn't need anything right now. Kat needs you – alive. Now, I managed to grab the doc alone in the hall. I'm gonna put you on with her.'

'Wait, I—'

'Mr Wingate?' A cool, feminine voice. 'This is Dr Cha. I'm a trauma surgeon. We have Annabel stabilized. That's the good news.'

'Stable? I was with her when she died. She had no pulse anywhere. She was *blue.*'

Kat was crying, Mike holding up a hand for her to wait, just wait. It was going down fast and wrong, exactly how he *didn't* want to break the news.

Dr Cha was talking in his ear already. 'The blade slipped between her sixth and seventh ribs, slicing her spleen and puncturing a lung, causing it to collapse. The collapse is called a tension pneumothorax – that's what made her lose breathing and pulse. The hypoxia – low oxygen – is what caused her to look blue. The paramedics needled her on site, got that lung inflated. She had some blood in her chest from a nick in the artery. We rolled her to the OR and got her spleen out, but I didn't move on the artery. I'm hoping it clots off on its own so we don't have to crack her chest. She's only lost a few hundred cc's of blood over the past few hours, and it seems to be slowing down. We're continuing to transfuse her, of course.'

Kat was on her knees on the bed, her face focused and alert. Mike circled the room like a caged animal, rubbing the back of his head, emotions sawing back and forth, cutting him to the quick. His wife, alive. But alone and injured. And him not there. He started for the door, his feet moving him before his brain slammed into drive. He halted.

'The bad news?' he said faintly.

'She's not coming fully back online. We're looking for her to initiate her own breaths – she's intubated – and show some pain response, wiggling toes or fingers, anything. Right now she's not. It's early yet, and we hope that it's temporary, but only the next couple of days'll tell.'

'How . . . what does that mean?'

'The longer it goes, the worse it'll look. Now, as her husband, you're her health-care proxy, is that right?'

'Yes.'

'You might want to get down here.'

He fought with himself, excruciatingly aware of Kat, her pained face hammering home his responsibility to protect her. Annabel's voice came at him again, a ghostly imprint: *Promise me.*

'I can't. I – There's a threat. To me, my daughter. The people who hurt my wife—'

'There are plenty of police officers here.' The silence spoke volumes. 'I see. That side of it is not my concern. I am Annabel's advocate here. Not the cops'. And I need to make sure I can talk to you if we have to make a tough medical decision.'

'Can I transfer—'

'Health-care proxy responsibilities? No. Are you reachable?'

'I don't know.'

'You might want to figure that out in a hurry.'

'Okay. I can be. Through Shep.'

'Is he family?'

'Sort of,' Mike said.

'Just so you know, if there's a major decision, we need to see you in person, or we're going to require something in writing, a fax, whatever. If not, the decision making passes to the backup proxy.'

Annabel's father. Jesus.

'I'm handing you back to your friend now.'

And she was gone.

Mike reached for the bed, lowered himself down, light-headed with relief and a new host of concerns.

Shep again. 'The doc told me there'll be security and on-call nurses with her through the night shift, so she's safe through morning. No one's gonna pull anything with this many bodies around.'

'I need . . .' Mike lost his train of thought, found it again. 'I need you to call Hank Danville, my private eye. He's former LAPD.'

Kat was rocking herself and moaning. He lowered his voice so she wouldn't hear. 'See if he can find out why dirty cops are gunning for us. What they want from me.'

Shep said, 'Where are you?'

Mike gave him the hotel name and room number.

Shep said, 'Contact no one. I'll see you in three, four hours.'

Mike hung up. Kat was staring at him, her face ashen. He fought for focus. 'Your mother's injured. She's at the hospital.'

210

'Is she gonna be okay?'

'We don't know yet.'

She stiffened, recoiling from the words. 'What happened to her?'

'She was stabbed.'

'Like in the movies?' She stood abruptly, hugging her stomach, shifting from shoe to shoe so quickly it seemed she was stamping her feet. 'I want to go see her.'

'We can't, honey. Daddy's in some trouble. I'm not sure what's safe right now.'

'Why don't we call the police?'

'I don't know. I don't know which cops we can trust.'

'You mean *they* hurt Mommy?'

'I don't know, sweetheart. I don't have many answers. I know that must be really scary. But I'm going to figure this all out and keep you safe. We're gonna be fine.'

'And Mommy, too?' He swallowed hard.

Her face seemed to collapse. He sat on the corner of the bed and rocked and shushed her until her jagged breathing settled.

He said, 'We need to stick together. I won't let anyone hurt you. But I need you to be strong as we figure out what to do. If you can be strong, we'll get through this. Deal?'

She nodded against his chest, her face flushed in streaks. Her tiny hand poked up, and they shook. 'Deal.'

Fifteen minutes later they were in Target, a dead-on-their-feet march through the aisles. Wonder Bread, peanut butter, baby monitor and batteries, a powder blue child-size sleeping bag. He wouldn't let Kat out of his sight, not around a corner, not for an instant. She trudged beside the cart yawning, scratching her head, rubbing her eyes. The black vinyl bag, filled with cash, strained on his shoulder. It occurred to him that Kat had left her eyeglasses back in his truck, but there was nothing he could do about that now, and besides, she only really needed them to read. In a bin on the checkout lane, Beanie Babies stared out with doleful stuffed-animal eyes. Mike plucked a polar bear from the heap, wiggled it at Kat. 'Snowball II: Bride of Snowball?'

She read the tag. 'Its name is Aurora,' she said flatly.

Its.

He bought it anyway.

The checkout lady said, 'What a pretty girl you have.'

Mike's thumb had moved to the cool gold of his wedding band. He had to concentrate to get his mouth to move. 'Thank you.'

The woman looked at him, uneasy, and rang them up without another word.

Back at the Bates Motel, he loaded batteries into the baby monitor and tried the reception with the connecting door closed and Kat on the other side. 'Testing one two three,' she intoned. 'Testing one two three.' Some static, but it worked well enough. The parent unit had a belt clip, which he hooked onto his waistband. It maintained a decent connection to the edge of the parking lot and down to the front desk.

When he came back, Kat's face was gray with exhaustion. On the little counter, he made her a peanut-butter – no jelly – sandwich, grateful to have something to do, some way to provide *something* for her. Meticulously, he spread the peanut butter and cut off the crust. His hands were shaking, and he thought of his father's arms in the station wagon, his arms shaking as he held the wheel. For the first time, Mike felt a stab of empathy for his father's situation: the blind panic of watching one's life come unraveled. The feeling felt forbidden, threatening; he tamped it down with anger. After all, his father had captained his own fate.

Mike focused on the sandwich, centering it on the plate and slicing it on a neat diagonal. What did he think, that a lovingly made sandwich could mitigate the hell his daughter was going through? Yes, that was his hope.

He gave her a half, and she took a few nibbles before setting it aside.

He was crestfallen. 'Can you eat any more?'

'It'll make me throw up.' She pulled her legs in Indian style and scratched at her head.

'Okay, sweetheart. Okay.'

She was really digging at her hair behind her ear and it hit him: head lice.

He sagged against the counter. For some reason this above all else seemed an insurmountable obstacle. It reminded him of those endless first nights they'd had Kat home from the hospital, the baby cries, the feedings and changing and burpings. He remembered the comprehensive exhaustion, himself and Annabel lying there in the dark, trying to rise to the wails, reaching back for more that they just didn't have but that as parents they had to produce, because if they didn't, no one else would.

Slurping at a leaky juice box, Kat was having trouble keeping her eyes open. He went over, turned her head, and parted the fine hair at her nape. 'Honey, your head lice are back.'

She had fallen asleep against him.

'Sweetheart, we gotta run back to Target. I have to buy mayonnaise and Saran Wrap and get this taken care of.'

'Can't I just stay here?' she mumbled. 'Can't I just sleep? Please, Dad?'

'I'm sorry,' he said, and her shoulders rocked with dry, soundless sobs.

An exhausting forty minutes later, she was curled in her new sleeping bag atop the starchy sheets, her head wrapped in mayo. Mike nestled the baby-monitor transmitter into the sleeping bag right beside her. And then he retrieved the polar-bear Beanie Baby from the Target bag.

'This isn't just an ordinary polar bear.'

Her eyes slid over, found him.

'This polar bear has magical protective capabilities,' he said.

'A magical polar bear.'

'That's right. He will keep us safe.'

'If we get attacked by animal crackers.'

'We have to name him. Do you like Aurora?'

'Hate it.' She picked it up by the tiny scruff, studied its face. 'Snowball II. Like you said.'

'Snowball's Revenge.'

Reluctantly, she tucked the Beanie Baby into her sleeping bag. She scratched at the plastic wrap on her head, doing her best not to look miserable. 'Will you read me a story?'

They didn't have any books, but he couldn't bear handing her another disappointment. Desperate, Mike opened the nightstand drawer, and there, instead of Gideon's Bible, someone had left a dog-eared copy of *Green Eggs and Ham*. It might as well have been water into wine. He ran his hand across the beloved orange-and-green cover, then held it up triumphantly.

Kat said, 'Dad, I'm *eight*.'

'Oh,' Mike said. 'Too old for it.' He made a show of putting it back.

'I mean, if you *really* want to read it.'

'I do,' he said.

'Then okay.' She yawned, half asleep.

'I heard Dr Seuss wrote this after someone bet him that he couldn't write an entire book using only one-syllable words.'

'"Anywhere."'

'What?'

'"I will not eat them *anywhere*." Three syllables.'

'Oh. I guess I heard wrong.'

'Mom does the best voice for Sam-I-Am.'

He collected himself. Read the first page. And then Kat was out cold.

He brushed an eyelash off her cheek. For a time he sat watching her sleep, waiting for the lump in his throat to dissolve.

Finally he crept into the connecting room with his vinyl bag of cash, easing the door shut behind him. He adjusted the volume on the receiver clipped to his belt until he could make out the faint whistle of Kat's breathing. Slanting the blinds a half inch, he pulled a chair around and sat for a good half hour with his feet up on a rickety radiator beneath the window.

At last the Mustang's headlights swept the glass, scanning bars of light through the blinds and across Mike's face. He rose and opened the door before Shep could knock. Shep wore an army-green rucksack over his shoulder.

Mike peered out at the night. 'Were you followed?'

'No.'

'How do you know?'

'I know.' Shep took in the room, his gaze moving from the dark seam beneath the bathroom door to the interior door to the baby-monitor receiver clipped to Mike's belt. He nodded faintly, putting it together, then said, 'Hank wants to see you face-to-face. He's gotta make sure he doesn't have a tail, but he should be here within a few hours.'

Shep dumped the contents of the rucksack onto the bedspread. Soap, a razor, a brush, women's deodorant Mike assumed he'd bought for Kat though she was at least a few years away from needing any, and a stack of Safeway phone cards.

'Prepaid cards go through a central calling center, so they can't be tracked.' Shep's hand dipped beneath his shirt, then he held out a .357 Smith & Wesson revolver, like the one Mike had left behind at the house but with a black rubber handle. Mike stared at it a moment, then took it.

Shep stretched out on the bed, closed his eyes.

Mike moved the cash from the black vinyl bag into the rucksack. He returned to Room 9, pulled a chair to the bed, and sat before the small bump of his daughter beneath the covers. Her back rose and fell, each sleeping breath giving off the faintest whistle. He felt something inside him give way a little. He swallowed, a dry click in his throat.

His hand, he realized, had tightened around the grip of the Smith & Wesson.

Chapter 31

The morgue smelled unnaturally clean. William walked the hall, his shuffle step pronounced, shoes squeaking on tile. He couldn't find an elevator, so he labored down a flight of stairs to the basement.

Two cops and a coroner awaited him, standing before a picture window covered from the inside with a blackout drape. The big cop produced a card with a flourish. 'I'm Detective Markovic. This is my partner. And the coroner.'

Everyone nodded awkwardly.

'I'm sorry for this,' Markovic said. 'There's never anything useful to say.'

'No,' William said. 'There isn't.'

'When's the last time you saw your brother?' the black cop asked.

'Months.'

'What was he doing down here?'

'Hanley was a drifter.'

'Fortunate you were in the area.'

'I was in San Diego for business. I drove right up when you called.'

They'd found William's cell-phone number in Hanley's wallet. The brothers carried each other's number in case of emergency since they were purposefully hard to locate; the house and land were still under their grandma's maiden name, which she'd gleefully gone back to after the old man succumbed to liver cirrhosis.

The call, dreaded as it had been, was not a surprise. William had known that something was off right away, of course, but with the cavalry en route to the crime scene and no call from Hanley, he and Dodge, waiting in the van a few blocks away, hadn't had many options.

'We found your brother in a house. With a severely injured woman. Annabel Wingate. Any idea of his relationship to her?'

'He was always something of a ladies' man,' William said.

The black detective made a noise deep in her throat that implied a lack of surprise.

'Did she die?' William asked. 'The injured lady?'

'She's critical.'

William scratched at the stubble of his neck, the rasp pronounced off the concrete walls. 'Huh,' he said.

Markovic nodded at the coroner, who cleared her throat nervously. She was an attractive woman, blond. 'I'm going to push this button, and the curtain will rise. The body is lying inside on a table. I'd like to forewarn you that there was some trauma to the head, so—'

'Do it,' William said.

She clicked the lever, and the curtain rose. There lay Hanley on his back, presented like some ceremonial dish, his gray skin catching reflections off the stainless-steel table. A medical-green sheet was draped over him, folded back to his chest. Though his head was in the correct position, it was all wrong, as if it had been popped off and screwed back imprecisely. The left side of his face was dented, flesh draped like parchment over the space that bones should have lent form to.

William reached over, touched his fingertips to the cold glass. Though Boss Man had confirmed Hanley's death already, William realized he'd held out a fantasy of a mix-up. It took him a moment to find his voice. 'Yeah. That's Hanley.'

'I'm sorry for your loss,' Markovic said.

'I want to touch him.'

'I'm sorry,' Elzey said. 'There's an active investigation—'

William wobbled over to the door. 'I want to touch him.' His voice wavered. He waited, stooped, pathetic, eyes on the floor.

The silence was thunderous.

Finally the coroner said, 'He could use latex gloves . . .?' A box was fetched. William pulled on the gloves, stepped inside. The room, a good twenty degrees cooler, smelled of bleach, metal, and musk. The odors seemed to lodge in William's lungs. The detectives and coroner kept their respectful distance, if respectful was watching him pay his last respects through a picture window. He put his back to them, blocking their view, and slid off one glove. Reaching out a steady hand, he laid it on his baby brother's cheek. It never ceased to amaze him how devoid of life dead flesh felt.

'Hanley,' he murmured.

He pushed his brother's eyelids down, then wormed his hand back into the glove.

He stepped out, passed the others without a word, and labored down the hall. Getting up the stairs, he broke a sweat. His grip on the railing felt arthritic, and he tugged at the fabric of his pants to hurry his legs up a step at a time.

Walking out, he let the nighttime breeze blow through his face into his lungs to drive out all those scents. Dodge was waiting in the van, hands on the wheel, staring ahead as if driving.

William struggled into the passenger seat, cranking down his window. He reached for the sunflower seeds on the dash, then thought better of it. Dodge stuck two cigarettes into his mouth, lifted a cheap plastic lighter from the breast pocket of his unbuttoned shirt, and lit them up. He passed one across to William, who took it with trembling hands. They sucked, breathed smoke. William flicked his yellowed nails against one another. He rubbed his eyes, then finally looked over and nodded at Dodge.

'When we get him,' William said, 'we'll take our time with him.'

Dodge dropped the steering-column gearshift into reverse. He said, 'Course.'

Ten minutes later, even with the freeway air blasting in his face, William couldn't get his lungs clear.

Chapter 32

Mike opened the interior door, towel-drying his hair from the shower. Kat was awake in the darkness, hugging her pillow, her own hair a white swirl of mayo and plastic wrap. 'I didn't know where you went.'

Mike pointed to the monitor at his hip, which gave off a soothing rush of white air. 'I got you, sweetheart.' He gestured next door. 'And Shep's here.'

At this her face lightened a touch.

Shep waited for Mike's nod, then leaned through the doorway. 'What's with your head?'

'Lice.' She made a face. 'I know.'

Shep vanished for a moment and returned with his Dopp kit, the same one he'd had as a kid. He rooted around, produced a pair of clippers, and tossed them to Mike.

'*No.*' Mike shoved the razor back at Shep, as if it could cut Kat's hair itself.

Shep held up his hands in surrender, came in, and took up on a chair in the corner.

Mike's mouth moved a few times as he tried to put his gratitude into words, but Shep cut him short. 'Handle your business.'

Mike closed the door quietly after him.

Kat jerked awake in the darkness with a cry.

Shep didn't move from his chair. 'You're okay,' he said.

'Where's Dad?'

'Meeting a guy next door. You've only been asleep a few minutes.'

'Someone who'll help us?'

'Sure.'

'Did you see her?' Kat asked.

'Yes.'

'What'd she look like?'

'Chalky. Peaceful.'

'Is she gonna die?'

'I don't know.'

Her bottom lip started to go, but she got it under control. 'Can I . . . can I have a hug?'

'I don't do that,' Shep said.

She flopped back down and curled up in a little ball. Within seconds she was asleep again. She fussed, eyelids flickering. Shep rose from the chair and moved silently across the room. He stood over her. She fussed some more. He reached out and rested a large hand on her back.

She stilled.

A moth landed on the window by Mike's face and spread its leathery wings. Rain started up, a patter on the motel roof that grew to a constant thrum. Just as he started to doze off, the rumble of Hank's Oldsmobile outside jarred him awake.

When Mike opened the door, Hank ducked into the room, pulling off driving gloves, rainwater dripping from him. 'It's like a cow pissing on a flat rock out there.'

Slanting rain smudged the streetlights. Steam rose from the hoods of idling cars. A seam of straw-colored light fringed the eastern horizon, interrupted by the blocky rise of Universal City. Mike took a long look outside before closing the door.

Hank brushed off his coat, his trousers, the drops big enough to tap the carpet. 'I'm sorry about Annabel. You know there's nothing you could've done differently.'

'Does anyone ever say that when it's true?'

Hank tugged at his jowls – point taken. He scratched his shin.

'They ID her attacker yet?' Mike asked.

'Hanley Burrell.'

Mike pictured the angled view he'd had of the guy from across the kitchen. That unshaven cheek, the hunch over Annabel, those fingers fussing obscenely at the strap of her bra. Mike couldn't manage to attach the name to him. It conferred a humanity, a real-worldness to a figure who seemed to have crawled out of a nightmare. Mike turned the name over, came up blank. 'Where's he from?'

'No address. I guess he was a transient.'

'He have a brother, William?'

'Indeed he does.'

'Lemme guess – no address for him either.'

'No. His last-knowns put him in Redding, but that was two years back.'

Mike exhaled, fighting to concentrate. 'North-of-Sacramento, middle-of-nowhere Redding?'

Nodding, Hank hacked into a fist, a rattling cough that went too long and left him winded. His head drooped, and he pasted a few stray hairs back over his scalp with a palm. Then he drew himself upright, finding again that proud posture. Still, he looked as fragile as a newborn's neck.

'Listen,' Mike said, 'I know this is about the last thing you need right now—'

But Hank showed little interest in taking that detour. 'There's more,' he said, cutting Mike off. 'William's got a robust record, as you can imagine, a good list of known associates. One is Roger Drake, a six-foot-six piece of work, like a Mack truck with no one behind the windshield.'

'Dodge.'

'That's right. Now, when the cops searched the blocks surrounding your house, they didn't find a vehicle registered to Hanley. So someone dropped him off.'

'Or he rode with Rick Graham. The cop I—'

'Shep mentioned that.' Hank drew in a breath, mouth corkscrewing to the side. 'When the ambulance and first responders arrived, they said there was no one at the house but Annabel. And there's no Rick Graham working for any law-enforcement agency in this county.'

'Can you check other ones?'

'There are a lot of counties from sea to shining sea. Could the badge have been a fake?'

'He had an exempt government vehicle. Plus, I got a read on him. The guy was a cop. A lifer, too – he had the swagger, the demeanor, the whole thing.'

Hank pulled his gaze to the ceiling, as close to an eye roll as he'd allow. He wobbled on his feet a bit, and Mike realized that he needed to sit but was too proud to ask, and Mike had been too dense to offer.

Mike sat on the bed and gestured, and Hank, grimacing, eased himself down into a chair. The effort left him short of breath again, his eyelids sluggish when he blinked. What kind of meds was he battling just to be here, just to be upright? A wave of gratitude washed over Mike. He wanted to express it somehow, but, as if reading his thoughts, Hank spun his hand for Mike to proceed, a curt, irritated gesture.

Mike continued. 'I'm thinking Graham was the backstop in case things got sticky and the authorities got involved. That's why once he caught wind of the 911 call, he went in instead of Dodge and William.'

'If he's really a cop, then why did he take off?' Hank said. 'Why wouldn't he have just shot you and filed a false report?'

'Maybe he was planning to after he finished sweeping the house. I think he figured he'd see if he could handle it quick and easy. If he gets spotted, he explains his way out of it. If he can sneak away, even better.'

Hank frowned skeptically. 'A cop executioner? In bed with a lowlife like Hanley Burrell?'

'I figure Graham for the guy who put out that alert on me.'

'So the original plan was to send in Hanley alone to do the dirty work?'

'I think so. Hanley kicks in the door, overpowers Annabel, has time to set up and wait for me. When I get home with' – Mike's fingers nervously tapped the monitor clipped to his belt – 'Kat, he's got privacy and my wife and daughter there to make me cooperate with whatever the hell they want. Then he cleans up afterward. Kills me.' He pictured the drop cloth, wadded on the living-room floor. 'At that point Annabel and Kat would be witnesses—' He severed the thought. 'But Hanley couldn't keep it under control until I got there.'

A cry wavered through the thin wall. Kat. Mike tensed.

'Go,' Hank said.

Mike hurried next door, patted Kat back to sleep, and returned, now with Shep at his heels. Shep crossed his arms, leaned against the bureau.

Hank said, 'Shep, I presume?'

Shep nodded.

Hank turned to Mike. 'Look, I'm a second-rate investigator with a foot in the grave. But I know a little.' With thumb and forefinger, he pinched off an inch of air to show how thin his expertise was. 'And what little I *do* know, I know about crap like this. The longer you leave things the way they are, the harder it's gonna be to get back.'

'Get back where?' Mike said.

'You left a corpse and your wife's body behind, went on the lam with your daughter, and pulled half a mil out of the bank.'

'Three hundred thousand.'

'Oh. Well then.'

'It's not what you think,' Mike said.

'I haven't told you what I think.'

Mike said nothing.

'Every hour that passes, you look more suspicious,' Hank said.

'You're acting like a seasoned criminal.' He shot a glance at Shep. 'No offense.'

Shep shrugged. 'None taken.'

'If you stay in hiding, you will be vilified,' Hank continued. 'You will lose control of what story gets told and which leads get investigated.'

'Spoken like a cop,' Shep said.

'I can't walk from my bed to the toilet without wheezing anymore, son. I'm too tired to play sides.' Hank's focus shifted back to Mike. 'I want to help you. Maybe I need a distraction. Maybe it's more than a distraction. Hell, if I can do one right thing before . . .' He made a noise, amusement at his folly, and Mike couldn't help but wonder if Hank's steadfastness was tied, somehow, to the worn school picture of the young boy thumbtacked to his office wall. Hank continued, 'I spend my days staring down the barrel. I see things with a certain clarity now. Perspective, I think they call it.'

Mike started to interrupt, but Hank held up a hand, cutting him off. 'At the moment, you're merely a person of interest in this case. You have not been formally charged. You've got a very limited window to step back from the edge. Now, the situation is drastic, and you've never struck me as someone who wanted only convenient facts, so I'm gonna lay out the picture, and let's skip the part where you're outraged and emotional, because, Mike, you don't have the time. There are whispers of infidelity, you walked in on your wife . . .' His hand churned the air. 'You can guess how that script'll play. Ninety percent of the game right now is how you look, and you *look* guilty. Even your name: Michael Wingate. You created a fake identity—'

'No,' Mike said sharply. 'I was never Mike Doe. I *left behind* a fake identity.'

'If they charge you with assaulting your wife—'

'Charge *me* for that?'

'They can take away your health-care-proxy rights. Then who

makes the choices for Annabel? And what are you gonna do with Katherine? Raise her on the run? Bonnie and Clyde, eating beans and franks under the open western sky? There's no play like that, not in this day and age. Especially not for a parent. We've gotta find someone we trust and get you with the authorities.'

Shep said, 'Bad idea.'

Hank swung his head over to take in Shep. 'Don't get stuck on stupid, son. This ain't you against the world.'

'It might be,' Shep said. 'He killed the man's brother. These guys weren't exactly agreeable *before* that.'

'You're right. They're bad news, it's hunting season, and they don't have a little girl slowing them down.'

'Hunting season,' Shep said. 'I like that.'

Hank kept his stare on Mike, as if Mike had made the last remark instead of Shep. 'So that's it? You gonna track them yourself? With an eight-year-old girl?'

Mike looked away, fidgeting.

'She's precocious,' Shep answered.

'So are William Burrell and Roger Drake. And you know what else? They've got more practice at this.' Hank heaved a sigh. 'The authorities will be able to protect you and your daughter better than you can out here on your own.'

'Unless the authorities I land with are in with Graham,' Mike said. 'In which case I'd be walking myself – and Kat – into the lion's den. I can't protect her in custody.'

'All cops are not corrupt,' Hank said wearily. The dappled skin over his temple twitched. He looked suddenly brittle, as though he might shatter if you threw the wrong words at him. 'I gotta see my doctor at eight. If you give me a few hours after that, I will find you a department with honest cops who can protect you, alert or no alert.'

'I watched a cop come back from searching Kat's bedroom wearing latex gloves and holding a throw-down gun,' Mike said. 'She's a witness. She saw two of these men.'

'As did everyone at that country club the night of the awards,' Hank said. 'Look, this thing hasn't gone according to their plan. Kat hasn't seen anything incriminating *yet*. You still have a shot to excise her from all this.'

'Not with these guys. They've used her for bait once already.'

'Can you get her to your in-laws?' Hank asked. 'Grandparents?'

Mike choked on the thought, swallowed to moisten his throat. 'They wouldn't know how to protect her.'

'So how about Annabel?' Hank stood and tugged his gloves from his pocket. 'You think they'll go after her to get to you also?'

Shep said, 'Yes.' He checked his watch. 'Shift change in an hour. I need to go back to the hospital.' He crossed and opened the front door, letting in a spill of pale gray light, the bleakest edge of morning.

Hank crowded him at the door, neither man giving way, a momentary logjam. Hank shouldered through first onto the walk and turned back. His gaze stayed on Shep, though he was addressing Mike. 'I'll call you in six hours with a name and a station.'

Shep pretended not to hear him. 'Don't trust the cops,' he told Mike. He gestured politely, and Hank stepped aside to let him pass.

Their respective cars waited on opposite ends of the lot. Breaking apart, they headed out into the storm. Mike stood in the doorway long after they'd driven off.

Chapter 33

'Look at this. Come here.' Her black hair arcing across her face, Dr Cha beckoned Shep closer, leaned over Annabel, and rubbed two knuckles in to her chest, hard. Still unconscious, Annabel shifted on the bed and grimaced.

'Sternal rub,' Dr Cha said. 'The bone's beneath only a millimeter of skin there, so people recoil from pressure. When they're responsive, that is.'

The surgical ICU occupied the east wing of the ground floor, so morning light suffused the double room. The dividing curtain had been pulled back to reveal the unoccupied bed, adding some breathing space to the cramped quarters.

'And check *this*.'

Shep looked up at the doctor, their faces close. Watching Annabel eagerly, Dr Cha pinched the pad of Annabel's finger. Annabel's hand twitched away. The doctor regarded the hand with wonder. 'Is that not the most beautiful damn thing?'

'Beautiful,' Shep agreed.

Dr Cha straightened up, and Shep took a step back. She cleared her throat and adjusted her wire-frame glasses, all business again. 'She's breathing above the vent now, which is good. We have it set for fourteen breaths a minute, but she's at sixteen. If this keeps up, we might get her extubated by the afternoon.' She cocked her head. 'Why the face? This is good news.'

'People will come to kill her,' Shep said.

'*Kill* her? Which people?'

'The ones who put her here. They'll want to finish the job.'

'We have good security here. It's not like anyone can walk into a patient's room.' She balked at the silence. 'You don't trust our security.'

'No.'

'So it's not her husband, like the cops say. Who did this.'

'No.'

'How do you know?'

Shep said, 'I know.'

'Is that why you're here? To stop whoever you believe is coming?'

'Yes.'

'You really believe—'

'Can we transfer her to a different hospital? An undisclosed location?'

'No. She's too unstable. Her blood pressure's labile. Plus, that artery nick is clotting off nicely. Any jostling in a vehicle might open it back up.'

'Can her husband force a transfer? Doesn't he have some legal say?'

'You're a devoted friend,' she observed. 'But no, I won't allow her to be moved. Not until she's more stable.'

'Like this afternoon, when she's off the ventilator?'

'Like a week from now.'

Before Dr Cha could reply, the door opened and Elzey and Markovic strode in with Annabel's sister, a big-boned, attractive woman. A weighty purse knocking about her hip, June paused a few steps from the bed, quivering, to regard her sister. She regained her composure, and introductions were made.

June shifted her attention to Shep. 'Who is he? Who are you?'

'Shep,' he said.

She looked at Dr Cha. 'He's not family.'

Dr Cha tapped the medical chart against her hand. 'I was told he's on the husband's side—'

229

'Annabel's husband doesn't have any relatives.'

'We were foster brothers,' Shep said.

At this, June's mouth came open a little. 'I thought family privileges were only afforded to *real* family.'

'Real family,' Dr Cha repeated evenly. 'It is our policy to consider foster siblings—'

'Given what's gone on here, why would you let *anyone* involved with Mike have access to my sister?'

'What *has* gone on here?' Dr Cha asked. She waited, the silence drawing out. 'I wasn't aware that any charges have been brought.'

June glared at Shep. 'Mind if I have some time alone with my sister?'

Shep said, 'What?'

'Mind. If I have. Some time alone with. My sister?'

Shep stepped out into the hall, the detectives flanking him.

'So,' Markovic said, 'you're very close to Ms Andrews?'

'Who?' Shep said.

'Annabel,' Elzey said. 'That's her maiden name. Which you know, of course, given how familial you are.'

'Right,' Shep said. 'Sure.'

A few feet away, Dr Cha jotted on the chart and slotted it into the acrylic rack mounted on the door. The detectives made no attempt to lower their voices.

'Shepherd White. Safecracking. Burglary. B & E. Quite a celeb you are.' Markovic grinned. 'You're in all the databases.'

Shep said, 'And still not wanted for anything.'

Elzey said, 'Currently.'

Markovic now. 'Mind if we frisk you?'

Shep held out his arms. Markovic spun him, planted him on the wall, hands pinching his ankles, sliding up his legs, patting his sides. 'You wouldn't happen to know where your dear foster brother is, would you?'

Shep turned, straightening his clothes, and nodded cordially at Dr Cha over the detective's shoulder. 'No.'

'If you talk to him, tell him this: If he doesn't produce himself in short order, he's gonna be charged for the murder of Hanley Burrell and the attempted murder of Annabel Wingate. Annabel's father has already started proceedings to enjoin your boy from exercising his authority under the health-care proxy. No judge is gonna uphold a fugitive's control over the life of a woman he put in a coma.'

'Mike didn't put her there. And he's not a fugitive.'

'Come tomorrow morning,' Markovic said, 'he will be.'

Chapter 34

Ensconced in a swirl of sheets and wearing a glazed expression, Kat watched cartoons. Absentmindedly, she rubbed her thumb across the back of Snowball II, working the mini-polar bear like a rabbit's-foot charm. Mike had done his best to put her hair up, but strays abounded and the ponytail had wound up off center. It was one of those things he could never figure out how to get right.

'I miss school.'

'I know.' Mike had pulled a chair around to sit, elbows nailed to his knees, his gaze stuck on the phone.

'I miss the *sun*.'

'Me, too.'

'I miss my bed.'

'I know.'

'I miss my mom.'

Mike's mouth opened, but no sound came out.

Kat was wearing the same blank expression she'd had on last time he'd glanced over. The phone rang, forcing him to switch tracks. He snatched it up.

Hank said, 'We're gonna steer clear of the sheriff's department, since we know they're hooked into the alert. But I found someone for you at LAPD. This is turning into a high-profile case, and I'm banking on the fact that LAPD'll want to keep it in their court if you go in to them. They've got more muscle than sheriff's.'

'Who there?'

'Jason Cayanne, a captain two in the North Hollywood Station.'

'Can I trust him?'

'Mike, this man will listen to you. That's the best you're gonna get right now. Let this thing go another twenty-four hours and the most you can hope for is a clean jail cell.'

'I need to know Kat will be safe.'

'LAPD will protect her better than you can.'

Mike hung up, pressed a fist to the edge of the desk until his knuckles ached. Then he found the Batphone and called Shep. 'How is she?'

'A little better. Some movement, pain response. The doc seems excited by that.'

'Movement. Movement is good. Pain response is good.' Mike realized he was babbling, chewing his thumb.

'But she's not out of the woods. Things could still go south fast.'

Mike swallowed dryly. 'How about her safety?'

'They're letting me stay with her right now,' Shep said, 'but visiting hours end at eight.'

'What are you gonna do?'

'I'll figure something out.'

'Okay.' Mike took a breath. It seemed inconceivable that he couldn't be at his wife's side through this. 'Can we transfer her?'

'Doc won't go for it. Says she's too unstable. The detectives were here, Markovic and Elzey. They said if you don't come in by tomorrow morning, you'll be charged for murder.'

'*Mur*—' Mike caught himself, lowered his voice. 'Murder? For that piece of shit who stuck a blade into my wife?'

'And for attempted murder on Annabel,' Shep said. Mike felt a surge of rage, but before he could respond, Shep had moved on. 'They also said Annabel's old man is trying to take over the medical decisions for her. Something about suing over the proxy. He's getting on a plane.'

'So he'd be the one to green-light a surgery?' Mike said. 'Or pull the plug? He can't do that. He *can't* do that.'

'He's trying.'

Mike looked across at Kat's zoned-out face, the glow of the TV rippling across her features. She had a red smudge on her chin from fruit juice, and she was sucking a thumb through her shirt-sleeve, a habit she'd left behind four years ago. He was barely taking care of her now. How could he take care of her if they were *really* on the run?

As if reading his thoughts, Shep said, 'Don't do it.'

'This only gets worse.'

'You'll be in jail,' Shep said. 'Helpless. And Rick Graham, William Burrell, and Roger Drake will be out here.'

'I'm sorry.'

He hung up. Shep called back immediately, but Mike muted the ringer. Then he rose and started packing up.

Kat asked, 'Are we going somewhere?'

'I don't know yet.'

They loaded up the truck and sat in the parking lot with the engine idling, Mike staring blankly ahead, the dusty windshield muting the early afternoon. Buckled into the passenger seat, Kat watched him; he could sense her keen stare. The rucksack of cash was an olive drab lump at her feet. Snowball II peered out from her fist, halved-marble eyes waiting on his next move. Panic rose in his throat like bile, but he stayed perfectly still, throat bobbing, choking it down. Eventually the heavy gray of the afternoon settled over him, leeching away all emotion, and then he didn't even feel panic anymore, just the dead, dismal weight of the air he was breathing.

After a time Kat said, 'What do we do when we're scared?'

It took him a moment to realize she was going for the Bad-Parenting Game. He couldn't get his heart into it. 'I don't know, Kat.'

More vehemently now. '*What do we do when we're scared?*'

He thought of Annabel lying in that hospital bed, the dark cigar hole between her ribs. His daughter beside him, needing to return to a life he was helpless to get her back to.

'We curl up into a little ball and surrender,' he said.

He put the truck in gear and started for the police station.

Mike couldn't settle his nerves. The instant he stepped into the North Hollywood Station, he was convinced that he'd made a terrible mistake. But it was too late.

A flickering overhead fluorescent seemed to set the ominous tone, casting one edge of the lobby in alternating shades of pale yellow. The desk officer no sooner took in his and Kat's faces than a back door opened and a uniformed cop appeared to frisk Mike. The guy would find nothing; Mike had left the .357 with the cash in the Toyota across the street. Shep could pick up the rucksack in case he needed money for Annabel.

Hands on the counter, legs spread, Mike made sure to keep murmuring to Kat, 'Don't worry, sweetheart. We're gonna be okay. We're gonna be okay.'

She clutched that miniature polar bear like a security blanket.

Before the officer was through with Mike, Captain Jason Cayanne appeared, a virile guy, sinewy and dense of mustache, to apologize for the pat-down. He even crouched and got eye level with Kat to tell her how glad he was that she'd come in.

Cayanne led them upstairs through a warren of hallways and offices. He moved light on his feet, like a dancer or a boxer. The way he took the turns – crisply, on the balls of his feet – said he was former military. The farther back they wound, the more Mike's apprehension grew. He had to remind himself not to squeeze Kat's hand too hard lest he hurt her. She glided at his side, silent and trusting. By being here was he breaking his promise to Annabel to get Kat away from all this?

Cayanne kept on, giving no indication that he noticed the sweat popping from Mike's forehead, until they reached his

235

office. Big wooden desk with facing armchairs, Rotary Club plaques, a striped bass mounted on a piece of driftwood.

Two officers joined them, Mike looking warily from one to the other, searching out signs of betrayal. He sat on an armchair, pulled Kat into his lap, and laced his hands protectively across her stomach.

Cayanne said, 'Get you a cup of coffee?'

Mike shook his head.

'Maybe it would be better if Katherine went with Officer Maxwell.'

Mike said, 'No way.'

Cayanne ran his fingertips thoughtfully through his dense blond mustache. 'We need to talk about the crime scene, and I think maybe it would be better for her not to have to get tangled up in the details. How about if we put her there' – he pointed through the glass door to the adjacent detective bullpen – 'where you can keep an eye on her the whole time?'

Kat started to get out of Mike's lap, but he didn't relax his arms. She said, 'It's okay, Dad,' and pulled free.

She settled into a chair in the next room and offered him an encouraging wave. Cayanne was waiting behind the desk, the picture of patience.

'You made a pretty good run there,' he said. 'Blipped off the radar.'

'There are people after us,' Mike said. 'Two ex-cons – Roger Drake and William Burrell, the brother of the man who stabbed my wife.'

Cayanne jotted the names in a black detective's pad. 'The brother of the man you killed.'

'Yes,' Mike said.

'I don't understand. Why are they after you?'

'I don't know.'

Cayanne's clear blue eyes ticked up from the pad and held on Mike's face for a beat before lowering again.

Mike said, 'And there's also at least one person gunning for me who's inside law enforcement. Rick Graham.'

'There appear to be a lot of people looking for you who are inside law enforcement.'

'Not looking. *Gunning*. This guy is working with criminals to come after me.'

Cayanne's pen ceased scribbling. 'Working with ex-cons?'

'Yes.'

'Bad guys and dirty cops makes a conspiracy. And you have no idea why this conspiracy is centered on you?'

'Look, I know how this sounds. But it's the truth. I don't have any idea why I've been targeted, but I will work with you and do whatever it takes to figure out what's going on.'

Cayanne set his pad down on his desk. Folded his hands on the leather blotter. 'And in return?'

'I need to protect my daughter. I want the right to make decisions for my wife, medical decisions. That's all I care about, how they can be taken care of. Nothing else. Do you understand me?'

'I do.'

Mike's throat opened up a little at that, as if he'd loosened a tie. 'I have put my family in your trust. Will you protect them, no matter what happens to me?'

'Of course we'll make sure they're safe.'

The muscles of his neck unclenched. He fought his shoulders down, stretched his neck, the burn somehow underscoring his relief.

Officer Maxwell reentered the room. 'Mr Wingate, you have a call.'

'A call? How does anyone know I'm here?'

'We alerted the hospital that you were coming in. And I'm afraid it's them calling. About your wife. They say . . . they say it's urgent.'

Dread, pure and simple.

In the next room, Kat was petting Snowball II soothingly, her

237

feet swinging a few inches off the floor. Her mouth was moving, and it took him a moment to realize what she was whispering to the bear: *We're gonna be okay. We're gonna be okay.*

When Mike spoke, it came out a croak. 'Okay.'

'You can take it at my desk.' Maxwell extended his arm, pointing to his station against the far wall.

Mike moved across the room on deadened legs. Five or so lines fed into the phone, but only one button was blinking. He rested his hand on the receiver, took a deep breath, and picked up. Steeling himself, he turned away toward the window, not wanting Kat to read his expression when he got the news. 'Mike Wingate here.'

Down below, he could see the gated side lot, filled with black-and-whites. The sight of a black Mercury froze him, his breath misting against the glass. The driver's door was open. His eyes tracked around the lot, found a broad black officer facing away, blocking whomever he was speaking to.

It took Mike a moment to register that it was Hank's voice on the phone. 'Mike. Mike. *Mike.*'

'*Hank*? What happened to Annabel?'

The cop in the parking lot was back on his heels, arms out, going submissive in the face of a reprimand.

A low heat prickled across Mike's neck.

'Never mind that,' Hank said. 'I had to say I was a doctor to get you on the phone. Listen, that alert that's out on you? It's at the *state* level. A counterterrorist agency. These guys have authority over sheriff's, LAPD, *everyone*. They can take you and your daughter into custody and move you wherever they see fit. And guess who's one of their directors?'

Down below, the officer stepped aside deferentially, and Rick Graham started briskly toward the entrance.

As the phone lowered to the cradle in Mike's trembling hand, he faintly registered the tin-can squawk of Hank's voice, saying, 'You gotta get out of there.'

238

Chapter 35

Mike forced himself not to sprint back to Cayanne. He had maybe four minutes before Graham cleared the lobby and navigated his way upstairs and back to them. Mike kept an even pace, nodding reassuringly at Kat as he passed her.

Cayanne said, 'Everything okay with your wife?'

'She took a turn. It looks bad.' Mike assumed he appeared shaken enough to be believable. What kind of plan could he generate in the next thirty seconds that would get him alone with Kat? 'Do you have a bathroom? I need a minute before I tell my daughter.'

'Of course. Around the corner there, second on the left.'

Mike rushed back, frantically scouting a way out. Offices let into offices, halls onto halls, a host of internal windows giving the entire floor a spotty transparency. In the bathroom he searched under the sink, behind the door – nothing. He threw toilet paper out of the rotting wooden cabinet, finally locating a first-aid kit in the back. He dumped it out and shoved aside the gauze rolls and medicine packets, plucking up a catheter-tipped syringe for wound irrigation. His shoes slipping over the supplies, he dashed across to the sink and filled the syringe with water. Dubious-looking, but if it came down to it, it would have to do.

Rushing back, he fought the plunger into place and shoved the syringe into his waistband. He slowed before the turn, tried to catch his breath. Cayanne was on his feet by his door, looking concerned.

Mike drew close, bowed his head. 'Can I have a moment alone with Kat? To tell her?'

'Sure, we'll leave you my office.'

That had been Mike's fear. He needed to get Kat out of the bullpen area entirely to make a move for the exit. Graham was probably on the third floor by now, winding his way back to them.

Plan B: out with the prop.

Mike walked over and crouched in front of Kat, slipping the syringe into her front pocket – they'd frisked him, but not her. She looked down, brow furrowed, perplexed.

He said loudly, 'My *God*, honey. Your color. Didn't I give you your insulin shot this morning?'

'What—'

'Honey, I know you hate needles, but this isn't the time.' He squeezed her shoulders: *Please go along with me.*

A familiar glint broke through her glassy eyes. She nodded.

He made a big show of checking her forehead, then turned, fearful that Graham was already barging around the corner, but there was just Cayanne and a few officers drawing near, concerned.

Mike channeled the Couch Mother. 'Cold and clammy, you need some candy. Dry and hot, you need a shot.' He patted her pockets. 'Where's your insulin? Do you have your insulin?'

Kat withdrew the syringe, and he made a quick grab for it, enfolding it in his hand, doing his best to hide the wide plastic tip. She went a little weak-kneed, overdoing it, but Mike grabbed her arm and stiffened her up. Listening for Graham's approach, he didn't find it hard to act concerned. 'I have to administer this in her thigh. Mind if I take her to the bathroom for a little privacy?'

'Sure,' Maxwell said. 'My mother-in-law's diabetic. I know how that goes.'

Nodding his thanks, Mike shepherded Kat through the cops

and around the turn, her hand clenching the polar bear. 'Dad, what was *tha*—'

They were flying up the hall now, past the bathroom. 'I need you to follow my lead so I can get us out of here.' He dumped the leaky syringe into a trash bin just inside a doorway. 'And I'll answer all your questions later. Deal?'

Through the open door and an interior office window, Graham flashed into view, charging up the parallel hall on the opposite side of the floor.

'Dea—'

Mike clamped a hand over Kat's mouth and jerked back, flattening against the wall. Cops buzzed in the surrounding offices; at some point someone was going to step through a doorway and see them hiding here.

He could hear Graham's elevated voice. '—known terrorist in your custody. Perhaps you can explain to me why a hospital clerk was able to get me his location before you thought—'

And the aggressively calm reply. 'He's back this way, sir.'

As Graham's voice drifted toward Cayanne's office, Mike propelled Kat down the hall the other way. It seemed their movement was linked to Graham's, two points on a pulley cable sliding in opposite directions.

They reached the terminus and stepped into a pass-through office, sliding behind two desk detectives hunkered into burritos. Neither raised his head. With Kat keeping pace at his side, Mike scurried through doorways and down corridors, waiting for red lights to flash, alarms to erupt, security barriers to lower.

At last a stairwell. They jostled down and spilled out into an open garage, a host of police cars pulled in for service or washing. To their right a wide ramp angled up to the side lot that Graham had been standing in moments before.

A faint ding-ding-dinging sounded from that direction, too subdued to be an alarm.

The overweight cop whom Graham had argued aside was

trudging right at them, lugging his bulletproof vest and shot-gun.

Mike froze, hand clamping the back of Kat's neck.

'Lost?' the cop asked.

Mike let a breath leak through his teeth. 'No. I'm doing some work.'

'Yeah?' The smile *seemed* friendly. 'What kind of work?'

The dinging continued relentlessly, a bird pecking on Mike's spine. The pause felt as though it dragged out several minutes.

'That flickering light in the lobby,' Kat said.

Mike scratched his forehead with a thumb, grabbing the life-line his daughter had thrown him. 'Right. Probably just a loose connection, but you always worry about arcing, you know? So we're off to check the breakers.' He pointed vaguely up the ramp.

The man flicked his chin at Kat. 'She your assistant?'

Mike shot a glance back at the stairwell door. 'It's Bring Your Kid to Work Day.'

'I thought that was in April.'

He'd *heard* of it?

'They changed the date,' Mike said. 'Conflicted with Talk Like a Pirate Day.'

The man studied him, head cocked, and then his serious expression broke and he gave a big laugh. Stepping aside, he swept a hand at the ramp.

Mike unlocked his muscles and headed for daylight. The ding-ing grew louder as he hustled Kat up the ramp. They stepped into the sudden bright, the sun winking harshly off the domino row of windshields. All those matching patrol cars, neatly aligned, as if for sale. Slanted in the middle of the aisle, door still flung open, issuing the nerve-grating dings, was Graham's Mercury Grand Marquis. A barbed-wire-topped fence hemmed everything in. On the ground before the exit at the lot's end lay a thick black sensor cable, requiring the weight of an automobile to open the imposing electronic gate.

An angry banging overhead.

Mike looked up. Hammering the window three floors above, his face tight and angry, Graham bellowed down at them. He stood where Mike had been minutes earlier; in fact, they'd reversed positions exactly. Graham's mouth wavered, spit flecking the glass, but his outrage, from below, was soundless. Standing beside him, looking not entirely displeased, was Cayanne.

Mike glanced from Graham to the electronic gate to the black Mercury. The door alarm meant the key was in the ignition. 'Come on.'

Before Kat could get the passenger door closed behind her, Mike was accelerating toward the gate. As it rattled arthritically open, he dug the truck keys from his pocket. His fist guiding the wheel, he squeaked through the gap early, the gate's edge grinding the side of the car and throwing up sparks. He screeched across the street and into the main parking lot, raking the tires the wrong way across the security spikes. The rubber shredded, Graham's car skidding sideways, throwing sparks and grinding to a halt. Mike and Kat leaped out and into the pickup, and then they were motoring away, his eyes clicking from rearview to side mirror. The rucksack full of cash and the few plastic bags of their stuff rolled at Kat's feet. Dusk was coming on, cutting visibility, making him feel incrementally safer. He accelerated through a red, cut up an alley, hit the freeway entrance on a slide, and ran the blacktop the length of two exits. Kat's eyes were bright, and Mike realized that this was, in a manner, exciting for her.

Back on darkening residential streets, he prowled like the teenager he used to be. He passed over the German makes. He'd heard they had fancy security systems these days, the antilock brakes kicking in and the steering shutting down before you pulled away from the curb. And even if you cracked a glove box and lucked into a valet key, there was still LoJack, GPS. He needed something from his era, something he could work like a Rubik's Cube.

A brown Honda Civic with a late-eighties body was nestled to the curb beside a high hedge, the nearest house quiet behind a substantial setback. Mike parked behind the car and hopped out. It occurred to him that each successive vehicle he'd taken was a stepping-stone to a prior time.

'Grab our stuff.'

But Kat was too fascinated to obey. As he dug in the wheel-well toolbox, she watched from the curb, swiveling one leg and chewing her cheek. He didn't find a crowbar, but there was a length of stiff electrical wire that he doubled, forming a hook with one end. His hands seemed to shape the wire by themselves, on muscle-memory autopilot. Clenching the wire between his teeth, he shoved a hammer into his back pocket and carried two flathead screwdrivers to the Honda. At the driver's side, he jammed both screwdrivers between the top of the window and the rubber guard, about two inches apart, opening up a small gap.

'Dad?'

The wire slid through, the hook grabbed the notched lock, and he was in.

'Dad?'

Three smacks of the hammer knocked off the plastic ignition keyhole, and the wider screwdriver fit the hole. A turn of his wrist and the engine purred to life.

'Dad?'

Finally he registered Kat's voice and looked up. She was standing a few feet off the driver's window, arms crossed, mouth slightly ajar with wonder.

'Where'd you *learn* that?'

Chapter 36

His back stiff, his gaze constant on the door, Shep sat at Annabel's side. Her chest rose and fell under her own power, the breaths long and sonorous. She was puffy around the eyes, bloated from IV fluids. The monitor ticked off hills and valleys.

The knob turned, and Dr Cha entered. Only Shep's eyes moved. It was late, and the halls were quiet.

She said, 'I'm sorry, Shep, but visiting hours ended forty-five minutes ago. You'll have to go now.'

'I can't.'

'There's nothing I can do. These rooms are for patients only.'

Shep reached over, plucked a Pyrex supply canister from the counter, and shattered it in his hand. Swabs and shrapnel fell at his feet. With a jagged shard, he carved a three-inch gash along the back of his forearm. Tendrils of blood snaked down his hand, running off his fingertips, drops pattering on the tile.

He parted the dividing curtain, moved to the empty bed across from Annabel, and sat. 'I need stitches.'

'You idiot. I should call security.'

'From what I've seen of them, go ahead.'

She stepped in, letting the door suck closed behind her. A stare-down. 'You're a real piece of work, aren't you?'

'What's that?'

'Oh, you heard me.'

Shep said, 'I will pay for the room. Cash – no HMO-insurance bullshit. But I want this bed.'

'This is a hospital, not a cabana at Skybar.' She snapped the phone off the wall, punched a button. 'Security, please.'

Shep pointed across to Annabel with a blood-wet finger. 'Your patient is in danger.'

Uncertainty showed on the doctor's face. Quickly replaced by anger. 'You don't know that. The cops said she's fine. That *you're* the criminal.'

'I *am* a criminal. But you don't want to wake up tomorrow morning to find out that they've killed her.'

She kept the phone pressed to her ear. 'Even if I *could* have men and women cohabiting in the same room, a few stitches don't buy you the surgical ICU. They buy you ten minutes with a first-year intern in the ER.'

The faint voice on the other end came clearly audible off the hard surfaces. '*Security. Security. Do you have a problem?*'

Shep raised the glittering shard to his face. 'Then what do I have to cut?'

Driving inland. A Honda Civic, his eight-year-old daughter, an unmarked revolver, and a rucksack stuffed with just shy of a quarter mil. The purple sky, half lit by the descended sun, had a portentous cast. An electronic billboard flashed a child-abduction alert, but they were past before Mike registered that it referred to Kat. He'd switched the license plates, keeping the ones he'd taken from Jimmy's girlfriend's Mazda, so the stolen car shouldn't raise any red flags. Freeway signs blinked overhead, waystations on a road to nowhere. He blazed past artichoke fields, a biblical swarm of grasshoppers unfurling from the crops and splattering against the windshield, Kat noting each plop with sickened delight.

Mike had explained to her, as best he could, what they were up against, but she mostly wanted to chatter about his boosting the vehicle.

'And then you were, like, *crack!* with the hammer, and the car

246

just *started up*. And then switching the plates like a *bank* robber. That was so cool.'

Her manic engagement with selective aspects of their ordeal, he figured, was self-protective, so he let her go, a windup toy that wouldn't unwind. She slapped at the old-fashioned radio. A scroll through static, voices burping from the speakers as the dial flew. Amy Winehouse wouldn't go to rehab, saying *no no no*, and Kat was digging through the glove box, captivated by the lipstick, the breath mints, a half-smoked pack of menthols. She posed, cigarette in mouth, to see if he'd comment, but he barely noticed her until she started in with the fake puffing. She was spoiling for a fight, wanting him to give her an excuse to let go and cry. But he didn't have it in him right now, so he let her air-smoke until she grew bored with it.

At the next rest stop, he climbed out, grabbed the rucksack, and headed for a pay phone. 'Stay close.'

Carrying Snowball II with her, Kat sat at a rickety picnic table nearby. Mike used the calling card to reach Hank on his cell.

'Hank—'

But Hank cut Mike off before he could get out another word. 'I'm camped out near a pay phone. Call me back at this number.' He repeated it twice.

Mike dialed the new number, and when Hank snatched up the phone, his voice was trembling. 'You're okay. You got out.'

'Barely. You're being monitored?'

'Dunno. But I'm a paranoid cop at heart. With the resources against you . . .'

Mike said, 'Who the hell *is* this guy Rick Graham?'

'A director at the State Terrorism Threat Assessment Center.'

'So I'm a *terrorist* now?' Mike said. 'This just keeps getting better.'

Over on the park bench, Kat glanced up at him.

'*That's* why I couldn't get a handle on that alert they put out on you,' Hank said. 'The routing request was so convoluted – it's all classified, higher-up shit. I finally reached a former partner's kid, a DA, who broke the code for me.'

'What's this center? Why have I never heard of it?'

'It's one of these multiagency deals. Graham's out of the main joint in Sacramento. They call it a "fusion center" to make it sound imposing.'

'It *does* sound imposing.'

'They pull the best and brightest from CHP, California DOJ, the governor's office – got the whole goddamned state under their thumb. The sheriff's an agent of the state, so that explains why his boys were first to the dance.'

An unhealthy wheeze punctuated each of Hank's inhalations. The scale of what Mike was confronting left him breathless, too. Graham had personally come down to L.A. to take him into custody.

A bitter laugh escaped Mike's lips. 'Green houses.' He punched the wall in slowmotion, pressing his knuckles to the splintering wood. 'When this started, I thought it was about phony green houses.'

Across the parking area, a family unloaded from a station wagon, stretching their legs and bucket-lining empty cups and wadded wrappers from the recesses of the car to a trash can. A golden bounded from his crate and peed, with evident relief, on the circle of designated grass. The teenage daughter emerged from an iPod trance to slap her little brother away. Mundane as the scene was, Mike felt like he was peering through the looking glass into a dream world.

Hank was talking again: 'Graham's out of Sacramento, and Burrell's last-known had him in Redding. Those cities are, what – two hours apart? That region of Northern California's looking interesting, but to be honest, I don't know what to do about it.'

Mike reined in his thoughts. 'So if it's a *state* agency, can I appeal to the feds for help?'

'No way,' Hank said. 'These guys coordinate heavily with the

Feebs, and Homeland Security, too. They're probably the only state agency with this kind of federal pull.'

'This is ridiculous.' Mike made an effort to lower his voice. 'Graham *can't* believe I'm a fucking terrorist.'

A door slam alerted him to the fact that Kat had gotten back into the car. She was sitting in the driver's seat, upset, hands on the wheel as if she were going to drive off.

'No,' Hank said. 'But labeling you a terrorist means he can pursue you like one. Your double background plays into it, makes you fit the mold. And now throw a few bodies into the mix – not exactly hard to build a case around you. Or an accident.'

'So he's looking for a fall guy for something?'

'Maybe. But given your family history, my gut says he's cleaning up a mess.'

'What mess? It's not like my father could've been an enemy of the state. We didn't even *have* terrorists back then. And even if he was, I was *four* when we parted ways. What could I have possibly known?'

'Seeing as how Graham's having Roger Drake and the Burrell boys carry out his dirty work, clearly this isn't official state business. Playing the terrorist card is just the most effective way to run you down.'

'So he's in someone's pocket,' Mike said.

'Given his stature in the law-enforcement community, it's a big pocket.'

'But he's got no real *evidence* on me. How's he getting everyone to fall into line? I mean, Elzey and Markovic? They were up my ass, now they're all over the hospital. Are *they* dirty, too? Did he bribe them?'

'You don't get it, Mike. Once you're fingered, you're fingered. The Lost Hills Sheriff's Station covers, what? A hundred eighty square miles? They've got rich assholes in Calabasas, Hidden Hills, Malibu, Westlake, and po' white trash, crackheads, and cowboys in Chatsworth. Now they get a notice from a state agency that you're on a terrorist watch list, you think they're gonna . . . what? Try 'n' prove you're a nice guy? No. They want to pick you up, kick the case to the state, and get back to the mound of complaints from the constituents whose vote the sheriff needs come election time. They're not gonna participate in patently illegal shit, but they will suspect who they're supposed to suspect and alert who they're supposed to alert. It's not a conspiracy – it's delegation and resource management.'

'There's gotta be someone I can tell my story to.'

'What story, Mike? That you're innocent?' Hank was less angry than distressed. 'I think they get that particular tale from time to time.'

Mike looked across at Kat in the stolen Civic. The glare of passing headlights turned the windows opaque. She flickered into view, gone, into view, gone again. Watching her ghost in and out of existence intensified the knot in his gut – all the deepest, darkest fears he'd swallowed over the years hardening into physical form. He thought about that morning he'd sat in his truck and watched her climb the fireman's pole at school, how she'd dinged the top bar with the tiny ball of her fist.

He felt like a third party listening to his own voice. 'So what do I do?'

The connection seemed to achieve a sudden crisp clarity, the static taking a rest. The rush of passing cars on the freeway was hypnotic, exhausting. When was the last time he had slept? He wet his lips, waited.

'Hank, *what do I do*?'

'I don't know what to tell you, Mike.'

Bickering, the family packed themselves back into the station wagon and pulled out on their semi-merry way. Breathing gas fumes and hot tar, Mike watched them merge onto the freeway, watched until the brake lights blended into the river of traffic.

'Mike? Mike? You there?'

A voice echoed in his head, Shep's reply when Mike had mentioned how they'd had stamina back in the day: *That's because we didn't have anything else.*

'Yuh. I'm here.' His voice was flat, robotic. 'I talked to Shep already.' When he had, Shep hadn't offered so much as a told you so. He'd just given Mike the update on Annabel and pushed forward as Mike was trying to now, moving the pigskin a yard at a time. 'He thinks the best play is Kiki Dupleshney.'

'Mike, you can't—'

'That's his world, so he put out word through his network that he needs a con woman for a heist he's pulling. He'll try to lure her in.'

'*Mike.* These men are looking to *kill* you. You can't drag Kat along with you.'

'What choice do I have?'

No answer but the gently falling rain that had started up without Mike's noticing.

'Good-bye, Hank.' He set the phone gently back in the cradle.

He trudged over to the car. Kat had locked the driver's door. He knocked, but she didn't look over at him; she glowered dead ahead at the raindrops tapping the hood. He walked around, climbed into the passenger seat, rucksack in lap, and sat, dripping, both of them staring at nothing, going nowhere, a stolen car parked on a rest stop off a freeway Mike couldn't name.

When Kat spoke, the intensity of her voice surprised him. 'What's the deal with Green Valley?'

He bent his head. Water dripped from his forehead onto his thighs.

'Phony green houses.' Kat wiped angrily at a stray tear, but her voice hadn't changed at all. 'You said "phony green houses." That's what you and Mom were whispering about before in the police station.'

'Given everything going on, this isn't important right now.'

'It's important to *me*. Right now.'

251

He realized that this was the end of the line, that there was nothing left to do but submit to the truth swiftly and brutally, but still, it took him two tries to get the words moving out of his mouth. 'The houses weren't really green. A guy laid in the wrong pipes. And I covered it up.'

She was shivering, pale. 'What about your award?'

'I didn't deserve it.'

Her voice now was weak, pitiful. 'You lied to me?'

His hands were shaking. His face numb. 'Yes.'

She choked out a little cry, and then her door was open and she'd vanished into the rain. He sprang out after her, sloshing through puddles. She was ahead, a wraith in the downslanting wet, faster than he'd imagined. She breached the grassy rise behind the bathrooms and darted down the far side, but he caught her, wrapping her up so they wouldn't tumble down the slope.

She kicked to get free, shrieking at him, 'What *else* have you lied about? What else?' She kept thrashing violently, and he lost his footing, skidding onto his ass, rainwater soaking instantly through his jeans. 'I *hate* you!' she yelled. 'You can't keep me in motels and cars for the rest of my life. I just want to go to school and have my room back and *Mom*.'

He held her frail little frame until she went limp against him, sobbing.

He spoke into the wet tangle of her hair. 'I will never break my word to you again. Never again.'

She murmured into his chest, half moan, half mantra, '*I want my mom I want my mom I want my mom*.'

He held her in the rain.

Footfall, slow and heavy, proceeded up the hospital corridor. It paused. Two blots interrupted the seam of light beneath the door. The lockless handle dipped silently. The hinges issued no complaint.

A wedge of light fell from the bright hall into the dark room, widening like a fan as the door swung inward.

A man's form, distorted and massive, stretched across the floor, a black cutout framed in a yellow rectangle. Inside, Annabel lay at rest, limp arms over a pilled hospital blanket, her mouth slightly pursed. The cutout hands twitched impatiently. Two shuffling steps and the door eased closed, extinguishing the light. Dirty boots moved across sterile white tile.

Uplit by the seesawing EKG line glowing from the monitor, Dodge stared down at Annabel's tranquil face.

Chapter 37

Dodge's hands twitched again. One moved to the tangle of tubes on the cart beside Annabel's bed, the other slipping into the thigh pocket of his cargo pants.

The partition curtain screeched back on its tracks, shrill as a scream. Dodge barely had time to pivot when Shep hit him on the side of the neck, staggering him. Dodge took a knee, broad fingers groping, clutching for air, his mouth agape. One hand settled on Annabel's bed, fisting the blanket into a black-hole whorl. Even with Dodge stooped, his mass dwarfed Shep, making him look, improbably, average-size.

Before Dodge could regroup, Shep grabbed him by the shirt collar and arm and rode him like a battering ram toward the closed door. Dodge twisted at the end, falling, ball-peen hammer magically in hand, steel head whistling past Shep's temple, just missing. The collision was titanic, both men bouncing back into the room. The door cracked but did not cave. Stunned, it wobbled open.

Dodge's breath came as an ongoing squawk, a reed-thin draw of air smothered in his throat. His Adam's apple jerked. Even drowning, he was finding his feet, hammer loose at his side like something mythological, something Nordic. He drew himself up, his back to the doorway, a head taller than Shep.

Shep had torn his St. Jerome pendant from around his neck. One worn silver edge protruded from the fingers of his fist like a push dagger. He drove flesh and metal into the high center of

Dodge's chest, a brimstone variation on Dr Cha's sternal rub. Dodge flew back through the doorway, arms and legs trailing weightlessly.

Shep slammed the lockless door closed, leaning all his weight into it. A thunderclap shuddered it in the frame as if a truck were butting the other side. Shep's sneakers left the floor, chirp-landed on the tile. He drove the door closed. Another thunderclap, the door yawning open a foot this time, then banging shut.

Silence. Shep panting, shoulder to the wood, waiting. The wound on his forearm had torn open around the stitches.

A nearby smash. Someone screamed down the hall. A bang, farther away. Footsteps and panicked voices.

Then the handle rotated again in Shep's grip, and someone shoved at the door. After Dodge it felt like a puppy nuzzling a palm.

Shep stepped back, and security and nurses spilled into the room, rushing toward Annabel. Two guards moved to grab Shep, but Dr Cha was shouting, 'No, no, he's okay!'

Shep shoved through and across the threshold. Dodge's wake told the story of his flight – a knocked-over patient tangled in his gown and IV pole, then a bleeding orderly picking herself out of an upended gurney, then a kneecapped security guard moaning and clutching either side of his leg as if to keep it from exploding. Finally, at the end of the hall, the stairwell door swinging closed, wiping from view the sliver of blackness beyond.

Dr Cha sat in the stillness of Annabel's room, restitching the cut on Shep's forearm. A drape of blood hung from the slit, dripping off his elbow. Her fingers moved nimbly, a blur of hook and Prolene. Two security guards were posted outside. The silence, long delayed, was welcome.

'Stitching a nick like this twice,' she said, 'is not the best use of a trauma surgeon's time.'

Shep said, 'Sorry I wasn't injured worse.'

'So am I.' She smirked, then repositioned his arm like a slab of meat on a grill.

They'd recounted the official version endlessly. Dr Cha had explained to the responding cops, as she and Shep had rehearsed, that she'd permitted him to go back to the room to pick up his good-luck pendant that he'd forgotten there. What fortunate timing that he'd been inside when the intruder had burst in.

On the bed Annabel stirred, her face drawing tight in a grimace. Progress.

Dr Cha went on alert, her hands pausing, then slowly resuming their work. She finished and wiped the blood from Shep's arm with some wet gauze.

Shep looped the thin silver chain back through his pendant and, ducking his head, secured it around his neck. His lowered gaze snagged on a small length of electrical wire partially hidden behind one of the medical cart's wheels. He retrieved it, held it to the light. He realized she was watching closely.

'A signal wire,' he explained. 'For a digital transmitter – a bug.'

'Why?'

'So they'd know when Mike came to visit. It's the one place they think he'll show up. Where they can trap him within four walls.'

Dr Cha cracked her knuckles, shook out a neck cramp. Her choppy black hair framed a swan's neck. She was quiet a moment. Then she said, 'This hospital isn't safe as long as she's here.'

'No,' Shep said.

'I spoke to Annabel's father this evening after he landed. The health-care-proxy hearing, I gather, is first thing' – a bleary glance at her Breitling despite the wall clock overhead showing a quarter past four – 'this morning. Proxies are very rarely reassigned, not without drawn-out legal battles, but I have seen the rights suspended.'

Shep stared at her patiently.

She continued, 'If Mike Wingate wants to make a request to transfer his wife, he needs to get me something signed in the next six hours.'

'I thought she can't be moved,' Shep said.

Dr Cha's smirk, this time, held an element of cunning. 'She can't.'

Chapter 38

The Batphone, charging on the nightstand, rattled Mike awake, harmonizing with the throbbing in his head. His eyelids felt gummy, his mouth filled with sand. He pried his eyes open, uncoiled himself from Kat's side. Slowly, his surroundings trickled into his brain. A motel. Somewhere in Glendale.

He answered, his voice hangover-rough.

Shep said, 'Dodge tried to get to Annabel.'

Mike felt a sudden temperature drop, an arctic wind blowing through the shoddy room. 'And?'

'He didn't get to her.'

'He was going to . . .'

'Maybe. He dropped an electrical wire. Maybe he was gonna plant a bug so they could ambush you if you visited. Either way they're watching her.'

Mike sat up sharply, Kat sliding off his arm, deadweight. Snowball II peeked out from under her shoulder, its bulging eyes a portrait of alarm. 'Is she okay?'

'Yes. I mean, for being unconscious.'

'So they want to use her to catch me when I surface?' Mike asked. 'You think that means they won't kill her?'

Shep said, 'They could always hope you surface at her funeral.'

The line hummed for a bit.

'There's a hearing on your health-care thing this morning,' Shep said. 'We've gotta get her moved before then, while you still have authority. You need to send a fax to Dr Cha

258

demanding that Annabel be moved. Get a pen. Write down this phrasing.'

Mike stumbled around, tripping over his shoes, found a pencil and a torn grocery bag to write on, and took dictation. 'Okay, but how am I going to find a place to transfer—'

'I'll handle it. Just get me the fax. Now.'

Mike did his best to rouse Kat, but she was out cold. He shook her gently, tugged at her arms, even lifted her eyelids with his thumbs. Finally, juggling their bags, the rucksack, and a page torn from the phone book, he carried her out to the Honda and laid her in the backseat. A few blocks from FedEx Kinko's, she woke irritably.

'What day is it?'

Early-morning gray. Few cars on the road. People smoking at bus stops. Drivers slurping from Starbucks cups.

'Friday,' Mike said. 'I think it's Friday.'

'Where *are* we?'

'I have to send a fax.'

'*Then* where are we going?'

Mike blinked hard, fighting off an image of his own father behind a different steering wheel, giving indistinct answers and nervous glances at the rearview. A fresh hostility spiked in his chest. In three decades he'd traveled only the distance from the backseat to the front.

Kat was asking something else. 'When do we get to go home?'

'I don't know.' His voice was half strangled, defeated.

She slumped against the window and blew out a sigh of despair. It struck him with renewed urgency that they couldn't keep up the nomadic routine for much longer. That they'd run out of time. Out of patience. Out of luck.

At Kinko's he prepared the fax on a rented computer. Kat spun in the chair next to him, her head tilted back so she could watch the ceiling spin. Before printing he let the cursor linger over the Explorer button. Hesitating, he looked at Kat, twirling, mumbling.

Something in his chest cracked open, and he glanced away quickly so she wouldn't see his eyes watering.

Through the American Airlines Web site, he booked a one-way ticket for Kat to St. Louis, departing at 5:30 P.M. Annabel's brother, whom Mike had always liked best of her family, had just gotten married and bought a house in the suburbs. A companion-ticket option popped up, and it took all he could muster to click *No*. He used Annabel's PayPal account to complete the purchase. Then he bought another ticket on the same route for Kat on the 11:45 red-eye and printed both boarding passes.

He gave the fax to the lady at the desk – "*I, Michael Wingate, do hereby request that my wife, Annabel Wingate, be released for transfer to a specialist management team which I have selected based on their ability to provide a higher level of care*" – and split.

Nosing the Honda onto the nearest freeway entrance, he put the pedal down, hard, wanting as much distance between him and the Kinko's phone, the number of which would be tattooed across the transfer request when they pulled it warm from the fax machine at the Los Robles Medical Center.

'Mom takes me to get ice cream every Friday after school,' Kat said.

Mike sliced between two semis, hit the fast lane on a slide. Around the bend they were greeted by a wall of brake lights. The front edge of rush hour. Mike jerked onto the shoulder, gauging the distance to the next exit.

'It's Friday,' she said. 'I know Mom's not . . . she can't . . . but maybe you and I could—'

'Not right now.' He struggled to hide his apprehension. His tone gave off more irritation than he would have liked.

'Why not?'

'*Because.*' He glanced over at her. 'Oh, come on. What?'

'You yelled at me.'

'I didn't *yell* at you.'

Vehicles clogged the exit. Two, three streetlight changes should be enough to shove them through onto residential streets. Then he could weave for a while, find another motel, hole up until . . . until *what*?

He risked another glance over. Kat's face was flushed, the skin puffy around the bridge of her nose, as it got before she cried. What could he do? Half the time she was more mature than he was, but right now she was eight and missed her mother and wanted ice cream.

Fifteen minutes and twenty constipated blocks later, he found a Rite Aid. Kat sat on a Lilliputian chair by the ice-cream counter. She ate her Rocky Road looking down into the cone.

He was not forgiven.

Watching her nibble around the scoop, savoring each bite with almost mournful focus, he realized that the scene felt like a last meal.

Back in the car, amped on sugar, Kat's anger boiled away. She strained at the seat belt, singing, '*Miiiss Suzy was a ki-iid, a ki-iid, a ki-iid. Miss Suzy was a ki-iid, and this is what she said—*'

Mike drove, fumbling at the wheel, cell phone at his face. 'The doc get the fax?'

Shep said, 'Just.'

'*Waah waah, suck my* thumb, *gimme a piece o' bubble* gum—'

'What now?'

'Don't know,' Shep said. 'But wherever Annabel goes, we can't keep tabs on her anymore. We have to sever all contact. It's the only way to keep her safe.'

'What if she—'

'You have to let her go.'

'*—was a tee-nager, a tee-nager, a tee-nager, Miss Suzy was a teenager, and this is what—*'

'I *can't*. She's my wife. I need to know how she's doing.'

'Even if that kills her?'

Mike fought his face back into place. Took a few breaths. 'Anything on Kiki Dupleshney?' he asked.

'I just put out the word twelve hours ago.'

'—*piece o' bubble* gum, *go to your room, oooo* aah, *lost my* bra—'

'I know, Shep, but—' Mike looked over at Kat, finishing the thought in his head: *But I don't know how much longer my daughter can hold up.*

Snowball II got into the song and dance now, swinging along, Kat kicking up the stuffed-animal legs, a Vegas revue gone polar. She was punch drunk, coming apart at the seams. She needed to run in circles until she fell down.

Shep said, 'Cat-and-mouse games take a lotta waiting, Mike. You know that.'

Traffic had loosened; Mike had a full tank of gas and nowhere to go.

Miss Suzy's life cycle had drawn to a close: '—*to heh-ven, to heh-ven, Miss Suzy went to heh-ven, and this is what she said.*'

He set the phone in his lap and watched the streetlights whip by overhead. All those people on the sidewalks, shopping and pushing strollers, going about their normal lives.

Seven hours until that first flight departed for St. Louis.

'—*oooo* aah, *lost my* bra, *help me, choke choke choke,* tra-*laaaaaa!*'

A nanosecond of silence.

Mike exhaled with relief.

'*Miiiiiiiiiiiss Suzy was a bay-bee, a bay-bee, a bay-bee—*'

They passed a public park with grassy hills and picnic tables and jungle gyms. Severing the third verse, Mike pulled off, and they used the bathrooms. He waited nervously outside the women's room until Kat reappeared. They sat at one of the picnic tables, Mike wearing the rucksack and digging through the grocery bags to come up with food. He found himself checking the parking lot, the trees along the perimeter, the guy in shades walking his dog. Kat picked at her food. He couldn't blame her; they'd had peanut butter for five straight meals, and the bread was stale.

'That sandwich isn't gonna eat itself,' he said.

'But if it did,' Kat replied, 'that would be *really* cool.'

'Want me to get you a hot lunch somewhere?'

'No. Really. This is fine.' Kat took a bite, made a big show of chomping to emphasize the hardship. He soaked in the smart-ass sight of her.

Clouds moved overhead, dimming the park a few watts. Mike thought about a one-way no-companion ticket to St. Louis. 5:30 P.M. Her boarding passes crinkled in his back pocket. He fussed with his fingers. Cleared his throat. 'Your mother and I, when we got married . . . Man, did we want a baby. We wanted you more than *anything*. Do you know that?'

Kat nodded impatiently, her eyes on the fenced jungle gym below. 'Can I play?'

He fought his voice steady. 'Of course, honey,' he managed.

She bolted down the slope, leaving her sandwich behind. He cleaned up and followed, watching from outside the fence. He indulged in a brief fantasy: her on a tire swing in an expansive St. Louis backyard, Annabel's brother waiting on the porch with his new bride and some lemonade.

He thought of that playground from his childhood, of the wail of that distant bell and how he'd emerged from the yellow tunnel to see the empty parking spaces along the curb. *Can you tell me who you belong to?*

His heart was racing. Needing to be closer, he circled the fence and pushed Kat on the swings. For a time there was nothing but the sand under his feet, a pleasant breeze, and his daughter rotating away and back, away and back. Her curly hair, flying up in his face, was badly tangled and smelled like fruit punch. The scene, this scene, never changed. She could have been two or five. He could have been twenty-nine or thirty-three.

He pushed her, his hands light against her back, letting her go, catching her, letting her go again.

Chapter 39

Holding Mike's faxed transfer order, Dr Cha appeared in Annabel's room, where she had left Shep, baffled.

'I will need to have a conversation with the receiving doctor. Then I'll require a signature from the critical-care transport team.'

Shep said, 'Huh?'

Dr Cha said, 'Do you think you could arrange that for me?'

Shep said, 'What?'

Dr Cha said, 'Excellent,' and disappeared.

Shep turned to Annabel to see if she was keeping up any better than he was, but she remained still on the mattress, hair matted, eyes closed.

The bedside phone rang. And again. And again.

Shep trudged over and picked up. 'Yeah?'

'This is Dr Cha. And this is . . .?'

A very long pause.

Shep said, 'Dr Dubronski.'

'Dr Dubronski, have the risks of transfer been explained to the health-care proxy?'

Shep picked at his teeth with a nail. 'They have.'

'Are you familiar with Annabel Wingate's case?'

'I am.'

'Would you like to discuss the plan of care now or once the transfer is complete?'

'Once it's complete.'

'Excellent. Will you be sending your own critical-care transport team?'

'No?' Silence. 'Yes.'

Click. Dial tone.

Light footsteps, a brief knock on the door, and then Dr Cha reappeared with a form on a clipboard. She tapped cheerily with a pen. 'I'll need a signature here.'

Shep scribbled something.

She glanced down at the page. 'Insert doctor-handwriting joke here.' She kicked the green foot pedal and wheeled Annabel's bed out from the wall, guiding it into Shep's hands. Steering the attached cart and IV pole, Dr Cha walked Shep down the hall and into the elevator, then leaned in and hit the button for the third floor.

A clerk jogged down the hall toward them. 'Dr Cha? An attorney is holding on line three. It's about Annabel Wingate, and he says it's urgent.'

Dr Cha winked as the doors slid shut, wiping her from view.

Before Shep could protest, he was rising. He stared down at Annabel. Fluids moved through tubing. Equipment beeped. She breathed, the skin of her neck fragile and translucent, showing faint blue veins beneath. He wondered what the hell was going to happen next.

The elevator stopped, the doors opened, and a team of folks in scrubs were waiting in a semicircle, a serious-looking young woman at the forefront.

'I'm Dr Bhatnagar. Is this the patient Dr Dubronski wanted transferred here?'

The doors banged shut on Shep as he wheeled Annabel out into their hands.

He rubbed his shoulder. 'Sure.'

The woman snatched the clipboard from where Dr Cha had left it across Annabel's shins. On the medical chart beneath, the personal information had been blacked out as on a CIA document. 'Do we have a name for this patient?'

An elderly man in a wheelchair butted Shep aside and punched at the elevator button impatiently. Shep said, 'No.'

She scribbled "*UCF 2*" across the chart. At Shep's look of incredulity, she said, 'Unidentified Caucasian Female. Yes, we already have one. They're falling out of the sky today.' A quick nod to Annabel. 'I understand she's a victim of domestic abuse.'

Shep said, 'Possibly.'

'We'll hide her in the pediatric ICU, then. Thanks so much. We got it from here.'

She nodded, dismissing him. Shep stepped back into the elevator, nearly stumbling over the man in the wheelchair. The doors closed, and they whistled down to the lobby. The entire episode had occurred in a matter of seconds.

Shep cleared his throat and said to the elderly man or the quiet confines of the elevator, 'I will never understand smart women.'

Kat splashed in the bathtub, which Mike had rinsed out extensively before filling. The motel, a variation of the ones they'd been ping-ponging through, was in a seedy part of Van Nuys, a stone's throw from the park where he'd smashed up that forest green Saab with a baseball bat.

He was sitting on the bed, a heavy old-school phone in his lap, his stomach all acid and dull pain. The dust that had risen when he'd sat on the rust-orange bedspread swirled and swirled, impervious to gravity. It danced along a shaft of light slanting through the sole window, which provided an alley view of plastic wrappers snared in a chain-link fence. Dusk came on in fast-forward, the shaft dimming even as Mike watched it, a flashlight losing batteries.

He'd already spoken to Shep several times. Annabel's transfer had squeaked through. When Shep had last seen her, she'd been stable, though her improvement seemed to have stalled out. Shep had made clear that being in contact with the doctors at her new location could put her or Mike – and, by extension, Kat – in harm's way. It was a needless risk, and though it felt like swallowing barbed wire, Mike had acceded.

The upshot was that Shep was turned loose, finally, to run down Kiki Dupleshney. But none of that was what had Mike's gut in an uproar.

It was the two boarding passes in Kat's name, folded and rumpled from his pocket, sitting beside him on the bed. One for the 5:30 P.M. flight, one for 11:45.

The beside clock showed 5:01.

Hands sweating, he dialed, routing through the prepaid card's calling center.

'American *Air*lines, LAX.'

'Will you please put me through to the gate for Flight 768?' he asked. 'I have an extremely urgent message for a passenger.'

His response was hold music. Daniel Powter was better than the usual, but Mike didn't need the reminder that he'd had a bad day. The blue sky *haaaw*-liday was cut short by a singsongy male voice.

Mike said, 'I have an important message for a ticketed passenger, Katherine Wingate.'

A pause. 'Okay. Yes.' Some rustling as the phone receiver was covered, and then, 'There is someone here who can help you with that. Let me hand you off.'

A cool feminine voice. 'Hello?'

Smart – they'd posted a female cop.

'Hello,' Mike said cautiously.

'I'm with Katherine Wingate,' the woman said. 'I was told you have a message for her?'

Mike hung up. He bowed his head. If they were checking Annabel's PayPal account and looking for flights under Kat's name, that meant they'd be monitoring trains and borders and extended-family members. Which meant that he had no idea, beyond the four walls of this shit-ass motel, where to take his daughter that was safe.

Kat splashed away in the tub, the water's reflection wavering off the open door. She was singing softly, the same off-key tenderness that infused Annabel's voice when Mike listened to it through the baby monitor.

'*Lulla-by and good-night, with ro-ses bedight* – Dad? What's bedight? Dad?'

His voice was husky. 'To decorate.'

'Oh. *Be-di-ight. Lullaby and good night—*'

He ripped the boarding pass for the 5:30 flight in half, then kept tearing and tearing, the hundred tiny pieces fluttering like snow to the carpet. The lump in his throat was making it hard to breathe.

'*Lullaby and good night, thy mu-ther's delight.* Mother's delight?'

'You, honey,' he managed. 'That's you.'

He tore up the boarding pass for the 11:45 flight that he was actually going to put her on if the first run had been clear, then stared down at the scraps.

What now?

'*Bright an-gels beside my dar-ling abide. They will guard thee at rest.*'

Mike tilted his head back, cleared his throat, wiped his nose. Kat was out of the bath now, drying off, her pink body stretched thin, elbows and kneecaps poking into sight at the towel's edges. Absorbed water had bubbled the cheap particleboard counter; rust ringed the faucets. He thought, *This is no place for her.*

He remembered the plea Annabel had made as dark blood drooled from the gash between her ribs. For him to get Kat away from all this. For him to keep her safe.

And he considered the hard reality of what he might have to do to fulfill that promise.

He scooped up the confetti from the carpet, dumped it in the trash, and went to Kat. The towel, draped over her shoulders like a boxer's robe, parted around the slight pout of her tummy. She'd dried her hair too exuberantly, the curls all ratted up. Of course no detangler spray, which Annabel would have thought to buy. He brushed patiently from the bottom up, working an inch at a time, the needling pain wearing Kat down until she was whimpering.

'Stay still, honey, I have to—'

'Ow. *Ow.*' She pushed away. He caught her hands, lowered them, started over. He got half the job done and did his best to fight a ponytail through a hair band. Her eyes were watering from the pain, and he was growing more frustrated, trying to force it, trying to make it right. 'Ow. Not like *that*, Dad.' She finally pulled away and put her back to the counter, like a combatant. She was digging at her scalp with her nails now, scratching hard enough to raise welts at the hairline.

A calm dread descended over him. 'Let me look.'

'I *don't* have lice.'

'Let me look.'

'No.'

'*Kat.*' He took her by a skinny arm, turned her, and tilted her head.

Tiny white dots at her nape.

Eggs.

She read his face in the mirror and fought out of his grasp. '*No.* Not again. No more mayonnaise on my head. I can't do it anymore. I can't. I can't.'

'*We don't have a choice!*' he yelled.

She flinched, her back to the counter, leaning away from him.

'We're *out of* choices. And the mayo doesn't even work.' His teeth were clenched. 'Gentle isn't effective, Kat. To fix this we have to consider harsher options. The chemical wash might sting and it might *seem* like it's not good for you, but sometimes that's what ... what's required ... if we're gonna keep you safe from ...'

He realized, with horror, that he was about to cry.

Kat had gone as white as the towel, which had fallen to her feet. Her mouth was ajar, lips trembling. Arms half up in front of her.

He pressed a hand to the wall, leaned over a little, tried to catch his breath. Clenched, she waited. He reached for her, and she drew back violently.

'I'm sorry. I miss your mom, too. She's so much better at—' His voice broke, hard. 'I miss her, too.'

Kat unfroze, shoulders lowering first, then the arms coming loose. She crouched, picked up the towel, and wrapped it tightly around herself. Her head was down, and tears were dotting the worn-thin linoleum. He reached for her unsurely, but she didn't push away, and then he drew her in and hugged her as she grasped his arm.

They watched bad TV for a while and ate a late dinner – 'Oh, swell, Dad! Peanut butter and fruit juice! Mm-*mmm*.' He did his best to smile, to keep things light, but his face felt wooden, the passing minutes a countdown to some terminal event. He took a long shower and dragged a disposable razor across his face. *The last time I shaved, it was in my own bathroom, thinking I needed to pick up more razor blades. Annabel was in bed, flipping through a magazine and humming out of key to Nina Simone.*

He shoveled cold water over his face to clear the residue, then returned to watch the end of *The Simpsons*. Finally he zipped Kat into the powder blue sleeping bag, checked the baby monitor's batteries, and tucked it between her and Snowball II. He and Kat both pretended not to notice her scratching her head.

The curtains barely touched in the middle, so he slid a chair over to trap them closed. When he turned, Kat's stare was focused and intense, and he realized that when his shirt had pulled up a moment ago, it had revealed the gun at the small of his back.

'I'm scared,' she said. 'Of dying.'

He crossed, sat beside her, and ran a knuckle gently down the slope of her nose. 'Everyone is.'

'You, too?'

A prescient question, given what he was considering.

'A little,' he said. 'Sure.'

'What scares you the most? Being dead or not seeing me and Mommy anymore?'

He said gently, 'What's the difference?'

After a moment her face changed, and she nodded. He kissed her cheek, breathing her in. She snuggled into the pillow.

He stroked her hair until she was asleep.

Pocketing the Batphone and clipping the monitor receiver to his belt, he locked Kat in the room, walked a few steps down the outside corridor, and crouched with his back to the wall. Across the strip of parking spots, traffic whirred past. The air was diesel fumes and fast-food grease. On the ground, ants overran an apple core. The monitor complained a bit, and he crab-walked a foot or so closer to their door so it would shut up.

A maid pushed a long-handled broom up the corridor toward him, head down. She was badly slouched, ancient, attired in a black, old-fashioned maid's dress, a stereotype unto herself were it not for the iPod headphones visible through the gray wire of her hair. The broom shushed its way down the corridor, a delta of dirt tumbling ahead of it. She did not acknowledge Mike, not even when she bent arthritically to pick up the apple and dust-pan the debris. She continued out to the parking lot, broom bristles scraping against the concrete soporifically – *shhoop shhoop shhoop*.

Shep picked up on the first ring. 'I'm getting close,' he said. 'Kiki Dupleshney. Everyone knows I'm auditioning con women for a job. Her name keeps getting tossed around. Sooner or later someone's gonna produce a contact.'

Mike said, 'Annabel's recovering, right?'

Shep did not respond.

'Can you watch Kat until Annabel's back on her feet?' Mike asked.

The old woman made her way around the parking lot – *shhoop shhoop shhoop.*

'What are you doing, Mike?'

'They want me. Not Kat. *Me.*'

'And if Annabel *doesn't* get better? And you're not around? You want me to explain to your daughter that her father gave up and that's why she's being badly raised by a safecracker?'

'I'm not giving up. I'm facing them. Maybe I get the drop anyway. If they win—'

'I've *seen* Dodge,' Shep said. 'He'll win.'

At Mike's hip the monitor whined, and he nudged down the volume. 'Then they'll have gotten what they want. And Kat will be useless to them. She'll be safe.'

'I will find Kiki Dupleshney,' Shep said. 'Soon. She will point us to them. Then we'll find them instead of them finding you.'

'And Kat'll what? Ride shotgun?' He was pacing the corridor, the cleaning woman's broom unnaturally loud, closing in on him, grinding at his nerves – *SHHOOP SHHOOP SHHOOP.* He turned, nearly tripping over her, but her head stayed bent as she squatted to touch dustpan to floor, the hollows of her eyes catching shadows. From the buds tucked into her pillowy, wrinkle-creased ears, music radiated faintly, a mariachi squall of violin and trumpet. He looked past a hunched shoulder to see, scattered in the spray of dirt and cigarette butts she'd shoved in from the parking lot, the hulls of innumerable split sunflower seeds, still gleaming with spit.

The phone was falling from his hand, turning in slow motion, shattering on the concrete.

The unit at his hip fuzzed Kat's yelp into something like the buzz of a wasp.

And he was sprinting, ten yards of panic scored by staticky commotion from the monitor, which he'd slapped to highest volume – a thud, the screech of metal on metal, hoarse, muffled bellowing.

He took the door clean off the cheap hinges.

The bed was bare.

Kat – and the sleeping bag she'd been tucked into – were gone.

Chapter 40

The bedspread, smeared to the right, pointed at the window. Curtains rolled on a breeze. A dirt smudge marred the chair cushion where a large boot had set down.

Something primal rose from Mike's bones, from the twisted ladders of his cells, firing his nerves, setting his skin ablaze.

The hip unit broadcast Kat's shrieking, the rumble of an engine, violent rustling. Echoes of the sounds floated through the open window, coming at him in stereo. He dashed across, hands on the sill, leaning out in time to see a receding white square at the end of the alley. The square turned, elongating into a van.

How? How had Dodge and William hunted them down?

Kat's cries warbled nightmarishly from his hip, and it took a moment for Mike to ground them in reality; they'd scooped her up in the sleeping bag and carried her off like a cat in a pillow-case, the baby monitor slipping unseen down with her.

He yelled after the van as it motored from view. Leaped through the window. Got six frantic steps down the alley before strategy flashed back into reach, and he backtracked, racing for the Honda. He left four feet of rubber peeling out and clipped the corner screeching into the alley.

The monitor gave out a steady roar of pure static. The van had traveled out of range, breaking the connection. He fishtailed out the far end of the alley onto a quiet residential street, but the van was gone. Reception stuttered back – Kat screaming for him –

and then was lost again in a sea of crackling. He accelerated, hit an intersection, took a hard right.

Pure static.

He swung into a U-turn, smashing into a parked Bimmer, and flew the other way. Crackling, cracking, and finally the faintest edge of reception broke through the fuzz.

William's voice, '—*better be quiet back there or else*—'

Gone. Static, full bore.

Mike locked up the brakes and reversed, sending the truck behind him veering up onto someone's front lawn. The blare of its horn faded as Mike zipped down a side street, the low-volume light bar of the monitor flaring, flaring, then catching fire.

Kat's shouting grew clearer as he accelerated, and he picked up the van on a parallel street, flicking into view behind fences and side yards. His head snapped back and forth – road, van, road, van – trying to keep tabs on the vehicle as it passed through cones of light dropped by streetlamps. The van peeled right, away from him, and the monitor light fell dead. He jumped a curb, skidded across a lawn, took out a side fence, and careened through a back-yard. A guy looked up from his barbecue, sod flying at him, his Doberman leaping to safety. Mike plowed through a fence and across an embankment, screeching north across two lanes of traffic, cars skidding, the monitor giving up nothing but roaring static. The edge of a scream fought itself audible, vanished into the white noise, then wavered back again. He revved, nosing around cars, flying around alley Dumpsters, desperate not to snap the spider thread connecting him to his daughter.

Reception grew clearer. He guessed on a left turn, and it grew clearer still. Leaving a wake of smoke, he floated through a gas station mostly sideways, the overburdened Japanese engine squealing at him in complaint. He swung to take in the whole road – no white van, no white van, no white van – as the car righted itself, the spinning wheels catching and ripping him forward into a strip mall's parking lot.

Kat's screams were torturously distinct, driving him to a razor-edged frenzy, but she could've been any direction on the compass rose, and he thought his head would explode from sheer terror-ized rage when he caught the flick-flick-flick of a white van through the slats of the fence at the parking lot's end.

He dropped the pedal to the floor, blasting into the fence. There was no impact separation between slats and van, just an instantaneous smash of wood and vehicle, the van crimping around the nose of the Civic and rocking to a halt, a cloud of splinters settling dreamlike over the steaming catastrophe. Mike kicked out of the car, gun raised, closing ground as William coughed and blinked dust from his eyes in the crumpled driver's seat of the van.

The dented side door was hanging open, Dodge filling the rear interior, the sleeping bag cinched like a heavy sack in one block of a fist, ball-peen hammer drawn back at the pinnacle of a windup. Tripping through the jagged mouth of the fence, Mike had no clear shot at Dodge, but he jammed the Smith & Wesson through the open driver's window into William's cheek.

Dodge froze in his windup. The powder blue sack bulged and writhed. William's hands were up, stiff-fingered, and he was saying, 'Whoa there, pal.'

Dodge shifted so the sleeping bag was pinned against the floor, the bulge of Kat's head isolated through the baby blue puff of the sleeping bag, a grapefruit grasped in his palm. Muffled cries and whimpers. The hammer wavered overhead.

Mike had no quick, clear angle on Dodge, but the men's eyes met above the seat back, and Dodge must have respected what-ever he saw, because he said, 'On three.'

Kat was coughing and sputtering. The whine of a police siren was joined by a few others, baying like predators.

Mike nodded faintly. His voice was steadier than he'd ever heard it. 'One . . . two . . . three.'

Holding his hands up, William began a graceless slide toward the passenger seat, Mike keeping the sights lined on the scruff of his neck. In the back Dodge lowered the hammer to his side an inch at a time. As the sirens grew louder, Mike became vaguely aware of movement in his peripheral vision, bystanders ducking behind cars and into the 7-Eleven just ahead. William pushed through the far door and spilled onto the ground, Mike leaning to keep his head in the revolver's sights.

Mike said, 'Annabel's cell phone. Two hours.'

Dodge heaved the sleeping bag toward Mike. Mike had to lunge to catch her and by the time he looked up, Dodge and William were vanishing around the corner of the 7-Eleven, sprinting away.

He shook Kat loose, grabbed her flushed face in both hands, savoring the blessed sight of her. She'd gone rubber-boned, and he held her until her legs firmed. She was intact. 'Come,' he said. 'Now.'

Stumbling after him, she grabbed Snowball II from the pavement and curled the stuffed animal to her chest. As Mike passed the van's driver window, his gaze caught on a fat manila file wedged by the seat's buckle guard, *Mike Wingate* written across the bright red tab in sloppy penmanship. Reaching through the window, he pried it free.

Ahead, Dodge stumbled around the building back into sight and paused, palm on the brick wall. Mike glanced down at the folder in his hand; Dodge had come back for it. Mike grabbed Kat, took a step back, away. Dodge tensed to charge.

Sirens screaming, closer. Closer.

Dodge conceded, fading back around the corner. Mike and Kat started running in the other direction. As they scrambled through a stand of bushes at the lot's edge, Mike caught flashes of blue and red spilling through the intersection a quarter mile away.

Backyards, alleys, streets – they ran for an eternity, alternating fits of speed-walking when they drew stares. Back at the motel, the manager and the maid were stupefied by the ruined door, surveying the damage. Mike shoved past them, grabbed the rucksack from the corner, and bolted.

Kat moved swiftly at his side, mute and blanched. Four streets over he found an old Camry parked in a tiny driveway, the house beyond unlit. He smashed the driver's window with a paver he plucked from the front walk. Reaching through the broken glass, he hit the garage clicker clipped to the visor. He told Kat to wait and ducked under the rising garage door. The interior door to the kitchen was unlocked, the car keys hanging on a hook by the light switch.

Driving the Camry through the neighborhood, he passed the aftermath of the chase – dinged cars, torn-up grass, cop cars gliding in all directions. Four exits down the freeway, he was still reminding himself to breathe. He realized that the baby monitor was clipped to his hip and quickly pulled it free and tossed it down by his feet as if it were scalding to the touch.

Leaving the Camry in a back lot four blocks away, they checked in to a motel tucked under a freeway ramp in Panorama City. He tried to talk to her, but she couldn't get words out past her jerking breaths. For forty-five minutes, he sat on the bed, rocking Kat as her breathing calmed and her whimpers quieted. She stayed in a semi-fetal position, burrowed into him, needle-thin veins etched into her closed eyelids. Even after she fell asleep, he held on to her, rocking her, marveling at her warmth, at the miracle of having stolen her back.

Finally he eased her gently beneath the covers and checked the clock. A half hour to his cell-phone date with William and Dodge.

From the rucksack he retrieved an unused calling card and the stuffed folder he'd swiped from the smashed van. He set them side by side on the wobbly desk in the corner and clicked on the gooseneck lamp.

When he opened the folder, information jumped off the page,

hitting him in the face. He stared down silently for a few moments, drowning in disbelief. A report on Annabel's parents, listing their phone numbers, addresses, vehicles, Social Security numbers, friends, former business partners, and places they'd traveled.

This was the first page. There were hundreds more.

With mounting alarm Mike leafed through the rest. Annabel's siblings and cousins, Mike's workers, subcontractors he'd used, doctors, neighbors, parents of Kat's friends, ex-spouses of Annabel's classmates in her teaching program. Page ninety-five solved the riddle of how William and Dodge had closed in on Mike and Kat. Beneath a picture of Jimmy's girlfriend, Shelly, was the number of the license plates Mike had borrowed from her Mazda 626. The same number he'd dutifully written down at each motel when registering to ensure that his car wouldn't be towed from the lot. A basic police flag on the plate number and a single phone call from a motel manager were all it took for Kat to be scooped off in the night.

The file also held credit-card statements going back years, red circles marking hotels Mike and Annabel had stayed at, towns they'd visited, stores they'd shopped at regularly, places they'd ordered takeout from. Then there were phone bills of friends, even a few transcripts from what he assumed were tapped lines, his name underlined where mentioned – *Wingate's ass been all edgy. Made me stop at a cemetery on the way back from the stone yard and he just float around like a ghost.* Further back the data reached into associates of associates, stretching through six degrees of separation, an aerial snapshot of the web into which the Wingates were nestled, a road map to their existence. There was information new to Mike: Kat's first-grade teacher's parents owned a cabin in Mammoth; Annabel's brother-in-law's cousin participated in a time-share in Jackson Hole; the Martins across the street had a second home in North Carolina.

Anywhere Mike would run. Anyone he'd turn to.

It struck him that this was how Rick Graham and the Threat Assessment Center closed in on terrorists.

He shut the file. Stared blankly down. His elbows and hands had marred the patina of dust on the desktop. The brutal reality of how outgunned he was hit home, setting his nerves on vibration. He had a bag of cash and a rusty aptitude for boosting cars, and his pursuers had the most powerful data-mining software available to the U.S. government.

Mike glanced over at the clock. It was time.

Routing through the prepaid center, he called Annabel's cell phone. He waited for the call to go through, sweat trickling down his ribs.

William said, 'Mike Doe.'

'William Burrell,' Mike said. 'And Roger Drake.'

'You been doing some homework.'

Mike gazed down at the file. 'As have you.' Silence. 'You came after my wife. To get to me.'

'Yes.'

'I can find out about your family, too. I can find out where they live.'

'Family?' William laughed. 'My notion of family's a bit different than yours. My people are nothing to me. Except for Hanley, and . . . well, he's not around anymore. Is he?'

'You've played a lot of games, but you've never said what you want.'

'To kill you.'

Mike's skin came alive – thousands of tiny insects crawling on legs of ice. 'So that's it?' He was incredulous. 'No information? No money? You just have to kill me?'

'Yes.' William sighed. 'We're foot soldiers, see? We have a mission directive. And you're the target. It's a bad state of affairs. I understand that. I wish it weren't the case. But there are two kinds of crooks, you see. Those with a code and those without.

We have a code, Dodge and I. We keep our word. I have never lied to you. And I'm not gonna start now.'

'What was my father to you people?' Mike asked.

'Nothing. He was nothing.'

'You're after me for something he did.'

'Maybe before I kill you,' William said, 'I'll tell you why.'

Mike glanced across at Kat, her chest rising and falling steadily. 'Then we can settle this face-to-face. I will come to you. But you leave my daughter out of this. She doesn't know anything. She's witnessed nothing.'

A faint little chuckle that held no amusement. 'You still don't get it, do you?'

The insects squirmed back to life, Mike's skin alive with movement. 'Get *what*?'

'Katherine's not a bystander in this,' William said. 'She's our other target.'

The line went dead.

Chapter 41

Mike and Kat were waiting at the front door of the mini-golf play center when the pimply-faced manager arrived to open the place. Mike had parked the Camry at the edge of the lot, its shattered window cleaned up. It sported license plates he'd swapped out with a Jetta.

In the video arcade, he got forty bucks of quarters and set up at the pay phone in the back while Kat played games in the nearest aisle where he could keep her in sight. The darkness and flashing lights were disorienting; they seemed an extension of the endless night they had emerged from. Was it really morning outside?

His eyes barely leaving his daughter, he made call after call, starting with 1-800 numbers, collecting referrals, then referrals of referrals. Given that he was dealing with emergency services, most places were open even though it was Saturday. Kat trudged from game to game, scratching her head, her vacant expression lit by the glowing screens. The arcade filled with kids until the aisles were jammed – all that candy and color and laughter surrounding Kat, a mocking vision of weekends past. Mike had to fight to stay focused. Slotting endless quarters into the pay phone, he ruled out fifty options and sniffed around fifty more, trying to zero in on a viable choice.

By the time he was done, the phone book was marked with sweat from his fingers. What if someone followed and lifted his prints? Could Graham, Dodge, or William pick a clue off the yellow pages that led to Kat? In a spasm of paranoia, Mike smuggled out the phone book and burned it by the Dumpster around back. Kat stayed in the car behind him, watching as if at a drive-in movie. Crouched in the cold morning air, warming his hands over the miniature pyre, he realized he was on the verge of sobbing with horror at what he was about to do.

He drove east through the afternoon, Kat with her face to the passenger window, watching the desert roll by. Juniper wagged in the breeze, lavender shuddered off purple dust, and Joshua trees twisted up, tombstones to unmarked graves.

Why would an eight-year-old be targeted by hired killers? Last week William and Dodge had scared Mike into grabbing Kat at school and bringing her home. He flashed on Hanley's fingers obscenely working Annabel's bra strap. *This is too messy, too messy. We were supposed to wait.* Wait not just for Mike but for Kat as well.

On that morning years ago in the station wagon, the horror in Mike's father's voice had been palpable. Maybe he'd feared for Mike's life as Mike now feared for Kat's. But *why*? His father was responsible for whatever mess he'd turned their lives into, at least according to that splash of blood on his cuff. A countering image popped into Mike's head – himself in the dim garage, using an old rag to wipe Annabel's blood from his arm. What if Mike hadn't been abandoned but *saved*? What if dispatching him to a new life was the only choice Mike's father had left to protect him?

But Mike didn't – *couldn't* – trust that explanation. It reeked of wish fulfillment, an origin story like Superman rocket-launched from Krypton. But worse, it seemed fueled by hope, by *longing*, and when it came to Mike's childhood, he'd decided that hope and longing were dead ends.

And yet how could he hold on to that lifelong outrage given what he was on his way to doing?

'Arizona,' Kat said dreamily as the sign drifted past on the side of the freeway. 'I always wanted to come here.'

When they reached the town of Parker, Mike took Kat to a diner. She ordered a stack of grilled-cheese sandwiches with french fries and a chocolate shake.

'Aren't you gonna eat?' she asked around a mouthful of food, and he just shook his head.

She ran out ahead as he paid the bill. When he dashed after her in a low-grade panic, he found her standing in front of a store window, hand to the glass, captivated. A yellow gingham dress floated on display, strung up by fishing line before a holiday backdrop, a dress without a girl. Mike took Kat inside and bought it, along with new shoes and a few shirts.

They went to the movies afterward, Kat boinging her arm along, as always, with the hopping Pixar desk lamp in the opening credits. For two hours, leaning back in his seat, Mike watched her instead of the screen. Openmouthed smiles, bursts of giggling, snorkel breathing through Red Vines. For a moment it was as though they'd skipped back in time and everything was normal again.

He found a boutique hotel that took cash for a deposit. The country decor was a bit frilly, but it was markedly nicer than the motels they'd been staying in. He bathed Kat, tilting her head back beneath the faucet to wash her hair. The lice were still in there, sure, but he didn't have the heart to cap the evening with a chemical rinse.

Tucked into bed, her skin flushed and clean, Kat said, 'Tell me a story.'

Mike realized that he'd pulled his flowery armchair bedside like a nurse on deathwatch. 'About what?'

'About next month. About us going home.' Her blinks were growing longer. 'Mom's been cooking all day. You know how she gets with Thanksgiving. And there's turkey. And pumpkin pie. And those oranges we stick cloves into. And we sit down, all together, and . . .'

She was asleep.

Mike remembered when she was first handed to him at the hospital, a fluffy bundle with a pink face, how he'd looked down at her and thought, *Anything you ever need for the rest of your life.* He rested his head on her chest, listened to the faint thumping, breathed her breath.

He stepped out onto the balcony. Smog had wiped away the stars. He asked Annabel if he'd be forgiven for doing what he was about to do, but no answer came back from the firmament.

In the morning Kat wolfed down a tall stack of pancakes, pausing only to scratch her scalp. Back upstairs, Mike packed her few things into the rucksack, laying aside his gun and a chunk of cash. Standing before the bathroom mirror, he brushed her hair slowly, meticulously, and drew it back, at last, into a perfect ponytail.

She smiled and flicked at it. '*Nice*, Dad!'

She lingered in the bathroom and came out wearing her new yellow dress. She pinched out the sides in a show of self-conscious theatricality. 'Well?'

He swallowed hard. 'It was made for you.'

He drove the route he'd been given over the phone yesterday as he'd sat in the back of that arcade. The referral chain to the address was too convoluted to remember – a caseworker to a social worker to a character reference – but that was partially the point. Somehow, through prevaricating, cajoling, and begging, he'd managed to arrive at a name he thought he could trust.

He looked straight through the windshield, his hands fastened robotically on the steering wheel, his gaze on the dotted center line, yellow streaks on black tar. He was heartless, insentient, a thing of steel and purpose. He sensed Kat's gaze tug over to him once, twice, then stick, and he felt his resolve melting away. But then they were there, parked across the street, and she looked out the window and saw the rambling ranch house and the backyard crammed with play structures and girls.

She breathed in, a sharp intake of air. 'Why are we here.' It was not phrased as a question.

He couldn't talk. He could barely breathe. *There is no forgiving a parent who could do that to a child.*

'Why,' she repeated, 'are we here.'

He forced words through the tangle of his throat. 'I need your help, honey.'

'Dad?'

'Mommy's in danger, and I need to . . . I need to go with Shep to help her.' He couldn't look over at her. 'And I can't do that and keep you safe at the same time.'

'No, Dad. *No no no*. You can't.'

'I need to make sure you're safe first. Before I do *anything* else.'

She was crying, little-girl crying. 'What did I do? It's not my fault I got lice.'

'No, honey, *nothing* is your fault. Remember that. Nothing—'

'I'm sorry. I'm *sorry* I got lice.' She was twisting one hand in the other like a wet rag. 'Please, Dad. *Please*. You can shave my head like Shep said. I don't care.' She'd popped up to her knees on the seat, eyes wide, pleading. 'You can protect me.'

'This is how I am doing that.'

'You *always* protect me. I'm safe with you. You'll take care of me.'

He struck the wheel. '*I can't.*' His words rang around the car. His fist throbbed. Choking back panic, he searched for words soft enough. Jesus – how to put this in terms she could grasp. 'This . . . this is what you can do to help Mommy right now.'

Kat wilted in the seat. 'How long?'

He lifted his hands from the steering wheel, spread his fingers, lowered them again. 'Whatever happens, you'll be okay. It may not feel like it. But you will.'

'What do you mean *whatever happens*? What does that *mean*? So if Mom . . . if Mom *dies* and they get you, then I . . . I . . .?' A breath shuddered through her, and then she was still for a moment, her shoulders curled, arms hugging her stomach. 'I'm eight,' she said. 'I'm only eight.'

He did his best to fight his throat open, his chest still. His jaw was clamped shut, but he could feel the muscle pulsing at the corners. Still, he could not look over at her. The silence lasted ten seconds or ten minutes.

'If that happens' – his fingers, clenched around the steering wheel, had gone white – 'you'll think I won't know how great you turned out and how you built a family and what a wonderful woman you grew up to be. But I do. I know already.'

'No. No no no no *no*.'

He had to get it all said before his will deserted him. 'However long you're here, you can't tell *anyone* your last name.' An echo from his childhood tore into him like a drill bit. 'You're Katherine *Smith*. Listen to me, Kat. You're Katherine Smith now, do you understand? Don't give my name. Don't give your mom's name. Don't say where you're really from. You have to make it all up and memorize it, and never forget it.'

Each word ground like broken glass on the way out. She had buried her head in her arms and was shaking her head violently.

He thought, *I am damned for telling her this. I am going to hell. My heart will fall out of my chest and disintegrate into a cloud of ash.*

'You need to be tough. Your life is at stake. No one can know anything about you.'

It was every lesson he wanted *not* to teach her, every Bad Parent caricature. But he steeled his back and drove on into the face of it. 'Swear it to me, Kat.'

'No.'

'You have to. They'll find you.'

'I'm not going.'

'There is *no choice* here, Kat.'

She looked up sharply, her face streaked with tears. Her words warbled through sobs. 'Then you swear to *me*. If I stay here and I keep my mouth shut about who I am then you *have to* live and come back for me. You have to. *Promise*. Or I won't go. I won't.' She stuck out her hand. 'Deal?'

287

He stared down at her trembling fingers, his blood rushing so fast and hard that it vibrated his vision. Was that a promise he could make? Did he have a choice?

She kept her hand pointed at him, her bruised gaze on his face.

He blew out a breath, pinched his eyes closed, then reached over. 'Deal.'

Her hand was warm, and it trembled.

'You will come back for me.'

'I will come back for you.'

'You swore it, now,' she said. 'You *swore* it.'

He lifted the rucksack from the backseat, and they headed for the house.

A plump woman answered the door, drying her hands on an apron. Behind her, four girls older than Kat were glued to cartoons while a toddler played with a one-legged Barbie. The sounds of the kids playing outside wafted through an open window – laughter and thumping and someone crying. A visceral reaction set Mike's gut roiling. He looked around to assess the surroundings, but past and present were fused. There sat the Couch Mother on the sofa, fanning herself with a TV Guide. There, the yellow cushion with its effluvium of cat piss. *Sure, shithead. My momz, too. All our parents is coming back.*

Mike's eyes stung, and he blinked his way back to the present. There was no Couch Mother, no cat-piss reek, but there *was* a bay window, put there as if to tempt kids to watch and wait. The couch arms were threadbare, the walls dented and scuffed, but the foster girls looked healthy and the house was suffused with the rich scent of tomato soup.

'Can I help you?' the woman asked.

He didn't know how long he'd been standing there. 'Jocelyn Wilder?'

The woman twisted her curly gray hair up into a knot. 'Yes?'

'Can we talk for a moment in private?'

Kat swiped at her nose with a sleeve. She was staring at her shoes. Jocelyn's gaze flicked to her, then back to Mike. 'Do you want to play outside, sugar?'

Head down, Kat walked through the open back door and sat alone on a bench. Warily, Jocelyn gestured toward the kitchen, and he followed her through a swinging door. They faced off over yellow peeling linoleum. Her handsome face showed that she'd dealt with a variation of this scene a time or two.

He said, 'We're in trouble. I need to take care of some business.'

'Sir, I don't run a—'

'I know,' he said. 'I know. But if she goes into the system, she'll be in danger.'

'A lot of kids are in danger.'

'Not like this.'

She blinked. 'What does that mean? Like she'll be *killed*?' Though she'd said it herself, the word made an impression. 'Why would anyone want to kill her? She's a little girl.'

'I don't know,' Mike said. 'That's what I need to find out. I have to go. I have to be gone. My car can't be out front. If they see the car, they'll know she's here.'

Jocelyn regarded him skeptically, but he could see the concern blossoming beneath the surface.

'I'm sorry to put this on you,' he said.

She made a sound that was a cross between a snort and a laugh. 'You're not going to put anything on me, Mr . . .?'

She crossed her considerable arms, legs planted, an immobile force. She was the kind of foster mom who'd take you by the ear and drag you to Valley Liquors to fess up to stealing nip bottles of Jack Daniel's. Mike knew her as he'd known the Couch Mother, which meant he could read her. The watery blue eyes. The feathered skin at her temples. The kindness etched into every crease of her venerable face.

He held a hand up, palm down, calming the waters or holding his balance; he wasn't sure which. 'Don't trust anything you might hear on the news. Don't trust anyone. *Anyone*, no matter who they say they are. If you turn her in, if you call the cops or Child Protective Services, she will be hunted down.'

'Well, that's quite a thing, isn't it?' She swallowed angrily, her neck clucking up and down, and looked away.

'You know kids. Talk to my daughter and you'll know I'm telling the truth.'

'How'd you find me?'

He swung the rucksack off his shoulder, letting it thunk to the floor. 'This holds two hundred thousand dollars in cash. It's not blood money. It's from our savings before all this happened. You can declare it as an anonymous donation, pay taxes, whatever. It's yours to keep. Spend it on the other kids, too, so they don't get jealous.'

'Donations don't work that way. I don't want your money regardless.'

'Keep it in case you need it.'

'You're not listening to me.'

'Then will you guard it for me?'

'Like collateral?' She practically spit the words.

'I *will* be back.'

'When?'

'Soon.'

'I won't do it,' she said, with grave finality.

'You will,' he said gently. 'I know that you will.'

'Two hundred thousand.' She set her hands on her hips, the flesh wobbling around her arms. 'Why so much money if you're coming back?'

His face felt unattached to him, a separate entity, a stone mask. If it cracked, it would crumble away and leave nothing behind. He heard a noise escape him, and Jocelyn's stance softened. She lowered her hands to her sides, seeming to take pity on him as he fought for composure.

'So she can have whatever she needs until then.' He gestured at the rucksack. 'Her clothes are in there, too. They're *her* clothes. Buy whatever for the others—'

'*All* my girls have their own clothes,' she said indignantly.

'And,' he said faintly, 'she has head lice.'

'Splendid.'

'I tried mayonnaise—'

'It doesn't work. You need the heavy-duty stuff.'

He toed the linoleum. It was no longer his right to object. 'Okay.'

'Any other problems? Drug-resistant tuberculosis, perhaps?'

'No.'

'I can't do this – I *won't* do this – for long,' she said. 'It's illegal, which puts the whole family at risk. I have no birth certificate for her. What am I supposed to do if—'

'You don't run a battered-women and children's shelter for seventeen years without figuring out how to give people a new life.'

A glare. 'You've certainly done your homework.' She took a deep breath. 'That was a long time ago.'

'Not so long that you couldn't get the right folks in the right offices on the phone. If it comes to that.'

'If it comes to that,' she repeated sharply.

She let out an angry laugh, and he saw it again, the steel in her eyes that said she was the kind of woman who could figure out just about anything she decided was necessary.

'And why should I believe you *are* coming back?' she asked.

'Because I told her I would.'

'Then you'd better goddamned come back, hadn't you?'

'Yes, ma'am.'

Turning to the stove, she dismissed him with a wave.

He pushed through the swinging door into the foyer. They were all as he'd left them, the girls fixated on the TV, the toddler twisting one-legged Barbie's remaining limbs this way and that, and his daughter sitting on the bench just through the open rear door, her untied shoelaces scraping the concrete. Her fingers fiddled with themselves autistically in her lap. Her lips were bunching; she was doing everything not to cry. He filled the doorway. He didn't want to blink – there was only this moment of seeing her, of capturing her image, and then it would be over. For a moment he thought he might just fly apart there in the doorway like a horror-movie effect.

Finally Kat looked up, fixing that amber-and-brown gaze on him. 'Please, Daddy.'

Tearing his gaze from her, he turned away.

He drifted numbly through the front door and back to the stolen Camry. Snowball II remained on the dashboard where Kat had perched him. He held the tiny stuffed animal in his hands and looked at the house but couldn't bring himself to go back in and deliver it to her. Resting it on the passenger seat, he drove off. A few miles up the road, he noticed the baby monitor down by his feet where he'd dropped it after the chase.

He threw it out the window.

Chapter 42

Mike blinked back to consciousness in a motel room with a vague recollection of driving for hours to put as much distance between him and Jocelyn Wilder's foster home as possible. Space, he hoped, would lessen temptation. Snowball II was mashed in his fist, and between his legs was a brown-bagged bottle of Jack Daniel's, though he had no memory of wanting to get drunk. He sat with the TV flickering across his face, pulling from the bottle, craving numbness, but he'd had no more than two gulps when he vomited in the corner. He saw himself from the outside – one shoe off, belt undone, curled on the coarse carpet. And then Annabel appeared, kneeling over him, hand on his shoulder, saying, *It's okay, I'm here, We'll get through this together,* but when he rolled over, she bled into a surprising blast of light from the high-set window.

He was cold in his bones where the rays couldn't reach. He thought he should shower, but he found he already was, the scalding water raising streaks on his chest and arms, though he couldn't quit shivering. Closing his eyes, he retreated into bleached-out memories of his mother. That yellow-tiled kitchen. Looking up as she'd bathed him, her black-brown hair draped along one tan arm. Patchouli and sage, the flesh-warm scent of cinnamon. That spot of blood – her blood? – on his father's cuff.

A dead patch of time.

And then the room was dark and he was trembling beneath an icy spout, the hot water having long run out.

Next he was wet on the floor, wrapped in a bedsheet, hugging the shopping bag containing the gun and his remaining cash. The room was a mess – splotch of puke, tipped-over chair, sheets pulled onto the floor to form a nest.

The door opened, and a fall of light from the corridor landed on his face, making him blink. Then the door closed, heavy footsteps padded across to him, and a man's shadow darkened his sight.

They were here, at last, to kill him.

'Get up,' Shep said.

A hand lowered into the fuzzy edge of Mike's vision. Mike considered it with stunned incomprehension.

His voice, hoarse from disuse: 'How'd you find me?'

'You called me. You told me what you had to do. Now get up.'

Mike took his hand. Shep hoisted him to his feet.

Shep crossed and set a worn brown paper bag on the crappy kitchenette counter. He removed a sleek black cell, a Batphone replacement, and tossed it at Mike. Next came the Colt .45 and a police scanner, which Shep plugged into the outlet by the microwave: '—*1080, you got a location? That's affirmative. I'm on scene at 1601 Elwood, back window looks to be broken. How many units we got in the area?*' He thumbed down the volume, leaving it loud enough to keep an ear on, then unpacked can after can of SpaghettiOs, setting them in a row by the sink.

'What . . . what day is it?'

'Monday. Eight-seventeen P.M. You're back in California – Redlands.'

Had he really left Kat just yesterday?

'Her glasses,' Mike murmured. Pushing a fist to his forehead, he rocked a little. 'I forgot. She needs a new pair to read—'

Shep opened a can of SpaghettiOs with a pocketknife, stuck in a plastic spork, and handed it to Mike. 'Eat. We got business to handle in the morning, and I can't have you all pale and shaky.'

'Annabel could be dead by now,' Mike said.

'Eat.'

'Tell me which hospital. I need to call—'

'You can't—'

'—just to know.'

'Then you're willing to kill her. And us. And Kat.' Shep grabbed the phone from the nightstand and, trailing the cord, held it out to Mike. A dare.

Mike stared at the phone hatefully. But didn't reach for it.

Shep set the phone down and extended, again, the SpaghettiOs.

Mike took the can and did his best. *Chew. Swallow. Repeat.*

He looked around, seeing the mess through Shep's eyes. The whole room was gravid with sullenness, as if it had been dipped in gray. The SpaghettiOs had turned to sour mush in his mouth. He gagged them down, wiped his lips angrily. 'Why are you here?'

Shep said, 'What?'

'You could've told me off when I first called. After how we left things back when. But I knew you wouldn't. I knew if I needed you, you'd be there in a heartbeat.' The sentiment was coming out, bizarrely, as anger, a slow boil of a resentment Mike hadn't known he was harboring. 'Maybe you *want* me to be a criminal again. Maybe you were lonely.'

Shep chewed his food. Scooped another sporkful. Paused. 'May*be*,' he said.

'You don't owe me,' Mike said. 'Not for serving three months' time for you.'

'You think that's why I'm doing this?' Shep was utterly, infuriatingly calm. Thoughtful, even. 'Because I owe you?'

'Why else?' Mike banged SpaghettiOs down on the TV, a blood spray erupting from the can to dot his forearm. There was relief in yielding to his temper, to using the old muscles in the old ways. He needed to strain and hurt and growl into the face of something. 'Why *else*?'

Shep took another hearty bite. Scraped the bottom of the can. 'Never gave it much thought,' he said, his mouth full.

'Of course not.' Mike felt his top lip curling. 'That would be *beneath* you. Because you're guided by unerring instinct—'

'That one o' your SAT words?'

'You're too pure to *think*. You've always known just who you are. Not like me.'

'No past,' Shep said.

'But I *do* have a past. I never left it behind. What was a lie was where I thought I was headed. The cover-up over those pipes, that bullshit award – I knew it was wrong. But I went along. And now.' A growl escaped Mike's clenched teeth. 'I don't know how you fucking stand to look at me.'

'That's what you never learned,' Shep said.

'What?'

'Acceptance.' Shep shrugged. 'It is what it is.'

'What is?'

'Everything.'

'The hell does that mean?'

'Take your father. You been holding a grudge against him for how many years now? Black-and-white world. Him playing the role of black. What's that leave you?' Shep cranked open another steel can and dug into it, his appetite unhampered. 'Your father's betrayal – that's been your North Star. And now? Leaving a kid behind?' He held out his hands, a rare superfluous gesture, the spork sticking out of the can, a little white flag. 'Black isn't black today. White isn't white. And maybe it never was. Maybe it's all a goddamned mess and we do the best we can.'

'That's what you've done? The best you can?'

'There was one time I didn't. I was beaten down and couldn't get up. And you made sure. You made sure I got up. And I vowed after that moment, *I will never stay down again.*' Shep wiped his mouth with the back of his hand and glared at Mike, as if he couldn't figure out it was a challenge.

All the heat went out of Mike. He took a wobbly step back and sank to the mattress. He tilted his cheeks to his palms and sat there, pouring his face through his hands. 'I remember when we went to Ventura Harbor to ride the carousel,' Mike said. 'She was three, and she wanted the chicken. But these other kids kept getting it. I mean, it *had* to be the goddamned chicken. Who puts a chicken on a carousel anyway? And we waited and waited, but I couldn't get it for her.'

'What are you telling me?' Shep asked.

'I picture her in that home and what will happen to her if I fail,' Mike said, 'and I think I might die.'

He couldn't look up, but he heard Shep set down the can, right the chair, and pull it over. An exhale as he sat.

'I never been responsible to or for anyone in my life,' Shep said. 'To take that on, it's a courageous thing. But you can't do it now. Not with what we're going into.'

He leaned forward so his head butted against Mike's. Same position, same posture, the two of them staring down at the threadbare carpet. Shep shoved a little, solicitously, crown to crown.

'You want her back,' he said.

Mike said, 'Yes.'

'Safe.'

'Yes.'

'Then you have to be nothing. *Want* nothing. You can't have them – Kat or Annabel – if you need them. You're not a husband. You're not a father. You're a man with a task. Understand?'

'Yes.'

'Get some sleep. We start early.'

Mike cleaned up the room a bit and lay on the mattress. Beside him Shep's eyes were closed and his breathing regular, but Mike couldn't tell if he was out or not.

The ceiling was cracked in infinite patterns, a tangle of tree roots.

Mike said, 'I will never turn my back on you again.'

Silence. Mike figured Shep was asleep, but then he answered,

'You done with your conscience yet? 'Cuz where we're going, it's gonna get in the way.'

They lay there in the darkness. Mike was unsure when he crossed into sleep, but when he awoke to the sound of the shower, the clock showed 4:14 A.M. Shep emerged from the bathroom a few minutes later, towel around his waist, the shower left running behind him like in the old days when they had to cycle six or seven bodies through on any given morning before the hot water ran out.

Mike said, 'I should probably ditch the car I stole.'

Shep tossed him a set of keys, then crossed and parted the curtains. Gleaming in the front spot was a forest green Saab.

Reluctantly, Mike matched Shep's smirk. He showered off, then swiped the steam from the mirror. Shep's Dopp kit was sitting there on the metal ledge, the electric clippers poking up into view. Mike lifted the razor and turned it this way and that, as if reviewing an old photograph. The plastic blade guards were loose in the Dopp kit. He found the right attachment, snapped it on.

Shep called out through the door, 'Ready?'

The clippers sat heavy in Mike's hand, like a weapon. The mirror had misted over again, so he cleared it with a washcloth and studied his reflection.

Then he turned on the razor and took his hair down to foster-home length. He toweled off his head and stepped out into the main room.

'Ready,' he said.

Shoulder to shoulder, they headed into the parking lot.

Chapter 43

Mike followed directions and asked no questions. He used the drive to iron out his thoughts, smoothing his resolve until it was as uniform and unwavering as the road ahead. The Saab blazed over the Grapevine through Bakersfield and the long flat tract of middle California, onion fields and truck stops, dust croppers feinting low over the 5 like something out of Hitchcock. Skirting the edge of San Jose, they pushed north through Sacramento and kept on toward Redding. *That region of Northern California's looking interesting*, Hank had observed, and Mike had a feeling that whatever Shep was steering him toward was going to make it more interesting yet. The Cascades loomed into view, Lassen Peak rising to the east, Mount Shasta dead ahead, both summits dusted with snow.

Around the nine-hour mark, Shep said, 'Exit here.' Mike pulled off in Red Bluff and followed Shep's instructions through the old-fashioned downtown. 'Left. Right. Your *other* right. Left. Park here.'

Before them a city registrar's office occupied a single-story adobe building. The L-shaped parking lot was long and narrow, hemmed in by concrete-block walls protecting apartment complexes on either side. It had exits on both ends, which could prove useful depending on what was going to go down. Mike cocked an eyebrow, and Shep said, 'Registrar's a good place for a con woman to work. Bogus building permits, fake deeds, notary stamps floating around.'

The Saab's idle was so smooth the car might have been turned off. From the passenger seat, Shep had the better view of the glass front door. The .357 pressed coolly against the small of Mike's back. They sat. And they waited – 5:03 P.M. . . . . 5:07 . . .

Shep pointed. Sure enough, the woman Mike knew as Dana Riverton emerged. She'd kept the same bland look she'd used when she'd met Mike at the café – librarian's spectacles, conservative blouse, brown hair in no discernible cut. He wondered if she powdered over the jailhouse tattoo on her thumb webbing every morning before reporting to work.

When Mike climbed out, Shep waited behind by some implicit understanding. The air felt cool against Mike's cropped scalp. He caught her a few steps from the door.

'Kiki Dupleshney?'

She turned quickly. A half-second delay while she placed him. A few colleagues scooted past, and she shot them a nervous smile even while her eyes blazed with anger. 'You must have me confused with someone else.' The others passed out of earshot, and she fumbled a cigarette from her purse and lit up. 'The fuck you want?'

'Who hired you?'

She grinned sweetly and blew smoke in Mike's face, her filter sporting a pink dimple of lipstick. She enunciated clearly, accustomed to talking to idiots. 'I don't know what you're talking about.'

'Why do they want to kill me and my daughter?'

'Gee. Dunno.'

'My wife is in intensive care,' Mike said. 'My daughter and I are on the run. You had a role in this.'

Kiki played an imaginary violin between thumb and forefinger. 'That's how the Darwin game goes. Sorry.'

'I'm going to find the men threatening us,' Mike said. 'I'm going to stop them. And you're going to help me.' Kiki started to walk away, but he grabbed her thick arm, hard. 'No matter what

300

I have to do, I will put my family back together. Do you understand me?'

She ripped her arm free, spilling her purse. 'I don't give a fuck about your wife. And I don't give a fuck if they *do* kill your daughter. But I'll promise you this: If you don't get out my face, I'll scream for the cops.'

She crouched and started collecting her things from the asphalt.

Mike walked back to the Saab. Set his hands on the steering wheel. He was breathing hard and could feel the heat of Shep's stare on the side of his face.

Kiki finished stuffing items in her purse and continued on her way. She aimed her keys at the far end of the lot, and headlights blinked on a maroon Sebring convertible. They watched her drop her purse in the backseat and flick her cigarette butt at a row of trash cans behind the building. She climbed in, breeze blowing her hair, and touched up her lipstick in the rearview.

Mike reached up and clicked a button, and the sunroof whirred open.

'Get out,' he said.

Shep said, 'What?'

'You heard me.'

Shep shrugged and stepped out.

Mike dropped the pedal to the floor, leaving two streaks of rubber scorched into the asphalt. The Saab fishtailed but held course, and Kiki was reversing out of her space when she looked up and shrieked. The Saab hit her at a straight perpendicular, T-boning the Sebring and driving it into the retaining wall. The Saab's air bag deployed with a sound like an upside-down bowl hitting water. Concrete crumbled around the convertible, chunks spilling through the open top into the backseat. Steam hissed up from the Saab's wrinkled hood.

Mike shoved aside the air bag. His door was crumpled, so he pulled himself up through the sunroof. The two vehicles were melded together. A continuous spray of wiper fluid shot in a poetic arc. Kiki lay flopped onto the steering wheel, the horn blaring, her seat belt still unfastened. A spurt of blood darkened her upper lip.

Straddling the two cars, Mike hooked her beneath the chin, ripped her up out of her seat, and flung her onto the pavement. He leaped down, grabbed her hair, and forced her face around to his. She was stunned, lipstick smeared down her chin, stockings torn and bloody at the knees, hand cupped beneath her draining nose. He felt a revulsion for what he was doing, but it wasn't close to stopping him. He tugged the gun from his belt and pressed the muzzle to the front of her shoulder, where arm met torso.

'Look at me,' he said. 'Look at me.'

Her pupils rolled to meet his.

'Do you care now?'

'Unh?' she said loosely.

'Do you care now?'

She nodded against his grip. 'Oh, God, yes, please stop.'

A few people had spilled out of the office, and tenants were at their windows in the apartment complex beyond the collapsed wall. What surprised Mike in the face of all this was just how undaunted he felt.

He said, 'Talk.'

'I don't know who they are I swear one big guy and a cripple never gave me a number or anything just showed up like fucking ghosts found me by reputation I'm the best female operator in the area up here I got pending charges they said they could get 'em wiped for me Jesus my nose—'

'*And?*'

'So they gave me a file with info and the whole play set up already for me to contact you as the will executor they wanted me to confirm who you were they weren't sure.' She was panting, blood spraying her lips. 'I have everything in the trunk there

there go get it you can have it I swear to *God* that's all I know.' She tipped her hand, blood drooling between her fingers to the asphalt. 'I need a doctor.'

The trunk had blown open from impact, the file box inside knocked upside down, trapping the folders in place. Mike found the red-tabbed file quickly. Jotted across the front, upside down, was "*4YCH429.*"

He walked back around to Kiki. She was on all fours, coughing. He pointed at the file, 'What's this license plate?'

'I wanted something in case they screwed me so when they drove away I wrote down the plate number of the truck but that was before I learned how they are.'

'It was a truck and not a van?'

'It was a truck you can't tell 'em they'll kill me.'

Shep had vanished. A small crowd was forming by the door of the office, and a few of the younger workers were whispering, looking like they were gathering their courage. The woman in the penthouse window across the way had a phone pressed to her face; she recoiled from Mike's stare, dropping to the floor. It would only be a matter of time before the cops rolled up.

'I guess you got a lot to worry about, then.' Mike paused over her. 'If you warn them I'm coming, you will see me again.'

'Okay.' She wiped at her bloody nose. 'Okay okay okay.'

File in hand, Mike stepped across the rubble through the hole in the wall and jogged along the side of the apartment complex. When he dashed out into the street a block over, a ragged Pinto with a rusted hood wobbled up beside him right on cue. Shep was hunched in the torn front seat like an elephant on a tricycle, the grocery bag with Mike's things waiting in the passenger foot well. Mike jumped in, and they motored away from the curb.

'I didn't think these things were still on the road.'

'After what you did to that Saab,' Shep said, 'this is all you're gonna get.'

The back of Mike's forearm was streaked with blood, and,

wiping it, he realized that it wasn't his own. He could feel it drying, a tightening on his skin.

Shep glanced down. 'Don't worry,' he said. 'You'll get used to it.'

Chapter 44

'Where are we?'

Boss Man's voice through the phone was so clear he might have been sitting on the porch of the clapboard house next to William. A hot-oil smell wafted over from the wrecking yard; when William and Hanley's grandfather had built the house, he hadn't factored in wind patterns, so on some days the very walls seemed infused with burned tires and battery acid. The clear-as-hell afternoon afforded a glimpse of Mount Shasta rising in the distance, speckled with an early snow.

'Wingate's a wanted man in his own right,' William said. 'The agencies are on alert. Anywhere he pops up, they'll deliver him straight to Graham.'

Behind him the rickety screen door banged and heavy foot-steps creaked the boards. Dodge carried with him the musk of the cellar. The mass of his shoulders bowed in a broad arc, he descended the steps and arrayed something on the crackly dead weeds of the front lawn. He shuffled over toward the side of the house, clearing William's view to the tools nestled in the weeds. Ball-peen hammer. Needle-nose pliers. Metal shackles.

'Even in his position, Graham can only do so much,' Boss Man said. 'The higher-profile this thing gets, the more cover smoke he has to blow. And the more it costs.'

'Well, that's why Graham has Dodge and me, isn't it? Once he gets a bead on Wingate and the girl, we'll make them vanish from all consideration.'

Trailing a black garden hose, Dodge moved back toward the weeds. Returned to the spout to crank on the water.

'You left the smashed-up van behind,' Boss Man said. 'Can anyone trace it to you?'

'Nah,' William said. 'Old license plates, no reg, VIN placard pried off the dash. If there's one thing we know how to do, it's strip vehicles.'

'But that's *not* the one thing I hired you for.'

Splitting the stream with a thumb, Dodge sprayed down the tools.

'No, sir.' William moistened his lips with the tip of his tongue. 'Wingate'll surface soon. You can't hide with a kid. He already tried to get her on an airplane to—'

'You should've killed her when you had her in hand,' Boss Man said.

'We were gonna use her as a lure first. In the 'Raq, our boys handed out a lot of sniper rounds through the spinal cord. You get someone down, screaming loud enough, and you can draw pretty much anyone out of the—'

'Your uncle would've handled them on the spot,' Boss Man said.

William bit his lips, overgrown stubble poking this way and that. A pulse beat in his neck, fluttering the sallow skin at the side of his throat. His right arm jerked a little. 'Maybe if the old man was more strategic, he'd be teeing off in Palm Springs 'stead of slow-roasting in hell.'

But Boss Man wasn't interested in clan history. 'And the wife?' he asked. 'She's our best path to him and the girl.'

'She was transferred.'

A displeased pause. 'Where?'

'We looked high and low. Nothing. Graham's running a computer search starting in Los Angeles and circling out in a spiral, checking every—'

'She was in critical condition. She can't have moved far.

306

Every hospital within driving distance. Every one. Understand me?'

'Yes, sir.'

Apparently satisfied, Dodge coiled the hose again by the house. Leaving the tools to dry below, he sat on the porch steps beside William and resumed reading the graphic novel he'd left facedown. The pear-shaped bruise on the side of his neck was changing from blue to purple.

'Where are you?' Boss Man asked.

William said, 'We came back to base to ready a few things, but we're good to deploy as soon as the bell rings.'

'I suggest you figure out how to ring that bell yourself.'

Dial tone.

William set down the phone and spit a scattering of seeds across the porch steps. The wind picked up, sending dead leaves rattling across the uneven boards. But aside from that, silence. The house wasn't the same without Hanley.

Still buried in the comic, Dodge turned the page, a rare smile twitching his lips. William glanced over at the facing page, where a scrawny guy with Orphan Annie eyes wearing a wife-beater exclaimed, "*Knife to the Eye!*"

William thought about what he'd just told Boss Man: *You can't hide with a kid.* Using the railing, he pulled himself creakily to his feet. 'Wingate got that file. He knows we're watching everyone who's ever been connected to him. I say he parks the girl somewhere safe. Let's check State Children Services.'

Dodge blinked twice and swiveled his head back over to his graphic novel.

William said, 'No – wait. Too obvious. And he'd want her below the radar.' Behind them the leaves kept scraping along the boards of the porch.

Dodge set aside the comic, lumbered down the stairs, and began towel-drying his tools with the oversize hankie he kept stuffed in a pocket. His attention was loving, absolute.

A scud of wispy clouds had materialized from nowhere to confer a halo on Mount Shasta's glorious peak. 'He's a foster kid himself,' William said. 'He'll go back to his roots.' He spit into the weeds and turned for the door. 'Let's start checkin' foster homes.'

Chapter 45

They'd put only a few miles between the car and the parking lot where Mike had left Kiki Dupleshney, but already his thoughts had migrated back to that look on Kat's face when he'd left her on the bench. Guilt came alive as an itch under his skin.

You're not a husband. You're not a father. You're a man with a task.

The red-tabbed file sat across his knees, "*4YCH429*" staring up at him.

'How do we run this plate number?' he asked.

They throttled along, Shep looking ridiculous crammed behind the Pinto's wheel. 'Hank Danville. License plates are a PI's bread and butter.'

'They're watching him. Tapped lines.'

'Call his cell. He'll give you a pay-phone number.'

Mike dialed. When Hank picked up, Mike said, 'Hey.'

'Maurice,' Hank said. 'You're looking for that shop number, yeah?' He rattled off ten digits. 'I hear they open in five minutes.'

Mike pocketed the phone. The file in his lap seemed to have taken on a weight commensurate with its potential significance. The air gusting from the vents smelled of hair spray. Cars flashed by. He stared down.

Shep said, 'Open it already. The thing won't bite.'

Mike complied. The glossy photo on top, the one Dana/Kiki had revealed to him at the café, captured his childhood house. And there were a number more beneath, taken from various angles. Some compulsion made him turn one over, as if checking the potter's stamp on a china plate. Taped to the white rectangle was a cutout of an undated real-estate listing, the newsprint brittle and faded but still legible enough for him to read the address.

Chico.

He'd come from the town of Chico.

Which was an overnight drive – about seven hours in the family station wagon – to the Los Angeles playground he'd been left at as a four-year-old. He thought about waking up in his clothes, not his pajamas.

Shep looked over at him inquisitively.

Digging in the glove box, Mike found a map buried beneath a raft of cassette tapes and fought it open across the dash. 'The house I grew up in. It's about fifty miles from here.'

'Which way?'

'Southeast. On the 99.'

Shep wheeled sharply left, Mike nearly banging his head against the window. When he looked up, he saw the freeway sign fly past on the ramp entrance. Within the hour he'd be standing on the front porch of his childhood home. It didn't seem possible.

A throb at his temples reminded him that he'd stopped breathing. He caught a glimpse of himself in the sun visor's mirror. His different-colored eyes – one brown, one amber – peered back from a face that had gone pale. A few deep inhales brought back a bit of color to his cheeks.

He found a red pen in the glove box and circled the towns that had popped up in name since Dodge and William had fastened onto his trail. Sacramento, home to Rick Graham's State Terrorism Threat Assessment Center. Redding, William Burrell's last-known address. Red Bluff, Kiki Dupleshney's stomping grounds. Chico, former home of Mike's parents. All within a 150-mile span of Northern California.

Shep kept driving and kept silent, and Mike loved him for it.

He pushed aside the map and flipped deeper into the file. That old Polaroid of his father, the sun-faded face so much like his own. And endless data on Mike and his friends and acquaintances, much of the same information he'd found in the folder he'd taken from the smashed-up van.

The bottom page featured a single typed note. No letterhead, no signature, no watermark.

Parent names: John and Danielle Trenley. Your cover: Dana Gage, the grown daughter of the Trenleys' former next-door neighbors. You are the Trenleys' will executor. You have significant assets to assign but can do so only once you've corroborated Michael Wingate's heritage and family history. If he is our target, he should prove emotional and unpredictable on the subject of his parents. He was abandoned by them at the age of four.

Do not try to contact us.

We will find you.

Mike was gripping the page too tightly, his thumb leaving an indentation. He relaxed his hand and read the note a second time.

The language seemed too crisp to have been written by William or Dodge. Mike pegged it for a document generated by Rick Graham out of his impressively titled state agency. As for "Trenley", Hank had turned up nothing for a John or a Danielle by that name. Had Graham given Kiki a fake name to foil any prospective searches?

Shep had said something.

Mike said, 'What?'

'You were supposed to ring Danville ten minutes ago.'

Mike placed the call. Hank answered in the midst of a coughing fit.

'You okay?' Mike asked.

'Pain meds have me shitting like a rabbit, but at least I'm not a terrorist on the lam.'

Mike gave him the broad strokes. He glossed over leaving Kat behind, trying to make it a fact like all the others. Nonetheless Hank offered a quiet, 'Jesus.'

'They still have an eye on you?' Mike asked.

'I checked the office phone yesterday, and it showed an extra voltage draw on the line. They probably have something up at the junction box. Which is noteworthy.'

'Why?' A highway-patrol car passed, going in the opposite direction, and Mike twisted to watch until it faded from sight.

'Because if it was legit,' Hank was saying, 'they'd tap the line from the phone company's switch or use electronic intercept, both of which are undetectable. So Graham's doing this without a warrant. If you can produce some evidence – I mean *concrete* evidence of corruption in his investigation of you, or his link to William and Dodge—'

'We're working on it. And along those lines, we got the plate number of the truck Dodge and William drove when they hired Kiki Dupleshney. Can you run it for me?'

'Course. I'll see if I can access the databases through a colleague's log-in so it won't be traceable. Plate number?'

Mike read it off.

Hank said, 'What's your callback number? Don't worry, I'll use a pay phone.'

Mike gave it to Hank, who recited it back twice, committing it to memory.

'Listen, Mike, with the medical costs and making my . . . arrangements, I'm running a bit low. And you can't exactly mail me a check.'

'Hank, I'm sorry.' Mike tapped his head in reproach. 'I have cash. Plenty. I've just been totally—'

'Of course. Don't worry.'

Mike opened the bag at his feet and surveyed the money. 'Is twenty grand enough?'

'Too much.'

'Not even close,' Mike said.

'I was thinking of slipping out of town away from watchful eyes anyway. And . . . well, all roads lead north, don't they?'

The windshield threw back the road guide's reflection, the red circles Mike had drawn standing out like a cluster of hives. He couldn't deny that he sensed it, too, a narrowing, as if the last thirty-one years were a funnel to this one square inch of map. 'Yeah,' he said. 'I guess they do.'

'I'll head your way, and we can settle up in person. Hell, maybe I can even be of service.' Hank gave a wry chuckle. 'A last hurrah. I'll call you when I've sourced that license plate. I have to figure out how to go about it covertly, so it could take a little time.'

A sign flew past. CHICO – 47 MILES.

'It's fine,' Mike said. 'I'm gonna need the time.'

The walkway rolled out before Mike like a concrete arrow leading to the front door. Standing at the curb, hands shoved in his pockets, cool wind biting at his ankles, his neck, he confronted the house.

His house.

Much had changed, but he recognized the porch and the asphalt roof shingles and the fanlike spread of the driveway. The louvered shutters, he realized, he'd inadvertently duplicated on the dream homes of Green Valley. The memory of this place pulled up through the murk, an anchor rising, dredging with it more details from the depths. He knew that the gnarled pine in the side yard smelled like Christmas when it rained, that the back patio dipped on the left side, that the gutter over the window there on the east corner used to drip patterns onto his pane. He recalled the large volcanic rocks that had once dotted the front walk, how he'd tried to tip one over once to catch a lizard, and

313

when he'd held up his palms afterward, they were covered with blood. His mother in the kitchen brandishing a magazine at a circling blowfly – *Let's wave him out of here, honey. This little guy's a bad omen.* He half expected to see his father sitting on the front step, sleeves cuffed, smoking a flaking cigar. If he was alive, what would he look like now?

Inside, a young family was pulled up to a kitchen table, the scene glowing out at the dark street like something festive. Mike could see that there were no more yellow tiles *sage incense* and the mother clearing the dinner plates was smiling and joking *her skin, tan even in winter, scented faintly of cinnamon.* A minivan was parked in the driveway *You like our new station wagon, champ? They have wood paneling, see, but it's not real wood. Run your fingers there* and he turned his face into the teeth of the breeze, eyes drifting across the Gages' house *mint trim Doberman bit the Sears repairman* and taking in the old lady rocking on the porch swing, patient and lined like time itself. He looked down the length of the planned-community street to a fenced lake – yes, there *was* a lake *he slips on a mossy rock and his father's hand clamps down on his shoulder, firm and steady, saving him from a wet spill* and it carried the odor of algae, giving the breeze its wet weight. The other way a hill fringed with dense stands of trees was crested by a yellow sign, rusted and battered with age. The sign proclaimed DEER X-ING, that broad black X hooking something buried in Mike's thoughts and reeling it squirming to the deck *Hey, Joe, you know any street names start with the letter X? How 'bout Fuckin' Xanadu?*

Shep was at his side, long forgotten. He spit in the gutter and kicked at the curb. Mike's legs tingled. How long had he been standing here?

The old lady on the Gages' porch set aside her knitting and rose, grimacing into the effort of it. Mike hurried over. 'Ma'am, excuse me. I'm sorry to bother you. Have you lived here long?'

The woman paused, bunch-mouthed and wizened, at the

screen door. Despite the prominent veins, her hands looked young and strong, and the crocheted shawl thrown across her shoulders gave off the pleasing aroma of coffee and cigarette smoke. 'What's long enough for you?'

'So you're Mrs?'

'Geraldine Gage.'

His throat clicked dryly when he swallowed. 'I'm a reporter looking into—'

She let go of the screen, which snapped closed, and gestured next door. 'Saw you looking there. Been years since anyone came asking.'

'About the incident?' Mike asked carefully.

'Is that what they're calling it?'

'How would you describe it?'

'More like a *non*-incident. An entire family just up and vanishes one day? Not a trace left behind? After a while the bank quietly reclaimed the house, and then there was a new family in there, and then another. Life goes on. I suppose it has to.'

The porch swing jagged in the wind, creaking softly on its chains.

'Do you think . . . ? Did they seem the types to get tangled up in trouble?'

'You mean, did they bring it on themselves?' A dry chuckle. 'If life's taught me anything, it's that you never know anything. But no, they sure as hell didn't act like folks who played with fire. If they had any enemies, you'd never know it. That's what was so shocking about the whole thing. They just didn't seem the type that something like this would happen to.' She shook her head, annoyed at herself. 'Whatever *that* means.'

'What was my—' He caught himself. Cleared his throat. 'What was their last name?'

'Shouldn't you know that,' she asked, 'if you're writing an article?'

'I'm doing a retrospective on a few cases like this. I sometimes get them mixed up.'

'Their name was Trainor,' she said. 'With an *o*.'

Trainor.

He'd said it out loud, he realized, just to taste it in his mouth.

John and Danielle Trainor.

Michael Trainor.

After all these years, the childhood interrogations, the X-rays and dental assessments to determine his age, after the private-investigator bills, the database searches, the cemetery walks, after all that and more, at last: a name.

His.

The fake name given Kiki, "Trenley", was kept close enough to the real one that it might ring a bell. But the real name was just as unfamiliar, and Mike was crestfallen over his inability to make it resonate.

Geraldine Gage had turned again to tug open the screen door.

'What were they like?' he blurted.

She paused, one slippered foot on the threshold. 'Normal-type folks, like I said. Quite in love – they'd hold hands on walks, like honeymooners. We were fond of them. She was graceful, a little hippie-ish, and . . . I guess these days you'd say *spunky*. Long, beautiful black hair. And he was a nice fella. Used to lend Glen a hand with . . . you know, moving a couch, holding a ladder. A handsome guy. Looked a bit like . . . a bit like *you*, if memory serves.' Her gaze intensified. 'They had a boy.'

Mike nodded, since he didn't trust his voice.

'He'd be about your age now,' she observed. 'Michael, was it?'

'I think that's right.'

The wind brushed a leafy branch musically across the slats of the porch.

'Look,' she said, 'I really must be going.'

His voice sounded like it belonged to someone else. 'And him?' he asked. 'What about the boy?' His face burned. 'Did they seem close to him? I mean, no matter what happened, that's quite a thing to uproot a kid like that.'

She mused on this a moment, her back slightly curved, shoulders hunched into the breeze. She seemed to sense what was at stake, or maybe he was only imagining it.

'He was well loved,' she said.

The screen clapped shut behind her.

He stood a few moments, listening to the crickets.

Shep was waiting back in the car. Mike paused by the passenger door, looking across at his old house, pausing at the sight. The little girl stood on a stool before her bathroom sink, brushing out her hair before bedtime. Her motions were uncoordinated, the brush snagging on knots. She couldn't have been six.

The phone vibrated in his pocket, though it took a few bursts to break his trance.

'License plate traces to a GMC Sierra 1500 pickup.' Hank's voice was excited, driving. 'It's corporate-owned, registered to Deer Creek Casino.'

'A *casino*?' Mike repeated.

Hank said, 'And guess where it is?'

'Where?'

'You're in Chico, yeah? Look northeast. See that mountain?'

'It's dark.'

'Right. Well, it's Mount Lassen. The casino's there on the slopes. I'm sure you'll see billboards.'

'My family name,' Mike said, 'is Trainor.'

A long silence. In the house the girl had managed to work out most of the tangles. Her honey-blond hair looked soft and fluffy. When she clicked off the bathroom lights, she paused, noticing him standing there by the idling car at the curb.

Hank said, 'Trainor with an *o*?'

'That's right.'

'I'm getting on the road while the getting's good. But I'll see what I can find.'

The little girl raised her hand in silent greeting. Mike waved back. 'Me, too.'

Chapter 46

Deer Creek unfolded roadside, darting away and returning at flirtatious intervals, a freestone stream tumbling past lava shelves. Swaths of landscape bled by, the Pinto's weak headlights barely able to keep pace with the shifting topography. First splotches of orchard with sprinkler streams arcing across walnut and olive trees like tinsel. Then came the rolling foothills, blue oaks staking down vast tracts of golden weed. Finally Mount Lassen closed in on them, dense sagebrush crowding the hubcaps, fir and pine shoving up from red-clay dirt, rocky plateaus encroaching overhead. The night breeze through Mike's window cleared his lungs, his thoughts.

Signage was plentiful and traffic thick as they neared the Deer Creek Casino. At last the mall-like building floated into view, sprawled across a flat plane stamped into the terrain. The parking lot bustled, cars waiting on spots, community-center buses unloading seniors, workers on break gathering at the exits, staking out cell-phone reception. One van, labeled NEW BEGINNINGS ACTIVE LIVING CENTER and featuring a logo of a winking smiley-face sun, disgorged one wheelchaired patron after another on its mechanical lift. A few lonely picketers circled out front, smoking cigarettes, ignored by and ignoring the trickle of gamblers. There were no Vegas lights, no showgirl glitter; it might have been a Walmart.

Shep trawled the lot. To the side, next to the plentiful handicapped parking, was the section for employee vehicles, each space labeled by name and title. Shep parked in the CFO's spot, and they climbed out and walked the rear bumpers. Nearly every vehicle sported law-enforcement plate frames and multiple shiny stickers – CHP Foundation, Sheriff's Booster Club, Friends of Sacramento PD.

Mike would have plunked down money on one of the green felt tables inside that casino management had cultivated a close ally at the State Terrorism Threat Assessment Center as well.

He stopped before a black Sierra pickup and pointed at the license plate sandwiched between a D.A.R.E. bumper sticker and a fire-department reflective decal. The number matched the one Kiki Dupleshney had written down; here was the truck William and Dodge had driven to hire her.

Running a finger along the paint, Mike circled the pickup. A parking pass on a lanyard dangled from the rearview mirror. From a square passport-size photo stared William, his features softened by an affable grin. Model employee.

Mike said, 'We should—'

But Shep was already into the truck, tapping a pick set back into his breast pocket.

Mike crouched to read the stenciling on the bumper block – WILLIAM BURRELL, SECURITY TECHNICIAN. Shep rifled through the glove box, came up with a paycheck stub. He angled it at Mike, his thumb underscoring the job title Mike had just read off the concrete. A chilling euphemism for what William really did.

Mike glanced at the slip. 'No taxes taken out. Freelance makes for a tougher paper trail. That's why Hank couldn't find him.'

The faint chime of a jackpot carried across the parking lot, followed by excited squeals. 'So this here's the end of the trail,' Shep said. 'The place paying the killers who are coming after you and your family.'

Not an individual, Mike thought, *but a goddamned casino.*

'Only question left,' Shep continued, 'is *why?*'

The yellow and turquoise letters announcing the casino stirred something in Mike's gut, but he couldn't put a name to it. One of the picketers mistook his gaze and angled the sign so he could get a better read – WHY ARE <u>WE</u> PAYING TAX SO <u>CASINOS</u> CAN RELAX? Mike lifted a hand in acknowledgment – *Thanks, got it* – then tilted his head toward the entrance. 'Should we go have a look around?'

'I can't,' Shep said, poking around in the glove box. 'Casinos got me dead to rights with their facial-recognition software.'

'They run that stuff?'

'Course. They're looking for advantage players, card cheats, fast feeders, armed robbers' – an artful pause – 'safecrackers.' Shep came up from the glove box with a John Deere cap and a bag half full of sunflower seeds. 'But *you.*' He slung the baseball hat onto Mike's head and poured him a handful of sunflower seeds. 'You're not in the casino databases. Just in case they're plugged into the law-enforcement watch lists, though, chew up these seeds, store 'em in your lips and cheeks. Just enough to change the shape of your face so the software won't map it right.'

Chewing food intended for William's mouth left Mike a touch queasy. He worked a bit of sunflower meal beneath his lower lip like tobacco dip. He finished, his stare pulling across to the casino. They were in there.

'In case William and Dodge get me, I should tell you where Kat is.'

'No,' Shep said.

'No?'

'I don't want to know,' Shep said. 'There's just as good a chance they'll catch me out here. Every man has his breaking point.'

'And mine's higher than yours?' Mike asked.

Shep said, 'I'm not her father.'

Mike nodded once and started for the building.

Popping lights and chiming slots, stale smoke and bracing air-conditioning, salty traces of the sunflower-seed mush tucked into Mike's lips and cheeks – the whole adrenalized experience took on a disorienting hyperreality. Elderly folks jockeyed for position at the five-dollar tables. Wheelchair footrests clanked into overburdened standing ashtrays. Cocktail waitresses wore Indian-print shifts with dagger thigh slits. They circled with trays of vodka and Red Bull, Jack and Coke, bestowing cheer like debauched Disney Pocahontases. On the walls, oil paintings of soaring eagles.

A drop team shoved around a wheeled metal cart, collecting jingling cash cans from slot machines and lining them in the flat metal bed like mini trash barrels. It struck Mike that the drop-team workers were the only personnel not wardrobed by Sergio Leone. In their black slacks and white polos with Deer Creek logos on the breasts, they were meant to blend in so as not to remind you that the whole spectacle and experience was fueled by your cash, which was being conveyed back to the vault by the cartload.

The walkways blazing through the organized chaos had virile names like Strong Buck Path and Tomahawk Trail, but even these couldn't match wits with the blinking destination signs – FIRE-WATER! WAMPUM! RAINMAKER ROOM! The Pow-Wow Palace welcomed Lockheed Retired and Friends of Yuba City Jazz; a glistening sign on an easel showed off a prime-rib special for $2.95; and Earth, Wind & Fire were playing the Grand Teepee next month.

An obese man motored by, overflowing his mobility scooter, his wife ambling beside him fingering a gift-shop dream catcher. The man's gaze hooked on a bartender wearing a chieftain head-dress serving up Woo Woos to a bachelorette party.

'Christ our Lord,' he boomed, 'don't this bug the Indians?'

'Indians,' she sniggered, 'I ain't seen a worker yet wasn't a Mexican.'

Keeping a lookout for William or Dodge, Mike nearly tripped over an abandoned medical walker with tennis balls impaled on its back legs. Given his fatigue, the whole spectacle put him on edge. He had no idea what he was looking for.

Backing to a wall, he tugged the brim of the cap low over his eyes. A casino seemed a great place to disappear, but he was all too cognizant of the black domes in the elevated ceilings hiding the security cameras. His elbow knocked a glass pane, giving off a sharp rattle, and he turned to see Rick Graham's face staring out at him from a photograph inside a wall exhibit.

His breath quickening, he confronted that face, here, on display.

Graham had an arm flung wide to indicate a row of computers, showing them off like a game-show prize. That dense salt-and-pepper hair, the pucker at the lips, his pit-bull build. Mike pictured him at their front door, Annabel bleeding out on the floor at Mike's back. *Dispatch sent a request. I was the closest responder.* Bitterly, he remembered the blast of relief he'd felt at Graham's appearance – help, at last.

The *Sacramento Bee* article accompanying Graham's photo spelled out how Deer Creek Casino had donated facial-recognition software and multiple computers to the antiterrorism agency. Graham, a resident of Granite Bay, California, was praised as a local hero.

Dazed, Mike glanced up to the top of the display, where a cheery header proclaimed, DEER CREEK IN THE COMMUNITY!

He stepped back, overwhelmed by the newspaper articles wallpapering the bulletin board inside. POLICEMAN'S WIDOW FUND HITS JACKPOT WITH CASINO DONATION, TRIBE BACKS MEGAN'S LAW AGAINST SEX OFFENDERS, DEER CREEK PROVIDES STATE WITH SIX NEW DIGITAL FREEWAY BILLBOARDS FOR AMBER ALERTS. There were motorcycle helmets for CHP and gun lockers for sheriff's stations. The casino had donated new SWAT tactical vests for Sacramento PD. And for SFPD. And LAPD. An 8 by10 showed a man wearing an expensive suit and a cowboy hat, shaking hands with the governor himself. The governor had one armed draped across the man's shoulders and was smiling wide for the cameras just as Mike had. In Sharpie, across the photo – "*To Deer Creek Casino, friends of mine, friends of California*" – and then the intensive signature.

Even from the start, law enforcement had closed ranks against Mike and his family. Hank's words played in his head: *They will suspect who they're supposed to suspect and alert who they're supposed to alert.*

Deer Creek Casino had the connections and the pull to unleash hell on Mike's family. But what was the motive?

Why did these people want to kill him and his daughter?

The notion was like a snake, coiled deep around his brain stem. It twisted, and he felt it again down his spine.

A cocktail waitress emerged from an unmarked door to his side, revealing a glimpse of hall stretching back to offices. Her tray now empty.

'Excuse me. Where can I find out more about the tribe?' He wondered if he was standing close enough that she would notice the sunflower seeds tucked into his lips.

She smiled from beneath her Indian-princess headband, the side feather nodding over her red curls. Her skin was pale and freckled; she might have been Irish. 'At the Tribal Shrine there off the stairwell landing.'

Mike drifted dreamlike up the stairs, through an archway labeled THE STORY OF THE DEER CREEK TRIBE and into what appeared to be a gauche history exhibit. The lights were dimmed reverently, faded photographs and museum-like captions set into black velvet fabric panels. A few tourists made their way around grudgingly, as if fulfilling some educational requirement. Through hidden speakers issued crackly chanting, sounds Mike associated with sweat lodges and Sunday-morning cartoons. The room, like the rest of the casino, recalled nothing so much as a Disneyland attraction.

A copper-faced Indian greeted comers from a mounted television. A computer-generated simulation, he seemed the archetypal Native American – high cheekbones, generous mouth, formidable nose, erect bearing. The stoic, lined face glowed with earth-baked wisdom. Mike found himself staring at the braided blue-black hair with disbelief and horrified recognition. All those fragments and inklings slid into shocking alignment.

'*Welcome, friends. Follow the trail and I shall tell you the tale of the Deer Creek Tribe.*'

Mike trudged along, his head thick and soupy, as if he were emerging from general anesthesia. Pinned photos and clippings related the promised tale.

'*The Deer Creek people,*' the Indian intoned from a new flat-screen, not missing a beat, '*have been in Northern California for nearly four thousand years.*' As the stilted voice continued, Mike did his best to focus on the exhibit pieces. Various sketches showed tribesmen hunting with bows and arrows, setting snares, using harpoons and fishing nets. The women were depicted gathering and grinding acorns and weaving their hair into figure-eight loops at their napes.

Mike's feet moved at a normal pace, but his blood had quickened, surging in his veins.

The next section covered the tribal member's beliefs. Woodpeckers symbolized wealth and good luck. Sleeping with one's face exposed to the moon was thought to be unwholesome. '*And a blowfly in the thatch house,*' the virtual Indian informed, '*meant evil was stalking the family.*'

A tingle crawled along Mike's skin.

A waft of tribal incense from the back reached his nostrils. Sage. The smell of his childhood.

His legs had locked up, but the digitized tour guide continued. '*At their peak, these proud Hokan-speaking people, distant relatives to the Yana tribe, numbered nearly two thousand. But then came the white man. Many of the Indians in this region were relocated in forced marches. Measles, typhoid, smallpox, tuberculoses, and dysentery thinned the ranks of those who remained. The 1860s saw endless*

324

raids and counterraids between Native Americans and white settlers, and many tribes were exterminated. But fortunately, a remnant group of the Deer Creek Tribe survived into the next century.'

More sketches – Indians mourning, their hair shorn, heads covered with pitch. The burning of the dead. Woeful faces. Mike willed the Indian to drop the cigar-store shtick and speak at a normal clip, but there was no speeding up animation. *'They were granted their own humble reservation, the government holding in trust for them title to two thousand acres. Then came the modern scourges. Suicide. Diabetes. Alcoholism. Over the decades the land was broken up and parceled out until precious little remained. By the 1950s many assumed that the Deer Creek Tribe was no more.'*

Dusty maps and laminated government treaties organized neatly in binders composed a history section. Agreements between sovereign Indian nations and the United States were public domain, and Deer Creek's were on proud display here. It took no time for Mike to zero in on a trust agreement buried inside a compact between Deer Creek Tribal Enterprises, Inc., and the federal government. The casino – and the attendant corporation – were being held in trust, just as what remained of the reservation was held in trust by the U.S. government.

He skimmed, legal phrases jumping out at him, confirming what he'd already grasped. Casino management had been appointed as trustee *'with all attendant general powers'* concerning the land and assets. Management would remain in charge as long as there was *'no member of the tribe able and willing'* to serve. Any tribe members who materialized would become the sole trustees and would enjoy *'full power and discretionary authority'* over the entire business.

Mike's mouth was bitter and dry with sunflower-seed residue.

With shaking hands he flipped furiously back a few pages to the definition of terms. *'"Tribe Member" shall mean a person, as defined in the tribal bylaws, with a combined minimum of one-eighth (1/8) Deer Creek Tribe blood quantum.'*

Mike's insides had gone cold.

The robo-Indian had been speaking for some time, Mike realized, his words repeating on a loop. '*One cold April morning in 1977, a hiker discovered a woman living quietly in a lean-to cabin. Her name was Sue Windbird. She was the last of the Deer Creek people.*'

Nineteen seventy-seven – just a few years before Mike was abandoned at that playground. His head abuzz with anticipation, he stepped around a small partition and beheld a photograph portrait of an ancient Native American woman. His breath left him.

Her hands curled like claws, resting on the woolen blanket drawn across her knees. Her sun-weathered face retained an impish liveliness. Teeth better than one would have thought. But it was her eyes that left Mike clutching for air.

One brown. The other amber.

Chapter 47

Mike's legs felt like stilts as he stepped out of the shrine onto the landing, the crisp air-conditioning welcome on the heat of his face. He leaned against the wall to catch his breath. When he mopped at his brow, his sleeve came away damp.

His mind remained fastened on that image of Sue Windbird. A brass plaque beneath her portrait had given her name, a question mark for a birthday, and the date of her death – August 10, 1982.

Yet Sue Windbird, clearly, wasn't the last of her people.

Though she was decades gone, those mismatched eyes might as well have been an arrow pointing from her through him to Kat. What had William called them? *Cat eyes.*

Mike couldn't remember if his mother, too, had heterochromia, but he could picture distinctly the view up at her when she bathed him as a child, her black-brown hair draped along one tan arm. The pronounced cheekbones. That golden brown skin, dark even in winter. A buried lineage to a culture he knew no more about than he did the Mayans or the Pennsylvania Dutch. But there it was, a birthright running through his veins. And Kat's.

The ramifications swirled around him, leaving him dizzy. As long as there were no Deer Creek tribal members living, casino management ran the show and kept all profit.

These people were willing to kill generations of a family to ensure that the tribe stayed extinct.

A few college kids bustled by, wisecracking and slinging cocktails, jarring Mike from his thoughts. He fought to reacclimate himself to his surroundings. Gripping the handrail, he descended into the confusion of the casino floor. Blinking lights and sweaty faces seemed to assail him, but he kept to the edge of the room, putting one foot in front of the other, his gaze trained on the exit.

Which is why he didn't see the shoulder until his face collided with it. Smooth calfskin leather jacket, black with a racing-red Ducati appliqué logo.

A hand pressed him away. 'Watch where you're going.'

From a distance the man would have looked much younger, but Mike was right up on top of him, so he could see the smoothness of the face lift and the too-black dyed hair – he had to be in his mid-sixties. He had perfect white teeth and the relaxed posture of a man secure of his place in the world. He'd given Mike no more than a cursory glance; he was focused on the high-stakes blackjack table across the way.

As were William and Dodge, standing just behind him.

Mike's legs tensed, locking up, the muscle cramping. He tilted his head, hiding his face beneath the cap's brim, and managed to turn away. The three men were clustered by the door leading back to the offices – the same door the cocktail waitress had emerged from earlier.

As Mike walked away, he heard the man in the leather jacket say, 'Results, boys. Soon.'

And William's raspy voice, like a fingernail down Mike's spine, 'We'll have 'em, Boss Man.'

Still riled, Mike hurried through the employee parking lot, Shep following him at a pace.

'As in customer-service Indian or many-moons Indian?' Shep asked.

Mike spit, the sunflower-seed chaw hitting the asphalt with a *wap*. 'Many moons.'

'Like peace-pipe, Manhattan-for-a-handful-of-beads Indian?'

'Yes, Shep. Like that.'

'*You?*'

There, in the cherry front spot, was a Ducati to match the man's riding jacket. Sleek and muscular, the motorcycle looked part fighter jet, part armored action figure. Mike crouched and read the lettering stenciled onto the bumper block. BRIAN MCAVOY, CEO.

Brian McAvoy.

Boss Man.

'Where to next, Big Chief Squatting Cow?' Shep said.

'Rick Graham.' Mike thought of the newspaper article inside describing the local hero from Granite Bay. 'Let's see if our boy's listed.'

Chapter 48

The white bedding, in the silver moonglow thrown through the skylight, looked like a pan of frosting. The giant cabin-style house was done to a turn – gable windows, antler chandeliers, steep-pitch roof for more headroom here, on the second floor. The place was way too pricey for a cop's salary, even if that cop was a state-level counterterrorist czar. The gated neighborhood, half an hour north of Sacramento, seemed more the domain of law-firm partners and vineyard owners.

A cold breeze blew through the open door letting out onto the unlit balcony. It riffled Rick Graham's salt-and-pepper hair against the pillow, and then he gave off a sleepy grumble, his hand thumping around the nightstand for the lamp switch. It clicked, and he released a yelp.

Mike sat bedside in a rustic armchair, the .357 resting casually in his lap, the barrel pointing at Graham's upper torso. Black leather gloves turned his hands invisible in the darkness.

'Do you have any idea whose house—' Recognition struck. Graham shoved himself up against the headboard. He was wearing flannel pajamas, perhaps in a nod to the decor, the top unbuttoned to reveal a swath of gray chest hair. 'Lemme guess – you came back to fuck up my tires again.'

Mike tightened his grip ever so slightly on the revolver.

'How'd you get past the gate?' Graham's hand continued a slow drift toward the pillow next to him. 'This house has heavy security. This is all being recorded.'

Mike pointed at the camera mounted above the open door, angled at them both. 'Digital save to the hard drive on the Dell in your study.'

Graham's Adam's apple jerked.

Mike said, 'Your affiliation with Deer Creek seems to go back a ways.'

Graham made a quick move with his hand and came up with a .38 Special. It was aimed at Mike's head before Mike's gun could leave his thigh.

Graham's lips stretched to one side, a half smile, and his thumb drew back the hammer.

Mike tipped his head toward Graham's pajama top. 'Your pocket.'

Holding the revolver steady, Graham moved his other hand across and tugged at the loose breast pocket. A metallic rattle. One of the brass-cased rounds tipped out onto the sheets, and Graham stared down at it helplessly.

Mike put a heel up on the edge of his chair, hefted the gun across his raised knee.

Graham swallowed again and lowered his hand, the unloaded weapon disappearing into the sheets. 'If I tell you everything,' he said, 'you won't kill me?'

Mike allowed a little nod.

'Give me your word.'

'You have my word.'

This seemed to relax Graham a degree or two. 'If you know someone's profile, you know as much about him as possible. I can read people from the data droppings they leave behind. And yours say you're not a liar.'

Mike lifted the gun a little, Graham's eyes widening to track its movement. 'Not generally,' Mike said.

'What do you want to know?'

'Your affiliation with Deer Creek.'

Graham moistened his lips. 'Me and Brian McAvoy go back to

the beginning. He was a fresh-faced kid out of UNLV's hotel-administration program. Family money, smarts to spare, and looking to use both. I was a young gun at Sac PD looking for advancement. We found each other useful. McAvoy funded an exploratory committee looking at expanding gaming outside of Vegas.'

'He stumbled upon Sue Windbird.'

'He stumbled upon a living, breathing lottery ticket. Tribes spend fortunes on legal petitions, lobbyists, lawyers, treaty experts, historians, genealogists – just to get what Sue Windbird already had.'

'Which was what?'

'You have no idea how big this is, do you?' Graham chuckled, taking his time. He was stalling, sure, but it was clear how much he relished the tale as well. 'The Bureau of Indian Affairs thought her tribe was already extinct. So in the seventies, Deer Creek slid right past all the tightened regulations for tribal acknowledg-ment. But just because a tribe has a surviving member, that doesn't mean it retains all its tribal rights. Unless' – his eyes gleamed with something like exhilaration – 'the tribal territory was never abandoned. And guess what? During all those years when Deer Creek land was carved up and parceled out, ol' Sue stayed hunkered down in her shitty cabin on a hundred acres of original designated reservation. A federally recognized tribe on sovereign land with one dying member left. Do you know what that means?'

'Tell me.'

'That land' – Graham's hands went wide – 'that hundred acres constitutes a tiny sovereign nation in the middle of California. It is not beholden to the laws of the United States of America.' He paused for effect. 'We're not just talking about having a monop-oly on gambling when it's illegal everywhere else in the state. We're talking about no zoning laws, no federal regulations. Hell, short of the right to pursue felons, the U.S. has shaky *criminal* jurisdiction on tribal lands. And the best part? Every single dime of profit is a hundred-percent tax exempt.'

Mike thought of those picketers outside the casino: WHY ARE WE PAYING TAX SO CASINOS CAN RELAX?

'And the location!' Graham continued. 'There's a planned retirement community nine miles up the road – disposable-income heaven. You're looking at seven thousand homes, one-point-eight people per lot. Those gomers might as well sign their Social Security checks directly over to Deer Creek.'

Mike thought about all the retirees he'd seen out on the casino floor, tugging on slot handles and throwing down chips.

'Indian gaming exceeds twenty-five *billion* annually – more than the combined gaming revenues of Las Vegas and Atlantic City put together.' Graham's face showed equal parts satisfaction and pride.

Mike's jaw ached with tightness. 'That buys a lot of influence.'

'You don't know the half of it. Indian casinos were the largest soft-money contributor in the last state election cycle. They practically greased the governor into office. Christ, Deer Creek *alone* bought thirty-five thousand dollars of tickets to Obama's inauguration.' Graham paused, wet his lips. 'McAvoy started with a high-stakes bingo palace. From there he moved into lotto, punch cards, and unregulated slots. It wasn't money like now – they were still fighting in the courts over slots and tables. Then the Supreme Court's *Cabazon* decision blew it wide open in '87. It was a whole new world. Remember when the California budget was overdue a few years back? The hundred-million-dollar shortfall?'

Mike nodded.

'Deer Creek made it up. As in paid for it *outright*. It's a pittance compared to what they'd pay in real taxes over the years, but they've been smart. They've made deals, spread less money around to the right people.'

'How . . . ?' There were more questions than Mike could keep

333

track of. 'How did they pull it off on the back of a ninety-year-old woman at death's door?'

'How does anyone pull anything off?' Graham said. 'With clever lawyering. McAvoy dug up some ancient clause that said that all reservation land sales were invalid unless preapproved by the federal government. Well, guess what? When the original Deer Creek reservation was parted out and sold off, no one knew to get federal approval. So McAvoy threatened to throw thousands of property sales – and titles – into question. We're talking two *thousand* acres of Northern California. We're talking lawyers calling up influential landowners and commercial real-estate holders, telling them they might not own their property anymore. Land development shut down. Banks stopped approving new mortgages. Didn't take long for McAvoy to get Sue Windbird what she deserved.'

'And he secured his own interest by promising to hold everything in trust for the tribe,' Mike said. 'So once Sue Windbird died, he'd set up his own tax-free ATM.'

'And why shouldn't it be his? You think Great-Granny was gonna up and build a billion-dollar business on her own? When we found her, she was still picking berries and shitting in an outhouse. That woman lived her last years like a *queen*. They paraded her around in ridiculous tribal costumes to ground breakings and ribbon cuttings. She drank single-barrel scotch and ate chateaubriand.'

'When did McAvoy find out she had a kid?' Mike asked.

'*Everyone* knew she had a kid. A drunk – typical full-blood Indian type. Died in a car crash in '59. What everyone *didn't* know was that he knocked up some white girl.'

'You uncovered that when you were doing the genealogy charts? To prove Windbird's stake on the land?'

Graham looked impressed. 'Yeah. We thought we were outta the woods, then *bam*! Turns out there was a little girl, born in '51. Took some searching, but we found her.'

'*We*,' Mike said. 'You keep saying *we*.'

'Like I said, I've been with Deer Creek from the gates. And even if I *didn't* dip my snout in the feed bucket, who do you think bankrolls half our agency? McAvoy's donated half the law-enforcement equipment in the state. So let's not get prudish over the distinction between public and private.'

'That's how you own all the cops.'

'I'm a director at the largest antiterrorist agency in the state. I don't *need* dirty cops. I finger "people of interest." That's what I do. If cops help me, it's not corruption. It's them doing their job, following directives. I point and they track.'

'The girl,' Mike said, steering him back on course.

'Danielle Trainor.'

'My mother.'

'That's right.'

If Mike's mother was half Indian, then Mike was a quarter.

And Kat one-eighth.

Graham ran a hand down his face, drawing his features into a droop, and for an instant Mike caught a glimmer of remorse in his eyes. But then Graham spoke hard, his words defensive, shoring up an argument it seemed he'd been making to himself for years. 'With the money McAvoy had invested, he couldn't leave a loose end like your mother out there. Just like he can't have some foster-home rube show up now and get the keys to the kingdom. Or your daughter – what's she, eight? – waltz in and stake a claim to the whole goddamned operation. I mean, can you really blame him?'

Mike just looked at him.

'Okay, from your position, sure. Of course. But you have to understand, there's a lot at stake.'

'An Indian casino with no Indians.'

'That's right.' Slyness bit into Graham's voice. 'We're just holding it in trust, see.'

'For an extinct tribe,' Mike said.

'Not so extinct, are you?'

Mike leaned forward, and again Graham's eyes tracked the barrel of the .357. A bead of sweat worked its way down from Graham's left sideburn. He held up his hands. 'Listen, I can be your friend here. Proving your claim will be really tough—'

'My *claim*?'

'You won't get shit without that genealogy report. That's why McAvoy keeps it buried in his private safe with all his valuable dirt, behind a painting of an Indian healer in his office. No one knows about the safe except him and me.' He mistook Mike's stunned expression for disbelief. 'I don't have the combination, but I could smuggle you in there and you could force him to open the safe. With that genealogy report, you could claim the casino and all its assets. I could help you navigate—'

Mike's voice was as cool and hard as the bullets he'd removed from Graham's gun. 'I don't give a shit about the casino.'

Through the open balcony door carried the buzzing of cicadas.

Graham wet his lips. 'Then why are you here?'

'You're the profiler. Look into my eyes and tell me why I'm here.'

Graham's fingers fussed in the sheets nervously. 'Your parents.'

'They're dead.' Mike couldn't bring himself to phrase it as a question.

Graham looked away sharply.

'Go on,' Mike said. 'Give me all those facts you add up to make a person. Because that's all I'm gonna get.'

Graham cleared his throat, still kneading that sheet. 'They were high-school sweethearts. Your mother was in the music society. She won Best Smile senior year – I think it was the contrast with her skin. Your father was voted Most Optimistic. He came from more money than her. Not that he was rich or anything – his dad was an accountant – but Danielle was raised by a single mother in a one-room apartment, helped her clean houses on weekends, wore thrift-store clothes. She identified

336

heavily with her father, though she knew him only fleetingly for her first eight years. She emphasized her Native American heritage, which fits with the idealization—'

'Which instrument?' Mike asked. Graham looked at him blankly, so Mike said, 'She was in the music society. Which instrument did she play?'

'Flute, I think it was.'

Mike's throat was dry, so he gestured with the gun for Graham to keep talking.

'They were married out of high school. John ran a fabric distribution center. He was fairly paid but didn't love his work. He loved baseball, western movies, and Mexican food. Danielle worked as a manager at a clothing store until he made enough, and then she stayed home. Family folks. Picnics on weekends, had a Dasher and a Ford station wagon – one of the Country Squires with the fake wood paneling?'

Mike could see the car, could smell the dust of the backseat.

Graham was still talking. 'She was a gardener, Danielle, liked her hands in the earth. She loved candles and Cat Stevens and incense.'

'Sage,' Mike said faintly. 'Sage incense.'

Graham looked suddenly agitated. 'How much do you need to know?'

'You killed them,' Mike said.

Graham looked at him steadily, though his fingers still fussed at the bedding. The bullet glinted into view, surfing the folds of the sheet. 'You gave me your word.'

Mike raised the .357 and sighted on Graham's forehead.

'Of course I didn't goddamned kill them. I'm a cop.'

'So you had people. Like Roger Drake and William Burrell?'

Graham's eyebrows rose with surprise. He said, 'Like *Lenny* Burrell.'

Mike set the revolver on the chair arm, keeping it aimed toward the bed. 'William's father?'

'Uncle.' That bullet rolled ever closer to Graham's fingers. 'He took care of your mother first—'

'*How?*'

'Shot her in the bath, I think. It was quick, painless. You were asleep in the other room, but your father chased down Lenny on his way down the hall to you. There was a tussle, and your father beat Len away. He had rage going for him, John. Somehow he'd caught wind of what was going on. That you were marked, too. He took off with you that night before Len could circle back with reinforcements. Len caught up to him a week later outside Dallas. We needed to know where your father had parked you – it wasn't like now, with databases and alerts and interagency communication around missing persons.' Graham rubbed his eyes wearily, his voice rueful. 'Len took his time with him, too. Leonard Burrell was a capable man. Your father had impressive stamina. Despite what he endured, he never gave up where you were.'

Mike looked up at the beams reinforcing the dark ceiling, his thoughts a haze. He said slowly, 'I've hated my father for thirty-one years.'

'Is it a relief?' Graham's dark-shaded face seemed almost paternal. 'That you don't have to anymore?'

Mike thought, *You have no idea.*

Graham cleared his throat. 'I'm sorry for what I did. There are nights where . . . Well, that's no concern of yours.'

Mike was aware, vaguely, of Graham's arm tensing, his fist working the sheet, the dark spot of the bullet against the pale cloth. Mike said, 'Why didn't anyone ever find them? My parents?'

'Len was expert at a lot of things. One of them was making bodies disappear. Easier that way. No murder investigation without a body. A lot less heat. No missing-persons reports in police files. People get into all sorts of trouble, pick up and go. Everyone just figured the Trainors moved on. No funeral service, no obit, much smaller splash. No one to miss them.'

'I did,' Mike said. 'I missed them.'

'What do you want me to say?'

Mike could see Graham's guilt quickening into anger, and he felt a powerful urge to lift the .357 from the arm of the chair and shoot him through the teeth. Instead he said, 'Tell me where they're buried.'

Graham turned back the sheet, his hand disappearing beneath the fold. 'I won't tell you,' he said, 'but I'll show you.'

'Okay, then.' Mike rose.

Graham swung his legs sluggishly off the mattress, but then at once his arms blurred, hands clamping together, that stray bullet seating in the wheel of the .38 with a clink. The revolver was up and aimed at Mike's face before Mike could snatch the .357 from the chair's arm.

Graham gestured for Mike to step away from the chair, and Mike complied. Graham said, 'I'm doing you a favor. If William and Dodge caught up to you . . .' He shook his head, gave a dying whistle. 'And they will. That team of them . . . well, sometimes the whole is greater than the sum of its parts. Those boys do something magical to each other. But I'm willing to settle this here. Leave Katherine wherever the hell she is. So what do you say? Is that a fair trade?' His thumb rose to the hammer.

Mike said, 'I wouldn't do that.'

Graham cocked the revolver.

A roar.

The blast of light from the balcony illuminated Shep's emotionless face behind the barrel of his gun, safely back out of the security camera's range. Before Mike could blink, the space beyond the open door had vanished into darkness again, taking Shep with it.

The side of Graham's neck went to red and white, a tailed dollop of blood rising like syrup, then falling with his body to land in a slash across his cheek and chest. The gun flash had seared into Mike's retinas, and he stood there a moment, breathing cordite, his

339

eardrums on tinny vibration. Staring down at the bone and exposed flesh, he felt nothing. He recalled a dinner not so long before with some parents of Kat's friends, roast chicken and Chilean Shiraz, how they'd all chatted and chewed and wiped their lips, resting happily in their assumption that they were decent, civilized folks.

What his father had gone through to protect him. The fear coming off him in waves that morning in the station wagon. The torn-open grief of losing a wife and leaving a son.

Just John. Just *John.*

Mike blinked himself back to life, returned to Graham's study, and downloaded the security footage from the bedroom onto a flash drive. He replayed the digital recording, double-checking that it had copied. Graham's face, clear as day: *With the money McAvoy had invested, he couldn't leave a loose end like your mother out there.*

Then Mike wiped the security files from the hard drive. As he was turning to go, he noticed a business card in the otherwise empty metal tray at the desk's edge. Brian McAvoy, CEO. On the backside he'd written *new cell* and a phone number with a Sacramento area code.

Mike stared at that number for a good long time, then withdrew his disposable phone and dialed, his gloved hand tightening around the receiver as it rang and rang.

A sleep-muffled 'Hnuh?'

Mike said, 'I got you dead to rights.'

'How'd you get this number?'

'That's the least of your concerns.'

'Who . . . who is this?'

'The guy who owns your casino. I have footage that will destroy you.'

'Footage?' A moist swallow, and then a breath blew across the receiver. 'How much do you want?'

'There is no sum.'

'Then why . . . ?'

'You're going to back off my family or I will bury you. Do you understand me?'

'Your *family*?' A whistle of breath. 'You sure you know who you're calling, son?'

Now that Mike considered it, the voice sounded a bit gruffer than he'd anticipated. 'Brian McAvoy,' Mike said.

'McAvoy?' A booming laugh, rich with age and tobacco. 'From the sound of you, you're probably the only person who hates that son of a bitch more than I do.' The man chuckled a bit more, fading out into a dead-serious silence. 'Wait a minute,' he said. 'Is this . . . is this Michael Trainor?'

A long pause. A ceiling vent blew dry and steady on the back of Mike's neck.

'Sue Windbird's great-grandson?' The voice filled with relief. 'I can't believe you're alive.'

Mike's fingers were cramping around the phone. He bent over, squeezed his forehead. 'Who is this?'

'I'm Chief Andrew Two-Hawks of the Shasta Springs Band of Miwok. I'm the CEO of a casino, but not the one you're gunning for. You and I sit need to sit down, son.'

'Why would we do that?'

'Because our interests align.'

Chapter 49

Andrew Two-Hawks had a jelly gut and a fish mouth, a goatee hiding the weak chin. He met Mike at a rear door behind his casino, his smile as broad as his handshake was firm. A leather vest overlaid a patterned button-up, the open collar looking lonely without a bolo tie to string the whole getup together. At Two-Hawks's side stood a guy nearly as wide as the doorway, a no-foolin'-around Indian with weathered skin and a crisply pressed black suit, his shaved head shaped like a blob of shaving cream swirled onto a palm. He began patting Mike down, and Mike shoved him away before his groping hands reached the .357 tucked into the back of his jeans.

Two-Hawks tugged at his face, the wrinkles pulling smooth, then nodded a dismissal at his bodyguard. 'Mike here's on *our* team.'

The bodyguard scowled and withdrew, keeping a junkyard-dog glare trained on Mike.

'Forgive Blackie there,' Two-Hawks said. 'The boy's so dumb he could fall into a tub of tits and come out sucking his thumb.' He gestured. 'Walk with me.'

The good-ol'-boy demeanor and his appearance, that of a Texas oilman who had enough money to dress better than he bothered to, caught Mike by surprise. What had he been expecting? A chieftain bearing tom-toms? They moved down a carpeted hall, the whirl and clang of the casino visible but muted by a wall of tinted soundproof windows. The place, a bit run-down, was considerably smaller than Deer Creek Casino.

Mike found himself sneaking glances over at the man.

'What?' Two-Hawks said.

Mike said, 'Nothing. You look . . .'

Two-Hawks grinned. 'As white as *you*?'

Over the phone Mike had conveyed the basics of his plight – the splintering of his family, the stakes for his wife and daughter – and Two-Hawks had listened patiently, issuing empathetic rumbles from somewhere deep in his throat.

'First thing you need to know,' Two-Hawks said now, ushering Mike around a turn, 'is that Deer Creek Tribal Enterprises, Inc., has staked a fraudulent claim to our historical tribal land.' He pointed down at the carpet. '*This* land.'

'They can do that?'

'No. But they are. And through the techniques perfected by Brian McAvoy' – a curl of upper lip at the name – 'they are in the process of turning that claim into law.'

'How?'

'Every tribe, you see, has gotta be formally recognized by the federal government to enjoy certain basic rights and protections. A couple of well-positioned politicians – backed, of course, by McAvoy – are claiming that our status was illegitimately shoved through under Jimmy Carter's appointees when the procedures were more ad hoc. They've put our tribal recognition under review, official arguments to begin early next year. If we lose, guess who's in primo position to take over our land?'

'And if McAvoy gets your land, he gets your casino.'

'Bingo.'

'That's why you've been looking for me. If another heir to Deer Creek was alive, you could use him to outflank McAvoy.'

'With you we have a chance to cut the man off at the knees.' A flicker of disgust crossed the shiny dark eyes. 'He and I are mortal enemies. I have quite a few these days. Does that make you nervous?'

Mike said, 'I don't trust anyone who doesn't have enemies.'

A smile rippled that close-shaved goatee. 'Then you'll *love* me.'

They stepped into a well-appointed office, Two-Hawks gesturing to a broad leather sofa behind a glass coffee table. 'Sit down. Put your feet up. You can't break the shit, and if you do, they make more of it.'

But Mike remained standing, crossing his arms as if bracing against the cold. A few sad relics adorned the walls – a frayed granary basket, a feather dance skirt, and a pair of tiny moccasins. Mike couldn't help but wonder if he was taking in the entire preserved history of the Shasta Springs Band of Miwok with a sweep of the eyes. Quite a contrast to the theme-park tribal shrine that Deer Creek had polished to a high gloss.

Two-Hawks set a cell phone on his desk blotter and stared down at it as if it were a half-crushed insect he wanted to put out of its misery. 'Brand-new phone, brand-new number. I got it after I found out that their lapdog, Rick Graham, was monitoring my old cell. I've given this number out to no one. And yet this is the number you called me on. Where did you get it?'

'It was in Graham's possession. McAvoy had written it down for him.'

Two-Hawks lifted a heavy brass lamp and, without anger, smashed the cell phone. He set the lamp back down and used the edge of his hand to brush the bits into a wastebasket. 'Let's have a look-see at this damning footage you told me about.'

Mike had taken a laptop and some CDs from Graham's house. Parked on a dark street, he and Shep had copied onto a disc the most legally damning section of the recorded conversation with Graham. They'd stashed the flash drive containing the entire episode with their remaining cash in the motel room's heating vent, leaving Snowball II to guard over it.

Now Mike withdrew the disc from his back pocket and handed it to Two-Hawks, who slotted it into his desktop computer. The black-and-white footage came to life on the monitor, Two-Hawks giving a growl of an exhale when he saw Mike sitting

344

in the chair across from Graham's bed, gun resting on his knee. Together they watched Graham spill the bloody history of his association with Deer Creek. The footage ended well before Graham's lunge and the gunshot that ended his life.

When it cut to black, Two-Hawks leaned back in his chair and eyed the blank monitor. 'A credible start,' he said.

'*Start?*' Mike said.

'This is just talk. Not hard evidence.'

'You're telling me this isn't enough to threaten McAvoy?' Mike said. 'A confession to multiple murders committed on behalf of a corporation?'

'Delivered by a man with a gun to his head during a home invasion,' Two-Hawks said. 'A man under duress, who would've said anything to save his life. Plus, if you want McAvoy, this is all just hearsay. He's got plausible deniability—'

'So I use this as a springboard.' Mike's tone was clipped, frustrated. 'I can get to *someone* in law enforcement who's clean. They could subpoena records, transactions that show payments to his goons—'

'Deer Creek Tribal Enterprises, Inc.' – again with the full corporate title – 'is a sovereign nation, just like ours. You can't subpoena shit from them. There is no agency in this nation or any other that can get them to release records. They run their business however they want because *there is no oversight*. And they've got judges and cops and DAs from *your* nation who are favorably inclined to their cause.'

Disgust welled in Mike's chest. 'They just plug into the government and use it like it's theirs.'

'That's what you don't understand,' Two-Hawks said. 'It *is* theirs. There was a pair of brothers who wouldn't sell land near a Deer Creek development site. They disappeared, couldn't pay the note on their property. There was some evidence at the site, but whoops, it up and vanished from the police locker. Everyone knows that McAvoy had them whacked, but how can you prove something when you can't dig into any records and when there are no bodies? I'll tell you how.' Two-Hawks leaned forward in his chair. 'With irrefutable evidence against them' – one meaty finger thumped his palm – '*in hand*.'

'I don't have it,' Mike said.

'Yes,' Two-Hawks said. 'But *we* do.'

Mike had the sensation of being left out of an inside joke, smiling dumbly while everyone else laughed. His lips parted with disbelief. 'Then what do you need *me* for?'

Two-Hawks's chair creaked as he rose, rocking behind him. He set his knuckles on the blotter. 'Because Deer Creek, in turn, has something *we* need.'

Mike's jaw shifted; he felt it crack at the hinge. 'Mutually assured destruction,' he said. 'If you burn them with what you've got on them, they can burn you back.'

'A version of that, I suppose.'

'So you have information that I could use to save my daughter, but you won't give it to me because you want something else?'

'I'm sorry. I truly am.'

Mike stared at him a long time, the gunmetal cool against the small of his back. Two-Hawks stiffened a bit, his eyes jerking nervously to the door.

Mike said, 'Maybe you should elaborate.'

'The information that we've acquired is our only ammunition against a corporation that is seeking to disenfranchise my people. If we had anything less on the line, I'd give you everything right now to protect your family.'

Mike leaned back. 'So what do you propose?'

'You have a legal claim on Deer Creek. Use your leverage to get us what we need. Then we can be free to give you what we have on *them*.'

Mike weighed this for a moment. 'Let me call my associate.'

'An associate.' Two-Hawks frowned, impressed.

Mike took out the Batphone and called Shep, who was waiting somewhere out beyond the ring of parking-lot lights. 'It's safe,' Mike said.

'You sure?' Shep asked.

'Mostly.'

Shep hung up.

Two-Hawks was on the phone himself. 'Be right there,' he said, and set down the receiver. He flicked two fingers at Mike. 'Come on now.'

They strolled down another corridor and wound up in a surveillance suite, the north-facing wall composed of maybe fifty monitors, each of which cycled through numerous perspectives. Staring vacantly at the wall of screens, three bored-looking men and one woman sat before a desk that ran the length of the room. Red Bull cans and empty Big Gulps cluttered the surfaces, and the smell of chewing tobacco hung heavy.

The woman said, 'Someone passed a chip cup at table nine.'

'Run the software,' Two-Hawks ordered.

She clicked a button on a computer, and a big screen on the side wall flared to life. A facial-recognition program began to map contour lines over the heads of the casino patrons, moving table to table. Now and then a double chime sounded and the patron's image was pulled into a subscreen and matched with a mug shot and a rap sheet. Connecting boxes listed aliases and associates.

'I'm getting no one who's worked chip cups before, but we have a couple slot-machine cheats,' the woman announced.

'Of course we do.' Two-Hawks sidled toward Mike. 'Manipulating a slot machine is a felony in Nevada, but it's only a misdemeanor in California, so everyone comes here to train.'

'What's a chip cup?' Mike asked.

'A weighted hollow cylinder with a real poker chip on top,' Two-Hawks said. 'The sides are painted to match the chip's edges. Since dealers don't break down chips that come in sets of five, you can pass off a single chip as five.' He directed his attention back to the woman. 'Let me know ASAP if another chip cup pops up, and in the meantime keep a close eye on the slot cheats.'

One of the men jogged a joystick, and four of the screens zoomed in tight on the suspects. Mike let his eyes blur, taking in an impression of seemingly every angle of the casino – blackjack table, vault, slots, parking lot – each screen clicking like a slot reel through different angles. 'You've got every inch of the place covered,' Mike said.

'Except the bathroom.' Two-Hawks grinned. 'That's about the only place in a casino you can have an "expectation of privacy," as the lawyers call it. If anything big goes down, of course, the first concern is—'

All four workers intoned wearily, "'*What's going on at the vault.*"'

With pride Two-Hawks said, 'We've got fifty-four cameras in the vault alone, covering the cage, the man trap, the count room, the fill bank where jackpots are paid out.'

The woman's back went rigid, and she swiveled toward a side monitor. 'Wait a minute,' she said. 'We got a safecracker up on Biometrica.'

Mike leaned around her to see who the facial-recognition software had pulled from the crowd.

'Oh,' he said. 'He's with me.'

Two-Hawks gave a hearty laugh. 'Please page Blackie. Have' – a glance to the on-screen data – 'Shepherd White brought back here.'

The woman nodded and picked up the phone. She was slender with elfish features, the bulge of tobacco in her cheek adding a fantastical flourish.

A minute later Blackie and Shep pushed through the padded door. They both looked mildly displeased, though Mike doubted they'd exchanged so much as a word along the way.

Two-Hawks said, 'You're a safecracker?'

Shep said, 'What?'

'A safecracker. You break into safes?'

Shep shrugged and looked away, disinterested. He took a few steps toward the wall of monitors and gazed at them, a fox in the henhouse. His head was tilted back, his mouth slightly ajar, the light of the monitors putting a spark into his flat eyes. He seemed to be drinking in all the flickering movement.

The workers and Blackie exchanged a round of glances. Blackie said, finally, 'You want to answer the man?'

Shep said, 'The broad on blackjack three's working a shiner prism to read the hole card. Two tables over, the black dude's counting cards on an iPhone app. You got a guy using a monkey paw on the bank of Hurricane slots along the west wall. And either your dealer on seven paid out a wrong hand accidentally or he's dumping the table.'

A long pause ensued.

The petite woman spit her cud of tobacco into a McDonald's cup. It hit with a little thud. 'You see anyone using a chips cup?' she asked.

'Obese Caucasian, floppy hat, roulette six,' Shep said. 'Watch her hands when she dips 'em into the front basket of her mobility scooter.'

Hands flew to joysticks, an entire quadrant of the wall's screens zeroing in on the woman from every angle. She'd rotated the mounted seat of her medical scooter to the side so she could pull right in to the roulette board, giving her easy under-the-table access to the mounted basket.

Two-Hawks nodded at Blackie, who drifted backward through the door to handle business. Then he said to Shep, 'Want a job?'

Shep looked away from the monitors for the first time, that crooked tooth slightly visible. 'You wouldn't be able to trust me.'

Two-Hawks swallowed, flustered and amused. 'Talk to you boys in private?'

They headed back down the hall and sat, Mike and Shep on

the leather couch, Two-Hawks in his chair, which he pulled around the desk to face them.

Mike said, 'Two-Hawks here has dirt on our boy McAvoy. But he won't turn it over unless we acquire the dirt McAvoy's holding on *him*.'

'How good is the dirt you're holding?' Shep asked.

'A no-shit smoking gun,' Two-Hawks said. 'Recently I had a man inside Deer Creek's operation. Someone with access.'

'How'd you flip him?' Shep sounded skeptical. 'Deer Creek's got more money than you. And more muscle.'

'Our guy was hired to do some freelance consulting for Deer Creek. He's a gambler, as the case often is. But you don't shit where you eat. So he came here, to us, to play cards. And he overdrew his credit line. Significantly. Unlike McAvoy, we don't maim people for that.'

'You just extort them,' Shep said.

'It was a beneficial arrangement, agreed to by adults.' Regret moved behind Two-Hawks's eyes, only for an instant, and then the game face snapped back on. 'He smuggled me documents. That's how we caught wind of you.' A nod to Mike. 'He told us about your name on the genealogy report.'

'But you weren't after that to start with,' Shep said. 'So what else did he get you?'

'Good hard evidence.'

'Of what?'

'No problems hearing now, huh?' Two-Hawks asked.

'Evidence of what?' Shep repeated.

'I promise, you won't be disappointed.'

'No,' Mike said. 'I need to know what exactly we'd be turning over to you.'

'That's not your concern.'

'If we're getting it, it is. I won't bring you something that'll wreck someone else's life.'

'It's nothing like that. That's all you need to know right now.'

Mike thought back to sitting in that armchair facing Bill Garner, the governor's chief of staff. The last time Mike's judgment was on the line, he'd folded, because what the hell, it was just an award and a couple of photos.

He stood.

Two-Hawks said, 'Think about your daughter.'

Mike was at the door now, Shep beside him.

'Okay, *wait*.' Two-Hawks was on his feet. 'They're just photograph negatives. But they're essential for us to keep our status – and our casino. I didn't want to explain them, because . . . in my business we see up close how greed affects people.' He scratched the back of his neck, hedging. 'Sometimes there's what's right, and then there's what's *smart*.'

'I'm a slow learner,' Mike said, 'but even I figured out there's really no difference.'

'Turning over those negatives – if you get them – to a competing casino is against your future financial interests as the heir to Deer Creek.'

'Do you have kids, Mr Two-Hawks?' Mike said.

'Five.' Two-Hawks drew a deep breath, chastened. 'Okay. Maybe I've been swimming in the shark tank too long.' He gestured back to the couch. 'Please stay, and I'll explain.'

Mike and Shep returned to the couch and sat, Shep plunking his boots on the glass coffee table.

'Unless I can pull off a miracle in the next few months before that formal review, we are going to lose our federal recognition,' Two-Hawks said. 'There's a higher bar for tribal acknowledgment these days, more stringent requirements. So far we've failed to produce additional physical proof tying our ancestors to this land. We've always had an oral tradition, so there's a paucity of evidence, especially from the first half of this century. Very little survives of our tribe.'

Mike found himself looking at those few humble relics adorning the office walls.

'Some months ago it came to my attention that there are antique photo negatives taken by members of a botany expedition or some nonsense out of Stanford during the 1930s. Those pictures show our people living on this very plot of land. I was told that the peak of Lassen in the background as well as a distinctive river fork just beyond the settlements made the precise location clear.' He crossed and threw the window curtains apart. There past the parking lot but still glittering under the outer lights was a narrow river, split into two streams around a massive, cracked boulder.

Gone was the down-home oilman. Indignation had heightened not just his language but his affect. Drawn erect, eyes ablaze, he seemed every bit the chief he was in title. He let the curtains flutter back into place. 'Of course, I arranged immediately to buy the negatives from the dealer. But somewhere between my hanging up the phone and arriving to pick up the film, McAvoy had stepped in and tripled my offer. He has the negatives. I need them. If we produce them as evidence – *irrefutable* evidence – of our tie to this land, the Bureau of Acknowledgment and Research will be forced to uphold our tribal status.'

'And you keep your casino,' Shep added.

'Hard as it may be for you to recognize, Mr White, this isn't only about money. McAvoy's aim is to dissolve our tribe and steal our land. And we've had enough of that in our time, thank you.'

Shep stared at the far wall. He seemed unimpressed.

Two-Hawks turned to Mike, a better audience.

Mike asked, 'So when McAvoy bought those photo negatives out from under you, you decided to go after dirt on Deer Creek and look for me?'

'I needed something to protect my tribe. McAvoy found out what I took from him, so he and I are at a standoff. For *now*. Next year's tribal-acknowledgment review puts a deadline on our little stare-down, one way or another. But given what I have on him, I'm not dumb enough to think he'll wait this out much longer.' Two-Hawks kicked the trash can, rattling the pieces of his smashed cell phone. 'They're intensifying their efforts to get back what I've taken. I relocated my family out of state.' His eyes found Mike. 'My five kids.'

'So why not make a move first?' Mike asked.

'McAvoy has made clear that he'll burn the negatives if any of the evidence I've collected against him sees the light of day. That would destroy our tribe as we know it. Plus, the thought of those pictures burning . . .' In the golden light of the office, his face took on shadow, and in his wrinkles Mike could see the faint etchings of his heritage. 'All we are is what we came from—'

At this, Shep snorted.

Two-Hawks continued, undeterred. 'Those are the *only* images of my early ancestors. I put this tribe back together one member at a time, driving around the state in a beat-to-shit Pontiac. Many were homeless. Most were destitute. But we built something for ourselves with our own hands. All of us living today, we've never seen the faces of our forebears. For us to be able to see where we came from, to validate our place on this earth . . .' He shook his head. 'You can't put a price on that.'

Mike studied his hands.

Shep merely looked annoyed. 'So what's the play?'

Two-Hawks went on. 'If McAvoy's faced with losing his entire corporation to your . . . bloodline, maybe you and he could strike a deal. You get him to turn over those negatives in exchange for some financial arrangement. You give me the pictures. I give you what I have on him. And then you sink him with criminal charges.'

'If he turns over the photos to me, he leaves himself unprotected against whatever you have,' Mike said. 'He won't do that.'

A silent sigh lowered Two-Hawks's shoulders. 'So what do *you* propose?'

Mike and Shep were both leaning forward, elbows on knees.

Their heads tilted slightly, their eyes meeting. Shep gave a little nod.

Mike said, 'I think I know where your photo negatives are hidden. McAvoy has a safe where he keeps all his valuable dirt.'

'A safe. So you're planning on . . . what?'

Shep flared his hands. Ta-*da*.

Two-Hawks let out a guffaw. 'Come on. A *casino* safe?'

Mike said, 'It's hidden in his office.'

'In his *office*?' Two-Hawks exclaimed. 'Why not the vault?'

Mike said, 'Think about it.'

Two-Hawks chuckled into a fist. 'Of *course*. The vault is filthy with cameras. Not exactly a choice place to hide dubious materials.' He stood, walked a tight circle, and leaned on the back of his chair. 'It's ballsy of McAvoy, I gotta say. But it makes sense, too. Keeping valuables in a secret safe in a locked room in a twenty-four-hour-surveilled casino on sovereign land – I suppose that'd make me arrogant, too.'

'Arrogant's good,' Shep said.

'But even then, you've got all the cameras on the casino floor.' Two-Hawks was still winding up. 'Plus, you can't possibly crack that safe there. The time, the noise.'

'No,' Shep said. 'I can't. How's your pull with the cops?'

'In the event that you get caught?' Two-Hawks asked. 'Good. But relative to Deer Creek's?' He blew out a dismissive breath. 'McAvoy has something we don't.' He jabbed a finger at his computer monitor, a reference to the footage Mike had shown him earlier. 'Rick Graham.'

Mike moistened his lips. 'Graham is no longer a consideration,' he said.

Two-Hawks sank thoughtfully into his chair, tilted back, studied the ceiling. Then he glanced at the disc lying on his desktop. He cleared his throat, then cleared it again. 'I don't want to know anything more about that.'

'Good,' Mike said.

'We have a police captain nearby who we're quite close with,' Two-Hawks said. 'Coupla DAs, too. There's no way I can get you off if you're caught red-handed, of course. But if Graham is no longer a factor, I can ensure that if you're taken into custody in the area, you won't be handed over to McAvoy's goons. There's one big problem, though: If you get hung up *at* Deer Creek, on sovereign tribal land, the authorities'll have trouble crossing territorial boundaries to make sure matters are handled above-board. Which leaves you at the mercy of McAvoy. And his attack dogs. In that event you'd better hope the cops arrive before the mallet falls.'

Shep said, 'Ball-peen hammer.'

Mike squeezed his eyes closed, remembering Graham's words: *Hell, short of the right to pursue felons, the U.S. has shaky* criminal *jurisdiction on tribal lands.*

Mike said, 'The cops can come in after Shep.'

A moment's delay, and then wrinkles fanned from the corners of Two-Hawks's eyes. 'You're a felon?'

Shep scowled, insulted. 'Course.'

Mike nodded at Two-Hawks. 'We'll be in touch with the plan.' He and Shep rose to leave.

'And I'll need a lawyer,' Shep said.

Two-Hawks asked, 'Why?'

Shep paused on his way out the door. 'Because I'm planning on getting arrested.'

Chapter 50

You will come back for me.
   I will come back for you.
   You swore it, now. You swore *it.*

Mike woke up with his head pulsing and the sheets twisted through his legs. His chest felt clammy beneath the motel vent, and sweat had pooled in the hollow of his throat. He shoved aside the sheets, ran a hand across the bristles of his cropped hair, and did his best to shake off the dream. Snowball II was wedged under the pillow next to him, glass eyes bulging as if from strangulation. Shep sat with his shoulder blades against the headboard of the other bed, spooning cold SpaghettiOs from the can, as calmly vigilant as ever. On the desk across the room, the police scanner gave off a steady stream of cop talk.

They'd returned to the motel at first light, it was 3:27 P.M. now, and the heist was set to go live at sunset, a little more than three hours from now. By then the darkness would offer some cover outside and the Deer Creek Casino offices, including McAvoy's, should be empty, at least according to the schedules Two-Hawks's surveillance men had pieced together over the past several weeks. But between now and then, Mike and Shep still had plenty to arrange.

'You believe in God?' Shep asked from around the spoon.

Mike realized that Shep thought he'd been praying. 'When it's convenient,' Mike said.

'Is it convenient right now?'

Mike pictured that cigar hole in Annabel's side, the black trickle leaking from the wound. Dodge's massive hand palming Kat's head through the baby blue sleeping bag, the ball-peen hammer drawn back for the kill blow. The bay window where Mike had waited as a kid, the one Kat might be sitting at this very moment.

'Yeah,' he said. 'It is.'

Motoring along on a medical mobility scooter, Mike wore a battered mesh 101ST AIRBORNE hat, oversize mirror sunglasses, and a fleece lap robe featuring a bald eagle glaring over a craggy mountainside. Shep strode beside him through the outer reaches of the Deer Creek parking lot, undisguised.

At 6:40 on the dot, a minivan turned off the main road and slotted into a space in the row farthest from the casino. A wholesome, all-American couple emerged. The man, a robust fellow in a Hawaiian shirt, offered a big grin. His wife fussed with the collar of her shirtwaist dress, her layered curls and teased bangs like something out of a Nagel print.

At the sight of them, Mike let off the throttle and hit the hand brake, the little scooter chirping to a halt. '*Them*?' he said. 'Those two are your big tough accomplices?'

'Yup,' Shep said. 'Bob and Molly.'

Mike's mouth was sour with fear and second thoughts. He was glad he'd delivered Hank's cash earlier in the day – one less thing to ride his conscience into the not-so-sweet hereafter if he got killed tonight. Hank had squeezed his hand an extra beat at the door and promised he'd be waiting by the phone. If Mike made it out to call him.

Mike readjusted his leather gloves nervously. The couple waved and started over. Bob's face was shiny and sunburned. Molly toyed with the strand of Mardi Gras beads around her neck.

As the couple neared, Shep asked, 'You got my gear to the warehouse?'

Molly's smile was improbably wide. 'That we did.'

Bob flipped Mike the keys to the van, then made cartoon running arms toward the casino doors. 'Shall we?'

Molly said, 'Okeydokey.'

Mike swallowed dryly and nodded. Splitting off toward different entrances, they headed for the building. At the south door, Mike got jammed up with a few other mobility scooters. There was a lot of angry huffing, either because the others were old and cranky or because Mike was lacking in scooter etiquette, but he managed his way through. Once inside, he puttered over past the cage, making sure that the empty metal drop carts were parked behind the low counter where he'd seen them on his last visit. There were three carts awaiting the next shift end, when they would be squired from slot machine to slot machine to collect the full coin buckets.

Steering across the vast casino floor, he did his best not to think of all the cameras angled down from the ceiling. He was the weakest link, the only nonprofessional. If someone spotted him, he was dead. And Kat was lost.

He buzzed into the bathroom, an elderly man holding the door for him, and steered into the wide handicap stall. He closed and bolted the door behind him, the lap robe slipping to the tile, revealing the Nike gym bag he'd hidden on the wide footrest platform beneath his legs. He ripped off his hat and glasses and dumped them, with the lap robe, into the scooter's front basket. In his innocuous black slacks and white gift-shop polo sporting the casino decal, he looked like your average Deer Creek worker.

As Two-Hawks had pointed out, a bathroom was the only place in a casino without surveillance cameras.

Except, Mike hoped, the CEO's office.

His watch read 6:53. Seven minutes to liftoff.

He shoved four squares of Bubblicious into his mouth, chewed rigorously, and worked the gum into his cheeks and lips. All the better to defy the facial-recognition software now that he no longer had a hat brim to hide beneath.

6:54.

Leaving the dead bolt locked, he shoved the heavy Nike bag under the wall into the neighboring stall, then followed it. Someone flushed a toilet, and then he heard running water. Bag in hand, he stood in the relative quiet and tried to remember how to breathe normally.

6:56.

Time to move.

He exited the bathroom, nodding at a few guys stumbling in, their free drinks slopping onto their wrists. Navigating through the clusters of slots and green-felt tables, he did his best to walk casually. Going on tiptoe, he stared nervously across the vast room at that door leading back to the offices. Two-Hawks's intel had predicted the rooms beyond to be empty by now. Predictions were helpful, sure. Not perfect.

Mike paused near the cage and put his back to the wall, his breaths coming harder now, puffing his cheeks. The heft of the equipment in the gym bag was reassuring, but still, there were more variables than could be accounted for with all the gear in the world. The drop carts remained behind the counter, so close he could reach across and tap one of them. His jitters sharpened until he was perched on a knife edge of panic.

Not a husband, he told himself. *Not a father.*

Just a man with a task.

6:59.

He closed his eyes.

That's when he heard the scream.

Bob gasped breathlessly, a giant plastic bucket of quarters slipping from his hand and exploding onto the carpet, sending out a jangly spout of coins. His face taut and red, he grabbed his left arm and pinwheeled off a Hold 'Em table, staggering forward, dragging the red velvet rope and the shocked dealer with him. A creak issuing from his mouth, he collapsed onto the pit table, which toppled, spilling tray after tray loaded with casino chips.

Molly clutched at her yellow curls and let out another piercing scream. '*My husband! Oh, my God, his heart, his heart! Someone help!*'

Everyone in the vicinity had frozen at once, as if by design. The only movement was that of the coins and chips rolling past ankles and chairs and beneath slot machines, forty thousand and change expanding like a swarm of rats across a hypnotically busy carpet pattern. An elderly man in a battered snap-brim hat crouched to pluck up a black-and-green hundred-dollar chip, and his creaky movement broke the spell, the statue garden springing to life, jostling, shoving, grabbing. Filled fists jammed into pockets. Coin buckets bounced cheerily on crooked arms like Easter baskets. Loafers and high heels trampled hands and kicked coins. The dealer was trying to untangle himself from Bob, who flopped and screeched, clutching his left arm as though it were going to fall off. Security swarmed the area, chasing down chips, manhandling patrons, shouting into radios. Molly's shrieks grew so strident that a few people, jostled along by the undercurrent, covered their ears.

Standing hip-deep in the chaos, the pit boss touched a finger to his earpiece and spoke into his sleeve. 'Surveillance, you better be getting this.'

The surveillance suite was pure mayhem, monitors flashing, hands toggling joysticks, frenzied pacing. Half the screens were focused on the commotion below, recording it from every slant.

The director was shouting, his voice high and thin, 'Could be a diversion! Get the software up and start grabbing faces!'

'Already running!' one of the supervisors shouted across.

'What do you got?'

'Nothing so f—' An alert chimed from the speakers of the supervisor's computer. He stood abruptly, one nervous hand mussing his spiky black hair, a deodorant ring staining his shirt beneath the arm. 'The guy having the heart attack is a twice-convicted con artist.'

The director stormed over. 'And the woman?'

There she was, listed under the con man's associates.

'Who else?' the director yelled. 'I want a sweep of the whole goddamned floor – *now*!'

Another alert sounded. 'Okay,' the supervisor said, 'we hit on another known associate.' The facial-recognition software pulled a third face from the muddle. Shepherd White, lurking by the bank, eyeing the vault through the crossed bars of the cage. 'This one's a safecracker.'

'Shift cameras ten through sixty to the vault,' the director said. 'I want every angle covered. Have security move now and roll up the crew. And get Boss Man on the phone. He's gonna want to hear this.'

Mike shoved the drop cart hurriedly across the floor, keeping to the perimeter as commotion reigned by the tables. The weighty gym bag resting inside the cart clanked as the wheels bounced from walkway to carpet. To his left, a bartender was standing on a stool for a better vantage, the FIREWATER sign blinking down on his crooked headdress.

Mike reached the door leading back to the offices and unzipped the top of his gym bag. First up, a spray lubricant, the thin red straw already inserted into the nozzle. He blasted the keyhole, then dropped the can into the cart and tugged from the bag a pull-handle pick gun. Slipping the thin tip into the lubed lock, he clicked the device on. The tip whirred, twisting in the metal channel like a snake in a fist, the internal pins clattering as they jumped above the shear line. With a click, the lock yielded and he was in.

He shoved the cart through and closed the door behind him.

Down the hall one door was ajar, a fall of light lying across the carpet.

Mike lost a heartbeat. He breathed in once, deep, then pushed the drop cart down the hall. As he passed the open door, a woman with wire spectacles glanced up from her desk.

Barely slowing, Mike said, 'We got a security mess on the floor. McAvoy called – he wants all nonessential workers to clear out before it escalates.' His voice was slightly distorted from the chewing gum, but she didn't seem to notice.

'Everyone all right?'

'I don't know,' he said. 'I heard that a few guys flashed guns.'

She grabbed her purse and bolted. He kept on down the hall. The end office had McAvoy's name etched across a brass placard. The lock was a fat Medeco – way too complex for the pick gun. But fortunately Shep had planned for this contingency as well. Mike reached into the gym bag and came up with an electric hand drill, already fitted with a hard carbide bit. He jammed the point into the cylinder core right above the keyway, tightened his finger, and shoved. The drill chuck screeched and sparks showered his forearms, but he made steady progress, decimating the lock pins, the tumblers and springs falling down out of place. The cored lock yielded, the door rotating inward before he even had to shove.

Wheeling the cart before him, he crossed the corner office. The furnishings were top-notch – walnut desk, Baccarat horse sculpture, gold-framed portrait of McAvoy with a fetching younger wife and twin boys.

And there was the painting, just as Graham had described. An Indian healer, rendered in oil, staring Mike down from across the room. The man's gaze was timeless and his hands raised to show his palms, a gesture that seemed at once passive and empowered. Mike grabbed the wooden frame, said a silent prayer, and ripped it from the wall.

An exhale hissed through his gritted teeth. Graham hadn't lied. Mike flattened a palm against the wall safe, feeling the cool of the impenetrable blue-steel facade.

Withdrawing a hammer from the gym bag, he punched holes in the drywall around the safe, then he tore it away, the leather gloves protecting his hands. The last item in the gym bag was a cordless reciprocating saw, the straight blade about six inches long. He clipped in the battery pack and revved it up. Rather than attacking the safe, he dug into the two-by-fours that the safe was mounted to, avoiding the thick bolts. The wood gave readily under the jagged teeth. Sweat ran into his eyes. At any moment Dodge could stroll through the office door with its destroyed lock. Mike forced himself to stop checking his watch. It would take however long it took.

He left the bottom two-by-four for last. Positioning the cart flat against the wall beneath the safe, he flicked the saw blade at the supporting beam until it splintered under the weight of the safe. The metal unit tumbled from the wall into the drop cart with a crash, denting the bed.

Too much of the last two-by-four had torn free with the safe, so he severed the protruding end, trimming it as close to the blue steel as he could. Opening the empty gym bag, he laid it over the safe, hiding it. Leaving the tools scattered on McAvoy's fine Persian rug, he shouldered into the drop cart. With a faint complaint from the wheels, it started moving for the door.

Everyone's attention, it seemed, was directed at the aftermath by the poker tables. A fresh outburst of excitement rippled across the casino floor, and Mike glanced up in time to see Shep on the run, sprinting between the craps tables, four or five security guards on his heels. He slid beneath a Wheel of Fortune table, popped up, knocking over a cocktail waitress in an Indian-print shift, and bolted into the keno lounge. Reinforcements followed. He didn't have long.

Wielding the drop cart before him, Mike wanted to sprint to the bathroom but forced himself to hold to a hurried walk. When he finally arrived, he used the end of the cart to bang open the door. He practically rode the thing across the tile, smashing into the far wall by the handicap stall. The place was empty, no one bothering with a bathroom break given the three-ring security circus raging on the floor.

Mike slid under the stall door, unlocked it, and drew the cart in beside the mobility scooter, still parked where he'd left it. Lifting with his legs and groaning under the weight, he transferred the wall safe from the drop cart onto the scooter's footrest platform. Donning his sunglasses and hat, he mounted the scooter, throwing the eagle lap robe over his legs and the safe. The safe was wider than he'd hoped, so his feet stuck out a little on either side, but he prayed that no one would notice.

He motored out of the bathroom and through the heart of the casino, heading for the nearest entrance. The jagged ends of the two-by-fours shoved splinters into his legs.

In his peripheral vision, he saw five guards drag Shep from the keno lounge, Shep letting himself go limp to make the job harder for them. 'I didn't do nuthin'!' he bellowed, playing up the impaired blur of his words. 'Lee' me alone. You're hurting me.'

A number of patrons watched with dismay and sympathy.

Mike kept his head forward and his hand on the throttle, but given the peewee motor and the weight of the safe, the scooter seemed to creep at a snail's pace. He realized with alarm that the cadre of guards surrounding Shep was moving directly at him, putting them on a collision course. His hand ached against the throttle, but he couldn't make the scooter go faster. For a brief stretch of walkway, their paths converged, Mike veering off onto the carpet to avoid getting knocked over. Shep's head reared up into sight for an instant, time enough for his and Mike's eyes to meet before the guards swept him off again.

Mike clanked back onto the walkway and pointed the scooter's nose at the glass doors twenty yards away. The safe shifted slightly, and he clamped his legs around it, the lap robe starting to slip. Up ahead he saw Dodge and William storming through the entrance, McAvoy between them. They started toward Mike, and for a moment he was terrified that he'd been made. Lowering his head so the brim of his cap blocked his face, he teased a lump of gum from his cheek and worked it anxiously between his teeth. The overtaxed engine gave off a whine. His leg was cramping under the weight of the slipping safe. He prayed his legs weren't sticking out too far, that the stupid eagle fleece would hold in place, that he hadn't in fact been spotted.

He didn't dare risk a peek, but he felt the weight of the wind as they swept past. His breath burst from him with a shudder, the scooter wheezing forward with comedic slowness. At last the automatic doors peeled open and he was out, the night air chilling the sweat on his face.

Near the knocked-over table, numerous guards had corralled Shep, Bob, and Molly, along with the majority of the casino chips. Despite management's best efforts, onlookers remained, standing a cautious distance back, pointing, and plucking the occasional quarter from underfoot.

Ducati helmet tucked casually under an arm, McAvoy approached the mass, offering Shep a collegial nod. 'Where's your friend?'

'Dunno,' Shep said. 'I thought you tribesmen hung together.'

McAvoy's left eye flickered a little. He turned calmly to one of the guards. 'Why haven't you moved him like I asked?'

The head security guard said, 'We just rounded 'em up.'

Bob waved to a concerned gaggle of older women. 'I'm feeling much better now, thank goodness.' He held up an orange bottle. 'Got my nitrate pill.'

McAvoy pointed at Shep, 'Take him.'

Dodge stepped into view, and Shep nodded at him. 'How's your neck?'

Dodge's head swiveled slightly, those eyes fastening on Shep but offering neither recognition nor acknowledgment.

'We can talk about that in a minute,' William said. 'In private.'

The guards grabbed Shep by the arms and tugged him forward.

The crowd stirred, and then several uniformed officers shoved through to the front.

McAvoy squared to them. 'I didn't authorize you to enter my property.'

A lieutenant flipped open his wallet, let his badge dangle. 'You're staring at three felons, Mr McAvoy,' he said. 'And they're wanted in custody.'

A stare-down seemed imminent, but McAvoy didn't let it get to that. Showing the lieutenant his palms, he stepped aside and smiled cordially. 'Officers.'

The cops took control of Shep, Bob, and Molly and started hustling them out through the crowd.

William stepped around McAvoy and put a hand on Shep's chest as he passed, halting the procession. 'Don't worry,' he whispered, 'Graham'll have you back to us in no time.'

'Yeah,' Shep said, 'good luck with that.'

Dodge followed them a few paces toward the exit, then stood, blocking the walkway, staring after them with dull, lifeless eyes.

By the time Mike reached Bob and Molly's van at the far edge of the parking lot, the safe and the scooter were barely holding on. He thumbed a button on the key chain, and the van's rolling door slid open automatically. A second button unfolded the wheelchair lift from the side of the vehicle. The dying scooter lurched up beside the lowered lift, Mike's trembling leg gave way, and the safe plopped out and landed with a clang on the metal. With another touch of the button, the wheelchair lift rose, conveying the safe, still bolted to the severed two-by-fours, into the belly of the van.

Leaving the scooter keeled over on the asphalt, Mike hopped into the driver's seat and pulled out, passing a second wave of arriving squad cars.

Turning onto the main road, he rolled down his window and spit his chewing gum to the wind.

The surveillance room smelled of coffee and body odor. McAvoy had the director play back the recording a third time. The footage showed Shep leaning against the wall near the vault, relaxed as could be, tilting his face up as if into a warm sun.

'That's it?' McAvoy asked. 'He just *stood* there?'

'Yeah,' the director said. 'He didn't make a move for the vault, nothing. I think it might have all gone down too fast for him.'

'And he had no gear.'

'No gear.'

McAvoy stared at the image. Shep pointing his face at the ceiling. No – at the hidden cameras.

As if he *wanted* the facial-recognition software to pick him up.

'Wait a minute,' McAvoy said. 'Give me that clip on screen twenty-seven again.'

The director complied. Five guards dragged Shep from the keno lounge and across the casino floor. 'Pause,' McAvoy said. 'No, back. Now. *Now*. There. Stop.'

A frozen image of Shep's head bucking up above the guards, his gaze focused.

'What are you looking at?' McAvoy mumbled. He stepped forward, traced a line in the direction Shep was facing until his finger hit the side of the monitor. 'Show me camera twenty-eight, same time stamp.'

The director complied. The screen showed an old vet, wearing a beat-up hat and sunglasses, riding a medical scooter. His legs poked out the sides as if they were broken. The hand on the throttle was gloved.

McAvoy paled.

'Boss,' the director said, 'what's wr—'

McAvoy bolted for the door, motorcycle helmet swinging at his side.

His pace was brisk across the casino floor. He barreled into the admin hall, keying immediately to his door at the end, slightly ajar. He stepped into his office, drawing up short at the edge of the rug.

The Ducati helmet slipped from his hand and cracked on the floorboards.

Chapter 51

When the ragged warehouse door screeched back on its tracks, Mike raised an arm against the light, though the pale dusk glow was far from bright. He'd been inside the dingy warehouse for seventeen hours, trying not to obsess over the limitless ways the plan could go to shit.

Given the low sun at his back, Shep was a perfect shadow, one arm extended, his hand hooked on the handle of the rolling door.

''Bout time,' Mike said.

Passing the day alone had been torturous. The smell of damp concrete had lodged as a taste in the back of his throat. Empty cans of SpaghettiOs rolled at his feet. The deserted warehouse was cavernous, which made the emptiness resonant, living, gothic. Bats in the rafters. Cobwebs. A rusty faucet dripping into a wide, paint-stained basin.

In the middle of the cracked floor was the pallet of heavy crates that Bob and Molly had delivered the previous day. Though Mike sat leaning against the boxes, he hadn't so much as popped a lid; he knew better than to handle Shep's gear. Pulling himself to his feet, he set a foot on McAvoy's wall safe, a game hunter posing over vanquished prey.

Shep stepped inside. 'Cops grilled me all day.'

'What'd you say?'

'"What?" mostly,' Shep answered with a faint smirk. 'I did nothing wrong. I was in a casino, minding my own business when I got manhandled. The bigger concern was my association with Mike Wingate. But of course that's all *years* in the past.' He rattled the door closed behind him. 'I'd never hang around with the likes of you now.'

'So that's it? They just let you go?'

'As promised, Two-Hawks lined up a pricey Injun lawyer for me.' Shep produced a taupe business card and flicked it, showing off the fine stock. 'Plus, it seems that the Shasta Springs Band of Miwok Casino bought a few new squad cars for the Susanville PD last year. For once in our lives, we were on the right side of a favor. With no Graham riding in to pull rank, they released me.'

'And Bob and Molly?'

'In the clear. Probably back in Reno by now.' Shep circled the pallet, appraising the boxes. 'Not that we haven't become "persons of interest," as they like to say. You are one wanted man.'

He started opening crates, unpacking equipment, most of which had been wrapped in moving blankets. Strings of floodlights hooked onto T-bar stands, which in turn plugged into a generator he had Mike wheel over from the rear of the pallet. With the click of a switch, the center of the warehouse was as bright as day. Shep positioned the floodlights around the wall safe, so it was lit up like some sort of industrial sculpture. Stepping this way and that like a finicky film director, he adjusted the floodlights to reduce glare. Watching Shep work brought Mike back to studying SAT vocab words while Shep whaled away on that wall safe from Valley Liquors, the Couch Mother bellowing down the hall. Not your traditional Hallmark moment, but still, the memory was a comfort.

Shep walked a few paces toward the safe and sat cross-legged, confronting it. 'We can't use explosives, since we're dealing with paper in there, not coins or gold bars.' His eyes were closed. 'The overpressure and detonation would torch the photographs.'

Mike said, 'Right.'

Shep lay flat on his belly and propped his chin on his fists, staring at the safe like a kid watching TV.

'Don't you know how to break into this brand of safe?' Mike asked.

'It's custom,' Shep said.

'What's that mean for us?'

Shep crawled forward and put his face flat against the metal door. 'It means we have to listen to it.' He fingered the combination dial. Fondled the thick handle. Knocked the walls, cocking his head at the dull ring.

Mike watched and stayed out of the way, trying not to worry about Shep's fussing and his troubled expression.

After twenty or so minutes of this, Shep said, 'The fact that it's a custom safe means it could be booby-trapped to destroy its contents if it's messed with. So there's that.'

'Okay . . .'

'It has at least three locking lugs. But I'm not sure where. And carving around the frame to guess would be risky business. Could set off that booby trap. Or fuck up the photo negatives.'

'So what are we gonna do?'

'We're gonna try to bypass the lugs altogether.'

'How?'

But Shep was already on his feet, digging around behind the circle of lights. From a footlocker he removed a futuristic-looking tool with the handle and motor of a chain saw and a white-silver circular blade emerging from a mouthlike guard.

'Looks like something out of a snuff film,' Mike said.

Shep held the tool out, his forearms cording. He'd donned eye protection and looked mildly deranged, which contributed to the effect. 'Rescue saw, used by fire departments. The blade here's tipped with industrial diamonds. Steel doesn't like it much.'

'I thought you said it's too risky to cut into the safe.'

'I said it was too risky to carve around the frame searching for the lugs. But if we can get the handle to turn, the camming-lever action will retract the lugs for us.'

Mike tried to hide his impatience. 'So how do we get the handle to turn?'

'The combination has three numbers, right? Each number corresponds to a disk inside the tumbler assembly. Each disk has a groove. And those grooves have to align to release the locking block and allow the door handle to turn. What I'm gonna do' – he revved the motor, the jagged blade morphing into a smooth blur and then back again – 'is cut away the locking block and skip all that other bullshit.'

'How do you know where to cut?'

'Experience. Feel. Instinct. It's like hitting a curveball. Sometimes it all aligns and you catch up to it.'

'And if you don't?'

'Then I mangle the tumbler assembly and we don't get in.'

After a few more adjustments to the floodlights, Shep braced himself and leaned in, blade biting into steel with a scream that made Mike's teeth throb in his gums. In the space between the combination dial and the door handle, Shep made three small equidistant cuts, no more than an inch deep. Mike was up, pacing, his hands laced at the back of his neck.

Finally Shep set down the rescue saw and wiped the sweat from his brow. He gripped the handle firmly and twisted. It rotated fully, giving off a dull thud.

Shep exhaled. Risked a glance at Mike. Then carefully turned the handle back into place.

'It's open,' Mike said.

'No. It's *unlocked*. We don't want to open it yet.'

'Right. The booby trap.' Mike blew out a breath and cracked his knuckles, his fingertips tingling with apprehension. 'I guess if it was easy, everyone would do it.'

Shep headed back to the pallet and, after protracted clanking, returned with a power drill fitted with a thick, carbide-tipped bit. Centering the bit on the roof of the safe, he set his full weight behind the handle and drilled down. This went on for ten minutes, then twenty. Every so often he'd stop and blow steel dust from the hole, the powder turning white when he hit a layer of concrete. Finally, he stopped to rest.

His lips tensed, that crooked tooth poking into view. Sweat and bits of shrapnel sparkled in his buzz cut. 'There is nothing better than this.'

Mike raised his eyebrows.

'Taking a hard nut to crack and cracking it,' Shep continued. 'Making it spill its secrets, nothing left but the light of day. Doesn't matter how much money you come from, how much security you pay for, what kind of custom safe you build. Any lowlife can grind past all that to the promised land. All it takes is focus and determination. Stamina, the great fucking equalizer. And when those doors swing open for me? Man. The release – the *triumph*.' He shook his head and whistled a single note. Mike had never seen him so alive. 'Half the time I don't even care what the take is. It's about the challenge, not the shit inside.'

'But tonight,' Mike said, 'it's about both.'

'Tonight's nothing. The nut isn't the safe. It's Brian McAvoy and Deer Creek Enterprises. Money, connections, power – they're the guys sitting behind all those doors that've been closed to us all our lives. But if we apply the right pressure at the right time, make the right incisions' – a nod to the cuts in the steel face – 'pull the right levers, we're gonna crack those mother-fuckers wide open.'

He resumed drilling, leaning on the handle, going through a second drill bit and then a third. At last, the resistance gave way, the drill chuck free-falling three inches to slap against the top of the safe. Shep blew the hole clear, then uncoiled a fiber-optic camera and fed the black wire through into the safe.

'You see the negatives?' Mike asked, the words coming in a rush. He had done his best to forget that every risk they'd taken was based on a hunch: that McAvoy had parked the photo neg-atives in the safe. Now they were inches away from knowing.

Shep studied the green footage on the tiny attached screen. His mouth drooped a bit, and then he leaned over the drill hole, sniffed a few times, and cursed under his breath.

Mike had the sensation of losing his stomach for a moment, a roller-coaster dip. 'They're not in there,' he said.

'Yeah,' Shep said. 'They are.' But his expression stayed dire.

Mike looked on the tiny monitor. All he saw were a few brittle papers and – thank God – the thin stack of film negatives. Then he noticed it – a stripped wire rimming the safe's interior. If the walls were tampered with or the door opened, the end of the wire would be pulled into contact with a bare wire loop. 'If those exposed parts touch—'

'They'll ignite,' Shep said.

'So how did McAvoy get in?'

'If you open the safe the right way, then the weight of the locking mechanism pins down the slack wire, moving it out of reach.'

'But you destroyed the locking mechanism,' Mike said.

Shep sat back on his heels, his hands resting on his stained jeans.

Mike wouldn't let himself fully acknowledge Shep's expression of defeat. 'So we'll just be ready to throw water in the minute the door opens,' Mike said.

Shep grabbed the back of Mike's collar and moved his face down toward the drill hole. 'Smell.'

An acrid scent singed Mike's nostrils.

'That's cellulose nitrate film,' Shep said. 'They made movies with it in the thirties and forties. But amateurs used to cut it down and use it for still photography.' He pushed the fiber-optic camera in farther, moving the lens right above the strip of negatives. 'See the horizontal dashes between every fourth sprocket hole?'

'How do you know this? What are you, the Professor from *Gilligan's Island*?'

Shep didn't smile, which heightened Mike's alarm. He just

poked his tongue into his lip and said, 'If you find it in a safe, odds are I've come across it. That shit is highly flammable – basically the same as flash paper. If it catches a spark, it's up in a puff.'

Mike exhaled and let his forehead bang against the safe. Those photo negatives were a foot away, sitting behind an unlocked safe door that he couldn't swing open. To have gotten this far, only to be undone by two lengths of stripped wire.

He swore sharply, a shout that echoed around the warehouse, rustling the bats in the rafters. Then he leaned back, spit into the darkness beyond the lights, and gave a bitter laugh. 'I'm never going to see my daughter again, and it's because some botanists from Stanford used cheap film eighty years ago.'

'There's no way I could've known.' Shep's voice was too loud, and his hearing had nothing to do with it.

'I know that,' Mike said. 'I'm not blaming—'

'I mean, of all things, cellulose nitrate—'

'—you. I'm just grateful—'

'—that shit's so flammable it burns *underwater*.'

Mike bolted upright, Shep's head snapping up. Mike jogged off into the darkness, shouting, 'Get some light over here!'

He found the faucet near the wall by feel and cranked the handle, water drumming the wide basin below. Shep directed one of the T-bars of floodlights over, nearly blinding him.

Mike said, 'We gotta drown the circuit. No oxygen, no spark.'

Shep came over, and they watched the rust-colored water slowly turn clear. 'And if the water ruins the negatives?'

Mike found a crusted rag and used it to plug the drain. 'We're out of options.'

As the water rose, he spread several moving blankets out on the floor beside the basin and angled a set of floodlights directly down onto them. 'We have to peel them apart right away.'

When Mike cut the water, the silence was pronounced, every plink from the faucet reverberating off the high rafters.

They crossed to the safe and lifted it from either side, careful to keep the door clamped shut. With some effort they carried it over and rested it on the lip of the basin. Shep's eyes were shiny and excited. 'Ready?'

They slid the safe over, and it hit the water with a slap, a wave rolling back and splashing their thighs. A spike of two-by-four gouged the underside of Mike's forearm, but he held tight, settling the safe gently on the bottom.

He stepped back and shook his arms, spattering the concrete with drops of blood and water. Shep stayed put, elbows resting on the edge of the basin, a dugout-railing lean. After testing that the blankets had warmed beneath the floodlights, Mike went to Shep's side, mirrored his position, and peered down. Bubbles streamed from the drill hole in the top of the safe. They made the faintest sound when they hit the surface, like guppies feeding.

Mike tried not to think of the water seeping into those photo negatives. He tried not to think about what would happen if they got ruined, if the wires sparked when the door opened despite the water, if they weren't the negatives Two-Hawks was looking for. His knee vibrated up and down, a nervous tic.

They waited, watching the safe slowly fill.

Chapter 52

William and Dodge sat in the musty kitchen of the clapboard house, flipping desperately through the list of foster homes in California and the neighboring states. They had narrowed the list considerably but still had a mile of addresses. Boss Man had been breathing down their necks, so William and Dodge had forgone sleep for two nights running. After last night's heist, Boss Man's impatience had turned to fury. William had been calling in favor after favor from various patrolmen in various departments, crossing names off the list with a bloody red marker. He had cops spreading out through four states, checking in on foster homes, looking for new faces.

The kitchen was so far gone that months ago he and Dodge had given up any pretense of trying to clean it. Grease spattered the wall above the stove, dust clouded the windows, spills of salt dotted the floor like mini pyramids. And yet somehow they managed, cleaning out a coffee cup or a plate at a time before returning it to the dirty dishes mounded in the sink or stacked along the counters. Perched anomalously atop the long-broken microwave was a fax machine, a few dead flies caught in the paper feed.

Dodge sat across from William, reading a graphic novel and sipping deliberately from a glass of hot tea. In the soft light, his features looked even more indistinct, the edges of his nose blurred into his cheeks as if smoothed out with a putty knife. Now and then he absentmindedly rubbed the broad pad of his thumb against his forefinger, giving off a rasp. That was how he showed impatience when he was itching to use his hands.

William had just plugged in his cell phone to recharge when it trilled. The movement of Dodge's thumb paused.

William checked the caller-ID screen, then picked up and asked, 'You got him for us?'

'Those bastards at Susanville PD aren't going to turn Shepherd White over to us.' Boss Man's voice was tense and driving. 'In fact, he was released nearly three hours ago.'

'Released?' Rattled, William sat on a waist-high stack of brittle newspapers. 'Dodge prepped the cellar already. Where the hell was Graham?'

'Dead,' Boss Man said.

'Graham's dead,' William repeated for Dodge's sake.

Dodge looked up, sipped his tea, and lowered his gaze again to the comic. His thumb resumed the gentle scratching motion.

'He'd gone offline, so I had Sac PD send over a car to take a look,' Boss Man continued. 'Shot in his bed.'

William realized what he'd heard in Boss Man's voice that had made him so uneasy. Something he'd never heard in it before. Desperation. William breathed out through his nose, scratched his cheek, quelled the rush of concern in his chest. 'It'll be okay.'

'Oh? You've handled this before, have you? You've dealt with state officials when they come knocking? You know how to pull strings inside a murder investigation of the goddamned director of an agency?' His breaths filled the receiver. 'Don't tell me what'll be fine. *I* say when it'll be fine.'

'Yessir.'

'Now, fortunately we still have plenty of friends. I'm sitting across from one of Graham's chiefs right now. It seems Graham sent us a little gift from beyond the grave. Our soon-to-be partner here has been monitoring a particular individual's activity. Once he caught word of Graham's death, he came here to deliver

378

the news personally.' A heightened pause. 'He managed to back-trace a signal.'

William shot a breath of relief, then said, past the phone to Dodge, 'We have an address.'

Dodge set down the graphic novel, smoothed his hands across the cover, and rose.

'The name is a familiar one,' Boss Man said.

William flipped over a piece of paper and held the bloodred point of the marker at the ready. He felt his lips stick to his teeth and realized he was grinning in anticipation.

'Go get answers,' Boss Man said. 'Any way you can.'

Chapter 53

The photo negatives – aside from the top one in the stack, which had disintegrated in Mike's hands – had emerged from the water surprisingly intact. They had stuck together at first, which actually served to protect the ones in the middle. Mike had been eager to deliver them, but Shep had forced him to let them lie for a time after drying so the floodlights could bake out any hidden moisture. Now it was a few minutes past midnight, and Mike sat alone with Two-Hawks in a sealed room behind the fill bank at the Shasta Springs Band of Miwok Casino, where jackpots were paid out. The table between them was stainless steel, and a matching cart in the corner held a money-counting machine, an accountant's calculator, a heavy phone, and a Polaroid instant camera. This was a room that changed the course of people's fortunes, and tonight, Mike prayed, would be no exception.

Shep was waiting nearby, parked on an unlit road, prepared to unleash hell if Two-Hawks failed to deliver what he'd promised. On the way over, Shep and Mike had stopped to make an addition to the growing stash hidden behind their motel room's heating vent – the Deer Creek tribe genealogy report. Back in the dank warehouse, with the footlights warming his shoulders, Mike had stared down in wonderment at his family tree, that official scalloped seal marking the top of the wet page. All those names and dates, the entanglements and forks, a history in which he was embedded. When he saw the place reserved for his own name, *Michael Trainor*, amid the vast and intertwined lineage, he had felt too overwhelmed to speak. But hours later, once the water had dried, leaving the pages stiff, it had struck him that the words were only ink on paper, that he'd already had a place in the world. The only path to reclaiming it ran through the man sitting opposite him now.

Two-Hawks raised each negative to the light and squinted up at it, his dark eyes moist. Wrinkles fanned through his cheeks. His tribe would keep their federal recognition, certainly, but it was clear that the images meant much more to him. He was soaking them in one at a time, and Mike's patience had grown thin enough to put a fist through.

'Thank you,' Two-Hawks said. 'These are amazing. I've dreamed about that settlement since I was a young boy. Did you see?' He offered a fragile negative across the table, but Mike just stared at him.

Two-Hawks's expression of wonder was replaced by sheepishness. He rode his rolling chair over to the cart and murmured something into the phone. A few minutes later, Blackie entered and set down a safe-deposit box on the table in front of Mike.

Though the room was cool, Mike felt sweat roll down his sides, tickling his ribs. He lifted the lid. What struck him first was how empty the box was – some papers sliding in the long metal case.

On top were surveillance photographs – Brian McAvoy with Dodge and William. Multiple meetings, each photo sporting a different time stamp. Mike looked up at Two-Hawks, unimpressed.

Two-Hawks said, 'Our man smuggled out the material beneath.'

Mike lifted the final few photos to reveal a stack of photocopies – cramped handwriting and figures filling lined pages.

A ledger.

Mike's heart quickened.

Two-Hawks's finger appeared beneath Mike's downturned face, one manicured nail tapping. 'These represent payments issued through McAvoy's personal slush account. Yes, that is McAvoy's handwriting. He must not have wanted digital files' – a note of irony – 'as they're too easy to copy.'

'Your inside man?' Mike said. 'You said he's an accountant?'

'Ted Rogers. A specialist in offshore bookkeeping. McAvoy brought him in to expedite the cash flow between offshore entities. In the process Mr Rogers needed to clean up some wires that had gone astray between accounts. So he was given limited access to this ledger. The recipients are identified by bank-account number – see there? You can probably guess who the most frequent fliers are.'

'Rick Graham,' Mike said faintly. 'Roger Drake. William Burrell.'

'And, if you reach back far enough, Leonard Burrell. I guess he's—'

'William's uncle.'

Mike riffled through the pages, the scrape on the underside of his arm throbbing. The dates trailed back through the decades. Next to certain payments were lengthy numbers without commas or dashes. Mike counted and recounted; each number had nine digits.

Mike said, 'Are those what I think they are?'

'Social Security numbers.'

Mike tried to swallow but found his mouth too dry to carry it off. 'Belonging to?'

'Your mother. Your father. Those brothers who wouldn't sell their land. A councilwoman in the way of a zoning law. A high roller who couldn't make good on a seven-figure marker. These payments are issued and the people corresponding to those Social Security numbers go missing a day or two later. To a one.'

Seeing it laid out so brazenly was sickening. Dollar and cents, human lives.

'Which ones . . .' Mike wet his lips. 'Which ones belonged to my parents?'

Two-Hawks pointed out the entries. Mike ran a finger across the dates. Stared at the Social Security numbers. Just John. Danielle Trainor. Two-Hawks cleared his throat, and Mike realized he'd zoned out for a time.

He flipped to the end of the photocopies, but the dates ended about a week before Dodge and William had stepped from the shadows into his life. The thought of the actual ledger still out there, sitting in some safe or locked drawer, chilled him. He knew what would be written there now in the same strained penmanship – his own Social Security number, and that of his daughter.

His eye caught on the last big payment. It had no corresponding Social Security number. 'What do you think that was?'

Two-Hawks bunched his lips, his stare dropping to the table. 'One of Ted Rogers's last acts was transferring the money to pay for his own murder.' He flipped back a page, pointed to two more entries. 'And the murder of his wife.'

The fact rang around the room for a moment or two.

'A few days went by, no sign of any of them. Cops were called, found the house empty. No trace of anything aside from a missing couch cushion from Ted's study. Dodge and William never leave a body behind.' Two-Hawks rubbed his eyes. 'Clearly, McAvoy had caught wind of *something*. For obvious reasons he left the Social Security numbers off the ledger, since Ted would have recognized . . .' He slumped back in his chair, a cheek clamped between his teeth, his eyes gone moist. Mike understood now the man's quick anger last night when Shep had pressed him on the topic of his inside man.

The scenario in the Rogerses' house was too close to the nightmares that had been playing out in Mike's head for the past two weeks. He averted his eyes. In the bottom of the safe-deposit box was a final stack of photocopied papers. He reached for them.

The top pages bore shadows where the originals had been folded like letters. Each had a handwritten date, one of the Social

Security numbers from the ledger, and a code of some sort. Midway through the stack, they switched to fax format, the codes scrawled in the middle of the page, the time stamp printed neatly across the top.

Grateful for the shift in attention, Two-Hawks said, 'I guess those were tucked in the back of the ledger. Each date corresponds with a payment and someone's disappearance. I figure it's confirmation that the job was . . . completed. On these later ones, the "sent to" phone number on the header? That's McAvoy's personal fax line. But we couldn't figure out what those codes mean.'

Mike glanced at a few of them. *FRVRYNG. MSTHNG. LALADY*.

Text messages? Nicknames?

The sealed room was making him claustrophobic. He was eager to get out and start formulating a plan with Shep and Hank for how to obliterate McAvoy and his men. Gathering up the papers, he slid them into the large gray envelope that Two-Hawks had provided.

He stood, leaning a hand on the table to steady himself. Two-Hawks gripped his arm in support. They headed to the back corridor, Mike continuing on ahead alone.

He reached the far door and shoved it open, the night air sweeping through his clothes, tightening his skin. He looked back. Two-Hawks was still there down the hall, standing in half shadow. He raised an arm, his palm out like that Indian healer from the painting.

Mike stepped out into the cold.

'You need a body.' Hank's voice over the line sounded hoarse and weak.

Cell phone pressed to his cheek, Mike sat shuddering in the passenger seat of the Pinto, Shep looking on. They were parked outside an all-night diner down the hill from Two-Hawks's casino, the gray envelope heavy across Mike's thighs.

'*What?*' Mike said.

'Why do you think McAvoy makes those people *disappear*?' Hank said. 'No body, no murder case. All that shit you got, damning as it looks, remains circumstantial. But a body, a *body* opens everything up.'

Mike was yelling: 'You're telling me that *all this*—'

'Look, there's no question this evidence changes the playing field. It's way too big for McAvoy to cover up anymore. He'll be stained – the payments to Graham a*lone*. Once this gets out, it'll drive a wedge between McAvoy and the law-enforcement community. You're gonna have whole agencies scrambling to distance themselves from the guy. It's all about appearances. And with that genealogy report, you can make a claim on the casino and put the asshole out of business. Dodge and William will be investigated and watched, and I can't imagine that the cops won't find something that'll stick. But you asked if this *hangs* McAvoy, and no, it doesn't hang him. A *body* would hang him.'

Exasperated, Mike pressed his temple to the icy window. A young couple in a vintage Mercedes coupe parked beside them and climbed out, so Mike resisted the urge to shout again. 'What do I do?' he asked quietly.

'You've done enough,' Hank said. 'We get a lawyer, leak some evidence, negotiate who you turn yourself in to. I'm thinking FBI. There's plenty you gotta answer for, too, Rick Graham's body being foremost. But we can get you in the system now. Check on Annabel. Get your daughter back, safe.'

Mike's head was tilted forward into the warm air blowing from the vents, his hand pinching his eyes.

'You've been out in the cold a long time,' Hank said. 'It's time to come in.'

Tears were falling through Mike's hand, tapping the gray folder. He managed to get the words out. 'How long? Until I can get Kat?'

'We'll get our footing with this as quickly as we can. A few days?'

'No. By tomorrow night.'

'Then let's get started.'

Mike swallowed hard. 'All right. I'm coming to you. We make copies of all this. Put them in different locations. Figure out a game plan, slow and smart.'

Hank agreed, and they signed off.

Mike tilted back his head and blew out a shaky breath. 'Okay,' he said. 'Okay.' Another breath, this one less wobbly. 'Let's hit the motel room, pick up the cash, the flash drive, and the genealogy report.'

'Motel's the opposite direction,' Shep said. 'I'll go, meet you there.'

'We only have one car,' Mike said.

Shep scowled at him, disappointed, clearly, by Mike's lack of imagination. Shep got out, swinging the door shut behind him. In ten seconds he was into the vintage Mercedes; in forty the engine roared to life.

He offered Mike a two-finger salute as he pulled out.

Mike slid across into the driver's seat and drove off.

The freeway, at this hour, was quiet. A few miles down the road, a lightning bolt of hope shot through the vise of Mike's chest, nearly splitting him in half. He steered off onto the shoulder, stumbled a brief ways into the brush, and bent over, hands on his knees, catching his breath. For so long he hadn't dared to let himself hope, and the sensation of it ripped through his bloodstream, a drug he'd lost tolerance for. He fought off thoughts of Annabel's touch, her hands intertwined in his against the bedsheets. The heft of Kat when he picked her up, that smooth cheek against his.

Not a husband. Not a father. Not yet.

The air was sharp and tinged with sagebrush, the wet dirt sticking to the bottoms of his shoes. He heaved twice, bringing nothing up, then returned to the car. He'd left the door open, the soft dome light spilling over the headrests. He buckled back in, put his hands on the wheel, and set off toward Hank.

As he exited the freeway, the Batphone vibrated in his pocket. He fumbled it out and open. 'Yeah?'

'I have to put through a call.' Shep's voice sounded weird.

'What? Who?'

There was some background noise and then an electronic click.

Annabel said, 'Hello?'

Chapter 54

The first thought to break through Mike's delirious relief was that Dodge and William had found her and forced her to call. He didn't know what he was saying, but in between the rush of his words and the thrum of his thoughts he registered his wife's replies: 'Yes, I'm alive. I'm alive. I'm right here, babe.'

And: '—need you. Need you here. I'm so scared.'

And: 'No, no one's got me. I'm safe. Laid out, sore as hell, and I smell like a nursing home, but I'm safe.'

His brain finally caught up to what was happening, sounding a single clarion note over the din of their voices: *She's alive.*

She was sobbing, her voice cracked and aching. '—was terrified when I woke up yesterday. Thought you were—'

She's alive.

And: '—almost twenty-four hours to get my voice working. I had Shep's number, the one you gave to me back—'

Alive.

And: 'No, I haven't called anyone. They told me my father's been on a scorched-earth campaign to find me, but I knew to wait, to only talk to you. Shep told me some crazy stuff – an Indian tribe? – and that no one can know where I am. That you guys are on the run.'

Her next question brought him crashing back into his body, stilling the background buzz of his own words. It sent him into a kind of reverse shock, his senses heightened to a painful clarity.

She asked, again, 'How's my baby?'

There was nothing but pure, raw sensation. The plastic bumps of the steering wheel digging into the meat of his fingers. Windshield condensation blurring the edges of the yellow sign of Hank's motel up ahead. The wrinkles of his shirt forming ridges against his lower back.

Mike cleared his throat, hard. 'Shep . . . Shep didn't tell you?'

'Tell me what?' All the warmth had gone from her voice.

He forced out the words. 'I had to leave her.'

'Leave her? *Leave* her? How long ago?'

Five days, fourteen hours, and seventeen minutes.

He said brusquely, 'Couple of days.'

'*Days*? Did you say . . .'

'Annabel, I promise you—'

'Have you checked on her?'

'I . . . I couldn't. I can't. There were—'

'She's been alone? Without you?' Her words deteriorated into something unintelligible. Her breath came in loud puffs across the receiver. 'You *know* she's okay, though? Right now?'

He heard himself hesitate a beat too long. '. . . Yes.'

'No.' Her voice had turned fragile, tiny, pleading. 'Uh-uh. No. Where is she?'

Shep said, 'Um . . .'

Mike had forgotten they were on a three-way call. The sound of his wife's voice had overwhelmed all other considerations, but Shep's interjection knocked him back to harsh reality.

He said, 'I can't . . . I can't tell you.'

Annabel was breathing hard, maybe hyperventilating. In the background he heard the beep of a cardiac monitor. 'What does that *mean*?' she said.

'You're on a hospital phone,' he said.

'I can't *walk* yet, Mike.' Her tone had gone flat. 'Where else would I be?'

'They're still looking for us. And you. They came after you

once to get to me and Kat. We don't know if they're monitoring your line right now. I can't tell you over this phone.'

'*Where's my daughter?*'

'They could be listening. Right now.'

'Does Shep know where she is?'

'No one knows.'

'Except you.'

'I'm getting her tomorrow, Annabel. We're almost out of this. We are one step from nailing them and starting to put our lives back together. Hours away, honey. *Hours.*'

She was crying again, hopelessly. He imagined her, injured and bed-bound in a strange room, pumped full of drugs and terror.

Without registering it he had pulled in to a parking space by Hank's door and set the car in park. 'I will pick her up tomorrow,' he said, 'and bring her to you.'

'Please just tell me where she . . . that she's . . .'

He summoned all of his strength to harden his heart to her. *Not a husband.*

'Tomorrow,' he said. 'Everything will be okay.'

'I need to know.' Her words, drawn out through sobs. 'I just need to hear my baby's voice.'

'I'm sorry,' he said. 'I love you.'

He snapped the phone shut. 'I'm sorry,' he told it. 'I'm sorry I'm sorry.' Heat rolled up from his neck into his face, and he punched the steering wheel. Once, twice, three times. His knuckles screamed.

He sat panting. *Hours away*, he reminded himself. *Hours.*

Annabel was alive. Impossibly, he had even more at stake now.

He grabbed the gray envelope and hurried across the parking lot to Hank's room. When he knocked on the door, Hank called out, 'Yeah, come in.'

The door was unlocked. Mike pushed in, the room led to by a brief hall. It was dark, lit only by the laptop, which sat open on the tiny desk, throwing off a lavender swirl of screen saver. Hank sat on the bed, facing away, his shoulders slumped. 'Yeah, come in,' Hank said again. The screen saver threw dappled light across half of his body before the glow shifted to the ceiling.

Mike stopped at the verge of the room, felt the smile bloom on his face. 'We did it, Hank.'

A meow came out of the dark, and Hank's fat tabby oozed from the blackness to rub against Mike's leg. It sat on his foot and began assiduously licking its front paw.

Mike held up the envelope. 'It's all right here.'

The screen saver kept on, mapping blocks of light on the far wall, the lampshade, Mike's shoes. A section of warped floorboards flashed into sight ahead. A trail of tiny paw prints, rendered in smeared black, led from around the side of the bed to the cat at Mike's feet.

Icy horripilation moved up Mike's arms, crawling across the back of his shoulders.

He dropped the envelope, reaching for the .357 tucked into his jeans. The envelope slapped the floorboards, and the cat started, scampering off, leaving fresh prints of blood.

Mike brought the revolver up, aiming, pivoting to take in the half dark around him. Across the room Hank sat as still as marble, facing away. Only then did Mike see the microcassette recorder on the comforter beside him. Hank's voice issued again from the tiny speakers: '*Yeah, come in.*'

Mike put his back to the wall, barely hearing his thoughts above the roar of blood in his head. A faint rustle came from the unlit bathroom between him and the front door. He was pinned in the brief hall. Inching forward into the room, he charted a trembling course toward a corner. The screen saver kept on with its disco alteration, bringing the walls and ceiling to life, making them bulge and contract like lungs. In the watery light, he noted the Ethernet cord trailing from the back of the laptop to the outlet beneath the desk, and he knew with fierce, distraught conviction that they'd tracked Hank to the motel when he'd logged in.

The cat bolted back into view, a whisper against the dust ruffle, and Mike started, a quick movement matching him in the space beside the curtains. He pivoted ninety degrees and pulled the trigger, the muzzle flash lighting the wall mirror already spiderwebbing around the bullet hole.

Too late he heard something whistling through the air behind him, and then the warped floorboards rushed up and hit him in the face.

Chapter 55

Janine, the oldest, kept a cocoon on a twig in a giant pickle jar, which Ms Wilder set on the ledge above the kitchen radiator in hopes of warming the chrysalis to fruition. Before every meal the girls watched it for signs of life. Traditions, though few and plain, were adhered to with rigor.

Kat slept in the fourth bedroom on a mattress laid between two bunk beds. She slept fitfully, and by the time she did drift off, she was trampled during the morning bathroom stampede. The other girls were neither nice nor cruel, though in some ways their indifference was worse. As if Kat were no more than another in a long line of undistinguished bodies that had rotated under this roof, no different from the countless that had predated her and the countless more that would arrive to displace her. She slept curled up like a puppy and smoothed out the top sheet before breakfast in a semblance of making a bed. She realized that she was doing her best to leave no imprint behind.

Most of the girls were swept off to school, and Kat cherished the relative quiet brought by the days. She sat in the family room, watching Ms Wilder through the kitchen doorway, shifting to keep her in sight as she moved to the stove or the little letter desk to pay her bills. Finally Ms Wilder looked over at her and said, 'Honey, you'd better find something to do afore your eyeballs fall out,' and Kat had skulked over to the bay window, plopped herself down, and stared at the road, reparsing her father's last words to her, searching out hidden meanings and nuance.

You'll think I won't know how great you turned out.

There were so many gaps and spaces, and it was too late to ask him to fill them in.

You need to be tough. Your life is at stake. No one can know anything about you.

She was Katherine Smith from San Diego – they'd been there a few times for SeaWorld and Legoland, and she could describe the smell of the mist coming off the ocean. But so far no one had asked, not even Ms Wilder.

I will come back for you.

Nothing uncertain about that. Was there?

Staring at the occasional passing car, she strained her mind but couldn't remember if her father had said anything about *when* he'd come back. Two weeks? Two years? When she was a teenager?

Kerry Ann, the three-year-old, was tattooing Kat's knee with a drumstick. Kat brought the drumstick over to a broken xylophone and tried to play her the Orphan Annie song she'd practiced a lifetime ago with her piano teacher, but she couldn't get it right, and besides, Kerry Ann was distracted chasing the cat.

When everyone got home from school, Kat tried to disappear into the walls. She sat at the bay window as the girls stormed around with their backpacks and hair bunchies and rambling stories. Her scalp itched from the chemical treatment; she had been pleasantly surprised that no one had made fun of her when Ms Wilder had combed the gunk through her hair on the first night. They'd all been there before.

Janine took note of Kat staring at the street and halted. She was pretty in a bug-eyed sort of way.

'Don't waste your time,' she said.

'He's coming,' Kat said. 'He swore it to me.'

Janine pushed out her bottom lip with her tongue and applied a bright swath of lipstick. 'You'll learn,' she said, and pranced over to join the cluster of girls at the pickle jar.

Their conversation washed over her, but she barely heard.

'Maybe it's a monarch.'

'Ms Wilder says it's the wrong season.'

'Oh, 'cuz Ms Wilder knows everything?'

'She knows more than you.'

'There are lots of kinds of butterflies. Besides, monarchs are too Halloweeny. I hope it's yellow instead of orange and black.'

'Just as long as it's not a ugly *moth*.'

It was as if Kat were underwater, the voices warped and distant. She pressed her nose to the glass. There was just her and the street and a caught-in-her-throat prayer that her father would show up with a stolen car and a smile.

During dinner Kat did everything not to cry. She chewed and swallowed, forcing food through the stricture of her throat. She tried not to meet anyone's gaze, because she knew if she did, she'd break and start crying and then that's who she'd be forever after: Katherine Smith, the Girl Who Cried at Dinner. So she directed her gaze at the twig and the cocoon. As the girls rose to clear – her job was silverware – she saw it pulse once.

That secret got her through after-dinner chores and teeth brushing. When she prepared for bed, she saw that one of the girls had stepped on her pillow with dirty feet. A dark smudge right in the middle. She padded down the hall. Ms Wilder was in the family room with the older girls, watching a *Hannah Montana* rerun – Jackson pouring cereal from the box into his mouth, half of it making it in.

'Sorry to be trouble,' Kat said, 'but can I have . . .? My pillowcase is dirty. Can I have another one?'

A few of the girls tittered, and Kat's face grew hot.

Ms Wilder said, 'Honey, what we got is what we got.'

They turned their focus back to the TV. Kat stood there feeling stupid.

Ms Wilder said, 'Something else?'

'I . . . Do I get to go to school?'

Ms Wilder said, 'We're working on that.'

'I wouldn't complain if I was you,' Janine offered. 'Not about *school.*'

As Kat passed the kitchen, she peered in at the cocoon and saw a seam where it had cracked. She went back to bed with her heart pounding and flipped the pillow over so it was clean side up.

Lying there, she stared up at the bunks towering on either side of her. The younger girls were all asleep – Emilia even snored some – but Kat couldn't so much as close her eyes. Sometime later she heard the TV zap off with a crackle, and there were footsteps and creaks and doors closing, and then there was nothing but the hum of the radiator.

Kat lay as long as she could and then slipped out and tiptoed into the kitchen. The cocoon was laid open, curled on the twig like a dead leaf, but she couldn't see the butterfly anywhere. Slowly, it dawned on her that it wasn't a butterfly at all, that what she'd mistaken for a fat bulge on the twig was really a newborn moth.

It was brown and fuzzy and very ordinary.

She thought about the pet lizard she'd wanted to keep and forgotten in the truck and how her dad had brought it in at night and how it had slid stiffly around in the jar. Before she'd really considered it, she had the pickle jar under her arm and was creeping out into the backyard, the night snaking up her sleeves and pajama legs and raising goose bumps. Pulled tight to the fence was a parked cop car, which made her feel safer even though there was no one inside. At the back of the lot, beyond the play structures, rose a line of thinning trees, and Kat couldn't help but think about how much lusher the ones were that lined her own backyard.

She remembered her father's words – *I will come back for you* – but she couldn't remember his expression when he'd said it, and she realized that soon she might not remember his face at all. And then the words might blur, too – what he'd said and what she thought she remembered – and it hit her with horror that one day, one day she'd really *become* Katherine Smith of San Diego.

He's coming, she told herself. *He swore it.*

She looked down at the pickle jar, her little secret that no one else had seen, the girls' sneers returning: *Just as long as it's not a ugly* moth.

It had spread its wings against the glass, and even here across the road from the streetlights she could see the tiny patterns, beige against chestnut, like a masterfully inlaid floor.

She thought about the disappointment and cackling that would ensue once the girls discovered that their butterfly was a common moth, and she ran her thumb across the sharp spots on the lid where breathing holes had been gouged with a screwdriver or a knife.

You'll learn.

With a savage twist, she removed the lid and held the jar aloft. The moth hesitated there on the side of the glass, and then it flicked once and cleared the mouth of the jar. She watched it jerk its way around the nearest tree trunk, rising, rising, and finally losing itself against the pitchblack sky.

No more than twenty feet away, among the trunks of the trees, an orange dot flared to life.

She froze, zeroing in on the point of light, suddenly aware of the silence, her isolation, the charcoal air that had blanketed the shadows at the edge of the yard. The faintest crackle of burning paper rose above the evening hum.

A cigarette.

Now gone.

Suddenly sweating, one uneasy foot half set down on dirt, she squinted at the grainy air beneath the dip of the branch, unable to discern much in the gathered darkness by the trunk. Whoever was there, she had come right up on him. Her breathing had gone all jerky.

The ember burned back to life, illuminating a sliver of face – edge of chin, cheek, temple. And a uniform collar. A police uniform. The man went with the cop car. She didn't recognize his face and didn't know what he was doing there in the dark.

No one can know anything about you.

The cherry died, the face vanishing back into the deep dusk.

Kat took a quick step toward the house, her sandal catching on a bulge in the asphalt. 'Oh.' She laughed nervously, trying for casual. 'I didn't see you for a long time.'

A voice came at her from the darkness, calm and low. 'Longer than you think.'

The words froze her.

'It's okay, sweetie. I'm a cop. I patrol this area. Make sure everyone's safe. You're new here, right? What's your name?'

She forced her mouth to work. 'Katherine Smith.' She managed a polite smile and took a step back, and then another.

'Now, smile pretty.' A camera flash blinded her.

She turned and broke for the house, breath firing her lungs. Something in the act of running stoked the terror, and she sprinted blindly, with abandon, her ankles throbbing, her chest burning. The trail up to her lawn, fifty yards away, might as well have been a mile. When she reached the rear door, she stopped, panting, and finally risked a look back. The yard was still.

An instant later the cop car roared to life at the curb. It pulled out, its headlights strafing the fence and casting a swath of broken light across the now-empty space between the tree trunks.

Chapter 56

First there was sensation. His head pulsing, filled with so much blood it seemed it might explode. Dust on his tongue. A slab of cushioned plastic shoved to his face, mashing his features to one side. A scent of decay, drawn into his mouth with each rasping inhale.

Then sound, strained as if through a filter. Water sloshing. Shuffling boots. William's voice – 'I got the technique down. I been rewatching that C-SPAN Senate inquiry. Why? What do *you* prefer?'

And then Dodge. 'Fingers.'

'Knuckle by knuckle, like *Sharky's Machine*? No, we should give this a try. I mean, military-perfected, right?'

None of this seemed to be related to Mike; it was as though he were listening to an old-time radio show, fictitious characters discussing fictitious outcomes. He forced his eyelids to part. The movement, however minuscule, sent daggers of pain back through his head. But finally: sight. It was like being reborn, acquiring one sense at a time.

The room rotated on its axis for a while, and slowly it dawned on Mike that he was lying supine on a downward slant, his face turned to one side. It took a few minutes longer for his eyes to adjust to the dimness and sharpen the focus on the whitish blob five feet away, staring at him. It was Hank's face, paled to an ashen white. His lips were bruised and mottled, puckered out as if for a last kiss.

His daughter's name roared into his head: *Kat. I have to scrub the memory of her location from my brain so no matter what they do to me, I've got nothing to tell them.*

When he shifted, fire roared through his chest and arms. His bound hands were a knot in the small of his back and his head screamed. He twisted his wrists and noted through his mind-numbed stupor that the restraints rubbing against his raw skin felt like cloth. He appeared to be at a forty-five-degree angle, his knees visible above. His thighs burned, and his calves and feet were installed into a contraption of some sort. Gradually, he recognized that he was hooked into an incline sit-up bench.

The voices continued, a calm rumble. Dodge and William were behind him?

With great effort he rolled his head, the dark ceiling scanning by, and faced the other direction. He was in a big concrete box of a cellar, the only light thrown through the open door at the top of a splintering wooden staircase. Standing between Mike and the stairs, visible only as a slice of shoulder, cheek, forehead, was Dodge. Mike blinked a few more times, the cellar coming clearer, William resolving from the darkness at the big man's side. They were huddled, conferring. Mike's gaze pulled to a square of burlap spread on the concrete floor, various tools laid out like devices on a medical tray. Beyond the burlap was a large, old-fashioned dunking-for-apples wooden tub. The water filling it to the brim looked black and forbidding.

Dust trembled in the column of light thrown from the open door above.

'Oh, you're up.' William came toward him, making lurching progress, an empty plastic milk jug floating in each hand.

Mike turned his head away, the only movement he could muster, bringing him again face-to-face with Hank. His sprawled body lay at an odd angle to his neck, a plastic drop cloth already cocooning his lower half. One foot protruded, the worn black dress sock incongruous here, in this context. The line of flaking white skin showing at Hank's ankle underscored the awful tableau, the frailty of this life, of any life, which, despite all the sweat and work and best-laid plans, could end in a windowless cellar, half rolled in a strip of plastic sheeting.

Beside the body was another drop cloth, which Mike realized had been reserved for him.

When he turned back, Dodge loomed above him, winding a piece of terry cloth the size of a gym towel around his hand. His shirt was unbuttoned, curled back from a wife-beater worn to near transparency. William crouched, letting out a little pained moan, and began to fill the gallon jugs with water from the tub. The bubbles gave off a faint, comic-book repeat: *glug glug glug*.

'Okay,' Mike said, still trying to grasp what was happening. 'All right.'

William stood, a bottle dripping in either hand. Staring up at the faces overhead – Dodge's drawn back, glinting eyes set in the wide skull, and William, stooped to favor his left side, all wisps of facial hair and bunched lips – Mike felt something break open inside him and spill heat.

'I heard about you years ago,' William said, 'from my Uncle Len. You were the one who got away. The Job. But Boss Man, he woulda let it lie. Finding you. He stopped looking. Stopped caring. Figured whatever life you'd made, you'd never put it all together. But then your buddy Two-Hawks kicked the hornet's nest, found out about your name on that genealogy report. Boss Man caught wind, and guess what? You were back on the table.'

He neared. 'These are glossies of Ted Rogers, the guy who did the stealing for Two-Hawks.' He produced some photographs from a back pocket and held them for Mike to see. The soft pink skin of a middle-aged man in various forced contortions. William fanned through several taken within these same cellar walls before Mike turned his head and gagged. William leaned over him, breathing down. 'My uncle worked on your dad some. What yer daddy went through? Made this' – a shake of the photos – 'look like a tickle. You know what? Why'm I talking so much when I can just show you.'

Horror came on like a toothed blade, sawing its way through the shock.

'Okay now,' William said gently, and Dodge let the small towel flutter down over Mike's face.

Mike jerked in an instinctive breath, the towel adhering to his mouth. He sensed William lean in close, and the cloth grew wet and heavy. Water moved up his nose, a slow trickle at first, and then soaked through the terry, sealing out oxygen. The effect was instant, comprehensive. Mike jerked and screeched, shaking his head, but the towel clung to his face like a film. His lungs and throat spasmed uselessly. Just when he thought he might go out, the towel peeled back and he found himself gasping and gagging, Dodge staring down at him, the towel dripping onto the floor.

Mike's shoulders cracked in their sockets, and he realized he'd pulled himself up to a sitting position. Also that he was screaming. He twisted off the backboard, one leg tangling in the pads, the bench rocking up on two legs and settling with the clop of horse hooves on cobblestone. He hit the floor with his shoulder and lay there, exhausted, pain blurring his vision.

Dodge leaned down and lifted Mike as easily as a grocery bag. He laid him back on the bench, manipulating his legs and torso with stern efficiency, totally absorbed in his task. He might have been threading a needle or tying his shoes. When Dodge moved Mike's feet through the leg pads, Mike bucked, trying to get upright again, but Dodge placed a thumb on his chest and flattened him down onto the decline backboard. Blood rushed to Mike's head. His chest heaved against the pressure.

Dodge finished with Mike's feet and eased his thumb off. Mike gasped for air, his ribs aching.

'You got information you don't want to tell us, right?' William said. 'So we need to extract it from you. It's not gonna be easy – on you *or* us. It's just something we gotta get through together.'

Mike made some garbled noise.

William's eyes trembled back and forth, as if his gaze were wavering, though it was not. 'Where's Katherine?'

Mike said, 'I don't know where she—'

William went to a knee over the tub, grimacing. *Glug glug glug* – the sound of round two.

It was over now, Mike knew. He was going to die. He just had to figure out how to get them to kill him before his stamina gave out. He pictured Kat where he'd left her, sitting on that little bench in the foster home, her untied shoelaces scraping the ground. *Please, Daddy?*

William said, 'We know you wanted to put her somewhere safe. Somewhere hidden. But Boss Man needs her, see, you *and* her out of the picture.'

'Shep got your address from Graham,' Mike said. 'If I don't check in with him, he'll call the cops and head up here.'

William shook his head with disappointment. He nodded slightly, and the terry cloth slapped back over Mike's head. Mike's panicked inhalation dimpled the cloth into his mouth, up his nostrils, and then the slow bleed of water invaded his face, drowning him into contorted silence. His thighs burned against the pads, but when he tried to shove himself upright, the steady pressure of Dodge's thumb smoothed him back down. There was fire and agony, the cloth suctioned to him like a sea creature, leaking a calm stream of water into him, shoving his own breath back down his throat.

At last he tasted oxygen and felt light on his face. His eyelids were fluttering as William leaned close, that sour breath moving across his cheeks.

'Ouch, ouch, I know, pal. I'm sorry. I know.' William watched closely, his face soft with empathy. 'But you see, I'm an expert in this. I've taken a lot of folks to the edge. I been here before. And you haven't. So I know the stories they tell, the lies they spin. There's a pattern to it, see? The fake answers, the money they promise, the friend who's gonna call the cops.'

'Okay . . .' Mike panted. 'I lied about Shep.'

'Where's Katherine?'

'I don't . . . I don't know.'

William hoisted a filled jug. 'Ready for the next round?'

'No,' Mike said. 'No no no.'

But it came anyway. The even influx of water up his nose, the airless choking and heaving, the head-shaking blindness – a fire-and-brimstone hell imported from some past, barbaric age. Somewhere between screaming soundlessly and passing out, his instinct to detach, cultivated since the whitesouts of his early childhood, kicked in.

He slid out of himself and observed the proceedings. He made himself impervious. He was a collection of parts, of bone and flesh. He was a rock. Unthinking. Unfeeling.

As Dodge tried to pull the towel free, Mike clamped his teeth down on it, and it tore a little. William laughed, 'He's bitin' it?' And then Dodge's fist hit Mike's forehead like a battering ram and the cloth was ripped from his jaws.

William said, 'Feisty, huh?'

Mike sputtered and drooled water. Because of the slant, it ran up his cheeks, over his eyes, through his hair, and tap-tap-tapped on the concrete.

William said, 'Where's your daughter?'

Mike said, 'I have no daughter,' and something in his voice made William draw back, shocked or perhaps a touch awed.

Dodge scowled impatiently and William bobbed his head, winded. A foul odor pressed in on Mike, and he thought for a moment that he'd messed himself. But then he realized it was the decay of Hank's body, picking up strength in the dank cellar air.

They did another round. And another. He would have preferred to die, but that was the point, to take him to a place where he would've pled for a bullet and to make him stay there awhile. And then to bring him back to life, again and again.

When he came into himself the next time, he was breathing

404

and William and Dodge were standing side by side, arms crossed, William wearing an expression of frustration that would have been gratifying under different circumstances. The little towel hung like a dishrag in Dodge's hand, and Mike was pleased to see that it was ripped in several places; he must've bitten down on it a few more times. The smell of Hank's body was stronger now, mixed in the airless room with the stink of sweat and fear. Reclined half upside down on the exercise bench, Mike hacked water through his mouth and nose, his throat raw, his chest an unremitting ache. His arms were as numb as posts beneath his back.

Dodge produced two cigarettes and set them beside each other between his lips. He dug a cheap plastic lighter from his shirt pocket and lit up, tilting his head to a cupped hand out of habit. He passed one to William, who sucked a long, eyes-closed draw.

'Fucking stinks in here.' William armed sweat off his brow. 'Before we take it to the next level, we should check with Boss Man.' His left leg was trembling. 'I'll get the phone.'

He labored up the stairs and returned a few minutes later. His gait had worsened from the effort of climbing and descending, one foot dragging, pigeon-toed. He reached Mike, squatted, and held the phone to Mike's ear.

Brian McAvoy's smooth voice. 'She's in a foster home, isn't she?'

Mike said, 'Who?' The syllable like a claw raking his throat.

McAvoy laughed. 'With the money at stake? We'll check every last one in the state. And then we'll move to the next state. And the next.'

'So all this,' Mike said, 'is about money?'

'You think I'm just a casino?' McAvoy said. 'I am a *nation*. I made something where there was nothing before. My daughter etched her initials into the front step when we poured the foundation. I know you think your life, your daughter's life are a big deal. But as far as collateral damage goes when it comes to nation building? There's no choice. This isn't my fault any more than it is yours. Or Katherine's. So let's handle this like men. Men with a decision to make. Here's my proposal to you: You tell us where she is, and we'll make it humane. For you, now. And more importantly for her.'

Mike's breaths were shallow across the receiver. He said, 'No.'

'We're finding her either way. All you'll be doing is sparing her a scared, miserable existence between now and then.'

'No.'

'So what's your plan?' McAvoy said. 'You're going to *outlast* my two guys there?'

'Yeah.'

'Bring 'em down through force of will?'

'Sure,' Mike said.

A guffaw. McAvoy had intended it to be dismissive, but there was surprise in it as well. 'And then?'

Mike said, 'You're next.'

A very long silence ensued. Then McAvoy said, 'Tell William I'd like to talk to him.'

Mike rolled his head. 'Wants . . . to talk . . . you.'

William stood up with the phone, cigarette dangling between his lips. 'Uh-huh, uh-huh, uh-huh.'

He snapped the phone shut and tossed it to Dodge, who slid it into the thigh pocket of his cargo pants. Something passed between their eyes, and then Dodge crouched, picked up the ball-peen hammer from the neat square of burlap, and tapped it into his vast palm.

William said, 'Why don't you get rid of our pal there first. He's makin' my eyes water.'

Dodge shuffled over, rolled Hank's body a few more times in the plastic sheeting, and hoisted him onto a shoulder. Mike's stare lingered on the remaining drop cloth that he'd soon be occupying.

William said, 'Leave me the rag.'

Dodge tossed it over, and William held it up in front of his face, his small eyes and patchy beard visible through the holes. He shot a stream of cigarette smoke through the towel and said, 'This ain't gonna work no more.'

Dodge swung Hank's body down, which struck the floor, sending a vibration through the sit-up bench. He tugged off his shirt and dipped it into the tub of water, his shoulders and biceps bulging beneath his wife-beater. On his way back to the body, he dropped the sopping shirt onto Mike's face.

Darkness. Mike had managed to suck in a breath before the shirt hit, and he fought the wet fabric with his mouth and tongue, moving it around. Breathing was difficult, but without fresh water pouring through he was able to draw some air.

William's voice floated down at him. 'When we're done with you, I wonder if you'll see my brother. If you do, tell him I'm sorry. I should've looked out for him better, like he looked out for me. Tell him we sent you.'

Mike heard Dodge's heavy boots creak the stairs as he carried the body up. He heard William's knees crack as he crouched and then the *glug glug glug* of the milk jugs filling. From upstairs came the muffled ring of a phone, then the screech of a fax. A moment later Dodge's voice called down – 'Look' – and something soft hit the cellar floor. The sound of paper uncrumpling, then a shrill laugh escaped William.

'Wow,' William said. 'Wouldja look at that. Okay, go on and take care of the body. I'll fill in our friend here on the recent developments, and then we'll go handle business.'

Heavy footsteps moved overhead, and a screen door banged. Mike kept manipulating the shirt into position. His teeth locking into the fabric, he blew out hard and managed to suck a few drops of air around his lips. Then he kept working the shirt across his face – almost there.

A singsong voice. 'I got something to show you.' Another laugh. 'Looks like a cop who owed me a favor came through.

Little girl found. In a foster home. He was good enough to fax over a picture so we could confirm. Before we . . . you know, saddle up and ride all the way out to . . . Arizona.'

Heat spread through Mike's chest, out through his limbs. A prickling panic, suffused with rage. Images flickered through the darkness – Dodge and William rolling up in their truck. Snatching Kat off the playground. Her little body, fighting and twisted in panic.

He forced his focus back to the wet shirt. A few drops tapped the fabric, increasing the pressure above his nose, quickening to a thin stream; William was playing with him, drizzling water. 'Wanna see?'

William reached for the shirt, and then the weight was lifted from Mike's face. A grin twitched around the cigarette. 'Ta-da!'

Mike caught a flash of the uncrumpled fax in William's hand – a photo of Kat in the backyard of the foster home. The picture had been taken at night, the flash severe, and Kat was recoiling, terrified, her skin bleached a sickly white.

Mike breathed through his nose, his nostrils flaring, his mouth clamped around the acid liquid burning into his tongue.

Cigarette smoke unspooling up the side of his face, William looked down at the object clattering on the concrete floor, freed from the wet shirt.

A cheap plastic cigarette lighter.

Chewed open.

The cherry on his cigarette flared with a shocked intake of breath, and William lifted his eyes just as Mike wrenched himself forward in an excruciating sit-up and blew a spattering of lighter fluid into his face.

The cherry erupted into a sparkler, embers flying into William's eyes and beard. One side of his face caught, the wisps crackling, giving off an acrid odor. William screamed, a high-pitched feminine wail, and stumbled blindly to the tub, with the fax, aflame, fluttering after him.

Mike fought to keep himself bent up into the incline, and as William dunked his head into the tub, Mike flopped off the sit-up bench, landing across William's shoulders. The bench flipped with him, the pads clinging to one calf.

William bucked and fought, Mike struggling to keep his weight on him so his face would stay submerged. But without the benefit of his arms, Mike could only pin William so long. William slid out from under him and collapsed on his back, sputtering and moaning. Mike rolled off as well, the wooden lip digging into his side, and spun over to the square of burlap. With the cloth restraints biting into his wrists, he felt for the tools behind his back, his fingers fussing over metal rods and rubber handles. William writhed on the floor, holding his eyes and thrashing. Something stuck one of Mike's fingers, and he reached for it again, holding the blade even as it opened the pad of his thumb. Trying to will the tingling from his fingers, he got the knife turned and sawing against the restraints. His panicked stare moved between William and the door at the top of the stairs.

Silently, William shoved himself to a sitting position. One eye was open. His teeth showed as a slash carved out of red flesh and black, curled hair. He struggled to his feet and lurched toward Mike.

Mike rocked to aid the movement of the blade, his shoulders aching, his hands cramped and barely holding on. William was almost on top of him. There wouldn't be time to saw through, so Mike rolled to his side, bent his legs, and tried to swing his wrists down under his feet and in front of him. The cloth restraints snagged on the bottoms of his shoes, and he tugged harder until his hands popped through. He barely managed to get to his feet before William swung at him. Mike ducked the blow, grabbed the back of William's shirt with both bound hands, and tugged it over his head to tie up his arms, an old schoolyard trick. Pressing his fists together, he hammered them down across William's face. A ribbon of blood slapped the concrete, and

William fell to all fours over the canvas. Mike wrenched his arms apart, straining as hard as he could. The restraints finally gave way with a wet rip just as William hoisted himself up and slipped a knife into Mike's side.

The motion was silent and smooth, all pressure and no pain, just the slice of a shark cutting through water.

And then William wrenched.

The sensation was electric, Mike arcing like a hooked fish, a current of pain running so hot and intense up his left side that he thought for a moment he'd somehow caught fire.

He staggered back a step and then another, William keeping on, the blade low in his hand, his breath fluttering the charred tufts of beard around his lips. William jabbed and Mike skipped back, the current coming to life again, making him cry out. Mike unhooked his belt and wrapped the soft end around a fist. William lunged with another thrust. Mike dodged and whipped the buckle, catching William at the side of the jaw, knocking him forward too hard and quick for his left leg. He stumbled, landing on a knee. Mike threaded the belt back through the buckle to form a snare and lowered the loop of leather over William's head. Yanking the makeshift leash tight, he dragged William choking and screaming across the floor to the patch of canvas. William's resistance, coupled with the tearing pain in Mike's side, brought Mike to his knees short of the mark. William's hands scrabbled at his throat, loosening the belt. As he turned to claw at Mike, Mike snatched up the first tool in reach, a flathead screwdriver, and drove it through the side of William's left knee, crushing the fragile bone. William howled, veins popping on both sides of his neck, and curled on the floor, coughing and weeping.

It took a few minutes, but Mike forced himself up. Stepping over William, he started for the stairs, his elbow brushing the wound, blood streaming down the outside of his leg. He left a scarlet footprint on the bottom stair. A few steps up, he almost lost consciousness. He pressed his bloodstained knuckles against the wall for balance and then sat.

He whited out for a minute, drifting back to Shady Lane. Charles Dubronski waited in the darkness, thick bully head protruding on his stout neck, except this time he was leering not at Shep but at Mike. *Stay the fuck down, runt. Stay* down.

Somehow Mike was at the top of the stairs, stumbling into the wreckage of a kitchen, shocked to see daylight streaming through the dusty windows. The smell of grease clogged his throat. Every surface was littered with rotting fruit, pots, and pill bottles – so many pill bottles. But no Dodge. The house felt empty, and the walls threw off an old-lady vibe. Peeling floral wallpaper. Old pictures in rose-colored porcelain frames. A posy of fake flowers, dust caking the gingham bow. Mike tilted into the table, sending sheets of paper airborne and knocking over a stack of old newspapers. His Batphone was on the table, dissected; clearly, given how they'd questioned him, they hadn't been able to retrieve whatever data they were looking for. He swung his leaden head around, searching for another phone. The charger at the outlet was empty, and Mike remembered Dodge slipping the phone into his pocket. Panting, Mike leaned on the counter, coming face-to-face with a fax machine perched atop a cracked microwave.

It had no telephone function, but the piece of paper in the feeder had Mike's Social Security number and another of those crazy codes – *FST14U*. He clutched the page, his fingers leaving bloody smears. There was another page behind, also waiting to fax, with another Social Security number – probably Hank's – and another code, *6D8BUG*. In sofar as he could think anymore, Mike thought, *So that's it.*

William's moans climbed up the stairs, but there was no way he'd make it up and out. As Mike turned to go, he spotted among the mess of papers on the table the big gray envelope Two-Hawks had given him. Its contents had been pulled halfway out, bringing the stack of photocopied ledger pages into view. He told himself to pick it up, and a minute later he listened. He staggered across the corroding tile of the foyer and out into the vivid white day. A vast field of weeds, hilltop wind roaring across his ears, and on the other side of the hilltop, a wrecking yard from which issued a blacksmithlike clanging over the low drone of machinery.

He lost his footing on the porch stairs and had to hug the banister, worried that his intestines were going to spill onto the rust-colored dirt. But then he was balancing cautiously, tightrope-walking across to the laid-open gate of the wrecking yard. His throat and nose still burned, salt-tinged wetness stinging the abraded flesh. He spit a mixture of blood and lighter fluid. The weight of the envelope tugging at his left hand reminded him, every instant, of the knife gash in his side.

The walk was interminable, the wind rising to a maritime whistle. Purple spots appeared across the sky. The glare of the sun turned into a five-pointed star. The banging continued – metal on metal – and as the mechanical drone grew louder, Mike pegged it as a big diesel engine of some sort.

He passed into the yard, tasting the rust in the air, and followed the *clang clang clang* through two rows of crushed cars stacked higher than the fence. He came into a clearing, one arm numb at his side, his legs wobbling.

A giant electromagnetic crane loomed ahead, the enormous circular magnet up on the boom still swinging from recent activity. But the cab was empty, the door ajar. A battered, rusting station wagon waited below the hoist, an ant beneath a raised boot. Its old-fashioned black-and-yellow license plate was barely holding on: *FST14U* – the code paired with Mike's Social Security number on the fax back in the kitchen. Staring at the plate, Mike blanked out, the heat rising from the earth through the soles of his shoes. But a fresh clanging broke him from his trance.

He oriented toward the sound, which came from an ancient, top-loading automobile crusher – a cross between a giant

Dumpster and a bear trap. A fat cable ran across the dirt, connecting the two machines so that one man could work the yard by himself, operating the crusher from the cab of the crane. In the crusher Dodge's massive bowed shoulders reared up into view. He was hammering away with his ball peen, trying to dislodge a piece of shrapnel from the metal jaws.

Mike stood frozen, no more than twenty yards away. But given the rattle of the crane's engine and the pounding of the hammer, Dodge was oblivious. He stopped swinging, evidently satisfied with his progress, and stooped, disappearing from view beneath the high wall of the crusher. A moment later he heaved back into sight, Hank's wrapped body tilted across a shoulder. He readjusted the corpse, letting it slide down and away. Then he stood with his hands on his hips, catching his breath and regarding his handiwork.

Mike threw the gray envelope through the open rear window of the station wagon for safekeeping, the pages coming free and scattering across the backseat. He stumbled around the tailgate, crossing the faded set of tire tracks pressed into the loose dirt, and staggered right past Dodge, heading for the crane. His side was warm, so warm, and his left shoe squished with each step. He fought not to scream as he hoisted himself up into the high cab, his wound tearing open a bit more. His shirt, matted to his side, felt dense and heavy. The rumbling of the cab was agony.

From the higher vantage, he could see down into the crusher and piece together what had happened. With the crane Dodge had hoisted the car – a '68 Bug as the license plate proclaimed – into the crusher, but the machine had jammed, popping the vehicle onto a tilt and jogging the body half out a smashed window. Dodge had climbed in to fix the snag and slide the body back into the car.

Mike reached for the control, popping the clear plastic lid over the wide red button. Down below, Dodge finally turned, hip-deep in the huge bucket of the crusher, his legs lost in the snarl of the partially crumpled front wheel well. Their eyes met across twenty yards of dust-filled sunshine.

Mike pushed the button.

The hydraulic crushing cylinders hummed to life, the contraption beginning to clench. Like a dumb animal, Dodge moved deliberately and without panic toward the edge, trying to climb out. But then he stiffened, and it was clear that the jagged metal had folded in on him. With his flat gaze fixed on Mike, he started his descent without whimper or complaint, descending until only one hand remained in sight, lifted as if for a life preserver. It quivered once and vanished slowly into the metal crush.

Pressing a hand to the wound in his side, Mike slumped forward over the controls, his vision spotting. It occurred to him how very nice it would be to go to sleep. His blinks grew longer.

A faint movement registered through the black-and-white speckling before his eyes, and he blinked several times, squinting through the cab window.

William.

His left leg trailed lifelessly behind him, the screwdriver still jammed through the side of his wilted knee, but he was tugging himself forward with his forearms, making herky-jerky progress, like some awful stop-action film. His face scraped along the ground, his mouth and nose powdered with dirt.

Mike stared for maybe a full minute in disbelief. William bellycrawled, arm over arm, past the rows of smashed cars and into the clearing. He paused now and again to catch his breath, his head wriggling on the yoke of his shoulders.

Mike's hands twitched forward onto the console, moving across the steering levers, the joystick, the pushbuttons. Having worked a lot of big construction machines, he found the controls familiar. The magnetic hoist hung high in his field of vision, maybe forty feet above the ground. Mike clicked the joystick, and the boom whirred over toward the car crusher, the hoist rocking at the end of the giant cable.

He tried three buttons before he found the servomotor. The entire crane vibrated from the massive charge, the generator shooting a jolt of current to the magnetic hoist at the cable's end. Mike rode the joystick left a few beats more and dropped the boom, undershooting the release to compensate for the skewed perspective from the cab, a trick he'd learned from years on wheel loaders and hydraulic shovels. The giant magnet clanged onto the roof of the crushed VW Bug. Mike lifted the neat bale of metal and flesh from the vise of the crusher and began to swing it across the clearing.

William paused to take note, his raw face tilted to the early-morning sun.

The rectangular shadow fell across him, and he began tearing at the dirt, trying to make quicker progress, but it seemed his arms had nothing left.

Mike pulled back on the control and raised the compacted car to the clouds. Seventy feet, eighty – he kept on until all he saw was the underside of the vehicle, the wheels smashed up into the box of the frame.

William lay still, panting, glaring across at Mike through a tangle of fallen hair.

A moment of perfect tranquillity stretched out and out.

Then Mike tapped the button, cutting the power to the magnet above. The car detached from the hoist without a whisper of noise and plummeted in absolute silence. William let out a bark of a cry and had just enough time to cover his head.

An explosion of dust, pluming like the aftermath of a bomb. The cloud rose halfway to the hoist and then began to dissipate. The warmth of the sun slanted through the glass, and again Mike was tempted to set his head down on the console and doze off.

Mustering strength, he shoved open the door of the cab and tumbled to the dirt. He lay there panting, holding his side, the flesh tacky and warm. Parked before him was the station wagon that William and Dodge had planned to crush him in, but his

415

slanted view also took in the swirling brown mist in the air, thinning by degrees. Emerging from the dust, stacked against the chain-link across the lot, was a distinct stack of smashed cars, clearly set apart from the other rows. Some were newer, some so rusted that no color was discernible. The dust thinned further, and he saw, wired to the front of every neatly baled car, a license plate – FRVRYNG, MSTHNG, LALADY. Metal coffins, a body interred in each one. Just John. Danielle Trainor. Ted Rogers.

Mike's breath kicked up little puffs of dust, Indian red and oddly beautiful. His hand, lying a few inches in front of his face, was caked with layers of blood, slick and bright over dry and black.

A snowy patch blotted out all sight, and then somehow he was standing, leaning heavily against one of the crane's high, hot tires. He staggered forward, falling onto the back of the station wagon and then shoving himself along its side, leaving mime handprints in blood along the dusty windows. The driver's door groaned open, and his legs went to water. He fell into the soft cloth seat, the springs sighing beneath him. He would not be able to pull himself from the car, so he prayed the broke-down piece of shit ran. His arms felt heavy, filled with gravy. He swatted a hand forward once, twice, his fingers somehow hooking onto a key, but he didn't believe it was real until he twisted and the engine sputtered irritably to life.

He'd been driven into this mess in a station wagon; now he'd go out in one.

Yanking the stick into drive was a herculean task. Tailpipe dragging, the car shuddered around the dropped bale of VW, out of the yard, down the harsh slope of the desolate dirt road. The turns were punishing, the switchbacks agonizing.

He realized halfway down the hill that he was probably going to die.

Chapter 57

Time became a wash of movement, a confusion of images. Impressions swam through his head. A house on a shady lane at the end of a road, jungle-gym bars, a faded salmon-pink shirt, the yellow cushion reeking of cat piss, him with his elbows propped on the sill, waiting. Mike Doe at the bay window blended into Katherine Smith at the bay window. *My dad's coming back.*

You swore it, now. You swore it.

A film reel turned in his head, the run-on sentence that was his daughter's life.

– *her fist, hours old, around his pinkie, Where's Kath-a-rine?, rocking her to sleep to the* na na nas *from 'Hey Jude', her baby tongue fluttering, scorched with thrush, the soporific pulse of the breast pump at midnight, goodnight chair and the red balloon, holding on to his leg, reaching for him to pick her up, him looking at—*

—the sunlight through the windshield, so strong that he had to fight to keep his eyes open so he could see—

—*a plaster of paris handprint, the* pchhhhht *sound of pouring imaginary tea, that No Tears scent, her going boneless in a grocery-store aisle, him struggling with the jointless arms, like trying to pick up water, crying the first time she watches Annabel get her hair cut, the movie-theater seat popping up beneath her tiny legs until he reaches over and holds it down, covering her eyes when the teapot shrieks, walking in his sneakers, in Annabel's high heels, in his boots, and—*

—the station wagon was off the road now, stopped, and he

417

was slumped forward, his lips smashed against the top of the steering wheel. He looked down through the rip in his T-shirt and saw the glittering stick of his rib in the wash of blood at his side. The surrounding skin was fish white. He closed his eyes again and dreamed about how lovely it would be just to keep them that way.

You will come back for me.

I will come back for you.

He set his hands on the wheel and pushed himself upright. He was shuddering; his *flesh* was shuddering. He willed his arm to move, to throw the car into reverse. The station wagon thumped its way up out of the roadside ditch and onto the road, and he gritted his teeth, blinked the sweat from his eyes, took a creaking breath, and—

—then she is five, jumping rope, smiling at him, missing eye-teeth, the lavender dress with the flaking Disney princess iron-on she sleeps in until it grows brittle, the first time she can read her own fortune at a Chinese restaurant, round red-framed spectacles, the spring break she wants to eat only licorice, orange slices at half-time, the Abominable Snowman on the Matterhorn, High School Fucking Musical. *You swore it, now. You* swore *it—*

—a horn blared, bringing him back to life, but by the time he lifted a sluggish arm, the driver had skidded angrily around him and kept on, leaving him behind, coasting down the wrong side of the road. A flash of awareness told him he was driving about five miles per hour, and he did his best to send a signal to his foot to tamp down on the gas pedal. Sometime in the past few minutes, the pain had shifted to numbness. His flesh felt as hard and cold as ice. Vaguely aware of the loose photocopies fluttering around the backseat, he cranked the wheel, righting the station wagon's course. The road looked wider, a real road now. The sun had notched a few clicks higher in the sky. Pins and needles pricked his fingertips and his breaths were shallow, almost delicate, the breaths of a newborn.

He closed his eyes for a quick prayer, but then, like magic, he has flown forward in time. He sees the future, and it is present. It floats out of reach, as fragile and elusive as a butterfly, and—

—there she is at graduation, the free spirit with the peace sign stitched to her gown who busts a dance move on the dais before shaking the principal's hand, the pale blue sky filled with graduation caps, and then her wedding night, a speech from a younger sister, or brother maybe, Annabel squeezing his hand beneath the table, and the first strain of the song for the father-daughter dance, him rising, cameras winking from the surrounding tables, and there she is, his daughter, in a shower of white, he takes her gloved hand and—

The collision hammered him into the dashboard, his eyes flying open. He rolled to the side, his forehead leaving a smudge on the driver's window. He noted the clean little homes spaced on the landscaped slopes outside, the old folks in their yellow golf shirts and beige walking shoes, pointing at him.

Through the wobbling sheet of steam rising from the crumpled hood, he saw the barely dented stucco pillar of the activity-center building and realized he must have been going only about three miles per hour. The car had ended up on some shrubs a few yards through the rear gate, a sad little terminus to a slow-motion journey.

A photocopied ledger page drifted dreamily past his face and settled on the dashboard. His lips barely moved. 'Help me,' he said to the wall of steam.

He heard whistles and footsteps, the rattle of a gurney, and at once a medical team was there, guiding him out of the driver's seat, pulling at his arms, questions raining down on him:

'Flank wound there, see?'

'Were you shot or stabbed? Shot or stabbed?'

'What's your name?'

'Any allergies?'

'*¿Hablas español? ¿Te pegaron un tiro o te apuñalaron?*'

'We need to roll him. Give yourself a hug now.'

'. . . can't . . .' He forced the words out. 'I can't die. You don't understand. My daughter . . . Katherine Wingate . . .'

'Don't move. Let us do the work.'

'Pain here? Here? *¿Dolor aquí?*'

'Tenth rib, midaxillary line. We're gonna need the blood bank.'

He heard what was left of his shirt rip away, and then leads plopped onto his chest. The pressure beneath his chin, he realized, was a cervical collar. '. . . in a foster home. Have to fix me.' His voice was so hoarse and weak that the sound barely reached his own ears.

'Open your mouth.'

'Deep breath. Again.'

Now he was being rolled down a walk, past puzzled elderly faces and manicured flower beds. He passed by the rear gate, a sign drifting by, cheerily announcing NEW BEGINNINGS ACTIVE LIVING CENTER. That painted smiley-face sun winked at him.

'Push six of morphine.'

'. . . so I can get to her. Tell her mother . . . Annabel. Jocelyn Wilder is the name.'

'Little pinch, okay? Good.'

Air-conditioning on his face. Overhead lights flying past, one after another.

'He's tachycardic, hypotensive, blood in his belly. He needs to get to the OR *now*. Who's on call?'

Mike's words were fainter yet. 'My daughter . . . she's hidden. Tell my wife . . . Annabel Win . . . gate . . .'

'Dr Nelson's in already with the shattered hip.'

'He's lost a lotta blood. I don't know.'

'. . . can't die . . . without . . .'

'CT?'

'No time – he'll bleed out in the scanner.'

A sturdy male nurse leaned over him, sliding a finger into his numb left hand. 'Squeeze my finger. Squeeze. That's good, that's good.'

Mike focused hard on forming words, shaping his lips. '. . . Jocelyn Wilder . . . Parker, Arizona. Tell . . . my wife . . .'

The nurse leaned closer. 'What's that, pal? Tell your wife what?'

Our daughter is with Jocelyn Wilder of Parker, Arizona.

Right before time stopped, Mike realized that the words had not left his head.

Chapter 58

The voice was blurred, as if Mike were listening underwater. 'Where's Katherine?'

He mumbled, 'I won't fucking tell you ever.'

Another voice said, 'Pleasant, ain't he?' And then he sank beneath another black swell.

This time he sensed the mattress beneath him.

'—press is climbing all over everything,' Shep's voice was saying. 'The state paid to medevac you in to Cedars-Sinai Med Center. And Annabel, too. Top care – bastards are scared of a lawsuit. They're relieved you lived. I guess you had a cut in your kidney vein. What? Okay – *renal* vein. Bleeds fast, but not as fast as an artery. Lucky for you, huh?'

Mike tried to make his mouth move, but it wouldn't obey.

Shep continued. 'The feds raided the wrecking yard, found your parents' remains in two of those crushed cars. McAvoy's in custody. Looks like he's fucked pretty good.'

'He can't hear you,' someone said.

Shep said, 'Yeah he can.'

Now his eyes were open, if barely, his vision blurry. His tongue was too thick to talk around. Metal pinched the skin of his stomach. A tan face was floating over him, saying, 'Congratulations, Mr Wingate. You just inherited a Class III casino.'

Mike said, 'Mmrm.'

'You'll be immediately commenced at a salary of three million.'

'A *month*,' Shep's voice added from somewhere. 'And the annual dividend? It's got more zeros than can fit on a check.'

Mike could discern the shape of Shep now, standing at the foot of the bed.

'Guess who's a leading expert in casino law?' Shep flicked his nail against something that Mike finally registered as a familiar taupe business card. Shep's face came into focus briefly, time enough for Mike to see the gleam of that crooked front tooth. ''Member that high-ticket lawyer Two-Hawks hooked me up with?'

Mike took in the man who'd spoken earlier as a collection of parts – sun-baked face, hammered sterling oval belt buckle with a turquoise inlay, Gerry Spence buckshin jacket with fringe sloping across the shoulders. The man nodded solemnly, a hint of wryness livening his eyes, and said, 'Chief Two-Hawks looks forward to a long era of peace and prosperity between our tribes.'

The scene blurred again, and a sharp female voice said, 'You can't be in here.'

Fading out, Mike heard Shep say, 'What?'

He came awake this time – fully awake – with a single thought branded across his brain: *Katherine.*

He sat up abruptly but a hot spear lanced his gut, flattening him back down onto a brace of pillows. Even tilting his head was excruciating, but he managed to look down at himself. The hospital gown he was wearing was thrown open to reveal a railroad track of surgical staples running from below his belly button to his sternum. The edges of the wound were purple-pink. It took some time for him to register the slit as a permanent addition to his body. A large gauze patch was adhered to his side with paper tape. With some trepidation he peeled it back. The stab wound was cleanly sealed, tiny black sutures sticking out like cat whiskers. The skin below was trash-liner black, a shade he hadn't known that skin could turn.

'They had to open you up.' The voice, from across the room, surprised him. A man sat in a visitor chair, picking a piece of lint from the thigh of his pressed slacks, a red tie sealed firmly to his throat. Mike recognized the clean-shaven face, but it took a few moments for him to place him as Bill Garner, the governor's chief of staff. He noted, also, that there was no one else in the room.

'Had to stop the bleeding, check your liver and bowel, all that,' Garner continued. 'You've been in and out for a few days. I guess you're recovering really well, but there's still gonna be a lot of—'

Mike tried to sit up again and cried out.

'—pain.'

Mike rolled his head, looking around. The door was open, nurses and patients walking briskly past in the hall. On his night-stand, blood-sopped bandages rested in a bedpan. Still processing the shock of the scar, Mike tried to retrieve memories from the slush of the past few days. Shep had been here. And Two-Hawks's attorney. Something about the state fearing a law-suit – Yup, there it was.

Groaning, he swung his legs over the side of the bed, the oxygen tube pulling out from beneath his nose. He tugged an IV from his arm, saline pattering on the floor, then tore some excess paper tape from his biceps.

'I wouldn't do that,' Garner said. 'There's a naggy nurse look-ing to live up to her adjective.'

Mike stood up and wobbled a bit until his legs firmed beneath him. 'They found Hank's body?'

Pinching his gown closed, he made progress gingerly toward the door, Garner following at his side. 'They did,' Garner said. 'LAPD's on the warpath – he was one of their own. Parker Center, FBI – everyone's shoehorned into this thing.'

'I can see that.'

'Hank Danville may not have looked like much, but he was very well regarded in the law-enforcement community.'

Mike paused for the first time. Looked over at him. 'Rightly so.'

'And with the evidence?' Garner shot a breath skyward, fluttering his bangs. 'Brian McAvoy might as well give *himself* the lethal injection. There hasn't been a case this airtight since O.J.' He scratched his nose. 'That was a joke.'

'Sorry,' Mike said. 'I'm still back on Hank.'

'You'll have a chance to say good-bye properly. LAPD's planning a big to-do, ceremony, all that. He'll go out a hero.'

Mike didn't trust his voice, so he just nodded and kept on toward the door.

'You really shouldn't be up,' Garner said.

'Feels like that,' Mike said. 'Which way's my wife?'

'Down that hall there.'

'Shep?'

'Around somewhere, I'm sure. He hasn't strayed far from your side since he was released.'

Mike leaned against the doorway, breathing hard. 'Released?'

'He's under investigation,' Garner said. 'Your lawyer turned over the security recording from Graham's house, as well as all the other documents. This is a high-order mess, clearly, but we've persuaded the AUSA and the DA to offer you full federal and state immunity in exchange for your truthful testimony and for your cooperation as pertains to the case against Brian McAvoy. Let me repeat: That's *full* immunity.'

'So I don't sue the state,' Mike said. 'Which I assume is why you're being good enough to check in on me. In a quiet hospital room before anyone else can get to me.'

Garner affected a bored expression. 'While they're willing to make some allowances for you given the early investigative . . . missteps, someone has to answer for the string of felonies you and Shepherd White left in your wake.'

Mike's lip curled. 'You need a fall guy.'

'There were laws broken. Stolen vehicles, battery, robbery, the murder of an important state law-enforcement agent in his bedroom at night. There's you, family man, honored community leader. And there's a convicted felon. *Someone* fired that shot from the balcony.'

'Graham was a murdering piece of shit.'

'It might be less complicated for everyone if it doesn't get advertised that way.'

'Less complicated for who?' Mike started forward again.

'Let's just stop a moment, Mike.' Garner placed a hand gently on his shoulder, halting him. 'You could end up in prison. This is no joke. You're gonna want to think carefully about what you do here.'

Mike steered Garner's arm away. 'There's a picture of your boss hanging in McAvoy's trophy case in the casino. He was even good enough to sign it – "To Deer Creek Casino, friends of mine, friends of California". You guys took in soft-money donations by the truckload from a guy who snuffed his opponents for *generations* with abandon while the cops, DAs, judges, and – yes – the governor looked the other way.'

'Lower your voice, please.'

'Not only is Shep *not* going down for any of these so-called crimes, but the governor has twenty-four hours to issue a full pardon or he can spend the last weeks of his campaign explaining why he's not responsible for his corrupt police force and how the hundreds of millions that McAvoy gave the state budget didn't have anything to do with how he got away with murder for decades.'

Mike stepped out into the hall, Garner scurrying at his side.

'We can still make your life extremely difficult,' Garner said.

'You don't know what difficult is.'

Two agents approached at a half jog, and Garner waved them off. They hesitated, not retreating, and Mike asked them loudly, 'Am I under arrest?'

'Sir, you're not to leave the—'

'*Am I under arrest?*'

The surrounding movement in the hall came to a halt. The agents looked at Garner. Garner looked back at them. They seemed to blink a lot, and then one of the agents said, 'No.'

Mike kept going.

'You're in the catbird seat right now,' Garner said, walking sideways next to him and doing his best to lower his voice. 'You and your family have won the lottery a thousand times over.' He skipped in front of Mike. 'You're prepared to throw all that away to protect a felon buddy?'

'He *is* family.'

Garner's stare stayed even, but his lips stretched a bit with concern.

Mike gritted his teeth against the pain. 'Now, get the fuck out of my way.'

Garner contemplated for a moment, then complied.

Leaving him in his wake, Mike continued down the hall. He grabbed a pair of scrub bottoms from a passing cart. Pulling them on hurt more than he could have imagined, but the staples didn't burst, and he finally managed, and let the gown fall to the floor. Every cough, every twist brought with it a fresh jolt of pain. He did his best to bend at the hips to avoid using his stomach muscles, but even that made his eyes water. Shirtless, he continued down the hall, eyeing the charts on doors, the names printed on the tabs, and finally, worn down by the pain and exhaustion, he started shouting his wife's name, turning circles.

He heard her faint reply from around the next corner and took one jogging step before the blast of heat in his stomach reminded him to walk. Around the bend, Detectives Elzey and Markovic were standing near a partially open door. Elzey had a gift-shop bouquet in her hand, probably wondering how much leniency a fistful of carnations would buy when it came time for Annabel's official statement. When the detectives saw

427

Mike tottering toward them, scowling and stitched together like a low-rent Frankenstein, they turned sheepishly and slinked off.

Heat roared in his face, in his chest, in the mouths of both cuts as he finally reached the doorway. She was on the bed, her skin pale and smooth, her hair lying limp against her scalp. One of her hands moved self-consciously toward her face but froze halfway up from the sheet, the tiny, instinctive gesture rending him. He gripped the door stile, wheezing against the pain, the two of them drinking in the sight of each other. Her father faded from the room like an apparition before Mike had even registered his presence. Mike couldn't take his eyes off her, couldn't move; he was frozen in pain and ecstasy.

'You cut your hair,' Annabel said.

She mustered a smile, then immediately started crying, the sight sending him, finally, into motion. He pressed his face to the top of her hair, breathing her in, the scent of her still there, deep beneath the iodine and dried sweat. A nurse was suddenly at his side, talking at them with great agitation, but he wasn't processing her words.

Annabel hovered her fingers above his scars. He parted her gown, checked her bruised skin, the line of the wound. He felt helpless and grateful and full of rage, the emotions cycling through him like a tornado.

Annabel turned her pale face up at him, and he thumbed a tear from her cheek. 'Let's go get our daughter,' she said.

The nurse came in then at full volume, 'You are not going *anywhere* with that nicked artery, Mrs. Wingate.' She wheeled on Mike. 'And you. You'd best march back up that hall and get horizontal. And you're due for some Percocet.'

'Can't take it,' Mike said. 'I have to drive.'

'*Drive?*'

Annabel said, 'Go.'

He kissed her softly on the mouth and walked out.

Shep was waiting in the hall, slumped with his shoulders against the wall like a Chicago gangster.

Mike said, 'Can you get me some ibuprofen?'

'How much?'

'A million milligrams.'

Shep put a hand across his back, and they started for the elevator. Mike said, 'You got a car?'

'What kind you want?'

'No, Shep. I want to *borrow* yours.'

Shep pulled the keys from his pocket. 'It's not a Pinto.' He plunked them in Mike's hand. 'With your driving record, I'm just sayin'.'

Shep leaned over the counter at the nurses' station and swiped a bottle of Advil from the back shelf. Mike swallowed six pills dry, and Shep shoved the bottle into the pocket of his scrubs, along with something else. Mike saw the furry white arm protruding and smiled.

Riding down in the elevator, Shep nodded at the bruises covering Mike's torso. 'What you did for your family . . .' He shook his head with admiration.

'You idiot,' Mike said. 'I learned it from you.'

The doors dinged open, and they walked across the lobby and outside, the breeze reminding Mike that he was, inanely, barechested.

The '67 Shelby Mustang was waiting across the lot, spit-shined, the wide grille sneering. Shep said, 'Gassed up and ready to go.'

A town car eased up to the curb nearby, and a white-haired man in a gray linen suit emerged quickly, waving at Mike and hurrying over to catch them. He had to walk briskly to match their pace.

'Mr Wingate?' he said. 'I came immediately to offer our condolences about this terrible situation.'

'You are . . ?' Mike asked.

'Now that Brian McAvoy has been detained for his egregious crimes, I am the senior trustee of Deer Creek Tribal Enterprises, Inc. And I come here on behalf of the board to tell you that we had no knowledge of any of Mr McAvoy's indiscretions. And that we cared for your great-grandmother at the end of her life. I knew her personally, in fact. She wanted for nothing. If there's any way we can assist you in this transition or anything you need—'

'Yeah,' Mike said. 'I need a shirt.'

The man's mouth came ajar, the fringe of his white mustache hanging over his upper lip.

Mike said, 'Give me your shirt.'

The man pressed a smile onto his face. Shep helped him out of his jacket, and then the man loosened his tie, unbuttoned his shirt, and handed it to Mike.

Mike pulled it on, grimacing, and began pushing the buttons through the holes. 'Thanks. You're all fired.'

He and Shep continued on toward the Mustang.

'You need us,' the man called after him. 'Who will run the casino?'

Mike said, over his shoulder, 'You'll have to talk to my chief of operations.'

The man, bare-chested beneath his suit jacket, climbed back into the town car, and the dark car eased away. They came up on the Mustang, and Mike ran a finger along one of the racing stripes.

Shep said, 'Chief of operations?'

Mike tilted his head at him.

'Yeah?' Shep said. 'How much?'

'How much you want?'

'Can I still pull jobs?'

'No.'

'I'll think about it.'

Mike tugged open the door, and Shep gripped his hands and

430

helped lower him down into the bucket seat. Shep tossed in a wad of cash and his cell phone – the sole surviving Batphone – and Mike rested both by the e-brake and swung the door closed. The engine roared to life, but before Mike could back out, Shep tapped the glass.

When Mike rolled down the window, Shep said, 'They always say it doesn't solve anything. Revenge. But when you killed them, did it feel good?'

'Yes,' Mike said, and drove off.

Chapter 59

The few times he stopped for gas, food, or caffeine, he drew odd stares. Fair enough – with his dress shirt, scrub bottoms, and bare feet, he did look like he'd escaped from an asylum. He popped Advil for the pain, but it was mostly adrenaline that kept him pushing through. The drive was long, and he dreamed a little.

He'd get immunity or wouldn't, but either way he'd return Kat and Annabel to their home and they'd have enough money from the casino to be taken care of for the rest of their lives. He could repay his countless debts of gratitude – to Hank's survivors, to Jocelyn Wilder, to Jimmy. Hell, he could repipe all of Green Valley with vitri-fucking-fied clay or pay back the fraudulent green subsidies. Those houses would be the first place he'd spend the casino's money, a public penance for the lie that had put all this into motion.

And whether as a free man or on prison release, he would have a quiet little ceremony for his parents. John and Danielle Trainor. Proper caskets. He would lay them in the ground and turn over the first spadeful.

At long last he would put them to rest.

At a truck stop an hour away, sipping Coke and eating a Snickers, he caught a glimpse of himself in the rearview mirror. A few drops of blood, probably from a dripping IV line, had dried on the lobe of his ear, and whoever had shaved him had missed a patch of stubble at the corner of his jaw. He licked his thumb and tried to wipe the blood off, and it wasn't until he saw how badly his hand was shaking that he realized how nervous he was. He went into the bathroom, washed his face, and did his best to make himself look human again. Still, by the time he got the Mustang back on the road, his pain had taken a backseat to the hum of fear running like a current between his ears.

He entered Parker, Arizona, passing the movie theater where he'd taken Kat, the little dress shop, the diner at which they'd eaten their last meal. Nausea returned like a muscle memory, and, flustered, he lost his way. He got turned around, winding through suburban circles, his frustration bringing him to the verge of tears.

The Batphone rang. Praying for help, he answered.

'Graham, it seems, was shot during a random home-invasion robbery.'

It took him a few seconds to place the voice. Bill Garner.

Garner continued. 'Would you like to contradict that account?'

Mike thought of how far back it all went with Graham. Mike's father, Just John, struggling to the death. The last name that Mike had been saddled with as a four-year-old, assigned by a faceless smart-ass in Social Services. And now it had come full circle. The record would show that Graham had been killed by an uniden-tified suspect – a John Doe.

'No,' Mike said.

'I had to go to the wall to get Shepherd White included under your immunity deal,' he said. 'It was closer than you'd ever like to know. I'll say one thing, Mike, you've got stamina.'

Mike said, 'And loyalty.'

A street opened up off a curve. He'd looped past it twice before but somehow not seen it.

Garner was saying, '—DA can send the documents on to—'

Mike came off the turn, and there ahead was the rambling ranch house and the backyard filled with play structures and girls in motion. 'I have to go.'

'We're talking about your immunity,' Garner said. 'You got somewhere more important to be?'

'Yeah,' Mike said. 'I do.'

He eased in to the curb where he'd parked before, where he and Kat had struck their dire deal.

You will come back for me.

I will come back for you.

Before he could brace himself, he saw her, off the front porch, pouring water from a plastic bucket onto a wilted fern. She was wearing the yellow gingham dress he'd bought her, though the sleeve was torn and the hem ragged.

He got out of the Mustang, his legs barely able to sustain him. At the slam of the car door, she looked up, a smudge of dirt on her cheek. She looked right at him.

And then she turned and walked inside.

A breeze blew across his face, an empty, desert sound, and for a moment he actually thought it would shatter him. He stood trembling. He did his best to put himself back together, piece by piece, before he felt steady enough to follow her in.

An older girl answered the door. 'Are you . . .?'

He said, 'Yes.'

A husband. A father.

The girl stepped aside.

Over on the couch, Jocelyn took note of him and beckoned the swirl of children in the room, corralling them magically around her. They hushed and looked with darting eyes.

Jocelyn said, 'She's outside.'

Mike's mouth moved twice before he could speak. 'Thank you.'

Kat was sitting past the swing set on a patch of cracked asphalt, playing with a doll. Legless Barbie. She was mumbling to herself, manipulating the arms this way and that. Her hair was uncombed and her nails dirty.

Mike reached her. She did not look up. Given the staples and sutures, it took him a while to lower himself to the ground opposite her. He watched her play. Still she did not raise her head.

He reached into the pocket of his scrub pants, tugged out Snowball II, and set it on the ground between them. In a burst of anger, Kat picked up the tiny stuffed polar bear and threw it off into the weeds at the base of the fence.

Mike said, 'Okay.'

The staples gnawed at his skin, but he wouldn't move. He watched her hands, the scab on her knee, the top of her head. He was aching to hold her, but he forced himself to sit still, to let her arrive at this moment on her own time. She tilted her head, and he caught a glimpse of her cheek. It was quivering. She banged Barbie against the asphalt.

He said, 'How's she feel about having one leg?'

Kat said, 'She's angry.'

'I bet.'

He wanted so badly to reach out and touch her arm, to stroke her hair, to take her hand. Overhead, a woodpecker knocked its face against a telephone pole.

'It's okay now,' he told her.

Kat banged the doll a few more times, then set it down. Tentatively, keeping her face pointed at the ground, she crawled across into his lap. She curled against his chest, and pain rocketed through to his spinal cord, but he didn't give a damn. All he cared about was her head tucked beneath his chin.

'Look at me,' he said gently.

She didn't move.

'Honey, look at me.'

Slowly, she lifted her eyes.

He said, 'It's okay now.'

And then she was sobbing, screaming, pulling his shirt and pounding her fists against his collarbone. He held her, grunting against the pain, his forehead pressed to hers, rocking her. It was gray with dusk, and still he sat, aching, legs splayed out awkwardly before him, holding her as she quieted, holding her until the only movement was the shuddering of her breath moving through her, holding her, holding her, holding her.

Acknowledgements

Several experts took time to offer valuable guidance on matters medical, logistical, editorial, and tactical. Thanks to Kristin Baird, M.D., John Cayanne, Philip Eisner, Tyler Felt, Marjorie Hurwitz, Missy Hurwitz, M.D., Don McKim, James Murphy, Bret Nelson, M.D., Andrew Plotkin, Emily Prior, and Maureen Sugden. Any flaws in the book are due not to them but to the author's inherent obstinacy.

Thanks to my supportive and untiring representatives: attorneys Marc H. Glick and Stephen F. Breimer, and agents Rich Green, Aaron Priest, and the irrepressible Lisa Erbach Vance. Incisive (and patient) editor Keith Kahla and my crew at St. Martin's – including but certainly not limited to publisher Sally Richardson, Matthew Baldacci, Jeff Capshew, Tara Cibelli, Kathleen Conn, Ann Day, Brian Heller, Ken Holland, Loren Jaggers, Sarah Madden, John Murphy, Matthew Shear, Tom Siino, Martin Quinn, and George Witte. Additionally, I'd like to acknowledge David Shelley, Daniel Mallory, and rest of the UK Sphere contingent, as well as my other publishing partners around the world. Also my Rhodesian ridgeback, Simba, present for the vast majority of the keyboard's rattling.

And Delinah, there for me every day with a smile that, ten years later, I still feel in my hip pocket.